SWEET AS HONEY

AN ASTER VALLEY NOVEL

LUCY LENNOX

Happy Birthday Nico!
(the blue baby)

Companion in adventures,
my personal videographer, my 24/7 doctor,
artistic baker, smart funny
and caring.

I love you to the moon and back

You will always be my "chiquitito"

Ita

April 26, 2021

Copyright © 2021 by Lucy Lennox

All rights reserved.

No part of this book may be reproduced in any form or by any electronic or mechanical means, including information storage and retrieval systems, without written permission from the author, except for the use of brief quotations in a book review.

Cover Art: Natasha Snow Designs

Cover Photo: The Cover Lab

Editing: One Love Editing

Proofreading: Victoria Rothenberg

Beta Reading: Leslie Copeland, Molly Maddox, Sloane Kennedy, May Archer, Shay Haude.

KEEP IN TOUCH WITH LUCY!

Join Lucy's Lair
Get Lucy's New Release Alerts
Like Lucy on Facebook
Follow Lucy on BookBub
Follow Lucy on Amazon
Follow Lucy on Instagram
Follow Lucy on Pinterest

Other books by Lucy:
Made Marian Series
Forever Wilde Series
Aster Valley Series
Twist of Fate Series with Sloane Kennedy
After Oscar Series with Molly Maddox
Licking Thicket Series with May Archer
Virgin Flyer
Say You'll Be Nine

Visit Lucy's website at www.LucyLennox.com for a comprehensive list of titles, audio samples, freebies, suggested reading order, and more!

1

SAM

Everything was going fine until I saw the bumblebee. It was the third day of my road trip from Houston to Aster Valley, and I'd finally arrived. It was as picturesque as any other ski town in Colorado was in late spring, but smaller and with noticeably fewer tourists since there wasn't any actual skiing here anymore. Considering I'd never heard of Aster Valley before my best friend, Mikey Vining, and his very rich, very good-looking, very adoring football player boyfriend, Tiller Raine, had left me behind in Houston and bought themselves a giant ski lodge in town earlier this year, I wasn't surprised.

But I was surprised when I saw the teen-sized bumblebee being chased through a large patch of wildflowers on the side of the highway by a man who looked at least twice his size. The last thing I wanted was to get involved in someone else's drama—hell, I'd left Houston specifically to get away from my own—but if there was one thing I couldn't abide, it was bullying. I'd gotten enough of that myself as a kid from my own father.

I wrenched my bike over to the side so fast I almost crashed into an old, half-broken-down billboard advertising a ski resort that must have been just the thing in the 1980s.

"Let go of him," I shouted. "Leave him the hell alone."

My friends teased me for my deep growl, saying I sounded annoyed at the least and angry at best, but in times like these, it came in handy.

The bigger man stopped and stared at me, and the bespectacled guy in the ridiculous bee costume froze like a squirrel caught stealing from the bird feeder. "Mind your own damned business, asshole," the bully said.

I glanced at the bee. "You okay?"

His eyes were wide with fear, and his antennae were trembling. Despite both of those things, he was trying very hard to smile as if everything was normal. "Um, I'm fine."

He was clearly not fine. I pulled out my phone and pretended to dial. "How about I call the police just in case?"

"Yeah, good luck with that." The bully shoved the bee until he fell on his fluffy yellow ass. "This isn't over, Truman." He shoulder checked me hard on the way past and disappeared around a bend in the road. I noticed a heavy trace of alcohol coming off him.

I reached out for the bee's hand and realized he was an adult and not the teen I'd first assumed him to be. "Let me help you up," I grunted, suddenly feeling oddly attracted to the little bee. He had a pretty face with delicate features and cherry-red lips almost hidden under a crazy tumble of dark brown curls.

"I'm sorry to bother you," he said in a soft voice, getting to his feet. "You could have just kept on going. He probably wasn't going to hurt me very badly. And, really, everyone has their issues, you know?"

Just then, a tricked-up truck with a heavy metal push bar on the front came careening around the corner from the direction the bully had gone. It deliberately headed straight for my bike, pushing it into the stone base of the town sign with a sickening crunch. The asshole shot me the bird, called me a few choice names, and then did a three-point turn before hauling ass away from us.

I looked back at the bee, who simply stared after the pickup. "Oh no," he said faintly. "No, no. He wasn't supposed to do that. He... that wasn't fair. You were just trying to help."

"Who the hell was that guy, and what the hell's his problem?"

"That's Patrick Stanner," he said, like that should mean something to me. When I shrugged uncomprehendingly, he added, "Brother of Craig Stanner? Son of Kimber and Gene Stanner? Nephew of Erland Stanner? Still no?"

He must have noticed the blank look on my face, because he cleared his throat and continued. "Huh. Well, anyway, his family fell upon some hard times and lost everything to the banks. And it was kind of because of me, so whenever he gets in a certain kind of mood... he finds me and gives me what for. Usually it's not so bad."

I opened my mouth to ask him why the hell he thought any of this was his fault, but he let out a nervous laugh and said, "I can't believe I just told you that. Please forget I said anything. It's not... it's... it's fine."

He looked everywhere but at me, and I couldn't tell if he was embarrassed or nervous. I knew my large frame and stern face, not to mention the bike, could give off the wrong impression of me, so I stuck out my hand. "Sam Rigby."

The bee's eyes widened even more behind a pair of dark-framed glasses when he slid his hand into mine. "Oh, uh... Truman Sweet." Suddenly, a pink blush appeared on his cheeks and his dark eyelashes flitted softly as his nerves got the better of him. My throat suddenly felt dry.

His skin was cool and smooth, and his slender fingers disappeared into my beefy grip. I was almost afraid of breaking the poor guy like a twig.

I shifted on my feet and forced myself to let his hand go. "I'd offer you a ride into town, but I'm not sure if my bike is up for it."

I wanted to beat the shit out of the asshole who wrecked my bike and hassled this little man, but I'd do the right thing and report him to the cops instead.

Truman glanced around as if trying to remember where he was. "We're only a half mile from town. It's a little hilly, but walkable. Plus, it's a beautiful day, isn't it?"

I nodded absently while looking him up and down, trying to find some reason a grown man would be alone in a field of wildflowers in a bee costume. I opened my mouth to ask him but quickly snapped it closed. The whole point of this vacation road trip—after a quick stop here in Aster Valley to visit Mikey and Tiller—was to relax and unwind before I had to return to my responsibilities in Texas. Truman Sweet and his problems were none of my business.

"Guess I'd better get moving, then," I said gruffly before stretching my head side to side and grabbing the backpack out of my saddlebags. I hadn't brought much with me, but I didn't want to leave my laptop and what little clothes I had to whoever might come along.

When I turned back to head toward the little town, I caught Truman staring at me. He blushed a deeper pink and looked away. The antennae bounced adorably on the headband he wore.

"There a good bike mechanic in town?" I asked, trying to ignore the way his pink cheeks tightened my gut.

"Oh! Yes, sir. Of course. Mr. Browning at the Chop Shop." His eyes widened. "I mean, it's not an actual chop shop, like with criminals. It's just called Chop Shop. I think it stands for something like Chopper. Is that a thing? Like, a kind of bike? They do cars and trucks, too."

I nodded and bit my lip against a smile. "Yes, a chopper is a style of bike with a long fork and..." He looked lost, so I stopped there. "Thank you."

"Anytime, Mr. Rigby. Happy to help."

I tilted my head at him. Had I misjudged this guy? "How old are you?"

"Twenty-four. Why?"

"I'm thirty. Why are you calling me sir and mister? Do I look that much older?"

He blushed again. "Oh no, S-S-Sam. I just know that some men demand respect, and I don't ever like to make assumptions. Besides, one can never go wrong with good etiquette. At least that's what they say. Although... I've never really understood who 'they' are in this scenario."

"Not all men deserve respect even if they demand it. Why does that man think his problems are your fault?"

Truman frowned and looked down at his feet. The yellow tights he wore ended in a pair of black Converse that looked as clean as they could be for the mileage they seemed to have on them. I regretted asking the question as soon as it caused his cheerful smile to disappear.

He flapped his hand in the air. "It's a long story and would probably bore you to tears. We should get you to Mr. Browning's place before he closes up for the day. I'll show you where it is."

He spun on his heel and started walking down the side of the highway. The fuzzy black stinger on his butt wiggled back and forth as he moved away from me. How could someone that innocent and sweet possibly be responsible for an asshole's personal problems?

I followed him for a while in silence before I couldn't stand it anymore. Maybe I could let Truman be my business for as long as it took to get to the mechanic.

"I don't mind long stories," I said.

He turned his sunny smile on me again. "Then you'll love this one. Did you know that Indian Paintbrush—that red flower there—was called 'Grandmothers Hair' by the Chippewa and was used to treat women's diseases? The Navajos used it as a contraceptive, and the Menominee used it as a love charm. Obviously, it was used to make red dye also, but I find it fascinating that the stories of its name vary from place to place. One story tells of a Blackfoot maiden falling for a prisoner, helping him escape, and then becoming homesick. The story goes on to describe her using her own blood to paint a picture of her old camp that she could never return to again. Where she dropped the picture, a flower bloomed, thus becoming the plant we know today. Then another story describes a Native American painter—tribe unknown—frustrated by his lack of the perfect colors to depict a sunset. He asked the Great Spirit for guidance and was given paintbrushes with all of the richest colors. He ran up into the hills to paint his sunset and left the brushes in the grass where they lay when he was done. The brushes blossomed into the plants we now know as Indian paintbrush."

I noticed as he talked, Truman became more and more comfortable in his skin. He used his hands to gesture wildly as he spoke, and the subject matter was clearly one close to his heart. Before today, I'd had no interest in learning about local flora, but hearing Truman weave his stories made me wonder for a hot second if I'd been missing something valuable.

It wasn't until we came upon the motorcycle shop that I even realized he'd never told me the story about the drunk who seemed to have it out for him.

"Anyway," Truman said happily, "here you are. Aster Valley's premiere mechanic."

I stopped and looked up at the arched sign above the garage, but before I had a chance to thank Truman for leading me here, the familiar whoop-whoop of a police vehicle sounded right behind us. I instinctively grabbed Truman and shoved him behind me, wondering if the local drunk driver was nearby and ready to take out his frustration on the adorable fuzzy bumblebee.

Last December, Mikey and another man had been involved in a hit-and-run that had landed Mikey in the hospital with a broken arm. Since the driver had never been identified, it was safe to say being a pedestrian in this small town wasn't without its risks.

The memory of Mikey's accident suddenly tweaked something in my brain. "Truman… are you the man with the spice shop?" I asked. Mikey had been on his way to see Truman when the car had swerved in their direction and knocked them down.

"Oh! Uh, yeah? I mean… yes. Yes, that's me. Spices." He bit his lip and blinked rapidly at the emergency vehicle.

The officer behind the wheel of an SUV marked as a Rockley County Sheriff's Deputy seemed to be staring right at me from behind a pair of mirrored sunglasses.

"Jesus," I muttered.

"Did you know that name is actually a variation of Joshua?" Truman's soft voice said from behind me. "Bible trivia is unnecessary, Truman," he muttered.

I wanted to laugh, but the sheriff's deputy stepped out of his vehicle and stared me down. He was fairly young with a slim frame, but his jaw was set like he was trying to appear tougher than he was. "You there, in the biker jacket. Hands where I can see them."

Truman made a little squeaky sound and pressed into my back.

"It's okay," I said quietly, raising my arms in the air. In a louder voice I called out, "I'd like to report a drunk driver as well as harassment and deliberate damage to personal property."

The deputy's forehead crinkled in confusion. "We've already had a report of those same things. What's your name, sir?"

"Sam Rigby. I'm a Texas resident, just in town visiting some friends."

The deputy tried to glance behind me without coming any closer. "Truman Sweet, is that you back there?"

"Cripes," he whispered without removing himself from where he was plastered against my back. "How did he recognize me?"

"Come on out here and tell me what happened."

I saw the antennae bounce into my field of vision before the rest of him. "Um... well, you see, there was a misunderstanding with—"

I cut him off. "No misunderstanding. Local resident Patrick Stanner as identified by Mr. Sweet here was physically harassing Mr. Sweet on the side of the highway. I pulled my bike to the side of the road to intervene when Mr. Stanner shoved Mr. Sweet, got into his vehicle, deliberately smashed my bike into an old billboard, and fled the scene."

By this time, several shop owners and customers from storefronts nearby had wandered out to see what the excitement was, no doubt alerted by the deputy's obnoxious and unnecessary siren.

"Now, calm down, sir," the deputy said, moving his hand to his service weapon. I wanted to roll my eyes, but I didn't dare make a move showing any disrespect. I was already the outsider, a biker who'd gotten into a scuffle the minute I'd arrived in town. What were the chances they'd take me at my word?

I looked over at Truman, expecting him to verify my version of events. Instead, I saw him practically chewing his bottom lip off with nerves. His face was pale, and his antennae had begun to wobble again.

"You okay?" I asked quietly.

"Not so much," he answered breathlessly. "Forgot to tell you that Erland Stanner, Patrick's uncle, is also the sheriff. I'm gonna probably pass out."

Even though he'd given me a warning, it took my brain a minute to process it. Within seconds, he was tipping forward toward the pavement. I lurched into action, grabbing him around the waist to keep him from breaking his face. But I must have spooked the deputy because suddenly, I was surrounded by two deputies with their weapons drawn, one of whom was shouting into the radio on his shoulder while various shopkeepers and customers screamed bloody murder and ran around like headless chickens.

When I straightened back up with the man-sized bee in my arms, I caught the eyes of an older, white-haired gentleman sitting at an outdoor cafe table a few yards away. He was sipping daintily from a porcelain teacup and had an overgrown purse dog curled up at his feet. His eyes sparkled as he looked me over.

"Oh good," he said in a lazy drawl. "We could use some excitement around here."

What the hell kind of place had Tiller and Mikey moved to?

Truman shifted in my arms. "Don't tell them I was the one tending the flowers," he said in a hazy slur. "Don't want anyone to know it was me. That's why I'm in disguise."

Was this one of those Colorado hippie towns where everyone was smoking weed all the damned time?

I glanced back up at the young sheriff's deputy, who seemed to be gathering his courage to try and take me down.

"Mr. Rigby, sir," he said in a firm voice. "Put the chickadee down and step away from him. We have you surrounded. You're under arrest for... for..." He tilted his head toward one of the other deputies, who stepped over to whisper in his ear. Then he cleared his throat. "You're under arrest for the destruction of private property and the taking of a hostage while resisting arrest."

I was in some kind of fairy tale, and they had it all wrong.

"First of all, I believe it's a bumblebee, Deputy," I corrected, stepping forward.

And that's when they pulled out the Taser.

2

TRUMAN

When Sam went down, I went down with him.

It was ironic, really, since I'd done my very best to avoid actually meeting the man in person up till now. But, because I had the worst luck in the world, here I was, lying flat on his chest with my nose pressed against his cheek.

When I'd first set eyes on Sam Rigby back in March, he hadn't noticed me, but I'd definitely noticed him. It had been snowing heavily, and Sam had been up on a ladder helping fix the sign out front of the diner. After asking around, I'd learned Sam was friends with the couple who'd bought Rockley Lodge. He'd come up from Texas to do some repair work for them over a long weekend.

I hadn't really decided how I felt about him at the time, which, of course, was a total lie. The truth was, I got all heart-fluttery around him. But I shouldn't have. Sam's shoulders were broad, and despite being devastatingly handsome, his face was set in a permanent scowl. He was big and mean-looking. In other words, he scared the bejeebers out of me. I was easily intimidated on my best day, but when I encountered a tall, strong guy with a stern face... let's just say my fight-or-flight reaction only had one setting.

And it wasn't fight.

But for some reason, I'd been drawn to him. I'd stared at him every time I'd seen him in town that weekend. I'd even kind of been introduced to him at the diner one day. He hadn't paid any attention to me. And that had been fine. Good, even. I'd tried to forget about him, and for a while, I'd sort of succeeded. He'd only appeared as a kind of daydreamy representation of the kind of man I wish existed in real life but didn't. And now here he was in Aster Valley again, trying to save me from an impossible situation.

Correction. Trying to visit his friends in peace. And I'd messed that up.

"Sam?" I asked, realizing he wasn't moving. "Sir, are you okay?"

My heart thundered with nerves.

"Truman, back away from the perp slowly." The sheriff's deep voice boomed, and I tried my best not to start shaking. If only he hadn't arrived on the scene, I might have stood a chance at de-escalating the tension.

"Sheriff Stanner, this man needs medical attention," I said, feeling for a pulse in his neck. It was strong and steady under bristly warm skin. I swallowed thickly. "He's not a perp."

"Don't make me repeat myself, son. Back away now."

I dropped my voice to a whisper and shook Sam's shoulders. "Please wake up. *Please*. You don't want to go to jail over me. You have to get up and talk your way out of it."

His eyes began to open. When they landed on me, for a split second they heated up and then softened into an affectionate warmth. He must have thought I was someone else. Sheriff Stanner's barked commands continued.

"Now, Truman. Or I'm hauling your ass in, too."

"It's okay," Sam mumbled. "I'll be okay. Not the first time."

I didn't understand that last part, but I trusted he could handle himself as long as he was at least lucid now. I nodded and stood, keeping my eyes on him as I backed away. Rough hands grabbed me and pulled me farther away. I squeaked and whipped my head around and saw Barney's round face full of concern.

"Why are you dressed like an insect?"

I blinked at him. "You know why. I told you yesterday it was time to put in the nasturtium seeds."

He sighed. "Not this again. Truman, I told you to let someone else handle it. Your job isn't to do free work for the town."

Barney Balderson was the town librarian, who'd also spent a time trying to convince me to be his life partner, a role to which I'd turned out to be not only not well suited, but also not particularly interested in. There were things I'd liked about the older man's offer. Stability, protection, companionship. But his idea of companionship had been slightly more paternal and controlling than I'd hoped for. Even though he wasn't physically intimidating—a feature I was grateful for—he'd turned out to have very strong opinions about how I should manage myself and my business. It had made me nervous, defensive, and apologetic so often, I'd begun to feel like I was dating my own disappointed and angry father. Regardless of how much I longed for someone to be there for me, Barney wasn't the one.

I'd tried making that clear to him, but he wasn't taking no for an answer. Which only made me more nervous around him even though we'd started out good friends. I missed having him as a friend, and part of me was relieved he was here. He'd make sure nothing bad happened.

I turned back to see Sheriff Stanner and one of his deputies cuffing Sam on the ground like some kind of criminal.

"He didn't do anything!" I cried, lunging forward to intervene. My forward motion stopped when someone grabbed my stinger. "He was the one helping me," I finished pathetically.

Barney pulled me back against him, wrapping his arm around my front to keep me from interfering again. "Let them do their job, sweet pea. That man looks dangerous."

I struggled against his hold to try and find my phone which was deep in my costume. "He's not. He's Tiller and Mikey's friend. We need to call them."

Sam turned and found me struggling against Barney's hold. His eyebrows lowered in an angry frown. "You okay?"

I finally pushed out of Barney's arms and rushed closer to Sam.

"I'll call your friends up at Rockley Lodge. They'll come help, won't they?"

Sam's dark blond eyebrows dipped even lower. "You know Mikey and Tiller?"

I nodded and felt the antennae bouncing on top of my head. Now that I was in the middle of town with everyone staring, I felt like a fool. "Yes," I whispered.

"How did you know they were my friends?" he asked. The younger deputy had a hand around Sam's arm while Sheriff Stanner made notes on the computer in his vehicle.

I shrugged and bit my bottom lip. "I'll call them for you, okay?"

Sam's eyes flicked from me to Barney and back. "That your dad?"

It wasn't the first time someone had asked me that, but it was the first time it made me feel embarrassed and uncomfortable. "No."

"Your boyfriend?"

I glanced around at the people standing nearby. Barney always said it was in my best interest for anyone associated with the Stanner family to think I wasn't alone, that I had protection. "Um…"

Sam let out a breath. "None of my business," he said gruffly like he was reminding himself of something. "Forget I asked."

I winced. "I'm sorry about all this. You shouldn't have stopped to help me."

He stepped closer, and the deputy's grip tightened on his arm. Sam lowered his face so he could meet my eyes. "Do you wish I hadn't stopped?"

I thought of what Patrick would have done to me if Sam hadn't run him off. As much as I didn't want Sam to be in trouble with the law, I couldn't lie and say I wished he hadn't stopped. I shook my head.

He studied me for another second before nodding and stepping back again. "I'd be grateful if you'd give Mikey a call."

Once the sheriff finished typing into his computer, he got out and walked over to me. "Would you like to press charges?"

I met his eyes and tried to be brave. "Against Patrick? Yes, please."

Sheriff Stanner's eyes narrowed. "Against this man right here," he said, pointing to Sam. "For assault."

"He didn't assault me. But your nephew did." I swallowed and tried to maintain eye contact. And there were witnesses this time.

Unlike the last time when Patrick and his brother, Craig, had assaulted me in the alley behind my shop one night after closing. When I'd reported the crime to the sheriff's department, they'd informed me it was a "he said, he said" situation with no evidence or proof of the identity of my assailants.

Which was true. But there was proof of the myriad injuries I'd sustained.

Sheriff Stanner made significant eye contact with me. "I think that part was a misunderstanding, Truman."

I took a bracing breath. "It wasn't. Patrick chased me, grabbed me, and then purposefully crunched Mr. Rigby's motorcycle with his truck. And I think he was drunk. If you find him and do a blood alcohol test, you'll have proof." I gathered up my courage for the big push. "Or... or, you could let Mr. Rigby go and we can forget about Patrick's assault."

Sheriff Stanner glared at me with flared nostrils. Behind him, Sam's voice came out low and controlled. "Truman, you don't want to do that."

I didn't dare look over at him. It was taking all of my guts just to confront the sheriff. If I saw Sam's dark expression, I'd lose my nerve and probably cry a little.

I tried again. "If the Patrick thing was a misunderstanding, then so was the Sam thing."

The sheriff turned around and faced Sam. "And you? Are you dropping your accusation of willful property destruction?"

Sam's face took on a dangerous, slightly amused glint. "No."

The air seemed to thicken before the younger deputy opened up his stupid mouth. "You don't need Truman's account, sir. We all saw it with our own eyes. The suspect grabbed Mr. Sweet and held him like a human shield as we attempted our arrest."

That was all Sheriff Stanner needed. He nodded and said, "You're right, Dodge. Book him and write up your report. I'll be back at the station in a few minutes."

They shoved Sam into the deputy's vehicle as the sheriff turned back to me. "I'll need you to make a statement."

I shook my head. "I don't have any statement to make. He didn't do anything wrong."

Barney came up to stand beside me, reaching for my elbow. "Then there's no harm in telling the truth."

I shrugged off his grip. "I am telling the truth."

The sheriff studied me for another moment. "What exactly were you doing out on the side of the highway, Truman? That's government property."

Well, heck.

"I dropped my spade and had to go look for it," I said as innocently as I could. "It must have fallen out of the car on my way home from the shop last night."

All of us knew that was a lie. I'd been trying to restart the highway wildflower program for years, and every time I brought it up at the county council meetings, it was shot down. It didn't help that the sheriff's wife was head of the council. The fact the sides and median of the highway were currently blooming with a riot of color indicated *someone* had taken it upon themselves to make it happen despite the county council's decision.

"And you're wearing a bee costume because…?" he asked.

"It's my shop mascot," I said as if it was a well-known fact instead of something I'd made up on the spot. The truth of the matter was that I loved costumes, and I loved spring. I thought Aster Valley was a magical place and wanted to add to the whimsy.

It was easier to be whimsical in disguise.

The sheriff glanced over my shoulder to where my shop sat on the corner of Main and Heath. The historic brick building that currently housed the Honeyed Lemon had once been the home of my great-aunt's herbal remedy and spiritual healing business. It had thrived back in the time when tourists had flocked to Aster Valley to take advantage of its popular ski resort. But after the resort had shut down... well, it hadn't thrived any longer.

I pushed down the familiar guilt that always accompanied those memories. *It wasn't your fault*, I told myself. But being told it was my fault so often over the years had clouded my memories until even I sometimes blamed myself.

I cleared my throat and made a mental note to schedule an extra therapy session with Greta. "Anyway," I said, "I'd better get to work. Have a good day, Sheriff."

I didn't wait to be excused, I simply waddled my way across the street to the shop and fished my keys out of the fanny pack I wore under my costume. As soon as I was alone in the store with the door locked behind me, I let out a breath and tried not to freak out. Instead, I scrambled for my phone and dialed Mikey's number.

"Hey, Truman," he said in a friendly voice. "I'm glad you called. I'm out of that smoked cinnamon already and wanted to see if I could come in and grab some more."

"Yeah, fine. Of course. But... you and Tiller need to get down to the sheriff's office. Your friend Sam was arrested."

There was a long beat of silence on the other end of the line. "Sam Rigby? My Sam?"

My heart did a little half beat of protest at his claim. It made me wonder, not for the first time, if he and Mikey had ever been more than friends to each other. Not that it was any of my business because it definitely was not.

"There was an unfortunate situation out on the highway. He was trying to help me, and... it was all a misunderstanding really. But the sheriff didn't think so and now..." Just retelling it made me feel horrible, like I'd inadvertently pulled poor Sam into my long-running Aster Valley drama. I felt terrible about it. "He didn't do anything wrong. Please help him."

My chin was wobbly, and I knew I was going to start crying any minute. The stress was too much. I'd tried so hard to stay under the radar since moving back to Aster Valley, but this was going to put me smack-dab in the middle of drama again. Which was only going to make the Stanners even angrier.

"We'll take care of it," Mikey said. "Are you okay? Did something happen?"

He was always so kind. The concern in his voice made my throat feel lumpy. "I'm fine," I said. "Just help Sam."

"Will do. Thanks for calling."

After hanging up, I reached out for the special set of mala beads that hung from a hook behind the register. The multicolored stones were cool and smooth against my fingers.

I took a deep breath and tried to center myself. I tried to remember the meditation exercises my aunt had taught me, but before I could get through the first set, the shop door jangled open and Barney rushed in.

I regretted giving him a key, but there was no way in heck I could get up the nerve to ask for it back, especially if I wanted to remain friends with him. Which I did. Friends were thin on the ground for me here in town, and I couldn't afford to lose a single one, especially the man who'd gone out of his way to care for me after the assault. He'd even taken care of me months ago when I'd had a horrible case of food poisoning. He was a good man. I just... didn't want to explain things to him right now.

"There you are. Everyone is in a tizzy out there. What the heck were you thinking?" His head swiveled between the crowd supposedly still in the street and me clutching the edge of the old wooden counter where the cashier stand was. "What part of 'stay out of trouble' did you not understand, Truman? You know how the Stanners are. The last thing you need is to bring Erland's attention on yourself."

Sheriff Stanner wasn't the only problem, though. It was his brother, Gene, who had it out for me. Gene and his grown sons. Gene had been the head ski lift mechanic back when the Aster Valley slopes were still running, and when the slopes had been shut down, he'd wanted someone to blame for losing his job.

Lucky me, I'd been the chosen scapegoat.

"I didn't ask for Patrick Stanner to come after me," I said, hating the defensiveness in my voice. "I was just planting flowers on the side of the highway when he came up ranting at me and chasing me around. He threatened to beat me up if I didn't stop making a spectacle of myself. I don't even know what he meant by that."

"I would imagine running around in a bumblebee costume on the side of the highway would meet the definition of making a spectacle of yourself," he said dryly.

There was no reason for me to argue the point, but I did anyway. "I wasn't hurting anyone. I was minding my own business when he attacked me out of the blue."

Barney gripped my arm. "Did he touch you?"

His grip was too tight, and I tried to pull my arm away. "That hurts," I said. When he loosened his grip, I stepped away and rubbed the sore spot left from his hold. "He pushed me down, but he was too drunk to move very fast. I got up and ran away from him. That's when Tiller and Mikey's friend showed up on his motorcycle."

Barney's eyes narrowed. "I don't like the look of that man in the motorcycle jacket. He was in town a few months ago right around the same time the diner sign was vandalized."

I almost laughed. "He was the one who fixed the sign. I saw him on the ladder during the snowstorm."

"Be that as it may, you should stay away from him. He looks dangerous. Besides, if the sheriff set his sights on the man, that's even more reason for you to stay out of it."

I was tired. Tired of being persecuted for something that happened eighteen years ago. Tired of feeling like I needed to do penance for something that wasn't my fault. Tired of being the focus of anyone's hatred when all I wanted to do was live my own life. More than anything, I was tired of always having to mind my own business and keep off everyone's radar in Aster Valley.

This was my home. Other than the years my family had moved to Durango to escape the whispers and threats, I'd lived in Aster Valley my entire life. I loved it. It was where I felt most myself, and I wished with all my heart I could live freely and happily here.

Enough time had passed now that most people had stopped thinking much about why the ski resort had closed down and how it had crushed the local economy for a while. Aster Valley had found a new normal somewhere along the way, and most residents seemed happy with the way it was here now. Even the people who still missed the resort or the tourists and jobs it had brought with it didn't seem to still blame my then five-year-old self for single-handedly ruining anyone's lives.

Except the Stanners.

"Maybe you're right," I said, deciding to mind my own business as usual. I forced a smile on my face. "I'll stay out of it. Mikey and Tiller can help him."

Barney nodded. "Precisely. You have enough to worry about without adding one more thing to your plate." He reached out and pulled off my antennae headband. "Hopefully you have a change of clothes here," he muttered. "This is ridiculous."

I felt my cheeks go slack as my smile dropped. He knew how much I loved costumes. I had an entire shed full of them at home. I'd bought or made most of them to entertain the kids at the library when I volunteered there for story hour. They loved my costumes, so it was disappointing that the librarian himself didn't. "Why is it ridiculous to want to make someone smile? Why is it ridiculous to want to make *myself* smile?"

He didn't roll his eyes, but that was only because the gesture was considered beneath him. "Don't put words in my mouth. But I do feel that you would be taken a bit more seriously if you behaved more like a grown-up."

Maybe he was right. But I wasn't sure it was worth the trade-off. During the years I'd spent growing up in Durango, my parents had made it clear life was less about having fun and more about working hard. It was my aunt who'd taught me otherwise.

Every summer when my parents had snuck me back into Aster Valley to help Aunt Berry on her farm during growing season, I got to escape their severity and learn a different way of life. Berry was a free spirit who believed in the power of the earth, positive thinking, and loving one another. She wore bright yellow stripes and dark purple paisley. Everyone in town came to Berry, not only for home remedies, but also for a kind word, gentle reassurance, and sometimes—if she deemed you special enough—a tarot reading, psychic prophesy, or love potion.

Aunt Berry had shown me that growing up didn't have to mean a life of drudgery. Was she taken seriously? I wasn't so sure about that. Plenty of people thought she was weird or quirky. But she was happy and successful.

"Speaking of behaving like a grown-up," I said, reaching around for the zipper on my costume. "I need to get to work. I have several orders due out today."

Barney sighed and reached over to yank down the zipper. I mumbled a thanks and made my way to the back room where I had extra clothes stashed. I peeled off the big fuzzy suit and stood there in nothing but yellow tights when I heard Barney's voice behind me.

"I shouldn't have complained about the costume," he murmured.

I gasped and turned around, holding the fuzzy suit in front of me like a shield. Barney's eyes were hungry in a way that made my stomach hurt. "D-did you need something?"

"I wouldn't mind a kiss or two," he said with a smile, stepping closer. "You sure are tempting me this morning, Truman."

I stepped back until I felt the worktable behind me. "No time," I swallowed. "I have to get these packages out before the scheduled pickup."

It was a lie. They were going out in the mail which meant I could drop them off at the post office anytime before closing.

"You keep putting me off, Truman," he said. "I thought we talked about this. We've been dating for months now."

"No we haven't," I said. "I told you in the very beginning I wasn't ready for a commitment or label, and then I told you I only wanted to be friends. I don't want a relationship right now."

He gave me a disappointed look. "And I told you to trust me. I know what's best for you, don't I? I can take care of you. Keep you out of trouble and whatnot. All I ask in return is for a little affection."

I shook my head and tried to remember Greta's words. "I'm not comfortable with that. I would like for us to be just friends."

His jaw tightened for a split second before he looked at the floor and sighed before looking up at me. "What am I going to do with you? You're scared, sweet pea. That's all this is." He reached out to take my shoulders in his hands. I tried not to notice how warm and damp they felt against my bare skin. "You've had a really bad day. I think you need a hug." He pulled me against him, the thick fur of the bee costume thankfully creating a barricade between his body and mine. I held my breath as he squeezed me tightly.

The jangle of the shop door broke through the awkward moment like the class bell at the end of a long school day.

"Truman? Are you here?" It was Mikey's voice, and I heard another masculine murmur as well. Probably his boyfriend, Tiller.

"Yeah," I said, gently moving away from Barney's grip. "Back here. Give me a minute."

I blinked an apology at Barney and scrambled to find my clothes. If Sam was somehow with them, I didn't want him to see my scrawny self in nothing but a pair of yellow tights.

But when I walked out to the main floor of the shop in jeans and a henley shirt, I didn't see the big biker.

"Did you talk to Sam?" I asked a little breathlessly.

Mikey came over and gave me a big hug. It felt a million times more reassuring than the one Barney had given me just a few minutes earlier. "Yes, he sent us to check on you while they finish taking his statement."

I closed my eyes and let Sam's concern warm me from the inside out. That was thoughtful of him.

Mikey pulled back and searched my face. "Are you okay? He said someone was trying to bully you."

Barney walked up and stood a little too close to me which made Tiller step closer to Mikey. Tiller Raine was a towering NFL player, who'd intimidated me when I'd first met him. But since then, I'd watched how tender and affectionate he was with Mikey. Not only had it put me at ease, it had helped me realize I needed to end things once and for all with Barney if I was ever going to have a chance at finding something like that.

Barney said, "He's fine. Everything's fine. It was all a misunderstanding."

Except it wasn't. And I could tell by the look on Mikey's face, he knew it. He glanced at Barney before looking back and me and taking my hand. "I'm making your favorite smoked paprika shrimp tonight. Will you come for dinner?" He seemed to realize his invitation hadn't included Barney, so he added, "Because I want to ask you some questions about the chemical effects of introducing bromelian as a pineapple-sourced protease to break down amino acids in—"

"Of course," I blurted before he had to come up with any more excuses. I already knew that tonight was Barney's model railroad club meeting anyway. "What time?"

It wasn't until thirty minutes later that I realized my mistake in accepting Mikey's invitation to dinner.

Sam was going to be there.

3

SAM

"How is he? He okay?" I asked, shrugging back into my leather jacket before grabbing my wallet and bike keys off the counter in front of me. They hadn't actually booked me, but they'd made me leave my jacket and the contents of my pockets at the security station before being led to the little space they considered an interrogation room.

Mikey and Tiller had returned from checking on the little bumblebee who'd been bullied. This entire situation was weird, and I was looking forward to returning to their house to ask a ton of questions.

"Truman's okay. His boyfriend was there," Tiller said, reaching out to pat me on the shoulder. "The question is, are you okay?"

I didn't like the idea of that young man dating the older man, not because of the age difference but because he'd looked annoyed by Truman at a time when the younger man had needed comfort and reassurance. The poor kid had been trembling. But it was none of my business, and I sure as hell didn't need one more person's welfare to concern myself with.

I'd had enough of that with my mom and sisters back in Houston. It was one of the reasons I'd finally convinced myself to take a vacation. I needed a break from the demands of both work and my family.

And maybe it was even time to consider making some changes. Hopefully time spent on the open road would help me clear my head about some things.

But first, I needed to get my bike fixed.

"I'm fine. They're not pressing charges. Obviously." I shoved everything back in my pockets except the motorcycle key. "I need to stop by the Chop Shop on our way to the house. My bike's fucked."

I hopped in the big SUV in the lot and tried calming myself down before we got to the motorcycle shop. It wouldn't do to go in there radiating the anger I felt after the way the law enforcement officers of this town had treated me.

Once I'd arranged for the guys at the Chop Shop to pick up the bike and give it a once-over, we made our way up the mountain to Tiller and Mikey's home. They lived in a giant mountain lodge that they planned to convert to a bed-and-breakfast as part of opening the ski resort back up. Tiller still had several years left on his NFL contract back in Houston, so their plan was to work on it during the off-season and ramp it up slowly to fit with their own travel needs. They'd asked me to swing by to consult with them about a few construction projects.

I'd originally planned to fly in in time for a party they'd thrown last week, but at the last minute, everything had changed and I'd decided to drive it instead. Only, now my bike was out of commission.

"Sorry again about the party," I said to Mikey from the back seat of the SUV. "You know how much I wanted to be there to help celebrate the launch of your cookbook."

Mikey turned around and frowned at me. "Yeah. You said something happened with your sister. Which one?"

"Kira," I said, thankful that my sister Sophie had finally settled down recently.

"Is she okay?"

I rubbed my face with my hands before letting out a breath. "Not really. She showed up at the Gillette jobsite while the project manager was there. She was high as a kite and ranting about our father and abuse and me not making it right and how she's fucked-up because of everything and it's all my fault. The problem is, she wasn't making much sense, so it came out sounding like my addict sister was accusing *me* of abuse and neglect."

"Oh shit," Mikey said in a soft voice. I nodded. "How did she even know where you were?"

Mikey and Tiller were close enough friends to know my family history. They also knew that I would never, ever jeopardize my career by allowing any of them access to a jobsite where I was working.

"One of my guys ran into her at a bar or something, I don't know. It doesn't really matter how she found it. She broke a seven-thousand-dollar ornamental window and then threw a brick at one of the guys who tried calming her down. He's okay, but the project manager called the cops. They arrested her, which of course gave her one more thing to blame me for. Then when I called my mom to tell her about it, she blamed me, too. It was a shitshow."

Mikey sighed. "She's going to have to do some time for this one, don't you think? That's... what? The third time she's been arrested in the last couple of years?"

I shook my head. "Fourth. I didn't tell you about the one at Christmas. That was when you and Tiller were going through everything. She was arrested for possession. I hired a lawyer who got it down from a felony to a misdemeanor, but I told her it was the last time I was going to help her if she wouldn't accept my offer of another rehab stay. Which of course, she refused. Again. So, yeah. This isn't going to be good."

Mikey reached back and took my hand in a squeeze. "I'm sorry, Sam. I know how hard you've tried to help her."

While that was true, I didn't want to think about it. My feelings about my family were so mixed-up and toxic, I was having a hard time dealing with them. It was one of the reasons I'd left town.

"I resigned the Gillette job," I admitted. "Handed it over to the Harding brothers."

Tiller's eyes caught mine in the rearview mirror. "You busted your ass to land that project."

It was true. But I was so tired. I hadn't taken a vacation in... ever.

And it was time for a change in my life. After watching Mikey take a big step toward pursuing his lifelong dream of opening a restaurant, I realized I'd let my own life become stagnant. Hell, I'd never even had dreams. All I'd had was work. I'd spent the better part of the past fifteen years busting my ass to make something of myself.

It had started as a scramble to make money to help my family. I'd started working construction at age fifteen and had worked my way up to becoming a contractor by apprenticing with a pair of brothers I'd worked for. They'd helped me get set up in business and had even pushed a few small projects my way to help get me started. Since then, I felt like I'd been trying to prove myself with every job I took on.

And I was so fucking tired.

"I need a break," I admitted. "I thought maybe I'd ride out to California and drive along the coast."

Mikey and Tiller exchanged a look before Tiller pulled the SUV through a large pair of elaborate iron gates. I knew that look was some kind of marital mind meld even though the two of them weren't married. Yet.

"You don't need to fix me," I muttered, looking around at the gorgeous plot of land they'd bought in this little town in the Colorado Rockies. "This is amazing."

And it was. Thick stands of trees made way for a more formal lawn of freshly sprouted green grass. The lodge itself was huge and solid, a long sprawling building made from heavy timbers and embellished with gas lantern fixtures by the welcoming double doors and plenty of windows sparkling in the spring sun. The slope of Rockley Mountain peeked over the roofline, and I could see the very top of the highest slope still held on tightly to its snow cap.

I'd been there before, but not since the winter snowfall had melted away and revealed everything it had hidden back in March.

"Jesus, is that an actual old-fashioned well?"

Tiller let out a soft laugh, and Mikey's face lit up. "Oh my god, yes! And wait till you see how adorable it is. The pump handle isn't just for show. Actual water comes out. I feel like I'm in a period drama when I use it."

Tiller pulled the vehicle to a stop in front of the lodge. "He thinks he's developing biceps from all the pumping."

Mikey smacked Tiller's arm. "I *am* developing biceps, jackass."

Tiller's eyes twinkled as they looked at his man. "Want to have a gun show?" He moved to roll up his sleeve, but Mikey slapped his hand away.

"Your pro-football muscles will never compare with my *Little House on the Prairie* muscles, so I wouldn't want you embarrassing yourself," Mikey said with a sniff. "Better to keep those little things under wraps."

Tiller leaned over and kissed Mikey on the mouth. "You know I love your muscles," he murmured against Mikey's mouth. Before he said anything else, I took the opportunity to hop out of the SUV and stretch my legs.

I was desperate for a long soak in their hot tub and a healthy dose of something alcoholic. No matter what else happened today, I knew I could count on those two things along with heaps and heaps of Mikey's gourmet cooking.

Despite the awkward start to my visit in Aster Valley, I knew I was in the perfect place to begin letting go of the work and family stress. Besides consulting with them on the construction projects they wanted my help with, I could spend a few days—or however long it took to get my bike back in working order—relaxing and enjoying the easy company of good friends before continuing on to sun and surf.

I ducked my head back into the SUV. "Show me how to work the hot tub, and then you can go have your fuckfest."

The afternoon spent lazing around the lodge with my closest friends did wonders for my mood. It all but wiped out the memory of watching my bike get crushed. I felt calmer and more centered, traits

I'd worked hard to embrace over the years so I would never become my asshole father.

But the minute I saw Truman walk through the door of Rockley Lodge, my calm disappeared in a puff of smoke. The side of his face was scraped and dusty, and a hole had been ripped in the knee of his pants.

"What the hell happened to you?" I barked, standing from my spot at the kitchen island and striding over to him.

Truman hadn't seen me yet, so when he heard my question, he jumped in surprise and clutched his chest with the hand that wasn't holding a bottle of wine. "Cripes, you startled me."

Mikey took the wine and set it on the counter on his way back into the kitchen from answering the door for Truman. "He fell on the driveway. Tiller, grab the first aid kit from our bathroom."

As Tiller disappeared down the hallway, I reached out to examine Truman's face. His big eyes were wide behind his crooked glasses, and his top tooth came out to pin his bottom lip. I reached up to straighten his glasses which made his eyes widen even more.

"Better," I murmured.

"It's fine," he said in a ragged voice. His entire body was coiled with tension, and his cheeks were mottled with pink patches as if he was flustered or embarrassed. "I just tripped. That's all. Stupid."

I glanced down at his feet and noticed the same black Converse sneakers he'd been wearing before, only one of them had a long pair of untied laces. I crouched down to tie it for him.

"So stupid," he muttered again under his breath.

"Pretty sure all of us have done it before. Distracted isn't the same thing as stupid," I said a little more gruffly than I'd intended.

He pinned his bottom lip even harder which made me want to kiss it better. And that thought brought lights and sirens of dire warning. *This adorably awkward man is not for you.*

If there was one complication I absolutely did not need in my life right now, it was interest in a man. I had more than enough things to concern myself with between my general contracting business, my troublesome sisters, and my friends' consulting needs.

Cute boys were off the table.

But he would look so good on a table.

I cleared my throat and stepped back, making way for Mikey to fuss over the spot of road rash on Truman's face. Tiller looked at me with a slight grin on his face which snapped me back to what we'd been talking about before Truman's arrival.

I continued what I'd been explaining before Truman's arrival. "You might not need replacements. The old lifts were manufactured by a company no longer in business. There are two companies in Colorado still making lifts. I think you should have them both send someone out to have a look and give their recommendations. From what I researched, it's possible you might only have to replace some drive terminals and possibly the chairs or pads at first."

Tiller asked, "I wonder if the original lift operator is still around. We could ask them."

It was a good idea. "Maybe. I can check—"

Truman cut me off. "No. No, I mean... no. That's not... Are you... what are you two talking about? The ski lifts?" His voice was pitched a little high and thready like he was upset but trying not to show it. Clearly, he was flustered. I watched him as Tiller responded.

"Yeah. Mikey and I are looking into reopening the slopes. Not right away, but we want to see what it would take to get everything up and running again by the time I retire in a few years."

Truman's eyelashes fluttered like frantic butterfly wings. "But why? Why would you do that? The ski resort? Why?"

"When we bought Rockley Lodge, we had the option to purchase the portion of the mountain the resort was on. I thought it would be a good investment in the town, give me something to do after I retire from the league."

Truman nodded and firmed his jaw. "I think that would be nice. I'm sure plenty of people in town would appreciate it." He seemed to be considering his next words. "But, um... don't... you probably don't want to hire the old lift operator. He's not quite right in the head. Well, that's not accurate. I believe he struggles with alcohol addiction now. But he was never the same after everything happened, you know?"

Mikey shot Tiller some kind of warning look I couldn't read. Tiller sighed and stepped closer to Truman which got my hackles up for some reason. "I'm sorry, Truman. I forgot about your history with the resort," he said in a gentle, kind voice. "I should have been more—"

Truman plastered on a big fake smile. "Oh no! It's fine. Totally fine. I think it's great. Super great. Really great."

What the hell was going on? I opened my mouth to ask questions, but Mikey shot me a warning look before the words could come out. I clamped my lips closed.

None of my business.

Tiller took Mikey's hint and changed the subject. "Truman, I meant to ask if you were growing any arnica this season. Winter told me you make an amazing salve for bruises that I need to stock up on before football season."

Truman's entire face changed, as if he was thrilled to be of use. "Of course! You definitely need some. I'll make you an extra-large batch to take home with you."

Mikey suddenly lurched at Truman and hugged him tightly. "We *are* home. And you're the best."

Truman looked flustered but happy. His eyes slid closed for a brief moment as Mikey crushed him in the hug. It made me wonder what kind of jackass boyfriend he had that he seemed touch-starved.

Not that it was any of my business because it absolutely wasn't, and I didn't care anyway.

Yeah, right.

It didn't take long for me to realize something about Truman Sweet pushed all my buttons in the very best way. He was a unique mix of shy and chatty. When the conversation centered around a topic he was familiar with, he came alive. He spoke with his hands and explained things in interesting detail. His knowledge was extensive. He seemed to know quite a bit about many different things.

When Mikey offered him tea after dinner, Truman's face lit up. "I would love some. Any kind is fine with me. Did you know there are four kinds of tea but they all come from the same plant? *Camellia sinensis*. And I just learned recently that tea bags weren't invented until the early 1900s. In fact, they were invented by accident. A tea merchant created little silk pouches to help him give out samples to his customers. Several of them thought they were supposed to dip the entire thing into the water instead of using a diffuser. Also, for the first three thousand years of its use, tea was only used as a medicine." He took a small bite of the chocolate mousse Mikey had made and groaned. The sound went straight to my dick.

I watched him like a hawk. His long slender fingers held the spoon delicately, and his red lips slid along the bowl of it like the man was deliberately baiting me. Clearly, he was not, because he continued talking about tea.

"And if you meet an English person who pours the milk into their teacup before the tea, they were most likely taught by the older generations who did that to protect the delicate china cups from the direct heat of the tea. It's not necessary anymore, of course. But cultural habits are fascinating, aren't they?"

He seemed to suddenly realize he'd been going on and on about tea. His face heated, and his eyelashes fluttered. He stared down at his mousse. "But enough about all that," he said quietly to himself. "I'm sure you don't need to know more tea trivia."

Mikey looked over at me with an expression of desperation on his face. I'd been best friends with the guy long enough to interpret it.

Do something.

I cleared my throat and took my best shot by making up a total lie. "I heard that in ancient China, tea was used as currency, but I don't know if that's true. Do you?"

Truman's eyes widened. "Um, yes? Yes, it was. The leaves were pressed into a brick, and it was scored on one side in case someone needed to break off a piece to make change."

"Wow, really?" I asked before I could temper my reaction. "I had no idea." Honestly, I'd made the whole thing up. Needless to say, his answer had surprised me.

Truman's brows furrowed. "But you're the one who told me."

Mikey jumped in. Finally. "What did you think of the mousse? I added the lavender like you suggested."

Truman's face lit up again with a kind of relief and quiet pride. "It's amazing. I can't believe you took my suggestion. What if it had turned out terribly?"

Tiller laughed and tried to reach for Mikey's unfinished mousse. "I would have eaten it anyway, so it's all good."

Mikey batted his hand away and curled a protective arm around the dessert. "You've surpassed your allotted carbs for the day."

Truman let out a soft giggle and blushed. It wasn't the first time I'd noticed him watching my friends display affection toward each other, and it made me wonder about his own boyfriend. Why hadn't Mikey and Tiller invited him here with Truman?

After remembering the man had a boyfriend, I spent the rest of the evening trying not to pay particular attention to him. I barely noticed how he smelled or how he shifted in his seat every time the subject of Aster Valley came up. I hardly noticed how his laugh got deeper when Tiller's humor got dirtier. And I definitely didn't pay much attention to the way he absentmindedly licked his spoon long after the last traces of chocolate had been scraped from his dish.

No, if I paid him too much attention, I'd want to rescue him from whatever the hell kind of trouble he was in, and it was definitely none of my business.

But later that night, after we'd enjoyed a nice dinner and plenty of good wine and Truman had left with his arms full of leftovers, I couldn't help myself.

"Why did he act funny when you brought up the ski resort?"

Mikey sighed and settled into the vee between Tiller's beefy thighs on the deep sofa. We were sitting in the den area attached to the big kitchen which seemed to be their favorite place to spend time. On my last visit, I'd quickly discovered they had this enormous lodge and barely used any of it. I wondered what it would be like when they turned it into a bed-and-breakfast. Mikey was eager to host guests and feed people.

Mikey swallowed a sip of wine. "Supposedly he's the reason the resort was shut down in the first place. His dad managed the resort for the family who owned it. When he was only like five or something, Truman snuck his grandpa's metal sled out to the slopes. I'm not sure of the details, but he got scared or something. Ran back home and left the sled behind. The snow fell all night, hiding the sled under fresh powder."

I winced, immediately sensing where this was going.

"The first person down the slopes the following morning was Langdon Goode, one of the best and brightest Olympic hopefuls for the Salt Lake games in 2002. He hit the sled at full speed, and the resulting injuries ruined his career."

Tiller shook his head. "Poor guy. Then his manager and sponsors sued the operation into bankruptcy. There went the Aster Valley Ski Resort. Meanwhile, the family had moved on to other things, or I think maybe they lived part-time in Chicago? That probably contributed to it as well. They kept the lodge here as a vacation home until the grandparents died last year."

"What happened to Truman's family? Surely they didn't blame a little boy for doing what little boys do."

Mikey looked peeved. "The town blamed him. I'm sure they blamed his parents plenty, but there are definitely people in town that still hold Truman himself responsible. It doesn't matter if your brain says a little boy isn't responsible for his actions, the end result was still the loss of a ton of jobs. It was a major blow to the local economy that's taken years to recover from."

"Where are his parents now?" I asked.

"They moved to Durango after a while," Mikey said. "Couldn't handle the gossip and blame. Truman grew up there, but I don't think it was a happy childhood after that. His parents blamed him, too. Probably more out of embarrassment than anything else."

None of this sounded okay. It sounded awful for the poor kid. No wonder he was such a shy, nervous type. "Then why the hell did he come back to Aster Valley? Who would voluntarily return to the viper's nest?"

Mikey sat forward. "He inherited his aunt's property, and it's amazing. It's a plant farm. I think his aunt grew veggies and herbal stuff for home remedies, but Truman grows plants for spices. He's the one with the spice shop I told you about."

I remembered. When Mikey had first told me about falling in love with Aster Valley, he'd described several men he'd met in town. The cutie in the spice shop had been wearing a bow tie.

I thought about it. "I still don't understand why he moved back here. And honestly, he doesn't seem like a farmer."

Tiller snorted softly. "No kidding. But he's super into it."

Mikey waved a hand as he talked. "He loves it, like really loves it. Plants are his thing. He's more of a botanist. He probably got it from his aunt, but regardless, that guy has a major green thumb. I'm sure the farm lured him back. I don't think he went to college or anything, so this was probably his best chance to start something for himself."

I leaned back in the wide leather chair and took another sip of wine while I tried to envision the prim man from the bumblebee costume getting himself dirty with fertilizer and sweat. "How does he manage both the planting and managing the shop?"

Not that it mattered. I was simply making conversation and showing an interest in Mikey and Tiller's new life here, even if that included their new friends.

"Most of his sales are through mail order. He closes the shop Monday through Wednesday during planting and harvesting seasons, and he has some help, too. But I've told tons of people about him in the cooking world, and lots of them already know of him from his company's reputation online. Pretty impressive for a kid, right?"

"He's twenty-four," I said without thinking. "Not a kid."

No one said anything for a beat while I realized I'd accidentally played a card I hadn't known I was even holding.

"Ahh," Mikey said carefully. "I see."

I groaned as I leaned over to set down my wineglass. "You don't see. There's nothing *to* see. I only heard him say it."

"Mm-hm."

I rubbed my face with both hands. "No. Stop *mm-hm*-ing. I know that sound. That's the sound my best friend gets when he's scheming."

Tiller grinned. "He's got you there, babe."

"I'm not scheming," Mikey said with false innocence. "Besides, I thought you were schtupping the pool boy."

I thought of Rico Moreno and his talented tongue. "No. Not schtupping the pool boy. That only lasted until your boyfriend won the Super Bowl—again—and Rico asked me if I could sneak him into your bed one night so he could say he fucked a Super Bowl MVP."

There was a beat of silence before Mikey scrambled up onto his knees and fisted his hands as if ready for fisticuffs. "What the fuck?"

Tiller grabbed him around the middle and pulled him back down, leaning in to nip at his neck. "Would have never worked," he assured Mikey. "I wasn't MVP."

Mikey let out a reluctant laugh and turned to pinch Tiller in the gut. "Ha ha, you're hilarious."

Tiller shot me a wink. He'd already known about Rico because it had necessitated firing him as the pool boy for security reasons. It hadn't been a big loss to me since the relationship had been purely physical.

"Anyway," I continued, "it's for the best. I'm not looking for love, and I'm not even sure I'm sticking around Houston at this point." It was probably just the wine talking, but I was feeling maudlin. I missed living in the same town as my best friend. Mikey and I had been like brothers since high school.

Mikey clasped his hands together in prayer. "Please move here. *Please* move here. We can set you up in one of the chalets."

Tiller nodded. "It's one of the projects I wanted to ask you about. There are three little A-frame chalets a little farther up the mountain on our property. We thought they'd make some good long-term rental properties. Maybe bring in enough money to cover the utilities on the lodge itself until we get the bed-and-breakfast up and running."

I looked at the man who'd already earned at least fifty million dollars in his pro career and was currently in the middle of another obscene contract with the Houston Riggers. Mikey met my eyes with an expression of suppressed laughter.

I couldn't resist teasing Tiller. "Don't worry, buddy. I'll help you get some money coming in. Give you a little breathing room in your budget for once."

Tiller grabbed a sofa cushion and launched it at me as Mikey finally let the laughter go.

It was nice to be among good friends. Comfortable companionship was all I needed. And if the image of Truman's sweet little body appeared naked and hungry in my dreams later that night, it was only an indication my balls were overdue for some much-needed relief.

That was all.

4

TRUMAN

Dinner at Mikey and Tiller's house was a little more awkward than normal because of the large, hulking presence of their moody friend from Houston.

It wasn't that Sam had a mean face, exactly, but he definitely didn't seem to think much of me. And I could hardly blame him. I'd gotten him into trouble with the sheriff's office before he'd even technically arrived in town. He probably hated me anyway.

But... but there had been one moment in the kitchen when the two of us were both bringing dirty dishes to the sink that he'd moved past me in a narrow space and put his big hands on my hips. His touch had been so gentle, so tender, I'd felt goose bumps erupt all over my body.

"Excuse me, sweetheart," he'd murmured so softly, I'd wondered if I'd imagined it. The words, whether they'd been imagined or real, had lit a fire inside my chest that had burned all night long.

But in the morning, I awoke to find the front door of my house hanging wide open and a hastily scribbled note sitting on my kitchen counter, held down by a dirty rock from the garden.

Tell your friend to drop the charges.

My hand shook as I made my way to the front window. There was no sign of Patrick Stanner or his brother, Craig, but it had obviously been one of the two. Their father wasn't usually sober enough to accomplish much of anything, and he'd even lost his driver's license a while ago.

I relocked and triple-checked the bolt on the front door and went around the old farmhouse making sure the window locks were also secure. For the hundredth time, I wished I had the money to fix the gate at the end of the driveway. As a single woman, Aunt Berry had taken her home security seriously, but a snowplow had bumped into one of the posts two years ago and knocked it out of alignment. The solution involved digging out the cement from the original post and replacing it completely, work I wasn't strong enough to do on my own or wealthy enough to hire out.

I decided to call my friend Chaya to see if she wanted to meet me for breakfast at the diner. My nerves were shot, and I really didn't want to be alone.

"Only if it's a quickie," she said. "I'm taking riding lessons from Nina at Crooked Bar Ranch before my shift at the shop this afternoon."

I agreed and raced through a quick shower before throwing on jeans and a hoodie. I normally tried to make a better effort, but I didn't have the time or energy for a dapper ensemble this morning.

When I got to the diner, Pim pointed me to a booth partway down the side wall where Chaya was already sipping coffee.

"Hey," I said, sliding into the red vinyl seat. "I like your hair like that."

She was almost a foot taller than I was, and her giant mane of dark curly hair had been tidied into two side braids like a little girl. It didn't match her brash personality at all, but it pulled her usually unruly mop away from her face enough to make her look fresh-faced and innocent. There was no way in hell I was going to tell her that, though. I valued my life too much.

"It's the only way to get it to fit under the helmet," she muttered. "I look like a damned milkmaid."

I snickered under my breath. "You said it, not me."

"Why do you look pale, hon? Did something happen? I heard from Mia there was a kerfuffle outside the shop yesterday."

I took a breath. Aster Valley was too small to keep anyone's secrets. There was no way to expect the scene from yesterday not to have already gotten around town.

"It's fine. A friend of Tiller and Mikey's got into some trouble with his motorcycle, that's all."

She opened her mouth to question me, but Pim appeared with a pot of coffee and cut her off. "Tell me everything. I heard you were stung by a rabid swarm of bees and had to be taken to the hospital by a miscreant on a motorcycle."

He winked at me, and I rolled my eyes. This town was crazy.

"It was nothing, I promise. Just a misunderstanding."

Pim set the coffeepot down and pulled out his order pad. "I heard it involved that hunk from Houston. What was his name? Simba? Sylvester?"

"Sam," I said. "And I'm pretty sure you knew that since you've met him before."

Pim's hand fluttered against his chest. "Those muscles. That ass. That brooding scowl..."

His husband Bill's voice came from the kitchen. "You think I can't hear you, but I can."

Chaya laughed. "Okay, I've got to see a woman about a horse, so will you please ask Bill to make me a breakfast combo with scrambled eggs, bacon, and hash browns?"

Pim jotted it on his pad. "And you, Mr. Sweet?"

"I'll take some dry toast. Thanks."

Both Pim and Chaya stared at me for a minute before Pim wrote something down and muttered under his breath. "Dry toast and a peanut butter, banana, and chocolate protein smoothie."

I opened my mouth to tell him I wasn't hungry enough for my favorite smoothie today, but he'd already bolted through the kitchen door.

"What's wrong?" Chaya asked. "And don't bullshit me this time."

"It was Patrick Stanner. He crushed Sam's motorcycle on purpose because Sam stopped to defend me against his harassment."

Her eyes narrowed. "That fucker. This has gone too far, Tru. We need to contact the State Police. Sheriff Stanner is never going to prosecute those sons of bitches for their bullshit harassment. Something worse is going to happen, and we both know it."

"I don't want to get anyone into trouble." It was something I'd already told her a million times, but the sentence was starting to sound ridiculous.

Chaya sat back and folded her arms in front of her. "Well, maybe this Sam will finally get Patrick into trouble. Someone from out of state is hardly going to accept them not bringing charges against him."

When I didn't say anything, she pressed me. "Surely, this friend of Mikey and Tiller is pressing charges."

I shrugged. "I mean... it sounded like he was. But when he mentioned it, the sheriff took Sam in instead. I found out later they didn't charge him with anything, but I think it was their way of trying to intimidate him out of accusing Patrick of the property destruction."

Just then Pim showed up with my smoothie and gave me a stern look. "Drink it. And if you want to know what Sam is going to do, simply ask the man." He looked over my shoulder with a tilt of his chin before returning to the kitchen. I turned around to see Sam sitting with Mikey and Tiller at the counter. He was busy scribbling notes with a pencil on a yellow legal pad.

I turned back around to face Chaya and tried not to look as flustered as I felt.

"Your cheeks are like little red apples," Chaya said with a shit-eating grin. "Funny, you don't get apple-cheeked about Mr. Balderson."

"His name is Barney."

"Babe, I grew up here. He's been our librarian for a thousand years. We always called him Mr. Balderson. No amount of nookie with my bestie is going to change that."

I shuddered. "No nookie, and you know that."

"That's not what Big Daddy told his model trains club," she singsonged.

"What?" I cried, unaware of how loud it came out. "What the heck are you talking about?" If Barney had told his model train friends lies about me...

"Gordon Iverson told me Barney had asked the group for a bed-and-breakfast recommendation. He said he wanted someplace special to take his beau for an intimate weekend alone."

I groaned. "I just want to be friends with the man. He's been so good to me, especially after everything that happened in December with the Stanners confronting me and then with Mikey and Pim's accident in front of the shop. How do I convince him I just want to be friends?"

I didn't have many friends as it was, and I didn't want to lose one of the few who cared about me.

Before she could answer, Chaya's eyes widened before a shadow appeared over my shoulder.

"You okay, Truman?" a familiar and delicious deep voice asked from behind me.

I looked up into Sam's handsome face. His blond hair was scattered about like he'd driven down the mountain in a convertible with its top down, and his eyes bore their usual intensity. I felt my stomach take a dive.

"Your eyes look like rosemary," I blurted.

No one said anything, so I scrambled to fill the awkward silence. "Ha, but not... not like... I only mean the rosemary plant has the same sort of dusty green color, you know? Rosemary? The herb? Do you know it? *Salvia rosmarinus*? Never mind."

Sam reached out and cupped my cheek gently with one of his hands before squatting down so he was on my level. His thumb brushed lightly across the remnants of the scrape from my driveway tumble the night before. He moved his mouth next to my ear, and I almost straight-up fainted onto the floor of the diner.

He smelled like pine and lemons... mint, maybe, from his

morning toothpaste. I wanted to inhale every single scrap of his scent I could get my nose on. Chaya stared in shock while my dick strangled itself in my jeans.

"Can I swing by your place later?" he asked softly against the shell of my ear. "This town seems to have eyes and ears everywhere, and I'd like to talk to you in private."

I turned my cheek against his, feeling the soft scrape of his whiskers. I let my eyes close for a second, just enough to savor the feel of his warm, bristly skin against mine.

"Uh-huh," I breathed.

As he pulled away from me, I swore I felt his lips brush against my cheek. My heart felt like it was going to thunder into outer space.

Chaya's eyes were wide and her lips made an o shape.

"Sorry to interrupt," Sam said calmly to Chaya. How he could remain so relaxed after that little interlude was beyond me. I felt like the entire universe had just cracked and shifted like a brand-new Rubik's cube. All the colors had been nice and tidy before but now they were mixed-up and jumbled. It would be impossible to get them put right again.

As he walked away, Chaya's eyes moved over to land on me like dual interrogation lamps. "That is the hottest man I think I've ever seen in my entire life."

I nodded numbly because it was true.

"And he practically made love to your face," she added.

I nodded again.

She patted her chest. "Jesus. I might need a little one-on-one time with my vibrator after that."

Pretty sure I was still nodding. She wasn't the only one.

"And he's friends with Mikey and Tiller?"

I swallowed. "Yuh-huh. He does construction for them." Or something. My brain wasn't quite all the way back online yet.

She snorted and reached out a hand to snap her fingers in front of my face. "Babe. Focus. I have to leave in like ten minutes, and I can't do that until you've downloaded everything into my drive. Got me?"

"That sounds dirty."

Now she was the one nodding. "Exactly. So now why don't you tell me why you're going to a B&B with Barney Balderson when that blond muscle beast over there wants to make bumblebee babies with you?"

I buried my face in my hands with a groan. "First of all, I'm not going to a B&B with Barney. I told you, we're broken up. Secondly, Sam does not want to make... whatever with me. He's just worried about me since he saw me getting bullied. I'm clearly the kind of guy who can't handle things himself. He feels sorry for me."

"Mm," she said, leaning back again with a thinking look on her face. "So why is he whispering sweet nothings in your ear?"

"He's not. He just asked if he could talk to me in private. He probably wants to make sure I follow through on filing a witness statement against Patrick."

"He'd be right. But are you going to do it? You know I have your back, for whatever that's worth."

I bit my lip nervously. That note was still fresh in my mind, and I knew if I pushed Sheriff Stanner to arrest his own nephew, things would go from bad to worse.

"Thank you. I think if he asks me to be a witness to the bike crash, I'll have to do it. Patrick will definitely retaliate." I thought again about how to beef up my home security. Maybe I could temporarily close the shop here in town and stay home until the whole thing blew over. I had plenty of work to do on the farm, and I could send my internet orders from home.

"If he does construction, maybe he can help fix your driveway gate," she suggested, as if reading my mind. "Might as well make himself useful if he expects you to put yourself at risk for his sake."

I glared at her. "Obviously he doesn't know I'd be putting myself at risk. And I'm certainly not going to tell him that. I'll just give the witness report and suffer the consequences. I owe it to him for stopping to help me. Besides, he's a friend of Mikey and Tiller's. I don't want things to get awkward with them if I refused to make a report."

And hopefully that was true. Sam might not believe me, considering I'd told him Patrick had it out for me. Maybe there was a way for me to downplay the whole thing like it was no big deal. I'd talk to him about it when he came to my place.

Sam was coming to my place.

Chaya grunted her disapproval and dug into her breakfast like some kind of feral dog. When she was done, she took a final gulp of coffee and threw some cash on the table for her share. "Sorry to eat and run. Call me later?"

I nodded and waved for Pim so I could pay the check and get moving myself. After dropping by the shop to pick up a few things, I wanted to stop off on the side of the highway and finish putting in the nasturtium seeds really quickly.

Despite everything that had happened yesterday with Patrick Stanner, I still wanted the wildflowers to bloom the way I'd envisioned so every visitor to town this summer arrived feeling happy and welcome. My plan to add the nasturtiums had a purpose. The mustard oil they produced attracted garden pests which would help protect the native wildflowers. They were also easy to grow and stayed low to the ground which made for a nice edging border.

My wildflower initiative was important, even if the county council refused to listen to me. They were going to let their stubbornness over my involvement in the ski resort closing keep them from realizing the economic benefits of a simple highway wildflower program. It was so frustrating to see grown adults cut off their noses to spite their faces.

But it didn't matter. They were getting the highway flowers whether they liked it or not. I had seeds in abundance from my own planting programs, so all it cost me was time and effort.

And a little Stanner harassment if I was caught again.

Not that I was going to let that stop me.

5

SAM

After breakfast and a few errands in town, the three of us drove toward the far side of the ski mountain. One of the ski resort equipment sheds was located on that side of the slopes, and we hoped to find an extension ladder I could use to inspect the roofs of the A-frame cabins.

"Son of a bitch!" I blurted when I saw Truman Sweet on the side of the highway again. "What the fuck is he doing?"

The answer was obvious. His little pert ass stuck up in the air while he bent over with a hand trowel to dig in the dirt. A small bag sat next to him, and I would have bet my bike it held wildflower seeds.

"Pretty sure he's planting something," Tiller said dryly. Mikey stifled a laugh.

"Stop the car," I demanded. "Let me out."

Tiller's eyes met mine in the mirror, and I glared at him. Mikey turned to stare at me. "We're not bothering my friend while he's doing something he loves. Why do you care? The man plants flowers for a living. If he wants to beautify the highway, let him. The poor guy needs a little happiness in his life."

That was all Tiller needed to hear to keep driving. I felt my back teeth grind together. "He won't be happy if that bully shows up again. He's going to get his ass kicked over a damned dirt patch," I said. "The kid has the self-preservation sense of a gnat near a bug zapper."

But Mikey was right. It wasn't any of my business. I'd already sworn off giving a shit about Truman's well-being. He was an adult. I was only passing through.

I let out a breath and rubbed my hands down my thighs. "Whatever," I muttered. "Stupid fucking idiot."

Mikey faced forward again and spoke to Tiller. "Did you catch how weird he smelled? What was that?"

Tiller glanced over. "Who? Truman? Why were you smelling him?"

"Yeah. I walked past him on the way to the men's room. He smelled like... I can't put my finger on it."

My teeth hurt, so I stretched my jaw open. And words popped out. "Cherries. He smells sweet like ripe cherries. Not weird. Just unique."

As soon as the words were out of my mouth, I saw the trap for what it had been. Mikey's face brightened in victory. "Ah-*ha*! I knew it. You like him."

"Wanting to lick him is hardly the same as liking him," I muttered.

Mikey's laughter made me happy, even if it was at my expense.

He danced in his seat and singsonged. "You like him. You want to lick him and fuck him and keep him safe in your arms for-*ever*."

I closed my eyes and drew in a breath of fresh mountain air. At some point Tiller had put the windows down in the SUV, and the warm spring day blew in and washed over me. Despite the hell my friends were giving me, I liked it here. There was something about Aster Valley that eased my soul. I could see why Mikey and Tiller had fallen in love with the place. Part of me wished I could stay longer than a few days.

"It doesn't matter," I said after a minute. "I'm only passing through, then I'm headed to the coast, remember? As soon as my bike is ready."

"We'll see about that," Mikey said. "My plan is to find a way to convince you to stay here with us. My only hesitation in leaving Texas was leaving you behind. If I can get you to move here with us, it will be perfect. All the people I love the most will be with me all the time."

He didn't realize the effect his words had on me. Or maybe he did. But I hadn't had a life full of people who cared. I hadn't had anyone looking out for me the way he had. Mikey may have been very different from his dad and brothers, but he'd still had them in his corner. No, they weren't perfect, and in fact, sometimes I wanted to kick their asses, but they'd still been there.

The only person who'd been there for me was Mikey himself, and I would never ever forget it.

"I'm not making any promises," I said roughly. "Not sure I can leave my business and Mom and the girls."

Mikey's expression turned serious. "No, I know. And I wouldn't want you to do something you didn't want to do. I just mean we love you. Whatever makes you happiest will make us happy, too."

Tiller nodded and met my eye again in the mirror. He was a good man. I was grateful beyond measure Mikey had found him.

"Well," I said, clearing my voice. "It will make me happiest to find a damned good ladder in the storage shed. How much longer till we get there?"

After finding the ladder we needed—at the local hardware store rather than the dusty old equipment shed—we made our way back to the lodge property where I spent a happy few hours inspecting the chalets. Tiller accompanied me and helped make a punch list of tasks, repairs, and upgrades the little cabins needed, but overall they were in fairly good shape. I could even knock out some of the work while I waited for my bike to be fixed.

Once I'd stuffed myself with Mikey's lunch spread that included custom turkey sandwiches on thick slabs of homemade bread, I borrowed the SUV and set off to town to check in with the Chop

Shop. Jim Browning assured me that he could fix it in the next few days.

"Are you sure? A couple of days seems quick for a bent fork and—"

"Never been more sure of anything in my life. Take my word for it. You're gonna be good to go in a jiffy." He beamed at me. "And if you need a loaner in the meantime, we have a good deal on a Kawasaki rental." He tilted his head toward a bike in the lot. I expected a cheap, banged-up piece of shit, so I was surprised to see a Versys in decent shape.

"Run well?" I asked, thinking it was too good to be true to get my own wheels in this tiny town without much fuss.

He nodded. "'Course."

"How much?" I asked Jim.

We settled on a rental agreement, but when I asked for the keys, he looked at me like I had two heads. "Key's in the bike. This is a small town, Mr. Rigby. If anyone else is caught driving that bike, I'll know who took it. Same goes with all our local customers' vehicles. They leave the keys in 'em, and we don't have to stick around for a late drop-off."

I laughed at the reminder I wasn't in Houston anymore.

When I finally walked out with an estimate for the repairs, I breathed a sigh of relief. At least I would be less of a burden to my friends while I was here. I'd be able to roam the mountains without feeling stuck in one place.

I left the bike in the Chop Shop lot for now and tossed my saddlebags into the SUV before continuing to the address I had for Truman's farm. My phone rang with calls from my mom, but I ignored them. Most likely my she was calling to beg legal help for Kira, and if it wasn't for that, she was calling to ask for money. I didn't even want to speculate as to why Kira wasn't calling, too. She probably knew I wouldn't answer and had asked Mom to call instead.

The first thing I noticed when I pulled onto the narrow road leading to Truman's place was a dilapidated sign that read, "Berry Sweet Farm." The second thing I noticed was half of a gate hanging drunkenly off to the side of the farm's driveway. I wondered if someone had crashed into it with their car. Maybe even the aunt who'd owned the property before Truman.

As I pulled down the drive, I passed open fields with row after row of various types of little green shoots sprouting through the tilled earth. A giant arc of water from a sprinkler shot through the air over the plants, casting vague rainbow apparitions in the afternoon sun. Motion off to the left caught my attention, and I saw the same tight little Truman ass I'd seen earlier sticking up from where he bent over a wheelbarrow. He'd changed out of his jeans and hoodie. Now that the sun was blazing warm in the sky, he wore a faded T-shirt and old cutoff shorts that had once been khaki pants but were now just a collection of wash-worn threads being held together with a hope and a prayer. I almost crashed the SUV trying to catch glimpses of his bare upper thigh through the holes in them.

After parking, I made my way over to him and noticed he had earbuds in his ears and had begun wiggling his butt to a tune only he could hear.

My dick urged me forward, and I could just imagine the way that gentle grind would feel if I grasped his hips and pulled him against me. I wasn't sure why my libido had formed such a quick and strong attachment to this man, but it clearly had. I wanted him naked underneath me, on top of me, any way I could get him. I wanted to run my hands over all of that sweet skin and then trace it with my tongue.

"Ahhh!" Truman screeched when he saw me out of the corner of his eye. Dirt and a hand trowel went flying through the air as he put up his arms in a defensive gesture.

We stared at each other.

Truman's chest heaved with labored breaths. He finally remembered to pull out his earbuds. "Holy crap, you... you..." His breathing seemed to make him light-headed because his eyes rolled back a little. I stepped forward and grabbed his arm as gently as I could in case he decided to tip over.

"Slow down," I murmured. "It's just me. You're okay."

"You scared me to death," he finally finished, pulling out of my grip. "You should… warn… a guy, or something."

I tilted my chin and lifted an eyebrow. How exactly was I supposed to warn him when he'd been listening to music at top volume?

"Maybe you should fix your driveway gate so no one can sneak up on you like this?" I suggested instead.

His eyebrows pinched. "That's easy for you to say when you have the muscles and know-how to do something like that."

Oh. The sweet little man had a backbone. I grinned at him. "Touché. Why don't I fix it for you while I'm in town?"

Truman's mouth opened, but nothing came out.

"It's the least I can do for helping you yesterday and having my bike crushed by your assailant."

His mouth closed with a click. "That's sarcasm."

"Indeed."

"Never mind, then. I don't need your help." He sniffed and turned around, accidentally knocking his knee into the wheelbarrow and yelping.

Christ, the man was adorable. I wanted to swallow him whole.

I moved over and crouched down to inspect Truman's hurt knee, trying my best to ignore the curved definition of his thighs and calves. There wasn't any blood, simply a smudge of dirt right below his kneecap. I brushed it off with my thumb and noticed movement under his threadbare fly. Bright blue briefs peeked out from the holes in the fabric and tested every ounce of my self-control.

I glanced up at him and saw two red spots on his cheeks. His eyelashes fluttered as he looked everywhere but at me. Fuck, but he was delicious.

"I'm fine," he said in a breathy voice. "Fine."

I stood up slowly, staying close to his body so there was only an inch or two between us. The sound of his sucked-in breath hit me in the gut.

"You sure?" I asked in a low voice.

"Do—" Truman's voice broke, so he started again. The apples of his cheeks deepened as he carefully stepped away from me. "Do you need something?"

I nodded. "I want to talk to you about what happened yesterday."

"Oh, uh, sure." He turned back to his planting, busying himself with whatever was close to hand. He was clearly trying to avoid looking at me, but I decided to allow it if it meant he'd relax and speak more freely. "What do you want to know?"

"Why Patrick Stanner is harassing you."

He froze for a split second before shrugging. "He's just a jerk like that."

"I don't think so."

"You don't think he's a jerk? I can assure you, the man has a reputation for being unhappy and causing problems."

I looked at his narrow shoulders and noticed the small swell of biceps and forearms as he used a long-handled fork tool to loosen the soil in an unplanted area. From the smell of the contents of the wheelbarrow, I guessed he was adding a fertilizer mixture to the soil.

I guessed Truman was stronger than his smaller size would indicate. If he did all of this planting and farming himself, he must have plenty of endurance and muscle mass.

"Are you even listening to me right now?" he asked.

I blinked up at his face which was pinched in frustration. "You said he was unhappy and a jerk."

He nodded and turned back to his tilling. "Exactly."

"So, if I had been the one planting nasturtiums, he would have harassed me?" I watched for his reaction and wasn't disappointed. His lips pursed in frustration.

"Obviously not."

"Why not? If it's just because the guy is a jerk, he would have done it to anyone, right?"

"No, not right. He wouldn't pick on someone so... so..." Despite his better judgment, Truman's eyes traveled up and down my body.

"So Texan?" I drawled, stepping closer. "So... blond?"

His nostrils flared. "So..." His hand flapped up and down,

gesturing to me. "Big and strong. There, I said it. Are you proud of yourself? Geez."

I enjoyed antagonizing him for some reason, but I suddenly realized I was being as obnoxious as Patrick Stanner. I didn't want to annoy him when he already had bigger men treating him with disrespect.

"Sorry. I didn't mean to tease you," I said softly.

Truman's eyes widened. He looked surprised by the apology. "It's fine. I don't see why you care. You don't live here. It's not your concern."

And that was true. But I could see something in his eyes that told me this was a bigger problem than he was letting on, and after what Mikey and Tiller had told me about the cause of the ski resort shutting down, I suddenly wanted to know how this guy was able to stand living in a town that held so many bad memories and grudges.

If Truman was regularly harassed by people in this town, why didn't he have friends protecting him? Mikey had never met a cause he didn't like, so why hadn't he taken it on himself to help Truman?

Was it possible he didn't realize what was going on?

"I'd like to fix your gate." The words didn't surprise me as much as they should have. I didn't do well with extra time on my hands, and the projects over at Rockley Lodge could keep. I didn't have much time in town, but what I did have could be put to good use here at the farm.

Not because I had an inexplicable desire to spend more time with Truman, but because I was never really good at sitting still, and working outside in such a beautiful location would be a great way to pass the time until my bike was ready.

My traitorous brain tried reminding me working on the Rockley Chalets would accomplish the same thing, but I squashed those thoughts down before they could take root.

Truman turned to face me again, and this time he leaned the tool against the wheelbarrow and put his hands on his hips. "That's not necessary. I was going to agree anyway."

Now I was confused. "Agree with what?"

"To file a witness report for the bike crash."

This seemed like a sudden about-face. But why? If Patrick bullied Truman regularly, why would Truman agree to bear witness against him?

"Thanks, but I don't need you to do that," I said before thinking it through. Surely my insurance company would need a police report, but I wasn't sure they'd need proof of fault in order to cover the damages.

"Why not?" He looked at me with suspicion in his eyes.

"There was another witness," I said stupidly. Why? Why was I making shit up? Why not just say I had plenty of money and didn't need to bother with insurance?

Truman's forehead crinkled in confusion. "Who?"

"Frank." I wanted to slap myself on the forehead. What the fuck was I doing?

"Frank Young from the real estate office? Or Frank Mosley who works at the nursing home?"

Shit. I remembered there was a real estate office next to the diner. Maybe I could find someone in there who'd cover for me if push came to shove.

"First one. Anyway, see? It's fine. I don't need you. It's all settled."

"Oh no! No, no, no," Truman groaned. "If Frank Young saw me planting flowers out on the highway, I'm done for. He's going to ban me from county council meetings forever. This is awful."

He stumbled to a nearby bench and sat down, burying his face in his hands. I stared at him. Guilt churned in my gut.

"Maybe... maybe it was the other one. I don't remember. Young... Mosley... who can tell the difference really?"

I shifted from foot to foot.

Truman threw back his head and wailed. "That's even worse! Frank Mosley is legally blind. Everyone in town knows it. His eyewitness account will be tossed out the minute he submits it."

What the actual fuck was happening right now?

I threw up my arms in defeat. "What do you want me to say? It's taken care of. That's all that matters. You don't need to worry about it."

Truman dropped his emotional act and stood up, pointing a finger at my chest and then striding close enough to actually poke it. "I want you to stop lying. Neither of those Franks exist. I don't know what Mikey told you, but I don't need you feeling sorry for me or trying to protect me out of some sense of—"

I couldn't stand it anymore. His feisty response lit a fire in my belly. I lurched forward and grabbed his face before leaning in to taste that sassy mouth.

6

TRUMAN

The first few seconds of the kiss, I was still angry Sam had lied to my face about another witness. The next few seconds, I was shocked to discover Sam Rigby was kissing me full on the mouth.

Why? Why was he doing it? And, like... why?

Then... then there were lots and lots of seconds where I didn't think much of anything. Regardless of what my brain would have chosen, had it been given a vote, I was at Sam's mercy. One of his giant hands spread across the middle of my lower back, and the other one held the front of my throat. His fingers and thumb tilted my jaw in whatever angle he wanted while he took complete ownership of my mouth.

I stood on tiptoes even though I really wanted to climb his body and wrap my legs around his waist. He felt so good. Strong and possessive, but gentle and sweet at the same time. It was a dangerous combination, dangerous for me anyway. The last thing I needed was to develop a crush on a guy who was going to breeze right back out of town as soon as the weather turned.

But that didn't mean I was going to end this kiss, because... well, I wasn't stupid. He was a darned good kisser, and I was going to drink in this experience as much as he would let me so I could replay it later like a favorite video clip on my phone.

The only warning I got before he ended the kiss was a slight tightening of his fingers on my neck before he let me go and gently pushed me away from him.

"Fuck," he muttered, wiping his mouth with the back of his hand. "Fuck. Fuck."

My heart was racing like a rabbit, and my mind was worse. Why was he so upset? Had it been a bad kiss? Had I disappointed him? Clearly, Sam was having regrets.

"Sorry," I said, spreading my feet a little wider and standing up straight. I wanted to be ready for the emotional blow when he full-on rejected me. I could take it. I was used to it.

"Why are you sorry?" He squinted at me in the afternoon sun. "*Are* you sorry?"

I firmed my jaw. "No, actually. I'm not sorry one bit. But you looked like you were, so I was sorry you didn't like it as much as I did."

I was surprised to discover myself more annoyed than insecure.

Sam's face softened, and he stepped closer again, leaning in until we were almost nose to nose. "Who said I didn't like it? I liked it, okay? I liked it plenty. I more than liked it."

For some reason, his growled words, spoken almost against his will, made me feel stupid. Like I'd made him angry by being kissable. My body flushed hot, then cold, and I began to feel numb. Ahh, here was the insecurity at last. It was a feeling I was familiar with. It meant I needed to get away from him before I did any more apologizing.

I flashed him a big smile. "I have to go," was all I managed to get out before bolting for the house. I heard him call my name, but I ignored him. In my mind I came up with all of the words I wish I'd said to him. That if he'd enjoyed kissing me, he wouldn't have scrubbed at his mouth like my lips had been poisonous. That if he recalled, *he* was the one who'd kissed *me*. It wasn't like I'd asked for it.

Had I?

Only with every fiber of my being. But unless he was a mind reader, there'd been no way for him to know it.

I reached for the front door of the house and pulled it open. Just as I was preparing to slam it closed behind me, I registered the sound of his heavy boots on the wooden planks of the front porch.

He got to the door before I could slam it.

"Truman, wait. Wait, dammit."

I shook my head and waved my hand over my shoulder. "I'm fine. Sorry to cut our time short. Bye!" I headed to the sunroom in the back where I had two large worktables set up to put together online orders. Cubbies with shipping supplies stood neatly below the thick wooden tabletops, and my laptop sat primly next to the small label printer.

I tried to focus my brain on what I needed to do. When I'd arrived home, I'd gotten distracted planting the last of the nasturtium seeds in my garden when I really should have been in here organizing today's shipments.

My body shook with a combination of nerves and frustration. I'd finally gotten the kind of sexy, breathtaking moment I'd only read about in novels. But then it had all been dashed to bits when he'd pushed me away.

Why had he ruined it? I wanted to scream.

I expected him to bark out my name again or grab my arm to force me to look at him. Instead, he simply followed me into the sunroom and sat on the edge of the old reading chair in the corner. I tried my best to ignore him and get to work, but the weight of my hissy fit became heavier as the minutes wore on.

The orders necessitated several trips out to one of the outbuildings that held inventory. Every time I returned to the sunroom, I noticed each completed package had been neatly stowed in the handled post office totes I delivered to the driver. With his silent help, I was finished in less time than it usually took.

When I began to carry the totes out to the front porch, Sam quickly jumped up and helped. Afterward, he followed me into the big farmhouse kitchen, the room of the house I was most uncomfortable in now that Aunt Berry was gone. It used to be the heart of her home, full of friends and family, pets and music, scents of new concoctions, and the taste of whatever cookie she'd made special for me.

Now... now it was just a kitchen. And I hated it.

"Lemonade?" I asked. My voice sounded a little scratchy from the hour and a half of tense silence.

"Yes, please." He waited patiently on the other side of the butcher-block island while I took down old Scooby-Doo drinks glasses from the 1970s. The decals were almost completely worn off from years of use and washing, but the memories were as fresh as they'd been when she'd first entrusted me with one.

I poured lemonade from the pitcher in the fridge and handed him a glass. "Sorry it's a mess. I had plans to put beadboard in here, but then..." I shrugged and sighed. I didn't owe this stranger any explanations or apologies.

Sam watched me as he took a deep gulp. After swallowing, he set the glass down and braced his hands on the counter between us. "I owe you an apology," he began. My hackles rose. I didn't want his apologies. I wanted him to leave me alone. Okay, fine. If I was being honest, I wanted him to kiss me again, but that probably wasn't one of my options.

"I shouldn't have kissed you like that."

Ugh, why didn't he just leave? Why did we need to rehash how wrong the kiss was? For god's sake, it was just—

"I know you have a boyfriend," he added.

My ears scrambled to hit the mental replay button on that. "But... I don't?"

The edge of his lip inched up. "You asking me or telling me?"

I took a breath. "I *don't* have a boyfriend. I'm single."

Suddenly, Sam's lips widened into a feral grin. "Well, now. That changes everything."

He was giving me whiplash. "Why? You seemed disgusted with yourself after kissing me earlier." Ugh, I wanted to kick myself for saying it out loud. I sounded so pathetic.

Sam began to move around the kitchen island. As soon as I

noticed it, I moved, too, creating a circular motion like hands on a clock. One moved faster than the other.

"Not disgusted with the kiss, Truman. Disgusted with myself for forcing it on an unwilling participant."

My heartbeat bounced around my chest irregularly like a handful of dice being shaken in a Yahtzee cup. "Not unwilling," I managed to say without also begging for more.

I mentally patted myself on the back.

We stared at each other for a protracted moment. Maybe Sam was sizing me up, and I was truly worried about coming up wanting. When was I going to get a chance to kiss another man this exciting, this dangerous, again?

Never. Because I didn't let big muscled guys close to me. Ever.

Thank you, Patrick and Craig Stanner.

Which reminded me I didn't know Sam. And, sure, he was friends with Mikey and Tiller, but honestly... I didn't know them very well either.

"But it's fine," I suddenly hurried to add as I continued the slow escaping shuffle around the butcher block. "You probably need to get going. I heard you're helping sort out the work that needs to be done at Rockley Lodge. That's really nice of you. I'm sure Tiller and—"

He caught up with me and pressed his body along my back. I sucked in a breath and squeezed my eyes closed. Sam didn't touch me with his hands; he only stood with the warm, strong front of his body pressed against the back of mine.

I felt the bulge behind the fly of his jeans against my lower back. I smelled the lemony-pine scent I'd noticed on him before. I heard the soft inhalations of his breath.

"I probably should get going," he said softly, leaning down to brush his lips against my ear the way he'd done in the diner. "But I really don't want to. I want to stay here and do things to you, Truman. Dirty, dirty things." He shifted in a way that brushed the steel-hard ridge of his erection against me. "And that's why I'm going to leave."

I could barely breathe, much less speak. No one had wanted to do dirty things to me before. Barney had wanted to do sexual things to me, I was sure. But not *dirty* things. At least, I couldn't picture Barney with those particular thoughts and desires. He seemed more like the kind of person who wanted to do clean and tidy things to me. Quickly, and without much spice.

I liked spice.

Not that I knew what it was like to have spice in the bedroom. Other than online, of course. With myself. But my real-life experience was limited to a sum total of nothing much with other people.

I got up the nerve to turn around and lean my forehead against the soft cotton of his shirt just below his collarbones. My head tucked perfectly under his bearded chin, and when his strong arms came around me, it felt as natural as breathing.

"I don't think I'm ready for dirty things," I admitted softly to his chest. "But just knowing you would want that is… really nice."

I mentally kicked myself. Nice? That was an incredible understatement.

But it was nice. It was so nice, I suddenly felt like I could fall asleep in his arms and sleep for days. Like I could finally let go of carrying all the weight of being me and just… let him take the watch for a little while.

And that feeling was terrifying. Because I knew from experience the minute you let your guard down with someone, they held too much power over you. Besides, there was a fine line between protecting and dominating, and a man like Sam Rigby had "domination" written all over him. I wasn't about to make that mistake again no matter how tempting it was.

I inhaled one last breath of him and then fortified myself before stepping back and plastering on a smile.

"Thank you for coming over and for helping with the packages. Hiram usually comes to pick them up around four thirty, so he'll grab them from the front porch, no problem. And I have loads of other work to do on the farm, so I really need to get out there. It's time to plant the cumin seeds so they can flower. The flowers are really good at attracting beneficial insects which is why I like to put them in fairly early in the process."

Even though I heard myself talking too much, I couldn't stop. I huffed out a desperate laugh. "They attract parasitoid wasps and ladybird beetles, so I plant it near crops that have problems with caterpillars and aphids. But I learned that if you water it too much, cumin can get root rot which isn't good." My breathing was getting shallower as I continued talking. Sam's face remained unreadable. His attention was focused on me, but I had no idea what he was thinking. I continued blathering on. "Obviously. And it has a longer growing season which helps me spread out the planting and harvesting."

I swallowed and tried gluing my lips closed. I failed. "And then I need to run by the shop to... do... things."

Sam finally nodded once before speaking. "I make a really good cumin chicken and rice dish. Mikey taught me how to make it, so you know it's good. Can I make it for you tomorrow night? I'll have to use your kitchen."

I stared at him. Hadn't he heard what I'd just said? "You want to cook dinner for me? Here?"

He nodded again. "I mean... you're welcome to come to Rockley Lodge, but I would prefer to have dinner with just the two of us. It's up to you. Whichever makes you more comfortable is fine with me."

Did he think cooking me dinner was going to lead to the dirty things he wanted to do to me? It wasn't. There was no way I would put myself in a position of making a fool out of myself in front of a man who probably had advanced certifications in dirty sexual acts.

I was still staring at him. Finally, Sam turned and looked around the kitchen before noticing a little pad of paper and pencil on the counter where the house phone still sat attached to the wall even though it didn't work anymore. He walked over to it and scribbled something down on the pad before turning back to me.

"That's my number. I'm going to be here at six tomorrow to start cooking. If you decide you don't want me to come, just call or text me, okay? Otherwise, I'll see you tomorrow."

He started to take a step toward me like maybe he wanted to mark his departure with a kiss or handshake. But he stopped himself and smiled instead. "Enjoy your time in the garden, Truman."

As he turned to leave, I finally found my voice. Rather, *stupid* Truman found my voice.

"You can use my cumin! I have... I have several kinds. Wild black cumin harvested by hand in Afghanistan. It's probably my favorite. And it has incredible health benefits." I ticked them off on my fingers. "Antidiabetic, antihypertensive, antibacterial, anti-inflammatory, neuroprotective, antimicrobial, antifungal... The list goes on and on. Even the prophet Mohammed said it could heal everything but death."

I bit my lip to shut up the info dump, but when I saw Sam's eyes spark with interest in what I was saying, I stopped biting my lip and allowed myself to smile a little.

"And if you want more eccentric spice trivia," I offered, "come back tomorrow."

At that, he grinned wide and nodded again before turning and walking out of the house in his long, possessing strides. I couldn't help but stare at his butt as he walked away. His jeans fit him perfectly. What did that body look like without them? What did it look like when he did *dirty things*...?

And would I ever get up the nerve to find out? Maybe it was possible to let him do those things to me without letting him get close enough to cause real problems.

Instead of heading back into the garden to plant the cumin seeds, I decided to head into town to give my eyewitness report to the sheriff's office before I lost my nerve. Hearing Sam lie about other witnesses made me realize how much of a coward he must have thought I was. The least I could do was support his complaint to have his bike repairs paid for by the responsible party.

Even if that party was someone who wanted to beat me to a pulp.

I ignored the nerves in my gut while I quickly changed into clothes that would bolster my confidence. Khaki pants, a plaid button-down shirt, and a deep blue bow tie Aunt Berry had sent me for my seventeenth birthday.

Thankfully, Sheriff Stanner wasn't there when I showed up to make my statement. A stern-faced deputy I'd never met before took me back to his small office to fill out the paperwork.

"I'm Deputy Declan Stone," he said, all business. "Tell me exactly what happened."

He must have been new in Rockley County because he treated me like a regular person. There were no derisive smirks or poorly disguised sneers. He simply took my statement as straightforwardly as possible, only stopping for a moment when I mentioned the driver of the truck.

"Patrick Stanner? Any relation to the sheriff?"

At that point, I was sure he was new. Everyone knew Patrick and his brother, Craig. They were troublemakers and assholes. If their uncle hadn't been sheriff, they'd have law enforcement files several inches thick by now.

"His nephew. You don't know him?"

Deputy Stone shook his head. "I transferred in a few weeks ago from LA. Just getting settled." He looked up at me. I assumed he was close to forty, but he looked good for it. Some salt sprinkled into his pepper and a few lines around his eyes. The man looked ex-military by the stiff way he carried himself and the closely shorn hair. Something about him gave me a tiny amount of hope that there might be at least one non-partial member of the department.

"Welcome to Aster Valley," I said politely. "It's a lovely place to live."

The twenty minutes I spent with him were cordial but professional. I wished I knew him well enough to be able to confide my history with the Stanners to him and ask for his professional help in dealing with the sheriff's bias, but I didn't. And I also had no desire to put the poor deputy between a rock and a hard place.

So I left the sheriff's department and headed back into town to check in with Chaya, who'd agreed to open the shop for the afternoon and do some inventory work.

"Hiya, sweet thing," she called from the back table when I walked in. The familiar scent of mixed spices and herbs was as comforting to me as sliding into my own bed at night. I took a deep inhale and let my shoulders drop.

"How was the riding lesson?" I asked, straightening a few bottles and jars on one of the front shelves.

"True confession time," she said, leaving her work behind and making her way around the display tables to where I stood. "I'm in love with one of Nina's cowboys."

I laughed. That explained why my friend who hated getting dirty was interested in a dusty horse ride. "Which one? Because Hank Jolly is married, and Mato Pietaker is intimidating as heck."

She grabbed my hand and danced me to the middle of the store. "Nick Humphrey, Nina's nephew from California. And he's neither of those things. He asked me back to the ranch for a cookout tomorrow night and said I could invite anyone I wanted."

The bell over the door rang, but I was too busy trying to clear my head from the sudden twirl and dip maneuver to greet the customer. Chaya threw a smile in the general direction of the front door before asking if I wanted to come to the ranch barbecue.

"No, thanks. I have dinner plans with Sam," I said while still a little dizzy from the dancing.

Chaya's squeal of excitement was joined by a familiar clearing of the throat.

Barney.

"Oh, sorry, Barney," I said, brushing my hair back from my eyes and straightening my glasses. "I didn't realize that was you."

"I guess not," he said with a sniff. "I came by to see how you were faring after your scare yesterday."

I tried to give him a reassuring smile. "Fine, thank you. How was the reading circle this morning?"

His forehead crinkled for a second like he didn't follow, but then he must have remembered how much I loved hearing about the kids' reading time at the library. "It was... normal? The same as always, really."

"Who volunteered today?" I asked, trying not to sound too eager. Reading to the children at the library was one of my favorite things to do, but Barney had taken me off the volunteer list a while ago, adamant that it would be "inappropriate" for his "special someone" to be involved in a library program like that. Maybe now that we were no longer together like that, I could get back on the rotation.

"Ellen Amana," he said with a wave of his hand as if it wasn't important.

It was. Ellen was the mayor's wife, who did a horrible job reading to the kids. It was clear she hated it and only did it for appearances.

I bit my tongue to keep from saying so. Thankfully, Chaya broke in. "Mr. Balderson, do you happen to have a book on how to become a kick-ass horsewoman in forty-eight hours or less?"

Barney blinked at her like she was an alien being from a faraway planet. "I'm not sure that's possible. Mastering the equestrian arts is a complex and nuanced endeavor. But I'm sure I have some picture books in the children's section that could get you off to the right start," he said, barely holding back a sniff of disapproval. "Not to mention several tomes about proper comportment for young ladies."

Chaya's nostrils widened in a silent laugh. "No need for that one, Mr. B. I'm good, thanks." She glanced back at me. "You should really get going if you want to shower before your dinner date with Sam."

I opened my mouth to remind her that the date was tomorrow night, and I wasn't even sure it was a date, but she winked at me. "Just kidding. Maybe you could stick around and explain whether I'm supposed to inventory the bulk spices by weight or container."

It was a ridiculous question because the Honeyed Lemon didn't sell spices in bulk, but thankfully, Barney took it as his cue to leave but not before pulling me aside.

"Tell me you're not having dinner with that man," he said in a low voice as if he hadn't found out about it from Chaya herself.

"I am having dinner with him."

He looked truly shocked. "He's a stranger. He's a drifter."

"He's friends with Tiller and Mikey," I corrected. "He's in town for a few days to visit them on his way out to California."

"You barely know those two either. Truman, really. Why this need to befriend everyone around you? It's like you're trying to prove something when you have nothing to prove. You're fine just the way you are, sweet pea. There's no need to make yourself into something you're not."

Was that what I was doing? I thought back to my interactions with Sam, Mikey, and Tiller. Had I been trying to be someone I wasn't? I didn't think so.

"They seem to like me as I am," I began, a little unsure.

"Be that as it may, I think you're better off letting me take you out for a nice dinner. We could go to that Chinese place you like."

Before I could answer, Chaya called out another inane question about comparing ounces to grams and why did the basil, bay leaf, and caraway blend sound like a folk band name.

Barney cleared his throat to regain my attention. "Perhaps you'll come see me at the library when you leave here so we can speak further?"

"Perhaps," I said.

But I didn't.

7
SAM

On the drive back to Rockley Lodge, I tried my best to feel regret over kissing Truman. It wasn't fair to lead him on when I was simply passing through Aster Valley. He didn't seem like the casual hookup kind of guy, and I was the king of casual connections.

But, god. Those full lips, that tight little body... the way his nose wrinkled when his glasses slipped down a little. The man was irresistible.

I'd noticed the broken gate again when pulling out of his driveway and had made a mental note to grab some supplies and come over early enough tomorrow to fix it before dinner. If Truman had people in town who didn't like him, he needed better security than he had now.

I wondered idly how the security was at his shop. Mikey had pointed it out to me earlier on our drive through town. The Honeyed Lemon was in a two-story historic brick building on the end of a string of similar buildings that made up part of the main drag of the little town of Aster Valley. Several of them had been abandoned somewhere along the way, but many of them had newish, seemingly thriving boutiques and restaurants in them. It was nice to see the town doing fairly well even without the ski resort running.

When I got back to the lodge, it was suspiciously silent until I heard enthusiastic sex sounds coming from the direction of the kitchen. I quickly turned on my heel and went right back out the front door, deciding a nice nature walk would do me some good before dinner.

It was hard not to be, well... *hard*... after hearing that. Tiller was a professional NFL wide receiver with a killer body, and Mikey was small and flexible. Even though I had no real-life interest in sleeping with either man, it was hard not to imagine how hot the two of them would be together. Tiller's hands were multimillion-dollar assets, and I was fairly sure they were just as talented on my best friend's body as they were on the football field. Mikey always got a dreamy look on his face when talking about Tiller's hands, and it was enough to set my imagination in motion.

I forgot the walk and threw myself down in one of the wooden rocking chairs on the front porch instead. The afternoon light was turning that magical golden color that signaled my favorite time of day. I propped my feet on the porch railing and tried to relax and enjoy the moment with a few deep breaths.

There was a fresh herbal smell coming from something nearby, and I wondered if Truman would be able to identify it with only a sniff. Probably.

And he'd lean over to sniff the mystery plant which would stick that sexy ass up in the air again. It hadn't been that long since I'd hooked up with someone, but for some reason, Truman Sweet's slim form was doing it for me. It had stuck to my brain cells like a very sexy Velcro strip, and I was having trouble plucking it off.

I forced myself to remember I was just passing through. Work had been hectic lately, and the situation with my sister had done a number on my stress level. All I had was my reputation as a hard worker and a contractor who came in on time and under budget. I didn't have a lot of capital. I had business loans that I was constantly juggling between sending out invoices and getting paid. My profits either went into the business or went to my mom and sisters.

I couldn't keep going like this. Something had to give.

Even though I knew I deserved a vacation, waves of guilt still came over me when I stopped to think about it too much. What if one of my clients had a catastrophe? What if one of my family members needed me?

But that was part of the problem. I'd spent the last several years dropping everything to either help my family or put out fires at work, and I'd spent even more years than that trying to protect my family from danger.

Was that why I was attracted to Truman? Because he needed someone to rescue him?

I pushed the porch rail with one boot to start the chair rocking. No. No, that wasn't why I wanted him. I didn't want to rescue him. I wanted to fuck him. There was a difference.

And then I was back to picturing Truman bent over a garden plant in shredded shorts.

There was no telling how long I sat out there trying not to jack off to thoughts of Truman's body and sweet blushes. I may have even dozed off a little bit, but eventually Mikey texted to ask where I was, and the buzz of my phone startled me fully awake. The air was much cooler, and the light was fading.

I made my way into the house and lifted a knowing brow at him. "Feeling better?"

Tiller snorted from inside the fridge where he was most likely doing recon to find out what Mikey had in store for us tonight.

Mikey nodded his head with enthusiastic exaggeration. "Soo much better. Thanks for asking. You should try it."

"Getting dicked down in the kitchen?"

He continued the nod but added a maniacal grin. It was Tiller who had the decency to blush. "How'd it go at Truman's?"

I told them about my visit, leaving out the part where I'd attacked his face with my lips. I also left out the part where I'd imagined bending him over his butcher-block kitchen island and sinking into his hot body. It galled me that my friends were living my fantasy while I'd had to settle for blue balls on the porch.

Tiller handed me a beer. "So, he's going to file a witness report for your bike?"

I took a deep sip of the crisp pale ale and shook my head as I swallowed. "No. I told him it wasn't necessary."

Mikey looked relieved. "Good. Because there's no telling what Patrick Stanner would do if Truman got him in trouble. The man's unstable, and his brother's just as bad."

Mikey got to work on dinner, moving around his kitchen with a kind of natural rhythm and grace he'd always had when cooking. I loved to watch him work. Watching someone do one of their favorite things was like getting a special glimpse into their true self.

"Why do they have it out for him?" I asked. "Was their family that affected by the ski resort closure?"

Tiller poured some nuts and pretzels into a little bowl and slid it over to me like a bartender. I knew him well enough to see this for the little deception it was, but I kept my mouth shut. Mikey did not.

"You eat those pretzels and I'm not letting you have dessert," he said calmly to Tiller.

Tiller blinked at him with faux innocence. "What? They're for our guest."

Mikey's eyes narrowed. "Then it won't be a problem for you not to eat them."

"It's the off-season." Tiller's voice bordered on whiny. "I can have pretzels."

"Yes, you could have. If you hadn't eaten half a pan of brownies for breakfast. And don't lie to me and tell me it was Sam, because I know his body is a temple." He shot me a wink.

The truth was, I'd ignored the brownies in favor of the leftover mousse. Being here with Mikey's cooking reminded me how much I'd missed hanging out at their house back in Houston.

"I think it was Sam," Tiller said, shooting me a look of false disappointment. "He's always making bad choices, aren't you, buddy?"

I laughed before taking another sip of my beer. Even though Mikey was no longer Tiller's professional nutritionist, he still managed Tiller's eating plan to help keep him in top training shape.

Tiller secretly loved it. He loved having someone who cared about his health and paid attention to him in that way. In return, Tiller looked out for Mikey and made sure he didn't run himself ragged with too many commitments cooking for others.

They made a good team.

"Can we get back to Truman and the Stanners, please?" I asked.

Mikey nodded and proceeded to explain that Gene Stanner, Patrick's father, had managed all of the lift operations and maintenance for the resort. As it was a highly specialized position, maybe he had a hard time replacing the lost job. But in Colorado, there would be several places to at least get similar work. It was hard to believe anyone could place that kind of long-term blame on a child. Why hold a grudge like that for this long? It didn't make much sense to me, but then again, I was an outsider. I didn't really know what the closing of the resort had done to the people of Aster Valley.

"What's your timeline for opening the resort?" I asked once we sat down to dinner. I wondered if their plan would make a difference to people like Gene Stanner, assuming he got his drinking under control of course. "You said you were going to aim to get it up and running in three or four years?"

Tiller and Mikey exchanged a glance before focusing back on me. "That's one of the things we wanted to talk to you about," Tiller began. "Originally we didn't want to even consider undertaking this project fully while I was still under contract with the league. But if we had someone here permanently overseeing the project who we could trust..."

Mikey jumped in. "And, just to be clear, that would be *you*."

I refrained from reminding them I ran a business in Houston. My family was in Houston. Besides, I'd never even skied before.

Tiller continued. "Then we'd want to go ahead and get started right away. I told you about that sports awards event we went to in Palm Springs, but what you may not know is that Mikey and I met several Olympian skiers there. One of them was Rory Pearson. Do you know him?"

I pictured the rugged alpine superstar who I knew more from

men's underwear ads than his actual career achievements. Even now that he was retired from skiing competitively, the man had a body that wouldn't quit. "Yeah, of course I know him," I said with a laugh.

"Right?" Mikey asked with a dreamy look on his face. "And to think there was a time I tried to swear off having feelings for pro athletes."

Tiller reached over and pinched Mikey's side. "Now look where you are," he teased. "Overflowing with feelings for them."

"For *one*," Mikey said, slapping Tiller's hand away. "Just the one. Tiller Raine for evah."

I loved watching them together. It made me so happy for my friend Mikey, who deserved to be adored exactly the way Tiller adored him.

"He might be old enough to have skied here," I said. "Isn't he pushing forty?"

Mikey nodded. "And he's looking to settle down and train other athletes. But he wants somewhere quiet where he can be a big fish in a small pond."

"I would think he could be the big fish at any resort around here if he wanted."

Tiller nodded. "True, but I got the feeling he'd be interested in investing in the resort if he could have a say in how to develop it from the beginning. Which would honestly be amazing considering the pull his name would bring to the project."

"No kidding," I murmured, suddenly considering the possibilities. Working closely with Tiller and Mikey here in Aster Valley was a completely different concept of my own future than I'd ever imagined. I'd planned on working construction in Houston my entire life. When it came to picturing myself with a long-term partner, I didn't even do much of that. I had a history of failing at relationships, in part because I'd ditched so many boyfriends or potential boyfriends to go rescue my mom and sisters from some kind of trouble or another but also because running a business like mine required working hellishly long hours and rarely taking time off. Somewhere along the line, I'd finally recognized I didn't have enough personal or emotional resources to meet the needs of a boyfriend in addition to my family and my career.

Hence the physical hookups only. As soon as things tried progressing into emotional or even much of a *time* commitment, I had to gently exit the scene in order to keep my sanity.

Tiller, Mikey, and I spent a long time at the dinner table brainstorming ideas for the ski resort and wondering how it would impact the town of Aster Valley.

"Is there a city planning council or something that might want to weigh in on this?" I asked.

Tiller nodded. "I've already met with the Aster Valley mayor, who pointed me to the county council. Technically, the mountain falls outside of the city of Aster Valley, which is actually very small. It's pretty much just the downtown area. So the Rockley County folk are the ones I need to deal with. Unfortunately, they're a little bit more..." He struggled to find the right word.

Mikey didn't struggle. "Assholish. They have strong opinions about absolutely everything. The good news is, they're on board with opening the resort back up. The bad news is, they want to have a say in every little aspect of it."

"They're going to be disappointed," I said, stretching my hands up and over my head. "Every city planning group I've ever encountered is hindered by existing zoning rules and standards. And if this resort already existed, most of what you need has an already approved precedent."

Tiller grinned. "Yep. And I've already brought my friend Julian up here to sit in on the meetings."

I barked out a laugh. Julian was one of Tiller's childhood friends from Denver. He was smart, gay, and gorgeous. And an absolute shark of a corporate attorney. He was the kind of man who would have enjoyed preparing for a meeting with the Rockley County Council by memorizing every shred of county real estate development law, history, and the major players involved. He'd come to Houston several times over the years to visit with Tiller, so I'd gotten a chance to get to know him a little.

Mikey's smug grin revealed just how much fun Julian had probably had protecting Mikey and Tiller's development rights in those initial meetings. The project would run much more smoothly with someone like that on board.

We finished up the evening going back over the list of the renovations needed at the chalets.

"But we'll have to find a crew to do the work," I added. "I'm going to be busy fixing a few things at Truman's house tomorrow and then stay for dinner."

My friends were oddly silent for a few beats while they stared at me.

I tried not to squirm in my seat.

Mikey hesitated before speaking. "I know I teased you about this earlier, but..." He glanced at Tiller like he needed help articulating his thoughts.

Tiller nodded. "I think Mikey's worried that you're going to hurt Truman. If you're only in town for a little while..."

The warning got my hackles up because they were right to be concerned. My pursuit of Truman was selfish.

"I'm just helping him repair his gate," I said a little too gruffly.

They exchanged another one of those damned looks.

"Stop that," I said. "I get what you're saying, but Truman is an adult, alright? Everyone acts like he's a kid who needs to be treated with delicacy. Give him some credit."

Tiller's brows furrowed. "Isn't he dating the librarian?"

I shook my head. "He said he was single."

Mikey continued to study me like I was a problem that needed solving. It reminded me of the methodical way he approached many of my challenges over the years. We'd been friends for a long time. When I'd had to get a job before it was even legal for me to do so, Mikey had gone through all of my options on how to get around the age requirements. When I'd gotten arrested for assault after finding my underage sister, Sophie, drunk and being manhandled toward a back room by a couple of assholes at a frat party, Mikey had miraculously convinced his parents to help pay my legal bills.

I trusted him.

And if he told me to stay away from Truman for Truman's own good, I'd do it.

"Maybe he just wants to get his cherry popped," Mikey mused.

Had I been drinking anything in the moment, I would have spit it across the table. I opened my mouth to ask if he was for real, or, more importantly, if he actually had information about Truman's virgin status, but I closed it again with a snap of teeth.

I wasn't going to discuss Truman's personal, intimate business at my friends' dinner table.

"Sam's going to crush him like a bug," Tiller murmured into his water glass before taking a sip. I glared at him.

"I'm surprised he picked you, of all people," Mikey continued. I bristled.

"What's wrong with me?"

He rolled his eyes and flapped his hand dismissively. "Calm your tits. I just mean, he's very intimidated by big muscular guys. The first time he saw Tiller, he edged away from him."

Tiller snapped his head around. "No he didn't."

"He did, babe. He was nervous around you. And not because you're a hot dish."

"Maybe it's because I'm a famous ballplayer," Tiller suggested before adding, "A celebrity."

Mikey gave him an exaggerated nod. "Absolutely. Because Truman Sweet lives, eats, and breathes professional football. He probably knew exactly who you were when you walked in and could regurgitate all your stats. RBI's, free-throw percentages, handicap, and whatnot. The man most likely has a poster of you on his—"

Tiller clapped a hand over Mikey's mouth. It drove him crazy when Mikey pretended not to understand football. "Fine. Point taken."

Mikey reached for Tiller's wrist to pull his hand away but not before kissing his palm gently. "I've noticed it a ton of other times. In fact, the first time he saw Sam at the diner, he went pale and bolted."

My stomach dropped. "You're kidding?"

"No. But he doesn't seem to feel that way anymore at all. At least, from what you describe."

I thought back to having surprised Truman in his garden earlier. He hadn't seemed scared because of *me*; he'd simply been startled that anyone had arrived without his notice. But then again... he had scooted away from me in the kitchen.

"Maybe you're right," I said, suddenly depressed about the idea of intimidating the sweet man. I hoped I hadn't truly upset him. "I'll have to pay better attention to make sure I'm not freaking him out, I guess."

Tiller stood up to gather the last of the dirty dishes from the table. "I'm sure you're fine. Besides, it's not like you're actually going to deflower the guy on the first date."

Mikey shot me a knowing grin. "I believe Sam's preferred euphemism is 'helping him fix his gate.'"

As Tiller laughed, I launched out of my chair to fake-tackle him, but before I got close, he shrieked and went running for the safety of Tiller's arms over by the kitchen sink. I called him all kinds of names before finally booting the two of them out of the kitchen so I could clean up in peaceful silence.

While daydreaming about helping a certain sweet virgin...

Fix his gate.

8

TRUMAN

How many kinds of cumin were too many for a cumin chicken date? And was Sam Rigby a briefs or boxers guy?

I glanced over at the pile of discarded underwear on my bed before taking another look in the mirror. If black made people look skinny, maybe black briefs weren't the right choice for a man to try and make his... assets appear more... assetty.

I shimmied out of the black briefs and tried not to lecture them about being a little *too* slimming.

Next came the pair I'd picked up at Macy's in Denver a month ago when I'd gone into the city for a supply run. These were little Calvin Klein boy shorts with a bright blue-and-green camouflage design. He wouldn't mistake me for some kind of hunter if I wore camo. Would he?

Don't be ridiculous. You hardly look like a hunter. Besides, he probably doesn't even want to see your underwear.

I thought back to the way he'd looked at me yesterday.

Sam wanted to see my underwear. Or, rather, he wanted to see me without my underwear. I was fairly certain of it. And the thought made the Calvin Kleins prematurely tight, enough to make me seriously consider touching myself in an effort to keep from humiliating myself when the man arrived.

The sound of tires on gravel suddenly sent me running in a frantic, confused circle. He was here. *He was here*, and I was in my underwear.

"Clothes," I muttered. "Any clothes. Put on clothes."

Thankfully, I'd already set out my top choice. I grabbed the blue jeans and hopped into them before sliding my brown belt through the loops. The jeans sat low on my hips which was my only nod to trying to be cooler than I was. For once, I'd eschewed my more formal trousers to try and appear a little less dorky.

But then I put on my favorite short-sleeved button-up shirt with tiny pink sailboats on it, so it was probably a wash on the dorky front.

I didn't have time to second-guess myself. I slipped my feet into my brown leather sneakers and raced out of my room, careening around the corner of the hallway before skidding to a stop by the front door.

He wasn't there.

I peered out of the glass panes in the top half of the farmhouse door and spotted Tiller and Mikey's SUV partway down the drive. The rear hatch was open, and Sam was busy rifling through various tools and supplies.

The gate repair.

I clapped my hand to my chest to calm my racing heart. I'd been so focused on the dinner date, I'd completely forgotten about the gate.

While I stood there catching my breath, I watched Sam's large, capable body move through his tasks. His ass looked amazing in his jeans, and the broad muscles of his back and shoulders stretched his T-shirt as he moved. The worn work boots he wore added to the masculine look of him, and I wondered—not for the first time—what it was about big strong men that made them so damned attractive.

Especially when they had the power to hurt you. Or control you. Or scare the bejesus out of you.

I hadn't heard from the Stanner brothers since filing the eyewitness report yesterday, and the silence sat heavily on my nerves. Retaliation was most likely coming, and part of me would rather it come in swiftly than have it hanging out there like the pall of doom.

I moved back to the kitchen to double-check everything was ready for his arrival. Had he left his groceries in the vehicle? Maybe I needed to grab them and at least put the chicken in the fridge.

Before heading outside, I grabbed one of my reusable water bottles and filled it with ice and water. It wasn't particularly hot today, but he'd probably get thirsty doing physical work. Also, I didn't know what to do with my hands.

On my way back to the front door, I caught sight of myself in the front hall mirror. My hair was a giant, flaming mess.

"Oh dear god," I said to the horrific reflection. I put the water bottle down and tried to finger-fix my wild curls into some kind of orderly coif.

One of the joys of living in Colorado was being able to avoid humidity-hair which was super-important when your hair was as curly as mine. But I'd let it get too long, and it had crossed the border from adorably wavy to lion's mane crazy about two weeks ago.

"There's nothing for it," I finally admitted to myself, pushing my glasses back up my nose. "This is going to be a disaster."

On that pleasant note, I fortified myself, grabbed the water bottle, and headed outside to greet Sam.

He didn't hear my approach until I was only a few feet away, but when he noticed me, his entire face lit up.

And my stomach exploded in a vat of drunken hummingbirds.

"Did you know that water is the only substance on earth found in three forms? Liquid, solid, and gas," I informed him, shoving the bottle at his solar plexus. "Also, a hundred gallons of water are used in the growing and production of a single watermelon. I find that fascinating. And since one in six gallons of water is lost in leakage before reaching a water customer, just think of how many more watermelons we could grow if we fixed the leaks." I glanced at him and tried not to assume he thought I was weird. "Not that we need that lost water for watermelons. I don't think there's a watermelon shortage or anything. But there's definitely a water shortage. In Africa especially."

Before adding the sad facts of time spent collecting water in Africa, I forced myself to stop talking.

Sam's smile grew until it lit up the entire farm. With the heat from that smile, I could grow an entire year's crop of anything. The hummingbirds swooped again.

"Hi," he said softly before leaning in to press a kiss on my cheek. "You look good enough to eat."

His lips lingered against my freshly shaved skin. I turned my face toward him the tiniest bit in hopes of "accidentally" brushing my lips against his, but he pulled back before I got there.

"Do you... do you need help?" I asked before realizing how ridiculous I sounded. "I mean, I could hold your... hammer?"

Why did that sound wrong? My face ignited while Sam's widened into a smile, and he held up his tool.

"It's a drill, but I'd love your company. How was your day?"

He moved over to the broken half of the gate and began to dismantle it. As he worked, I told him about finally starting the process of cleaning out the farmhouse attic.

"Even though she's been gone several years now, I haven't been able to bring myself to get rid of her things. But Barney's been encouraging me to tackle it, and it's the right thing to do."

Sam glanced up at me. "I'm sure it's not easy, though."

"No. Aunt Berry was sort of a local legend," I told him, moving over to prop myself against the other gate post. "People used to give her all kinds of things as gifts and payment for services rendered. She got this farm in trade if you can believe it."

He glanced up at me in surprise. "No shit? What the hell did she trade?"

"She was a naturopath. Apparently, she traded her healing abilities and saved the man's great-niece from a wasting disease. Knowing what I know now, I think it was probably celiac disease. But this was back in the sixties. Before coming through Aster Valley, she traveled around apprenticing with any natural healer who'd allow her to shadow them. She wanted to learn everything there was to know about using natural remedies to heal the body. My grandparents managed the Rockley Motor Inn back then—that's how my dad ended up managing the ski resort. He went into hospitality because of his dad. Aunt Berry—who was actually my great-aunt—came through Aster Valley to visit her brother and sister-in-law, my grandparents, just for a few days. It was all a fluke, really. She ran into a man while taking a walk. He was crying and praying on the ground in the woods."

I thought about the box of letters I'd found from Sid Staughton to Aunt Berry. Over the seven years he'd written to her, his words had morphed from eternal gratitude to a kind of hero worship. If I hadn't known better, I'd have thought Sid was half in love with my aunt. But Sid and his "best friend," Warren, had been as thick as thieves. When I'd finally grown old enough to see their relationship in a different light, I'd understood they were life partners, and it had made much more sense.

"Anyway," I said, trying to choke back the memory of how difficult it had been to learn about being gay on my own, without anyone to talk to about it, "Berry found out what he was so upset about and offered to help. The little girl, who'd been shuttled around from doctor to doctor with various diagnoses and ineffectual treatment plans, suddenly began to heal under Berry's care. Sid thought it was a miracle. He thought *Berry* was a miracle."

"She sounds like an incredible person," he said with a soft expression on his face.

"She was." I rubbed a little speck of dirt off my finger. "She always made the people around her feel like…"

Sam waited patiently while I searched for the right way to say it. I spotted the row where I grew sunflowers. It was located directly outside my bedroom window so I could see their tall sunny faces as soon as I woke up on summer mornings.

"Like the biggest, brightest bloom in a bouquet," I finished. "And I needed that. I needed *her*." My voice revealed too much emotion, so I stopped talking and focused on rubbing away the spot of dirt on my finger that I was starting to think was probably a freckle.

Sam's movements were slow and deliberate. He walked over to me and set the shovel down against the working half of the gate before sliding his arms around me and pulling me into his body for a hug.

The gesture shocked me. My brain blinked erratically a few times before shutting down. Then it was just his big, strong body against mine. The heat of him. The masculine scent of his sweat. The overwashed softness of his shirt against my cheek. And the wide span of his hands against my back and sides.

God, he felt incredible. I managed to pull my arms out from between us and wrap them around his neck. If he wanted to hug me, I was going to accept it for as long as he was willing to give me the comfort, even though I wasn't sure why he'd decided to do it.

When he finally pulled back, I expected him to go back to his task with the shovel, but he didn't. He kept one hand on my hip and used the other to brush back the curls that had fallen in my eyes.

"It's a mop," I muttered apologetically.

"Mops where you come from must be sexy as hell," he said with a slow grin. "I'd never get any cleaning done if my mop looked like this. I love your hair."

Oh.

Ohhh.

My breathing went low-key haywire. Sam's long fingers toyed with the same crazy bits that had driven me nuts only a few minutes ago in the house. His fingers twisted around a curl before letting it go and twisting another.

"Thank you," I breathed, trying hard not to break the spell.

He finally seemed to realize what he was doing and stepped back to reach for the shovel again. After clearing his throat, he asked, "So the man gave your aunt the farm?"

I took a deep breath to keep from tripping after him and plastering myself against his body with a whimpered plea.

"Um, yeah. So... right. The aunt farm. I mean the aunt... the farm for my aunt. My aunt's farm. Cripes."

Sam's laugh crinkled the edges of his eyes, and I thought for a mini-second it was worth accidentally making a fool of myself.

"I could eat you in one bite," he muttered, almost under his breath.

Yes, please.

I shook my head to clear it and continued on. "She refused, obviously, but then he offered for her to stay there for the summer to look after the place while he and his partner traveled to Hawaii to visit friends. She was a total free spirit who usually followed her nose, but that summer her nose told her to stay put here in Aster Valley. I think that was the same year my uncle Dave was born, so maybe Berry stuck around to help my grandmother through that. I'm not sure. But she took advantage of the planting season and grew all kinds of things. She hadn't had a plot to garden in the years she'd been traveling and learning, and she'd forgotten how much she loved it."

"That's where you got your green thumb."

"Exactly," I said, looking around at the freshly planted plots, the ones tilled and ready, and the ones that would remain fallow this year to prepare for the following year. "She taught me everything I know about that part of my business. She grew mostly medicinal plants and organic veggies. She gave most of the food away to families who needed it, or she sold it at the farmer's market when she needed extra money for something or other. When Sid and Warren came back from Hawaii, they told her they wanted her to stay on as the farm's full-time caretaker so they could retire to Hawaii to be with their friends. None of us knew at the time that Sid had already put the farm into her name."

"That's amazing. I'm surprised she stayed if she was used to traveling around. Did she ever marry?"

Sam continued his work, slamming the sharp blade of the shovel down into the ground and working clumps of dirt and rock to the surface.

"No. But she was always surrounded by friends. She traveled to Hawaii every few years to see Sid and Warren, and they would come see her, but eventually they both passed on. The farm had been Sid's parents' place. Berry tried giving it back to the family, but they refused to accept it. So she told everyone in town she inherited it when they died, but the truth makes for a better story," I said with a laugh.

As Sam worked in the late-afternoon sun, I told him more about my aunt, about the work she did through her shop that was half natural healing and half accidental psychotherapy. I told him about how she kept an old corduroy beanbag in the back of the shop that I could curl up on to page through picture books. Every afternoon during kindergarten, I would come straight here from school and spend the afternoon dozing in a sun patch like a contented cat—or an exhausted five-year-old. I remembered loving my life during those early years, but then it had all come crashing down.

I didn't tell Sam that part. I was sure he already knew the basics, about my supposed jaunt out onto the deserted ski slope that fateful night with my grandfather's old sled. About the ensuing disaster that befell not only Olympic hopeful Langdon Goode but also the very town itself.

Including my own parents.

"I missed her when we moved away," I admitted. "I think part of her wanted to come with us, but she would have hated it in Durango."

"What was it like there?" he asked as he finally levered out the giant block of concrete that held the gate post. My eyes were glued to his bulging arm and back muscles like I was in a trance. It took me a minute to realize he'd asked me a question.

"Not great," I admitted, moving over to where the water bottle lay forgotten on the tailgate of the SUV. I picked it up and handed it to him, watching every movement of his throat as he took large gulps of it.

"Thanks, sweet," he mumbled, handing it back. It took me a moment to realize he'd been using my last name. At least I thought that's what it was. If he'd called me sweetheart again, like he'd done the first night in Mikey's kitchen... well, I would probably have to beg him to try out some of those dirty things he'd mentioned.

I squeezed my eyes closed and tried to reset my brain from horndog to reasonable human mode. "My dad got a job as a manager for a hotel there. It wasn't bad, actually. At least... I didn't think it was a bad job for him. He manages one of the biggest hotels in town. It runs along the river and has great occupancy rates. It's owned by a national chain, so the benefits are good, too. At least, that's what my mom always says when he complains about his job."

"But it wasn't the same."

"No. It wasn't. It's almost seven hours away from here by car. And my mom missed her friends. I think she missed having someone to help her with me the way Aunt Berry and my grandparents did."

Sam found the water hose and began mixing concrete in a bucket. "Do you get along with your parents?"

I thought through my answer. "We have what you'd call a polite distance now. We're cordial enough for visits, but we're certainly not close. They resent my moving back to Aster Valley because they thought it opened back up a large can of worms that was better off buried."

Sam gestured for me to come help him hold the new post in place as he poured the concrete around the base. "Do you have siblings?" he asked.

I nodded. "My sister, Trinity. She's three years older than I am. She's an assistant dance professor at the university in Grand Junction."

"Oh, wow. It's not often you hear of someone pursuing a career in dance. Do you see her often?"

I shrugged. "No, but that's okay. She's happy. Moving to Durango was better for her in the end, so that's a good thing. She made it into an elite dance company that led to her pursuit of dance as a profession."

"Why don't you see her?"

I had to stand on tiptoe to keep the post upright as he moved around me with the cement.

"We were just never close. My parents were pretty miserable after the move, so I tried to avoid being at home. I spent a lot of time at the local library, and Trinity spent more time at dance. It's hard to be close to someone when you rarely see them."

I didn't want to talk about my sister or my family anymore. And I didn't want to talk about anything related to the *incident*.

"Do you have siblings?" I asked, shifting the subject slightly.

Sam's face darkened. "Mpfh."

Okay.

"Sorry. That was personal," I said. "I didn't mean to—"

"I have two sisters. You didn't do anything wrong by asking."

I clamped my lips together and stayed quiet, so the ball remained in his court.

"Sophie and Kira. They're... they have issues. Hell, who doesn't? But Kira is an addict, and she's been struggling lately. Sophie is a single mom, so she has it rough in a different way..."

He seemed to be paying a little too much attention to how he described them to me, as if he was worried about my reaction.

"It's okay," I said softly. "You don't have to tell me anything you don't want to. But if you do want to talk about it, I'm hardly one to judge."

Sam took over holding the post and indicated I could go back to my perch against the other side of the gate and relax. Then he continued.

"Okay, straight truth. Kira is an addict and a felon. She showed up high and ranting at my jobsite last week."

I winced, but before I could say anything, he kept going. "And she refuses to go to rehab, so I have to enforce some boundaries with her at this point. Which upsets my mom very much. Mom expects me to fix everything."

"Where's your dad?"

Sam's jaw tightened, and I knew right away I shouldn't have asked.

"Prison," he said. "Has been for a long time and will be for an equally long time."

He took a breath as if considering whether or not to say more. Then he did.

"He was a mean drunk. Violent, even with us. Anyway," he said, clearing his throat. "One night it went too far. Thankfully, the girls were at a sleepover. But I wasn't. I'd come home from football practice and was going to grab a bite to eat before doing my homework. But when it got really bad between them, I bolted. I called the cops, then went to Mikey's and hid in his basement. Like a chickenshit."

"Like a scared kid," I countered, defiantly.

"Yeah, well, I know that now."

But I wasn't sure he did.

Sam's eyes flicked upward. "The cops came, and it was bad. My mom went into the hospital for a while, and Dad went to jail. After that, it was just the four of us."

Even though he was still holding the post steady, I walked over to him and wrapped my arms around his middle. "I'm sorry." For once, the word was exactly right.

"Thank you. So am I. It's a longer story, but he ended up getting a life sentence," he said.

"Good," I said softly, extracting myself from the hug when I realized he was having trouble keeping the post steady. "But it must have put a lot of pressure on you and your mom to hold the family together."

For a split second, Sam's face was full of raw emotion. Grief, hurt, anger, resentment, helplessness. It was like a heavy blanket of horrible feelings he usually kept hidden away. The weight of it almost staggered me back, and my heart felt like it was going to burst out of my chest and wing its way over to settle into his chest in case he needed it.

I opened my mouth and stepped forward again, but his face quickly shuttered, and he turned away from me.

"Yeah. So anyway, that's life, right? You ready to cook? I could use a sous chef in the kitchen."

I almost continued my way toward him, to slide my arms around him from behind and press my body against his back just to let him know I was there, to pay him back in kind for the comforting embrace he'd given me earlier.

But I wasn't that brave.

So I did the expected thing instead.

I told him the etymology of the term *sous chef* and chattered nonstop on our walk back to the house about the history of Escoffier's kitchen brigade in the London Savoy hotel.

Nothing said "I want to take care of your giant sweet heart and make love to your incredibly sexy body" quite like the French words for fish and fried food.

9

SAM

I wanted to laugh at myself, and I knew for sure Mikey would laugh at me if he heard me chucking my emotional stew all over this poor guy.

What the hell was I thinking? This wasn't me.

Not only did I not share my personal shitshow with others, I definitely didn't share it with people who'd also had it bad. Sure, maybe... *hopefully*... Truman hadn't had the periodic physical abuse I'd had, but he'd experienced a different kind of trauma by being blamed for something that wasn't his fault.

I wanted to drive down to Durango and confront his parents, insist they apologize to Truman and confess just how wrong it had been to lay the harsh consequences of a childhood mistake at his feet.

But I wasn't a superhero. And, as usual, I had enough family drama on my own plate as evidenced by the nonstop buzzing of my phone.

"If you need to take a call," Truman said politely, "you're welcome to use the guest bedroom for privacy."

I shook my head as I followed him into the farmhouse kitchen. "No need. It's my family. They've been trying to reach me all week even after I told them I needed a break."

Hopefully, Truman didn't think I was rude for ignoring my own family on the phone. I had to assume he understood about having to set boundaries for the sake of your own mental health.

If only I did, too. Ignoring them was eating me up inside. I'd never been good at setting boundaries.

As he began showing me around, Truman loosened up a little. His slender arms waved around at the various cabinets and drawers as he indicated where certain items could be found, and I quickly realized I was spending more time watching his body than following along with where things were.

That was fine. I would make do once I got started. I wasn't afraid to poke my head around if I needed something, and watching his attractive form and his lively movements had a calming effect on me.

Truman kept up his endearing chatter as I began preparing the chicken. He told me about each variety of cumin he'd selected and why I might want one over the other. Obviously, I didn't have a preference since my only goal here was to spend time with him, so I followed his body language cues to select the one he seemed most excited about.

I asked a few leading questions in an attempt to learn more about him. Things like, "Did you always want to take over your aunt's farm?"

And I loved every minute of hearing his responses. He told me about being shocked by her death. "It was a car accident in Canada. She'd gone up to Calgary for a workshop and... the van she was in was run off the road by a tractor-trailer, I guess. They say she died instantly. There were four people in the car. Another one died at the hospital, and another had serious injuries but survived. The truck driver hit a patch of ice."

"How old were you?"

He turned to face me, and I saw traces of anguish hidden underneath a forced smile. "Can we not talk about Berry right now, please?"

I hesitated for only a second before following my gut and reaching out to him. I pulled him into a tight hug like I'd done out in the driveway earlier. It was completely out of character for me. Not only was I not one to show emotions, but I was also very careful not to lead anyone on romantically. After the number of relationships I'd squandered because of family commitments, I'd made a habit of keeping that shit buttoned up tight.

But, god. I couldn't help myself with Truman Sweet. I wanted to wrap him up in a fuzzy blanket and keep him safe. I also wanted to bend him over the kitchen island and pound his ass.

The whiplash of feelings for this practical stranger was unlike anything I'd experienced before.

Suddenly I realized the small body in my arms was struggling to get away. I lifted my hands up and stepped back, horrified to have advanced on him against his will. "Truman, shit," I began.

He must have seen the look on my face because he immediately began apologizing. "No, sorry. That's not… no. You didn't do anything wrong. Don't be nice, dammit! Don't. I'll start crying like a baby and never stop."

I was surprised by his response but relieved at the same time. "Okay, asshole," I said in a rough voice. "Then stop all this talking bullshit and get to work setting the table."

His face lit up with a smile, and he saluted me. "Aye-aye, captain." When he walked past me to get to the silverware drawer, he leaned over and brushed a kiss along the edge of my jaw. I was moving my head at the time, so it also brushed my ear and made me shiver.

Truman made a low humming sound in his throat as if acknowledging the sensitive spot. I closed my eyes and took a breath to regain my focus.

Cooking. I was cooking food.

After the chicken was finally marinating and the rice was measured and ready to cook, I retrieved the wine I'd brought from the fridge and asked if he'd like some.

"Yes, please," he said before rooting around in a drawer for the corkscrew. Once we each had a glass, he led me out the back door to a stone patio.

I hadn't seen this area before since it was hidden by the house from the front and by an overgrown cluster of shrubbery from the side of the sun porch Truman used as an office.

It was clean and tidy like the rest of Truman's house, but I could see he'd spent extra care setting it up for his enjoyment. Pots of colorful spring flowers lined the flagstones on both sides of the patio, and a solid wood chaise lounge overflowed with comfortable throw pillows in various shapes and sizes. On the right side, near the sun porch shrubbery, was a round table with four chairs. A cluster of candle lanterns and small potted flowers sat primly in the middle of the table, and I spotted a modern copper birdbath in a nearby flower bed.

I loved seeing this part of him, but at the same time, it made me realize how little of his personality was inside the farmhouse. It looked like a memorial to the woman who'd lived there before him, and I wondered what it would take for him to start making it his own.

I knew better than to ask. It wasn't any of my business. At least he would begin to make forward progress by cleaning out her things.

"This is really nice, Truman," I said instead. "Do you spend a lot of time out here?"

He reached over idly to pinch off some dead blooms from a nearby plant. "When the weather is nice. I've always loved this view."

We were on the low part of the valley slope which meant mountain peaks surrounded us on two sides. Most likely, every property owner in the area relished the view of the peaks.

Not Truman.

The view he loved seemed to be of town. From here, you could see the white church spire, the patch of green grass where the large statue of a mountain rescue dog took pride of place in front of the visitors' center, the oval shape of the high school track-and-field facility, and the red roof of the little historic covered bridge over the stream that ran behind Main Street. It reminded me of the one in Vail, and I'd meant to ask Mikey if Aster Valley had copied it for tourism reasons.

"Can you see the shop from here?" I asked, squinting at the brick buildings in the general area of the Honeyed Lemon.

"Right now you can. It's next to the building with the black roof in that strip of shops on the right." He pointed to a cluster of buildings I instantly recognized. From here, I could see green plants on the roof of his building. Why wasn't I surprised?

Truman continued. "But once this meadow starts flowering for real, there's usually a cluster of elephantella and purple coneflowers that obscures the view." He looked at me with pinkening cheeks. "Or maybe they just distract me from it."

I realized it wasn't necessarily the town that provided his favorite view, but the open meadow leading down to it, no doubt the blank canvas on which he could plant any number of things. His backyard was a wide swath of land he clearly set aside just for wildflowers.

Just to make him happy.

"I'll bet it's gorgeous in full bloom," I said softly, imagining it in the late-afternoon sun.

He looked back out at the land where only a scattering of pale purple and tiny yellow flowers covered most of the area. Most of the expanse of clear-cut space was still winter-ragged and barren, but I could tell Truman didn't see it that way. He saw it covered in a riot of summer color.

"It's amazing," he said with a sweet smile. "I can't wait to show it to you. I mean, if... if you come back for a visit. With Mikey and Tiller."

"I'll bet it's stunning." I wanted to reach out and pull him close, nuzzle into his neck, and plant kisses along his smooth skin. But I knew that if I started something now, there'd be no dinner. "Tell me more about the shop. What got you interested in spices?"

I made my way over to the table and took a seat before sipping more of the wine. Truman followed me and took a seat as well.

"I took over the cooking after we moved to Durango," he began. "It was one of the, um, extra chores that my parents decided I needed to do for the family." He quickly waved that conversational direction away with a flick of his wrist. "Anyway, I really didn't have access to much in the way of flavors. Money was tight, so we couldn't get premade marinades or spice blends. I ended up growing some herbs the way I'd learned from Aunt Berry. My mom was really impressed when I made rosemary chicken one night using herbs I'd planted and grown myself."

His smile was nostalgic as he remembered. "You couldn't have been old enough for all that?" I asked.

"I was probably seven."

"Jesus," I muttered, thinking about the boxed Kraft Mac and Cheese and frozen pizzas I made at that age.

"And I loved it. Probably at first it was because it seemed to make my mom happy, but then I just really liked the challenge of growing obscure spices that I could use in cooking. As I got into growing the plants, I reached out to Berry for advice and remembered the medicinal ones she always had on hand. So I began to grow those, too."

"Do you sell that stuff at the shop as well?"

Truman nodded. "Yeah, actually, I still produce and distribute several homeopathic products Berry was famous for. There's an arnica salve that I can barely keep in stock. It's been flying off the shelves for years. There's also an antioxidant tea blend, but I don't grow it. I order the leaves and make the blend. What else...? Oh. There's a hypoallergenic organic soap I still make from her recipe, as well as a spray household cleaner. Some women's remedies," he added with a blush, "and nutritional support blends."

"How do you manage all of this with so little help?" I worried about him. I knew from Mikey that Truman had a little part-time support at the shop, but it didn't seem like he had help here at the farm itself. That was a ton of physical work for such a small man who also needed to be in two places at once and manage the accounting and everything else.

Truman peeked over at me, hesitating. "It's not easy."

I wanted to laugh at the understatement, but he seemed worried about my response. "No," I said instead. "I can't imagine it is. Why don't you have more help? You seem to be successful. Hell, Mikey heard about the shop before he even came to Aster Valley the first time."

He tapped the side of his wineglass with a fingernail. "I tried to hire help when I was first starting out. No one wanted to work here. With me."

My jaw ground tight. "That's bullshit."

Truman's eyes widened in surprise. "No. It's true."

"I don't mean it that way. It's ridiculous that these dumbasses would let ancient history get in the way of decent employment. I don't get it. You were five fucking years old, for fuck's sake!"

As my voice raised, Truman leaned farther away from me until his chair was practically tipping over. "I'd better go check on dinner," he said quickly before scrambling for the house.

I'd scared him.

I'd scared him after he'd done absolutely nothing wrong. I was a fucking monster. He deserved better than someone with an anger problem. Better than someone like the Stanners.

Better than someone like my own damned father.

Memories of my dad's rage stormed into my mind against my will, making me nauseous.

My phone buzzed for the millionth time, and I no longer had a handle on my self-control. I answered it on speakerphone and then placed it on the table so I wouldn't throw it across the meadow.

"What?" I barked.

"Finally!" My mom's voice was relieved, but I also heard fear and desperation in it, a sound as familiar to me as the scent of her apricot hand lotion. "Where the hell are you, Sam? We need you here. Things are out of control."

No kidding.

"I'm in Colorado," I said.

"Well, you could have told someone you were leaving. And why now, when Kira needs you and Ethan is in the middle of tax season at work?"

While Kira had acted out with drugs, Sophie had acted out with men. She'd thrown herself at them in hopes of finding "the one," but, despite my attempts to keep her out of trouble, it had resulted in an unwanted pregnancy at the age of twenty and a string of asshole losers ever since. Ethan was the latest boyfriend, but I had to admit this time seemed like the real deal, not to mention, I liked the guy.

And my mother more than liked him. She thought Ethan was Sophie's only chance at a normal life, and she tried everything in her power not to burden him with our family issues.

I couldn't blame her. It wasn't Ethan's job to deal with Kira. But it wasn't mine either. Not anymore.

"You don't need to do anything. Kira made her choice. And now she's going to have to live with the consequences of her actions. We can't keep bailing her out, Mom," I said.

There was a long beat of silence on the other end. I thought I heard the tinkle of ice cubes, but I wasn't sure.

"She's sick," she said. "Addiction is a disease. It's not her fault."

I let out a humorless laugh. No, it wasn't. And that's why I'd spent several years dropping everything to help her and bail her out of trouble. That's why finally setting boundaries was the hardest thing I'd ever had to do. "The addiction may not be her fault, but her actions are. Where does it end? If she won't consent to treatment, we'll be right back here again in a month or two or six. Just like we're right back here after last time. And the time before."

"She didn't have an easy childhood, Sam," she reminded me.

I didn't either. I bit my teeth against all of the toxic responses that threatened to rain out if I so much as opened my lips.

"She needs you," she said softly for the millionth time. "We need you."

What about when I needed you?

"I'll be home in a few weeks," I told her. "I'm heading out to California for a break." I thought back to the way I'd just fucked things up with Truman. Even my vacation was going to be pathetic now since it was pretty clear I'd spend the entire time dissecting what I'd done wrong and how I'd never have a healthy relationship as long as I lived.

"Surely your family is more important than some fancy beach vacation," Mom snapped. This was the expected next stage of any manipulative conversation with my mother. First was the sweet, innocent plea. Next came the angry implication that I was selfish and snobbish. Finally, the sullen mother guilt would wrap it all up in a tidy bow. Sometimes followed by the bonus hanging up of the phone.

"Not right now, it's not," I admitted. "I've prioritized work and my family for fifteen years, Mom. It's not too much to ask for a week to myself."

"Must be nice," she said with a sniff.

I thought of my bike crushed against the sign. The look on Truman's face when I got angry. The possessive way Barney Balderson had held him when he'd tried defending me to the sheriff. The easy affection between Tiller and Mikey—the kind of relationship I'd never have with someone.

"Not really," I muttered.

"You can fix this," she said. "You've always fixed everything. It's your role. You're the fixer."

I hated this forced narrative. I'd done what I'd needed to do out of desperation, not some innate skill or calling.

"No. Not this time. If you want this thing with Kira fixed, then fix it. You're an adult. You have a job. You bail her out."

"You have no idea what I've been through, Sam. None."

I looked out at the streaks of color the setting sun was shooting across the clear sky. It was so beautiful here in the valley. It almost felt like I was protected from the full weight of my family responsibility. "I find that hard to believe. Look, Mom, I have to go. I'm sorry you're having a tough time, but Kira needs to learn to look out for herself."

"She doesn't need life lessons! She needs her brother. She needs family. And she needs a good lawyer. You know how awful the public defenders are! There you sit on your high horse with all your rich friends and fancy vacations, and you can't even spare enough money for your sister to stay out of prison?"

My face felt numb. I thought back to all of the thousands of dollars I'd spent over the years trying to keep my sisters out of trouble, trying to get them out of trouble, then trying to cover up the trouble they'd been in. I was so fucking tired.

"Bye, Mom," I said in a low voice before reaching out to hit the End button.

I leaned my head back and closed my eyes. How had I fucked everything up so completely, and how could I try to make things right with Truman? Should I even try? Or would it be better for me to spare him... whatever this was... by keeping my distance?

I opened my eyes and prepared to stand up to face the music, but I saw Truman standing over me.

"I'm sorry," I said with as much heartfelt sincerity as I could muster. "I didn't mean to scare you."

A wrinkle of worry marred his smooth forehead just above the dark frame of his glasses. At first, I thought it was his concern that I might have another outburst. But then he stepped closer and crawled into my lap until he was straddling me. He slipped his arms around my neck and hugged me tightly.

I froze for a beat in shock before wrapping my arms around his slender body and letting myself exhale.

10

TRUMAN

I'd heard it all. It had been easy to put together his mother's words with the little bits I'd picked up from both Sam and Mikey about Sam's past. She'd blatantly attempted to manipulate him, and it had made me want to spit fire in her general direction.

I'd felt so helpless. So I'd done what he'd done to me a few times already. I simply hugged him as hard as I could.

"I'm the one who's sorry," I said. "Sorry you're trying to handle this from afar."

"I'm trying *not* to handle it, though. That's just it. And it makes me feel like a horrible person," Sam said roughly, tightening his arms around me.

"Sometimes protecting yourself means you can't keep protecting everyone else," I said, as if I'd ever taken my own advice.

"Easier said than done," he said with a soft laugh against my hair. I could have stayed like that all night in Sam's arms out here on the patio, but I had to admit to wanting more. Lots more.

But then he threw a reality check at me like a dousing of cold water. "I'll be back in Houston soon enough. I can deal with it then."

"Yes. Right. Um, we should make dinner," I said, pulling back.

"Because I'm going to die of embarrassment when my stomach starts growling in front of you."

Sam's easy smile gave me an overwhelming feeling of relief. I knew he wasn't going to be able to drop the stress of that phone call as easily as that, but maybe I could at least distract him for a while.

He stood up and let me slide down the firm front of his body until I stood on my own feet again. Then he leaned down and pressed a long kiss against the edge of my lips. "I'm definitely hungry, Truman," he murmured.

My entire body shuddered because it was obvious he wasn't only referring to the food.

"Yes," I squeaked before clearing my throat. "Yes, well, then. Ha. Hoo-boy. Let's cook, then. Dinner. Chicken. Dinner chicken. Chicken for dinner."

Well, then.

Sam's smile took away some of my nervous fluttering, and when I felt the solid warmth of his hand on my lower back, I forgot all about being a bumbling idiot.

I was a horny idiot.

While he continued to make dinner, I asked about his business back in Houston, what he liked about working in construction, and what his dream job would be if he could do anything.

"I actually love what I do. Building things. Fixing things. Working with my hands and spending the day with other hardworking people. It's good. I think if I could change anything…" His voice trailed off while he focused on the food for a moment. "I guess I'd want to do those same things in a place I liked better than Houston. You know, it never occurred to me to ever leave, but now I see Mikey and Tiller and I see this place…"

"It's very different from Houston," I prompted.

He chuckled. "Yeah. Something about it…"

"Now you know why I came back." I watched Sam's face for his reaction.

Sam blinked up at me. "Yeah. I guess I do. It's beautiful. Peaceful. I almost feel like Aster Valley is set outside of real life."

I nodded because I knew exactly what he meant. "When I'm here on the farm, I feel like I can do anything I want. I'm close to the earth, and it's a bit... timeless. Sometimes I can almost imagine what it would have been like to be a pioneer or one of the original tribes who made their home here. That connection to the land and the weather, to helping others... that's what I inherited from Aunt Berry even if I hadn't inherited the farm, too. It lives inside of me, and I'm so grateful for it."

It was the most I'd ever admitted out loud to another person in regards to my true heart. Maybe it was because Sam was safe. He was a "dead end" as Chaya called it—someone who wouldn't or couldn't repeat the information in a way that would hurt me.

It felt good to share those thoughts, even if an urban construction worker couldn't understand what I meant about a connection to the earth. But I suspected he could. Not because he had experience bonding with nature or anything "woo-woo" like that, but because he seemed empathetic in general.

Sam's eyes met mine. "I'm grateful to your aunt for giving you a place to feel yourself."

I nodded again and looked away, fussing with the candles I'd laid out on the kitchen table so I didn't have to look at Sam's intense face and feel the laser-focused attention he gave me.

"So maybe you should leave Houston," I suggested. "Find a place that makes you feel yourself."

The silence was thick enough to cause me to glance back up at him. His green eyes pinned me in place. "Maybe it's not a place," he finally said. The low words slid between us like somnolent temptation. Did I dare wonder what he meant by that? Did I dare hope he was implying home was a person?

No. I didn't dare. Because men like Sam Rigby weren't for me. He was a flash of bright light, here one minute and gone the next. I would bathe in its warmth for that singular shining moment and then try my hardest not to wallow in the dark when he was gone.

I put on a big smile that didn't feel quite as comfortable as before. "Phenology is the study of the timing of natural phenomena as relates to the environment as a whole," I said apropos of nothing. "In other words, studying the timing of various features of the plant growing cycle can give us indicators into the effects of climate change. Well, that's one of the things it can tell us. But it's also critical to understanding how various natural phenomena interact with causative impact on other phenomena."

Sam stared at me. Because I was spouting ridiculous information. There was nothing to do but barge through it.

"Imagine if dandelion fluff appeared just in time for a season of no breeze. That would be nonideal timing, and it would have a great impact on the dandelion's ability to spread its seed far and wide. Now imagine if bears came out of hibernation after all of the fruits of the season were gone. Terrible timing. The bears would starve. So this timing situation is critical in nature."

I started to low-key panic because I really had no idea what my point was. Didn't matter. I carried on like a good little soldier.

"Phenology is a leading indicator of climate change. Birds time the building of their nests and the laying of their eggs with the hatching of insects to feed their young. Once these factors get out of whack, the gentle organiz—"

I hadn't noticed Sam's approach, but suddenly his lips were on mine, and the giant rounded muscles of his arms were wrapped around me once again.

Forget phenology. The timing of Sam's kiss couldn't have been better. I groaned my approval into his mouth as his lips and tongue took control. He kissed me like he did most things—confidently, assertively, silently.

Meanwhile, I was the one making all kinds of noises. Mewling sounds and rapid breathing, little whimpered pleas not to stop. It was like a quick summer storm—flashing in and throwing things around, drenching everything in reach, before leaving just as rapidly as it had come.

Sam stepped back and adjusted himself while I stood there gasping for air.

"Sorry," he said gruffly. "Couldn't help myself."

"Nor should you," I said breathlessly.

He grunted out a laugh and shot me straight through the gut with a devastating grin. "Then maybe I won't."

Oh please, oh please.

"Did you want to hear more about environmental science?" I teased. "Because I'm going to take that enthusiastic response as a positive indicator that I was on the right track to wooing you with my fascinating, albeit trivial, knowledge."

Sam laughed again. "You wooed me with something, alright."

When the meal was ready, we sat down together at the table and dug in. The food was amazing, and Sam asked more questions about the herbs and spices.

"You know a lot for someone who didn't go to college," he said. I wondered how he knew that about me.

"I didn't have much of a social life growing up, but I hated being at home, too. Honestly, I hated Durango full stop. But—and you're not going to believe this—Durango's library has a botanical garden."

"Heaven for sweet little baby Truman," Sam added, nudging his empty plate away and leaning back in his chair.

"Exactly. I spent as much time as possible there. I would check out books on every topic imaginable and read outside as long as the weather permitted. I planted thousands of imaginary gardens and grew metric tons of imaginary plants. The botanic society loved volunteers, so I worked with them as much as I could."

"Ahh, so those weren't wasted years. You were learning, practicing, and working in preparation for following your own path."

I'd never looked at it that way, but he was right. Even if I hadn't inherited this property, I most likely would have gotten a job at a nursery or garden center and saved up every penny until I could buy myself some land. It was nice to realize I might have been okay on my own without Aunt Berry's generous gift.

"Yeah," I said, feeling like something tight and creaky inside of me was finally able to loosen and relax. "Yeah, I think you're right."

"Are you doing well financially? Is the farm and shop income enough to make you comfortable and ease your worries?"

I was surprised by his question, not because it was a bit personal, but because of the way he'd asked. As if he wanted to make sure I wasn't burdened.

I shrugged. "The online business is very lucrative. I love having the shop in town because I think I'd be quite isolated and lonely if I was on the farm by myself all the time, but it's not nearly as successful financially."

Sam shifted in his seat. "That makes sense. Overhead and whatnot."

"Also, businesses in the town of Aster Valley have to pay a supplemental service fee to the sheriff's department, and it seems like it keeps going up every time I turn around."

I took another bite of chicken and rice and savored the flavor. I'd never had a man cook a nice meal for me like this. When Barney and I had shared a meal, it had either been at a restaurant or I'd cooked for him.

I looked up to see a storm in Sam's eyes. "What do you mean a supplemental service fee?"

"It's kind of a long story. The city of Aster Valley used to have a police department, but when the resort closed, there wasn't enough money anymore to sustain it. They disbanded it and put the city under the Rockley County Sheriff's Department instead. To make up for the extra work they were having to do, the businesses inside the city limits had to start contributing more to the department. At least, that's what I was told. It happened while I was gone."

"That's ridiculous. Weren't they now getting the taxes or funds that originally went to the Aster Valley Police Department?"

I stopped to think about it. "I guess so? I mean... that makes sense."

Sam's brows furrowed. "Truman, how do you pay this fee?"

"It's actually organized so we contribute to their retirement fund. So I guess we're not paying the department directly, we're helping fund their pensions."

His nostrils flared. "Truman, who do you make the payment to? How is the check made out?"

"I don't remember exactly. It's an acronym. It stands for the Rockley County Sheriff Pension Fund or something like that, I think."

Sam opened his mouth to say something else but stopped himself. "Okay. Maybe I'll ask the guys at the diner more about it since they were here when it first started."

"Pim and Bill would know more than I do, for sure," I said in agreement. "Do you want dessert?"

Suddenly, the subject of the sheriff's fee was long gone, and Sam's eyes were filled with decadent promise.

"I sure do," he said in a rough voice before reaching for my hand. I glanced at my smaller hand in his larger one. He was incredibly gentle with me, so much so it made me want to thank him. Which was ridiculous. I knew enough to know I deserved for men to be gentle with me, but I also recognized it wasn't always the case.

"Truman," he said carefully. "I'd really like to kiss you again."

I opened my mouth to enthusiastically agree, but he continued talking before I could.

"But I need you to know I'm not relationship material, and I'm only passing through town. I'll be back on the road in a few days. And I think maybe you deserve more than that."

I did deserve more than that. But I also deserved the right to have a one-night stand if that's what I wanted.

"I think maybe I deserve to make my own decisions," I said instead.

Sam met my eyes. "And what's your decision about kissing me?"

I stood up and stepped closer to him before reaching for his other hand. After urging him up from his chair, I led him to the giant sectional sofa in the den. This room was one of my favorites with a stone fireplace, windows on three sides, and several of Aunt Berry's old quilts folded neatly here and there.

"My decision is a resounding yes, please," I said with a smile as I sat him down on the sofa and straddled his lap again the way we'd done on the patio.

This time Sam's hands came around to grab my ass and use it to pull me closer. I felt a confidence I didn't recognize in myself. I leaned in and pressed a kiss to his cheek just above the line of his blond beard.

"Truman," he said softly. "You're in charge, okay? You tell me to stop and I stop."

I kissed him again, just below his bottom lip. I wanted to kiss every square inch of his face. "Mmhm."

His big hands moved up, sliding under the hem of my shirt and landing on the skin of my back. The feel of those warm, callused hands on me made me harder than I already was.

"Fuck, you're so perfect," he murmured, nuzzling the side of my face. "You're driving me crazy."

"Is this okay?" I asked, kissing his temple and then his ear and then his neck.

Sam groaned and arched up, pressing the bulge in his jeans against my own. "More than okay. You can do whatever you want to me, sweetheart."

I felt oddly bold and brave, like I truly could do whatever I wanted and he wouldn't judge me for it. Knowing it was a one-night stand was freeing. I could be brave.

I kissed his neck beneath his beard and then mouthed my way over to his Adam's apple. The scent of pine and lemon was stronger here, and it had enough of a commercial hint to it to confirm what I suspected. It was an aftershave or cologne of some kind.

Whatever it was, I wanted it. I wanted to spray it over my pillows and pour it into my bath. I wanted to spend hours trying to recreate the scent with organic sources and all-natural elements.

One of his hands came up to cradle the back of my head and hold it still while he ducked down to kiss me on the lips. Ahh, there it was. The brain-fog and belly-swoops that came from being kissed by Sam Rigby.

I gave myself up to it happily, letting my body sink against his as his tongue explored my mouth. The endearment he'd uttered a minute ago finally sunk in and twisted my heart in hopeful knots.

He's not relationship material, I reminded myself. *He's not sticking around.*

But oh, how irrelevant that was right in this moment. I didn't need long term when I could have this right now. I didn't need a future when I had *this* as my present.

I moved my hands down to his shirt and yanked it out of his pants so I could sneak my fingers up under it. I felt the crisp hair on his stomach and moved my hands up to explore his muscled chest. God, he was like something out of a construction worker pornography video, all chiseled muscle and hairy chest. I roamed my hands over every firm curve I could reach and enjoyed the noises he made in response.

"Fuck," he said before flipping me quickly onto my back on the sofa. The move took my breath away, and then his mouth on mine made it hard to get it back.

Please, please! My brain hammered out a silent litany of begging for more. More kisses, more touches, more skin, more time.

Sam ground his erection against my hip and moved a hand down to cup me through my pants.

"Oh!" I cried. "Oh god."

I sounded like a prim miss, but I was too overwhelmed with sensation to temper my words.

Sam rumbled out a low string of dirty talk I wasn't even sure he realized he was saying out loud as his belly pressed against my erection in a rhythmic cadence. "Want to fuck you. Want to strip you down and suck you off. Slip my fingers inside you and fuck you with them. Want to watch you lose control. Then I want you to sit on my dick and—"

Apparently, I was a sucker for dirty talk. The orgasm hit me like a roundhouse kick out of the blue. I grunted in surprise and cried out in complete horror.

"No! Oh, ahhh, oh my god. Oh. Oh god." It seemed like it lasted forever. My humiliation was impossible to miss as I gasped and wheezed and shoved myself against him in a heady combination of embarrassment and relief.

The silence that followed was horrendous.

"Keep going," I said stupidly.

Sam pulled back and stared down at me. "Did you just—?"

"Keep going," I said again. "Please! It didn't happen. I'm good. Keep going." I reached up to try and pull his face back down for another kiss, but he was stronger than I was.

Instead, he gave me a giant, shit-eating grin. "You came."

Cripes.

"No."

"You did. You came in your pants."

What would happen if I burst into tears right now? It would probably make for a really awkward goodbye followed by tires squealing as he peeled out of my driveway.

"I'm sorry," I breathed. "It's been a long—"

"That's the single hottest thing I've ever seen."

"—time for me. What?" I blinked up at him. "What?"

"If I so much as touched my dick right now, I'd come all over you. You're so fucking sexy, Truman. That was incredibly hot."

"Come all over me," I whispered, too scared to say it fully out loud. "Please, come all over me."

Sam's eyes turned molten and stayed riveted on mine. He reached down between us to unfasten his pants. "Stop me, sweetheart."

I shook my head.

"Touch me," he said softly.

Instead, I reached for the buttons of my own shirt and began popping them open as swiftly as I could. When I finally got them all undone, I opened the shirt all the way and bared myself to him.

I didn't need to say it again.

Come all over me.

Within seconds, he was above me, stroking himself and making low noises in his throat. His eyes never strayed from mine, and it made my heart stutter in my chest.

I reached out to run my hands up his powerful thighs, squeezing the muscles and feeling them respond to my touch. I wanted to feel the warm puckered skin of his balls, so I reached up with one hand and ran my fingertips under his sac. Sam made a choking noise in his throat and threw his head back. His cum splattered over my chest and stomach as he groaned out his release above me.

When he was finally done, he looked back down at me and fell forward onto one hand, propping himself above me. "I can't remember the last time I came that hard," he admitted. "You're so fucking sexy."

I wondered if he was going to leave then, prove my mom right when I'd overheard her tell Trinity that men only wanted one thing and when they got it, they were as good as gone. That had never made sense to me considering my father had never left her in all these years, but then I'd had my first kiss and furtive grope in high school and the guy had ignored me after that like I was nothing.

So I'd learned that maybe my mom had been right.

I braced myself for his swift departure.

11

SAM

I'd never seen anything as debauched and tempting as Truman Sweet covered in my cum. His skin was flushed with color, and his eyes were glassy. His warm brown curls stood out around his head like the quirkiest of halos, and his top teeth bit into his bottom lip, reminding me of what it felt like when I was the one who got to nibble on that plump skin.

"Let me wash you off," I said, leaning down to press a kiss to those incredible lips. "Shower with me."

His eyelashes fluttered for a second before widening. "Huh?"

I stood up and reached for his hand to haul him up next to me. "Which way to the shower? We need to get you cleaned up."

"But I... I can do it myself. You don't have to..."

"Truman, I know I don't have to. I want to. I'm not done touching you yet." I grabbed his hand and headed toward the hallway, assuming Truman slept in a main-level bedroom so he didn't have to heat the second floor of the farmhouse.

When I caught sight of a bed with a pile of men's underwear on it, I knew I'd come to the right place.

"Oh god," Truman groaned, racing ahead of me and gathering

them up to shove into a nearby dresser drawer. "Ignore this. Close your eyes. Stop looking at anything!"

He flailed around, looking for anything else he could clean up. I stood back and watched, especially enjoying the knowledge that my release was still branded on his skin.

"Truman, did you try on various kinds of undies for our date tonight?" I teased, leaning back against the doorjamb and crossing my arms in front of my chest.

He froze. "What? No. Of course not. That's... that was simply a load of clean laundry I forgot to put it away."

"You save up several weeks' worth of underwear and wash it all together, apart from the rest of your clothes?"

"Never you mind," he said absently, rushing over to straighten up the already made bed. "Stop being nosy. You don't need to worry about my underwear."

I strode over to him slowly enough to give him fair warning of my approach. "But I am worried about your underwear. Especially since I was the cause of its recent besmirching."

His jaw dropped down, and I laughed.

"C'mere," I murmured, pulling him close again so I could pull the shirt off his shoulders and undo his jeans. "I want to see the undies I ruined."

I could feel him getting hard again which reminded me how young he was. Shower sex seemed like a really good idea right about now.

"Let me wash you off," I offered again. "It's my mess. I should be the one to clean it."

Truman groaned. "Why do you make that sound so sexy?"

I pulled his jeans down to reveal a tiny pair of camouflage boy shorts.

"My, my," I purred, running a fingertip under the edge of his waistband. "Aren't these nice?"

The wet sticky front of the shorts moved. "You're killing me," he said.

I slid my hand over his cheek and pulled him in for a kiss. "If this is too much, I'll go."

Truman shook his head. "Not too much."

I distracted him with kisses as I moved us both toward the bathroom. It was surprisingly large and modern inside, but I didn't waste time wondering about farmhouse renovations. I simply turned on the water in the walk-in shower and kept kissing him as I peeled my own clothes off.

"It's not fair," Truman complained as I reached for his dark-framed glasses. "You're all fit and strong, and I'm..."

"Hot, sexy, beautiful, perfect," I suggested, setting the frames on the bathroom counter. "Young, fit, luminous, magnetic... *hot*."

"In the bathroom with a liar," he finished with a laugh. But I could see my words pleased him even if he didn't believe them to be true. And that was all I could ask for.

Truman stared at my dick after I stripped out of my boxer briefs. I wasn't shy at all, so his attention only made me harder.

"Well," he said nervously. "There's... that."

He was nervous enough about my dick to pretty much confirm his virgin status. "*That* isn't going to do anything you don't want it to do," I assured him. "I'm just here to wash the merchandise, sir."

He let out a relieved laugh. "It's not that I don't want... *that*... to do things. But I—"

"It's okay," I said, reaching for his own underwear. "I promise."

He let me strip the sticky pants off him and toss them aside. His pubic hair was the same kind of dark riot of curls I'd imagined, and his dick made my mouth water. "This might require extra special cleaning," I informed him. "I'm nothing if not thorough and dedicated."

His easy smile made me feel almost giddy. Had I known I could make this sweet man happy by joking around a little, I'd have tried it sooner.

We got into the shower and rinsed off, barely removing our hands from each other's bodies enough to grab soap and shampoo. The warm slick slide of Truman's body against mine was enough to make me wish he had a limitless hot water heater so I could spend the rest of my days wrapped around him like this.

We kissed and fondled each other lazily as the hot spray thundered around us. I finally dropped to my knees and looked up at him with a question in my eyes.

Can I please suck you off?

He nodded and bit his lip again. Fuck, what that did to me.

I began with long wide licks, watching his eyes for any sign of nerves or discomfort.

There were none.

When I sucked the head into my mouth and curled my tongue around it, Truman's hands landed in my hair, and he held on tight. Within moments he was gasping and spluttering, practically choking on shower water. I moved him away from the spray and doubled down on my efforts. I clasped his balls and ran a strong fingertip behind them, loving the way Truman's slim thigh muscles contracted as he fought to keep his balance.

His hands tightened in my hair, and his breathing lost its rhythm. His dick oozed salty precum that mixed with the water from his body. It was erotic as hell, enough to make me take myself in hand and jack off to the sounds of his pleasure.

When he cried out and shot into my mouth, it was fucking fantastic. I shot my own release all over the shower floor a few moments later as Truman's body was still shuddering from his orgasm.

This man was dangerous to my self-control. And I knew if I didn't get the hell out of here, I'd keep touching him, keep pushing him, until we did something he wasn't ready for.

I quickly finished washing us both off and bundled him into one of the large towels hanging on a nearby bar. With a clearer head, I finally noticed how tidy the bathroom was and how each product was in unlabeled glass pots or jars. I wondered if he only used items he'd made himself. It would explain why he smelled like actual sun-ripened cherries—different than the artificial cherry smell in store-bought products.

After drying us both off, I hustled him back out to the bedroom and pulled back the blankets on his bed. "I'm going to say good night and let you drift off," I said to the still-dazed man in my arms. He tried protesting, but I kissed the words from his lips. "Sweetheart, if I get in this bed with you, I'm not going to be able to keep my hands off you, and I don't want to rush things, okay?"

"But—"

I kissed him again. He was so beautiful, so sweet and kind. He was careful and considerate, interesting and responsive. I wanted to know more of him, to *touch* more of him. But I really needed to take a breath here. Even though I felt like I knew him, I really didn't. I knew enough to know he deserved to be treasured. He didn't deserve someone flying through town, fucking him, and bolting back out of town a few days later.

And that was still my plan.

"I'll come check on the fence tomorrow," I said, pulling the covers over him and kissing his clean-smelling cheek. Obviously what I really meant was that I'd come check on him tomorrow, but I was trying to be at least a little circumspect. After all, there were plenty of things that needed fixing around this place, and I could always kill two birds with the same stone.

After grabbing my clothes, I headed toward the bedroom door.

"Sam?"

"Yeah, baby?" I asked, turning back around. His damp curls were flipped this way and that around his head, and he squinted to see me without his glasses.

"Thank you for everything."

"I can't tell you just how much it was my pleasure, Truman," I said with a smile.

"No, I mean..." He sat up and rubbed his hands over his face like he was finally clearing his head from the orgasm. "You treated me like I was special, but you didn't treat me like a baby. You didn't treat me like a choirboy, like I was made of glass."

I strode back over to him and took his face in my hands. "Researchers at Caltech have created a form of glass that's stronger than steel," I told him. "Even if you were made of glass, you'd be tough as nails. You know how I know?"

He looked up at me with hopeful eyes. "How?"

"You never give up. You don't give up on your dreams, your friends, your family, or this town. You don't give up hope even when things don't go your way. You just keep being you. You're one of the strongest people I know, Truman Sweet." I leaned in and punctuated my words with a long, hungry kiss but then forced myself to pull away. "Sleep tight. See you tomorrow. I'll turn the knob lock before I go, but if you get up, be sure to turn the bolt, too, okay?"

He nodded and gave me a goofy grin. "I'm not worried anymore since you fixed the gate. No more notes in the kitchen."

I was busy pulling my clothes on when he said it, and it wasn't until I was halfway back to Tiller and Mikey's house before his words sunk in.

No more notes in the kitchen. What the hell did that mean?

I thought about texting him to ask, but I didn't want to run the risk of waking him if he'd actually let himself drift off to sleep. We'd eaten fairly late, then stayed at the dinner table talking for a long time. By the time I snuck back into Rockley Lodge, it was close to midnight.

I went to the kitchen to pour a glass of water and caught Tiller watching *SportsCenter* on low in the kitchen's sitting area.

"Hey," he said, stretching. "How was it?"

"Good." I moved over to the cabinet that held the glasses.

Tiller let out a surprised laugh and turned off the TV before joining me. He wore nothing but a pair of basketball shorts and his pro-football body was on full display. I'd always thought it was the height of irony that my best friend had ended up with a pro baller after spending a lifetime hating jocks.

Life was funny that way.

"Surely you're going to tell me more than that," he pressed. "You know Mikey's going to give you a full interrogation over breakfast."

He was right. Mikey was nosy as hell. We'd been friends for years, and we usually told each other everything. I wasn't as much of a talker as he was, but I was still expected to share my shit with him.

Shit like dates and hookups.

I shrugged. "I don't know what the hell I'm doing, to be honest. The man lives in Colorado. I live in Texas. I'm just here till my bike is fixed."

Tiller slid onto a stool at the kitchen island and reached for an apple from the fruit bowl between us. "That right?"

I sighed. "My whole life is back in Houston. My mom, my sisters, my business."

He nodded and took a bite from the apple. "True."

Silence descended between us. Talking to Tiller was a very different experience than talking to Mikey. I liked his quiet calm.

After a while, I said more. "But I feel like I need some distance from my mom and sisters. As long as they have me to rely on, they don't need to learn to rely on themselves."

He nodded again. "Seems likely from everything I've seen." He took another bite and chewed.

"And it's not like I have a man back there. Or even good friends besides you two."

"Mm." Tiller kept chomping on the apple.

"And my construction business is fairly transactional. I don't have any big projects looming right now. It's how I was able to finally take a break."

Tiller's eyes sparkled. I knew he was happy to hear me getting around to his point without him having to say it. We both knew he wanted me to move here and help with the resort remodel. But it was a large undertaking, and I wasn't sure I was up to the challenge. It would be easier to stay in Houston and keep building the business I'd already put so much blood, sweat, and tears into.

"Even if I lived here," I continued, "would I really be the best person for Truman? I don't think so."

"Why not?"

"He deserves someone more... I don't know. Polished? Educated? Interesting?"

Tiller's smirk dropped, and he leaned toward me over the island. "Do you remember who dropped everything to board up my house when a hurricane was coming and I was in Cleveland for a game? Do you remember who picked my parents up from the airport in the middle of the night when I was stuck in San Francisco? And by any chance do you remember who stood up to five fucking asshole tough guys who tried to beat the shit out of Mikey in the high school parking lot one night after band practice even though your dad had been arrested only a week before and your mom was still in the hospital?"

"None of those things imply polish, education, or interest," I said.

"True. They prove that you're better than any of those things. You have a giant fucking heart, and you take care of people. You are selfless and protective, kind and hardworking. You are one of the most steadfast people I've ever known, and in almost six years of leaving Mikey behind while I traveled for work, I've never once had to worry about him. Because of you. Because I know you're there and you love him as much as I do."

I couldn't meet his eyes. I didn't like being the center of this kind of attention. "With a hundred percent less dick involved," I clarified, in hopes of breaking the intense emotions of the moment.

He barked out another laugh. "Damned straight." Tiller studied me for a minute. "Truman may not want to be coddled, I don't know. But he could definitely use someone strong and protective in his corner, and he'd be lucky if it was you."

"Thank you. Now shut the fuck up."

"Detroit traded Owen Watson to Seattle," he said as if we'd been talking football all along.

"No shit? Who's going to replace him?"

Tiller and I spent a solid half hour speculating and talking smack about the league until a sleepy Mikey came shuffling out of the bedroom. "You two are not quiet," he grumbled.

Tiller grabbed him and pulled him in for a kiss. "Sorry, babe."

"How was your date?" Mikey asked with a knowing smile.

"Really fucking good. The man is an award-winning kisser. He showed me the view of town from his patio. I learned that he has a sister who teaches dance at a college, and his aunt actually got the farm in a trade from a homeopathic patient."

Tiller's jaw fell open in shock while Mikey begged for more details.

"You're kidding me," Tiller said. "I asked the same question, and you answered with a one-word grunt."

I shot Mikey a wink. "You have to know how to ask."

Tiller lifted his middle finger at me.

After I stopped laughing, I asked, "Do you guys know anything about a sheriff's department fee the shop owners in town have to pay for law enforcement service?"

Tiller's forehead wrinkled as he thought about it. "I don't remember anyone mentioning it when I went over the licensing and business fees associated with getting the resort back up. Maybe it's just for businesses in town? The ski resort is outside city limits."

"If we go into town for breakfast in the morning, would you mind asking your friends there?"

Tiller and Mikey both nodded. I stood up and thanked them before heading to bed. I got as far as the bathroom to brush my teeth when my phone buzzed in my pocket.

It was Truman. And he was sobbing.

"It's on fire! The shop. On fire, Sam. It's on fire. On..." I could barely understand him through his tears. I raced out of the room and barged into Mikey and Tiller's room without knocking.

"Fire in town at Truman's shop," I said quickly. "Taking the SUV."

Mikey quickly asked if we wanted them to come, too, but I didn't want to wait for them to get dressed. "No. I'll call you."

As I ran back through the house to grab the keys, I tried getting Truman to calm down. "Where are you, sweetheart? At the farm?"

"No, Barney came to get me. I'm at the shop. It's awful. Sam... Sam... can you... Can you come here?"

"I'm on my way, baby. Hang tight, okay? Stay away from the shop. Are the firefighters there?"

The drive to town seemed to take forever, and every hiccup of

Truman's slowed down the flow of information. I finally saw the commotion out front of the shop and pulled the SUV over to the side of the road before hopping out and making my way through the growing crowd of onlookers.

I finally found him with the older man's arm around his shoulder. I skidded to a halt, not wanting to upset him by yanking him out of his ex's arms. I didn't know their history. For all I knew, Barney Balderson was a great comfort to Truman. I'd known the man all of a day and a half.

"Truman," I said as I approached. He let out a garbled sound as he spotted me and then lurched in my direction. I wasn't sure if he'd intended to fly into my arms or not, but he tripped halfway there and landed against me anyway. I wrapped my arms around him and held on tight.

I could see the confused face of his ex in the shadows caused by the fire engine's swirling lights.

I closed my eyes and breathed. "Are you okay? You didn't get close, did you?"

I finally opened my eyes and looked at the building. It was completely engulfed. The windows were broken, and large columns of water shot through several of them from thick hoses managed by firefighters on the ground and in one of the truck's ladders.

"It's ruined," he breathed without even looking at the building. "Everything Aunt Berry worked for. Everything she built. I've ruined it all."

"How did you ruin it?" I asked, keeping my arms banded tightly around his back.

"They set my shop on fire because they hate me," he said in a small voice into my chest.

I pulled back and gripped his face so I could meet his eyes. "What? Who did this? This was set on purpose? Do you know that for sure?"

Truman's eyes were wet with tears, and his face was golden in the light from the fire. I looked around to see if anyone was close enough to hear us, and the only person was Barney.

"No, I don't know it for sure, but the building passes safety and code inspections every year. Why else would my store catch on fire?"

Barney stepped closer and patted Truman's shoulder. I wanted to snap and growl at him, break his fucking hand off his arm for even thinking of touching Truman right now, but I recognized that as entirely inappropriate and uncalled for. Barney was more of a friend to Truman than I was. I'd only known the man a couple of days, and I was heading back out of town before the week was out.

The older man cleared his throat. "I think Truman might be right. Plenty of people in this town have had it out for Truman for a long time. He needs to take better care of his safety. I keep trying to tell him, he's safer at home."

Truman pulled out of my hold enough to include Barney in the conversation, but I noticed he kept a tight grip on the back of my shirt with one hand.

Barney looked at Truman with parental-type affection. "Truman's going to come stay with me for a little while, aren't you, sweet pea?"

I felt Truman's hand tighten on the back of my shirt. "I don't think that's necessary," Truman said. "I'll be okay."

His words from earlier in the evening about not treating him like a child echoed in my head, and it took all of my self-control not to go full alpha on him by swooping in and making protective demands the way Barney seemed to be doing.

Barney pursed his lips. "But your gate is broken, and I don't feel comfortable letting you stay alone all the way out there."

"The gate isn't broken anymore," Truman said, turning to face me. "Sam fixed it for me."

I reached out and brushed an errant curl out from behind the frame of his glasses. "I was going to fix that fence tomorrow, too, so I'm happy to come bunk on your sofa and get started on that first thing in the morning if you don't want to be alone tonight."

At this point his grip on my shirt was nearly causing me to choke. I glanced over to see his body practically humming with tension. His eyes were fixed on the fire again.

"Yeah, maybe," he said absently.

Meanwhile, Barney's glare was still completely focused on me. I noticed he was sweating from the heat of the nearby fire. "I think he'd be better off at my place. This traumatic experience is clearly taking its toll on him, and he needs someone to care for him. I've been looking out for him for a while now."

He wasn't wrong about Truman needing someone to care for him. His slight body was swaying heavily against my side and trembling. I moved an arm around his shoulders to help keep him upright.

Two women I didn't recognize came hustling through the cluster of townspeople who'd gathered to watch the firefighters attempt to subdue the blaze.

"Truman, sweetie, no! Oh my god, what happened?" one of them cried before grabbing him in an embrace.

Barney sucked in a breath and stepped back to avoid being trampled on by the two women sandwiching Truman in a hug.

"I don't know, Mia," Truman said faintly. "I don't know what happened. It's all gone."

My heart broke at the sound of his voice, at the change from his happiness earlier in the evening when he told me about Aunt Berry and her special gift for healing and helping the people of Aster Valley.

"It's not all gone," one of the women said fiercely. "It's all in your head and in your heart, Truman Sweet, and we're going to help you rebuild it. Okay?"

They fussed over him as one of her words hit its target in my own head and heart.

Rebuild.

My specialty.

But first, I needed to figure out what the hell had happened here. And who needed to pay.

12

TRUMAN

I was numb. And for the first time in a very long time, I also felt completely hopeless. I'd tried so hard to keep my head down and stay out of trouble, not bother anyone or make waves in town. Now here I was with a ruined business and a heap of trouble on my doorstep.

I hated feeling like a burden or a child, so when Barney clucked and fussed over me, it grated on me. I tried to politely rebuff his attempts to have me stay at his house, but when he finally insisted, I lost my patience.

"I want to go home," I cried, sounding exactly like the baby I hadn't wanted to be perceived as. "Please just take me home."

Sam had wandered off to ask a nearby sheriff's deputy and firefighter a few questions, and seeing him with his muscular arms crossed over his chest watching the waning fire and talking to two of the officials was calming. He would be clearheaded enough to ask the right questions, something I sure as heck wasn't.

"Sir," another first responder said, approaching me from one of the nearby emergency vehicles. I recognized him as the deputy who'd taken my witness statement about the bike crash.

"Deputy Stone, right?" I asked.

"Yes, that's right. How are you, Mr. Sweet? Are you holding up alright?" His face held kind concern.

"Not really," I said with an attempt at a smile. "Is there any speculation about what caused the fire?"

"Not yet. We were notified through your alarm monitoring service to respond, but there was also a 9-1-1 call. Hopefully the rapid response will at least result in retaining the structural integrity of the building itself, but I would assume most of the contents are lost. I'm very sorry."

I nodded and swallowed thickly. "At least it was just inventory and not people."

Deputy Stone pulled out a little notebook and pencil. "How did you hear about the blaze?"

The question shouldn't have surprised me, but it did. "Barney came and got me. I was asleep at home when the gate alert woke me up."

Barney stepped closer and put his arm around my shoulders. "It was the least I could do. I didn't want him driving himself in such a state."

Deputy Stone glanced over at Barney. "And you are...?"

"Barney Balderson, director of the Aster Valley Library. I live here in town." He reached out a hand to shake, and Deputy Stone had to shift his notebook and pencil to one hand.

"And how did you hear about the fire, Mr. Balderson?"

Barney seemed taken aback by the question. He gestured to the fire trucks and other emergency vehicles whose lights were illuminating the entire downtown area. "It's fairly hard to miss, Deputy."

My attention drifted back over to Sam. It seemed like he'd asked the men beside him a million questions.

"When will you know if it was arson?" I asked Deputy Stone, not realizing I'd interrupted another one of his questions to Barney.

The deputy's brows lowered. "You suspect it was arson?"

I nodded and steeled myself. "Yes. In fact, I think it was retaliation for filing that report with you the other day."

Barney turned to me. "What report?"

Deputy Stone tilted his head. "You think someone would burn down your entire business because of a property damage report? You're talking about felony arson in response to criminal mischief."

He was right. I was being ridiculous. "Never mind," I said. "I think maybe I'm just upset. It's hard to wrap my head around the fact I could have lost my business because of some electrical fluke."

Barney nodded. "Quite right. You're responding with your emotions instead of your brain. Let's get you home and into bed. I'm sure the deputy can ask his questions tomorrow once you're feeling more yourself."

I wanted to tell Sam I was leaving, but I didn't have the energy to approach the cluster of people he was talking to. The group was now composed of several hulking firefighters, a deputy, and someone who looked an awful lot like a local reporter. I didn't want to go anywhere near such an intimidating group.

I gave Barney a weak smile. "Thank you."

He drove me home through the pitch-black night. A low hum of jazz music was the only sound filling his car as we made our way to the farm.

"Thank you for coming to get me," I told him. "I really appreciate it."

"Of course. I care about you, Truman, and I didn't want you to be alone when you found out about it."

He was right. It would have been awful to show up there alone and watch the place burn without anyone there to support me. It was thoughtful of him, even if he wasn't really the one I wanted comforting me.

I wondered if Sam had meant what he'd said about coming to sleep on my sofa. I didn't want him on my sofa. I wanted him in my bed, wrapped around me like kudzu.

But I was an adult. And if I wanted to be treated as such, I needed to act like one. That included fending off Barney's continued insistence that he stay over in case I needed him during the night.

"Obviously, Sam didn't mean it when he offered," Barney pointed out, somehow recognizing my own insecurities. "I don't see him here.

It just goes to show, you can't trust someone like that. As if you needed an itinerant worker lurking about the place. What do you even know about him? It's better to circle the wagons and stick with people you know and trust."

I wanted to laugh at him calling Sam an itinerant worker. From everything Mikey had told me, he was a general contractor who owned his own business and ran large jobs. He was hardly a seasonal apple picker.

But I was too tired to argue. "Okay. Thanks again for taking me and bringing me home. I'll call you in the morning." I tried closing the front door, but he reached out a hand to hold it open.

"Sweet pea, I'm worried about you," Barney said. "You need someone to look after you, especially if this was deliberate."

"I'm fine. The gate is fixed, and I have the bolt on the door." I didn't dare mention the bolt hadn't kept my note-writer away earlier in the week. But maybe I'd been lax and forgotten to turn it. Stranger things had happened.

"I don't just mean looking after your physical safety. This has to be upsetting you. I'd really like it if you let me come in and hold you tonight."

The image of that almost caused me to shudder. "I think what I really need is sleep," I said as gently as I could. "I'm going to get in bed and stay there as long as possible to avoid thinking about this right now."

He met my eyes and studied me for a moment before reluctantly nodding. "Lock the doors behind me. Don't open the gate for anyone but me. Call me the minute you wake up."

I gritted my teeth to keep from snapping at him to mind his own business. "Will do," I said instead.

Once he was gone, I let out a breath and locked up. I made my way back to my bedroom and changed into a T-shirt and a pair of threadbare pajama pants. I really was going to fall into bed and hope for hours of oblivion.

But then my phone buzzed.

Sam: *I'm at the gate.*

I felt the tears come as I pressed the remote to let him in. He was riding a motorcycle I didn't recognize. When he got to the front door, I flung it open and planted my feet to the floor to keep from also flinging myself right at his solar plexus.

"Hi," I said instead, quickly brushing the tears away.

Sam's eyes roamed all over me as if searching for something. "What can I do to ease your pain?"

I stepped forward and climbed his body until my arms were wrapped around his neck and my legs were wrapped around his waist. "Take me to bed and hold me all night."

So that's what he did.

He reached back and locked the door again before carrying me down the hall and laying me on the bed. He stripped down to his boxer briefs and slipped into bed next to me, pulling me close again. I let out a shaky breath and let myself fall asleep to the strong feeling of kudzu wrapped around me.

When I awoke, Sam was gone, but the spot beside me was still warm from his body. I went to the bathroom before making my way out to the kitchen where I found him drinking a cup of coffee and scrolling through his phone.

"Hi," I said nervously.

Sam turned to me with a soft smile. "Good morning. Sleep okay?"

I reached for a mug and poured myself a cup from the pot he'd made. "I slept like a brick. You?"

"Best sleep I've had in a while. Gotta say, I don't mind holding you all night. I think maybe I need to do it more often." He winked at me and went back to his phone. "They're going to investigate the fire to confirm its cause. I pulled up some information on insurance claims in the case of fire, and I'm happy to help make some of those calls for you today. It might be a good idea to try and get on a contractor's schedule for the repairs. Even if you're not sure about what you want to do, you can ask them for options and estimates. I can sit in on the interviews and help show you what questions to ask. If we call around today, we can get several of the interviews done before I leave."

Thinking about him leaving was definitely not good for my mental health today, so I dropped it from my mind like a hot potato.

Sam looked back up at me. "But that doesn't mean you're obligated. It's your business, your call."

I blinked at him for a minute in confusion before he laughed.

"Never mind. You're pre-coffee. It was stupid of me to bring it up yet. Sit and I'll fix you something to eat."

I moved to the coffeepot instead and poured myself a cup. After fixing it and taking a few sips, I let out a breath. "The insurance company will want to know what caused the fire. Do you know who I'm supposed to contact at the fire department?" I asked as Sam nudged me out of the way with his hip to get the eggs from the fridge.

"Yes, I have the investigator's info, but I wouldn't think they'd have an update for you until at least after lunch. They have to make sure it's cool and safe enough to enter before they can start the investigation."

"Do you think it's possible it could have been arson? Maybe one of the Stanner brothers?" I asked.

Sam held the egg he'd been about to crack in midair. "Because of the incident with my bike?"

"I filed a witness report," I told him. "And he probably found out from their uncle, the sheriff."

"I told you not to do that," Sam said with a sigh before cracking the egg and adding it to the collection in the bowl. "It's not necessary. It's certainly not worth putting you in danger."

I busied myself getting out some slices of bread for the toaster. "Well, it's done. But surely that wouldn't be enough to cause someone to burn down my entire business?" I quickly reminded myself that wasn't their only motivation. They blamed me for any number of things, all stemming from their father losing his job after the resort closed. Which, of course, they blamed me for.

Sam turned to face me. "Last night you said, 'No more notes in the kitchen.' What did you mean by that?"

He wasn't going to like it, but if I wanted his help figuring this out, I needed to tell him.

"The morning after your motorcycle was hit, I woke up to find a note on the kitchen counter warning me to make sure you dropped the charges."

Sam threw the stove nob to the *off* position and crossed his arms in front of his chest. It made him look bigger and broader, but for some reason, I wasn't intimidated by him the way I was by other men his size. "Where is this note?"

I retrieved it from a drawer in the sunroom and handed it to him. While he was checking it out, the gate buzzer blasted through the house over and over.

"Holy cow," I muttered, making my way to the intercom with Sam hot on my trail barking out cautionary warnings. "Yes?"

It was Chaya. "Let me in, asshole."

I pressed the button to let her in and made sure the front door was unlocked. Within seconds, she was barging in and grabbing me into a giant hug. "What the fuck? Why didn't you call me?" Once she saw Sam, she huffed out a laugh. "Oh, I see."

"It was the middle of the night," I told her. "I was hardly of sound mind."

She pulled back and studied my face, keeping a light grip on my upper arms. "Are you okay?"

I nodded. "Bruised in spirit but not in body."

"I was at the diner when I heard. Fair warning, I'm fairly sure half the town is on the road behind me. Everyone wants to know how you're doing." She flicked her eyes back over to Sam before adding, "And Mikey and Tiller were there asking about the sheriff's pension fund. Seems like some shit is going down."

Just then the sound of the gate buzzer blasted again. I needed to find a way to turn that down or I was going to go gray in my twenties.

I opened the gate and pressed the button that would keep it open if multiple people were coming. Besides, with Chaya and Sam here, I was plenty safe.

"Chaya, have you met Sam Rigby?" I stepped back to introduce the two of them. Chaya flitted her eyelashes at Sam which seemed to make him oddly nervous.

She grinned at him before reaching her hand out. "You were preoccupied when we saw each other at the diner the other day," she teased. "Nice to meet you. Thank you for looking after my brotato chip." She reached out and tousled my hair.

I tried explaining to Sam with my eyes that Chaya was an odd duck. He winked at me and reached to shake her hand. "It's my pleasure. I love brotato chips."

God, he was so fucking hot. And his voice was sexy enough to make me almost forget the Honeyed Lemon had burned down.

But not quite.

"Did you drive by the shop? How did it look?"

She frowned. "Not good. Except the brick looks solid. The windows are mostly broken. Part of the street is blocked off, and there were official-looking vehicles there. It looked like there might have even been a state fire investigator there."

"Good," Sam muttered. "Maybe a state investigator will be objective."

I glanced at him, knowing he was bound to be upset about the note I'd just shown him. "Agreed."

He held his coffee mug in one hand but used the other to reach for my hand, threading our fingers together and holding on to me as if we were boyfriends. Chaya's eyes practically bugged out of her head, and I felt my face heat.

I didn't want her getting any ideas. It wasn't a boyfriend thing, just a comfort thing.

Tiller and Mikey's SUV crunched to a halt outside next to Chaya's vehicle and Pim's Volkswagen. Mia and Mindy followed closely behind in their Subaru, and I spotted Nina's ranch pickup truck behind them. Even though the reason for the meet-up wasn't a good one, I was secretly a little excited to have everyone here. I felt cared for and supported.

Part of a community.

After stepping through the front door to wave everyone inside, I turned to put on another pot of coffee and see if I had any kind of food I could put out.

As soon as Pim and Bill came in, followed by their teenaged son, Solomon, I saw my worry over food wasn't necessary. Solo was loaded down with trays of breakfast treats.

"Where do you want these, Mr. Sweet?" he asked. I'd told him to call me Truman a million times, but he refused. Since he worked for me part-time at the shop, he insisted on treating me like a proper boss.

My heart dropped as I realized I wouldn't need him at the shop for a while, but then I quickly realized I could use his help here on the farm instead, if he wanted it. My face must have shown my roller coaster of emotions, because Sam squeezed my shoulder and asked if I was okay.

"Yeah. Just... adjusting, you know? It'll be a new normal."

He leaned in and pressed a kiss to my forehead. "You're strong as hell. You're going to rock this."

I turned to see my kitchen full of friends and neighbors, coffee and pastries, laughter and hugs, and gossip and teasing.

Within seconds, this kitchen had turned from a lonely reminder of the loss of Aunt Berry to a living memorial of the legacy she left and the hopes she'd had for me. By giving me her gift of healing and planting, by giving me the shop and the farm, she'd given me a sense of place, a community.

And now they were here in her kitchen surrounding me with the kind of friendship I'd always longed for but never thought I'd find.

I knew everyone in here because of my shop, because, despite my fear of rejection, I'd worked hard to be a quiet, contributing member of the Aster Valley community. Mia and Mindy owned the yarn shop a few stores down from mine, Bill and Pim owned the diner, and Nina owned a dude ranch on the edge of town. I noticed she'd also brought her friend Carlin, who owned the new tack store in town.

As we drank coffee and ate muffins, several more people arrived. I recognized most of them as fellow business owners in town. When Pim finally took the lead to get everyone's attention, I guessed what the common denominator was between all of us.

Business owners who weren't close to the Stanners.

Pim's usual joking manner was replaced with a serious expression. "Alright, everyone, settle down. It's come to our attention that some of us are being extorted by the sheriff's department for financial support that's completely off the books."

Out of the corner of my eye, I noticed Sam's jaw tighten. Tiller looked equally pissed off.

"So I think we'd better get to the bottom of this and figure out exactly how we want to go about fixing it," Pim continued. "Let's start by making a list of who's paying this fee, how much we're paying, and who's getting the money."

As we slowly began comparing notes, I realized not every shop was paying this "supplemental" fee for law enforcement. I was shocked, but I could tell Sam wasn't surprised at all.

"It's not legal," Bill said. He was normally the quieter man in their marriage, so when he spoke, people tended to listen. "I did a little digging into the county budget, and I don't see these payments listed anywhere. I propose we pool our resources and hire an attorney to look into it."

Pim added, "Someone from out of town. Because if we're wrong, several of us are going to make serious enemies with the wrong people. Bill and I are already on their shit list for refusing to pay it. We asked for the federal tax identification or charity registration of the pension fund for our records, and they never got back to us. We kind of forgot all about it. But we definitely deal with petty vandalism every few weeks. Not sure we even thought to connect the two."

Everyone grumbled their frustration and agreed to the idea of an attorney. Tiller offered up his friend Julian, who could come in from Denver again.

I could tell Mia was mad as hell. "We questioned this payment when we first opened the shop. A week later, the shop was broken into and a brand-new delivery of high-end yarn and notions was taken. When we tried filing a report, the sheriff made it clear that businesses who contributed to the fund were put at the top of the priority list."

Mindy rubbed Mia's back. "At the time, we thought it was homophobia, and we just decided to pay it to keep the peace."

Nina sighed. "Not homophobia. I was stupid enough to date Craig Stanner for about three months a couple of years ago. That's when he convinced me to contribute. Even though the ranch is outside the city limits, he told me that the department helps those who help their officers. I just thought it was a nice way to be a supportive member of the community. But now I wonder who's actually getting this money."

I spoke up. "There's a new deputy, Declan Stone, who seems like a stand-up guy. He transferred in from somewhere else. Once we get some more information, we might be able to ask his help."

Mindy sighed. "I don't know, Truman. I'd feel more comfortable if we called in the state bureau of investigations or something. Maybe the FBI?"

Bill nodded. "Let's wait and see what the lawyer says. In the meantime, we need to keep this real quiet."

Everyone agreed, and the conversation eventually moved off the topic of the corrupt sheriff's department. Nerves coiled in my gut, but there was a slice of hope, too. If someone could hold Sheriff Stanner accountable for not treating the citizens of Aster Valley equally, it would go a long way toward improving our lives here.

Pim landed a beefy hand on my shoulder. "Now, what are we going to do with the Toasted Lemon?"

It took me a minute to realize he was talking about my shop.

And all I could do was laugh to keep from crying.

13

SAM

I watched Truman come to life with all of those friends and colleagues in his kitchen. He was a natural host, bustling around offering refills of coffee or answering questions about the new plants he was growing on the windowsill. After a while, I noticed Truman was smiling and relaxed, even laughing at one of Pim's stories while the two older men held court at the kitchen table.

At one point, Barney Balderson showed up to check on Truman, and I could tell he was not a happy camper.

"Why are all these people here?" he asked Truman near the front door. I was trying not to eavesdrop, but my feet were glued to the floor.

I expected him to tell Barney about the pension fund situation since they were close and Barney was a member of the Aster Valley community as well as anyone, but he didn't.

"They came to check on me because of the fire," Truman said instead.

"You should be resting," Barney said. "All this attention must be making you uncomfortable."

Truman pushed up his glasses, and I noticed a furrow of confusion between his eyes. "No? It's nice, actually. It's really nice that everyone cares."

"Well, be that as it may, it's time for them to get back to work and allow you to get on with your day. We have quite a few tasks to organize to get the shop officially closed down." They moved into the kitchen where I was pretending to inspect a cabinet door handle that wasn't even pretend-loose.

"Closed down?" Truman asked. "You mean boarded up?"

"Hi, Mr. Balderson," Chaya said politely. "I think Sam here volunteered to do some of that work. He's certainly strong enough to haul those big sheets of plywood around." She reached out and squeezed my biceps.

I tilted my head at her. She hadn't been the least bit flirty with me, so why was she acting this way now?

Truman blushed. "He doesn't need to do that."

Barney looked annoyed. "Certainly not. I'm sure we can hire some manual labor to knock out those menial tasks. I thought we could make a punch list of what all needs to be done."

Tiller and Mikey wandered over, and Tiller chimed in. "We're happy to help. We have nothing scheduled today, so Sam can put us to work." He clapped me on the shoulder and met my eyes. "And we're going to go ahead and pick up another car so you can have full use of the SUV."

I opened my mouth to argue, and Tiller cut me off. "We need a second car here anyway, so this isn't about you."

They were good friends, and I loved seeing their support of Truman. Tiller and Mikey had always been the kind of friends to drop everything and come running. They'd helped Sophie with the baby plenty of times when no one else had been available.

"Call us when you know how we can pitch in," Tiller said before leading Mikey out. Everyone else eventually said their own goodbyes until Chaya, Barney, and I were the only people still sharing the kitchen with Truman.

I didn't want to make things awkward for Truman, so I decided to duck out. There was no harm in letting Barney help make a to-do list.

Truman needed friends who were going to be able to help him for more than a couple of days. "I need to run a few errands and pick up some supplies. Are you okay here for a bit?"

Truman looked surprised, but he nodded. "Of course."

"I'll swing by the shop and find out how much plywood you need. If you think of anything else you want from the hardware store, just shoot me a text."

I turned to say goodbye to Chaya and saw her give me a wink. I wasn't quite sure what it meant until she made a big deal about "sticking around to help out." Somehow, I was already on good terms with Truman's best friend, and it made me feel an odd sense of relief.

As I made my way into town on the rented motorcycle, I enjoyed the fresh mountain air in my face and the twists and turns of the road leading to town. The Honeyed Lemon looked even worse in the daylight than it had last night. From what I could see through the broken windows, the interior was nothing but a collection of black char. The front doorway was blocked with a pile of debris that looked like the twisted remains of the shop's heavy wooden and glass doors. The metal lock mechanism still looked intact which wasn't surprising considering any arsonist with a brain would have come in from the dark alleyway in the back.

I was surprised to see only one official-looking vehicle parked nearby. Maybe I could get a look inside and see if there was anything salvageable to take back to Truman.

After making my way around the building to the back door, I carefully stepped inside. Off to one side of the back hallway was a storage room full of shelves dripping with dirty water and the charred remains of cardboard boxes. Shattered glass jars covered the dirty wet floor, and a terrible smell with an acrid spice tinge permeated the place. I was grateful Truman wasn't here to see it.

"Stop right there," a voice boomed from further inside the shop. "This is a crime scene, and it's unsafe for entry. Remove yourself the way you came. Carefully."

A crime scene? Did that mean arson had been confirmed?

"I'm a friend of the owner. He wanted me to check to see what we needed to do to protect his assets," I replied.

A helmeted man ducked through the doorway from the main part of the shop. He was dressed in a protective jumpsuit and wore a face mask. I wanted to kick myself for not thinking about the possibility of toxic fumes or particulates.

I quickly did as he asked and waited for him in the small parking area behind the shop.

"And you are?" the investigator asked, pulling down his mask.

"Sam Rigby."

He seemed to relax before introducing himself as the state fire investigator and handing me his card. "Dirk Bromley. We'll be here most of the day completing our investigation. We'd like to ask Mr. Sweet some questions. Do you know if he'll be stopping by today or if we should plan to interview him at his residence?"

"He's at his farm today. He runs part of his business from there, too."

He nodded. "We'll head over to talk to him after lunch."

I texted Truman to make sure the plan was okay with him and then gave the investigator the farm's address. Dirk said I was welcome to begin boarding up the place, and when I asked if there was anything of value inside, he said that was something he'd only be able to discuss with Truman. He indicated that a sheriff's deputy would remain at the property until it was appropriately secured. That didn't ease my mind until I recognized the deputy Truman had described as the man who'd taken his statement the other day.

I hesitated for a few moments before finally deciding to give him further information. "If you determine it was arson, you need to know that Truman has an active harasser."

The man's eyes widened only slightly before he resumed his professional expression. "Can you give me the person's name and the particular details of this harassment?"

I summarized it as much as possible and told him that if the fire was set deliberately, it was most likely done by Patrick Stanner, which was tricky considering his relationship to the county sheriff.

The investigator nodded, but I could see I'd given him information he'd rather not have had. It made the situation much trickier.

"And does Mr. Sweet still have the note left at his house?" he asked.

"Yes. I'll make sure you get a chance to see it when you come by for the interview."

He nodded and reentered the building while I continued on to Mikey and Tiller's place to shower, dress, and swap out vehicles again.

Tiller and Mikey came with me to board up the shop, but rather than do the heavy lifting, Mikey took the opportunity to wander up and down the street and pop his head into most of the shops to chat up the owners. He was unassuming and social enough to put people at ease right away, and most everyone already knew him as "that famous footballer's boyfriend" anyway.

When he returned to the shop, he'd amassed a ton of helpful information.

"Bearwood Realty has had their sign vandalized five times this year. They don't pay into the pension fund. They assumed the vandalism was done by pranksters. The coffee shop hasn't had any problems at all. They don't pay into the pension fund, but Yasmin's brother is the sheriff's department accountant. Oh, and Dr. Allan's vet clinic doesn't pay either, but his mother is the receptionist at the sheriff's department. Small towns, am I right? What else?"

He took a minute to think about it while I got even angrier on Truman's behalf.

"Bolo's Market pays into the fund. When their alarm gets tripped, they get incredible response rates from the department, so they said they're never stopping their payments." Mikey sighed. "This place is fucked-up."

"I wonder what the mayor's involvement is," I said. "How does the county sheriff's department get away with running this town like it's their own?"

Movement out of the corner of my eye caught my attention, and I realized I'd said that in hearing distance from Deputy Stone.

Fuck.

The man politely looked away, but it was clear he'd heard. Was he going to go back and tell the sheriff what I'd said?

I thought about confronting him about the situation, but that would put him in a position where he couldn't simply forget what he'd just overheard. And, damn, did I want him to forget.

Had I just put an even bigger target on Truman's head?

"I've got to get back to the farm," I said, tossing my tools in the back of their SUV. "I don't want him to sit through the investigator's interview with just Barney for support."

Mikey asked what was going on with Barney. "I really thought they were an item."

"No idea," I admitted. "At first I thought they were dating. Then Truman said they weren't. Not sure the old man's gotten the message."

"It's creepy," Tiller muttered as he closed the hatch.

Mikey shrugged. "I mean, it's not creepy because of the age difference, really. But I agree it's a little creepy because Truman never shows the slightest bit of romantic or sexual interest in Barney, yet Barney seems to think they're an item. And they were, at least at one point. Why would Truman date someone he was that uncomfortable with?"

"My only guess is Barney wants Truman," I admitted. "And Truman probably wants to be wanted."

The whole situation put my teeth on edge, and my frustration mounted as my phone began to buzz with a new slew of calls and messages from my mom and my sister Sophie.

I waved Tiller and Mikey off before heading to where I'd parked the rental bike. I turned off notifications on my phone from my family members so I'd no longer get their interruptions. I could only handle one crisis at a time, and right now I wanted to help with this one as much as Truman would let me.

When I got to the farmhouse, I was disappointed to see Chaya's car gone and Barney's still there. The gate was closed, so I pulled up and pressed the buzzer.

Movement off to my left caught my attention, and I saw Barney's thicker form carrying trash bags out of a garden shed and stacking them up in a pile. As much as I disliked the guy, his helping Truman clean out Berry's things was a great idea.

The gate swung open, and I pulled down the drive before parking the bike. Truman came out of the front door and waved hello, his face just starting to widen into a smile before he spotted Barney.

And then it flashed through confusion to anger.

"What are you doing?" Truman called across the garden plot that separated the corner of the house from the storage shed. He hopped down the porch stairs and raced down the gravel path to yank the trash bag out of Barney's hands. "What is this?"

As Truman ripped the bag open to reveal what looked like brightly colored feathers, Barney crossed his arms and stuck out his chin. "We talked about this."

"About throwing my costumes away? No we didn't! You said you were organizing them, not trashing them. Why? Why would you do this? These are the costumes I wear to do story hour at the library."

"Well, you're no longer doing story time, so it's a moot point."

Truman's face showed a mixture of hurt and defiance. I wanted to soothe the hurt part and cheer on the other.

"Why not?" Truman challenged. "Give me one good reason I can't volunteer at the library again."

Barney sighed. "We've been over this. It's not appropriate. I could be accused of playing favorites because of our relationship."

"We're friends. This is a small town. You're friends with plenty of the volunteers. That's how we became friends in the first place! I signed up to volunteer."

Barney reached for the bag in Truman's arms and set it on the pile before grasping the smaller man by the shoulders. "I understand you're upset, sweet pea, but this is part of the cleanup we talked about. You asked for my help clearing things out, and I'm helping make some of the tough decisions. That's what people who care about you do. I know this isn't easy. None of it is. But you'll be happy when we're through. Just think of all the gardening tools you can keep in here. We'll get it organized as your very own garden palace."

Truman's brows furrowed. "I asked for your help clearing out Aunt Berry's things, not mine. And I already have a huge greenhouse for my gardening supplies, not to mention the barn. I don't need to use the goat shed for that. And since I don't have goats..." He flexed his jaw and pushed his glasses up his nose with a jab. "It's for my costumes. And they're not trash. They're special. I'm keeping them."

I moved forward and picked up a handful of bags before stepping around Barney and entering the little shed. The cramped and dark space was surprisingly tidy with several rows of hooks on one wall and utilitarian cubbies lined up along another. At the end was a portable clothes rack that stood forlornly with nothing but a few empty hangers swinging idly from its pole.

I began unpacking the trash bags and hanging the costumes back up as best I could, stashing shoes and accessories in the cubbies and hanging ties and belts from the hooks. Barney's attempts at lecturing Truman about needing to stop spending so much time and energy on silly things made my fingers itch, but I kept reminding myself Truman was capable of standing up for himself since he was the one who called Barney out in the first place.

When I returned outside to gather some more bags, the two of them were standing opposite each other with matching glares. Someone needed to break the tension.

"Is anyone hungry? It might be a good idea to grab a bite to eat before the fire investigators swing by for the interview."

Barney looked surprised to see me as if he'd forgotten I was here. "Interview? What interview?"

Truman lifted his hand up to fiddle with a curl hanging over one ear. I'd noticed him do it before and wondered if it was a nervous gesture.

"They think it's arson, so they want to ask me some questions."

Barney's face darkened. "That's ridiculous. As if Truman had anything to do with it. If it was arson, it had to be those Stanner boys. They've been hassling him for years."

I couldn't hold back the question that had been bugging me for a while now. "Why hasn't anyone stopped them?"

Barney's nostrils flared. "And who are you, again? A friend of Mister Moneybags?"

It took me a minute to realize he was referring to Tiller. "I'd like to think I'm a friend of Truman's now, also, but yes. And if this harassment has been going on for so long, why hasn't anyone gone to the state police?"

I could understand Truman himself not having the guts to go above Sheriff Stanner's head because the repercussions would be awful if it failed. But Barney was old enough and established enough in town to be able to go to bat for him with the authorities.

Truman opened his mouth to say something, but Barney beat him to the punch. "Not that it's any of your business since you're a stranger here in town for all of five minutes, but this is a delicate matter involving sensitive moments from Truman's past. There are quite a few people here in town who blame Truman for what happened to the ski resort and..." He stopped to pat Truman's shoulder awkwardly. "Not that it was your fault, sweet pea, of course. But because of that, Truman has many enemies. It's complicated. I wouldn't expect a newcomer like you and your friends to understand."

I thought about Pim, Bill, Nina, Mia, Mindy, Chaya, and anyone else who'd come by the farmhouse to check on Truman after the fire. He wasn't without friends in town, so what was I missing?

Truman cut in. "Actually, I'm feeling tired and think I want to take a nap before the investigators come. Barney, would you mind taking those orders on the front porch to the post office for me?"

Barney's eyes flicked between us. "I'm sure your friend Sam wouldn't mind."

"Actually," I said casually, "I'm here to fix the fence. But don't worry, I'll keep an eye on him."

Fine, I couldn't help a little jab.

"If he gives you any trouble," Barney said, turning to Truman and smoothing his thinning hair back, "call me. I'll return later this evening to check on you, and if I need to get the sheriff's office involved in checking up on this guy, I will."

The threat was particularly offensive considering how dangerous the sheriff's family was to Truman. This man made me sick, and I hoped like hell Truman would tell him where to shove it when his head cleared. In the meantime, I gritted my teeth and held my tongue.

"I'll be fine," Truman said wearily.

As soon as Barney's car had disappeared through the gate, I returned to the trash bag pile and began moving them back into the shed.

"Come lie down with me?"

I let out a breath and turned to face Truman. There was only ever going to be one answer to that question.

Hell yes.

I followed him into his house and back to his bedroom before stripping my jeans off and sliding into bed with him. I pulled his back to my front in spoon fashion. "Better?"

He surprised me with a laugh. "Ten thousand times better."

We lay there in silence for a little while, simply feeling the warmth of each other's bodies. I kept my desperate hands above his waist and distracted myself with cataloguing the texture of his arms and hands. At some point I realized his little round ass was making itself known to my dick with slight wiggles and presses back.

I sucked in a breath and reminded myself this poor man had just lost his entire shop. He was exhausted and vulnerable. The sweet man needed actual sleep.

"He means well," he said after a few minutes.

"Mpfh." That was about all I was capable when it came to Barney.

"I mean… he… well, I just wish…" His voice trailed off for a moment. "I just wish he listened to me. As opinionated as he is, he's actually been a very good friend to me in many ways. He's taken care of me when I didn't have anyone else, and he has the ability to be so thoughtful and sweet. After Patrick and Craig gave me hell one time last year and I wasn't feeling all that great, Barney volunteered to work at the shop so I could stay home and rest."

"That was nice of him," I admitted.

"And he's brought over dinner several times, even if I didn't ask him to stay and eat with me."

"Mm-hm."

"But when I asked him to clean out Berry's stuff today…"

It had been an odd departure from the attic cleanout Truman had probably had in mind. "Why would he start with your costumes?"

Truman sighed. The warmth from his breath washed across my arm and made my skin tingle. "He thinks it's childish. He's embarrassed by them. It was the same way with my dad back in Durango."

"What do you mean?"

"When I volunteered at the library there, they asked me to stand in for one of the ladies who worked at the botanical garden. She wore a caterpillar costume for her preschool visitation days, and the kids loved it. So that day I kept it on and read *The Very Hungry Caterpillar* during circle time in the library. Oh my gosh, you'd have thought I was Superman! The kids loved it. The librarian loved it. After that, I tried making or buying costumes to go with some of the books I read."

I pictured Truman as a shy, awkward teen waddling up to the library in his bumblebee costume with his stinger bouncing from side to side.

"I think that's amazing," I said, pulling him closer against me and pressing a kiss to the side of his face.

"My dad hated it. It was the closest he ever came to acting homophobic toward me. Comments about being flamboyant and how a town like Durango would never go for a drag queen library hour. It wasn't drag. It was Clifford the Big Red Dog and Winnie the Pooh, for heaven's sake. So I hid my costumes from him. And when I moved here, I spent an entire weekend cleaning out the goat shed so my costume collection had its very own home on my very own property. It was freeing."

His words hammered home just how painful it must have been

seeing someone he trusted throwing his beloved costumes in the trash.

"I'm sorry he did that. And I'm sorry your dad wasn't more understanding."

Truman was quiet for another moment. I enjoyed the feel of his warm body against mine. Providing physical comfort wasn't much, but I had a feeling it was more than he was used to.

"I promised myself when I moved here I would remember my promise to Aunt Berry. That I wouldn't let anyone try to turn down my sunshine."

I wasn't sure exactly what he meant by that, but I had an idea. Truman continued.

"She taught me how important it was for people to feed each other's growth. That we are all affected by the energy around us, and we thrive or languish based on that energy. I want to be the sunlight for others."

I turned him toward me and met his eyes. "You are. You are the brightest light I've ever known. And that's saying a lot because I'm friends with Mikey Vining."

Truman's face flushed, and his eyelashes fluttered a little as he lowered his eyes to stare at my chest. "Thanks."

"Why does Barney think you have enemies in town?"

His eyes widened. If it was possible, he looked even younger without his glasses on. "Because I do," he said. "The Stanners."

"But he made it sound like there were more than that. Who else still makes you feel bad for what happened all those years ago?"

He opened his mouth to respond but then closed it with a click. "Um…"

I brought a hand up and ran a finger along the side of his face. He was so beautiful. "Is it possible Barney exaggerates the fear to keep you close? He seems to like being protective of you."

"No. That's not about him. He's protective because it's justified. Anyway, can we not talk about this right now?"

"Mpfh."

Truman laughed. "I kind of like it when you're grumpy and vengeful."

"That man treats you like a wayward child. It's rude."

He held his arms out to the sides, and I noticed he was wearing a Rigby General Contracting T-shirt. It swam on him. How had I not noticed it before? "Maybe he was annoyed because I was wearing this," he teased.

Holy fuck did he look good in my shirt.

"Where did you get that?" I asked with a chuckle.

"You left it here last night after our dinner date. When you grabbed your clothes, you must have only taken the button-up shirt you had on over it. I hope it's okay I stole it." He gave me a cheeky grin that invited me right back into his bed.

"Hell yes," I said before leaning in and nipping at the side of this throat. He threw his arms around my neck and pulled me down on top of him. We kissed for a long time—slow, searching kisses and faster, hotter ones. I ran my hands underneath the shirt to the warm smooth skin of his slender body. Every time he sucked in a breath, I learned more about what he liked and vowed to repeat it.

Who knows how long we would have continued on like this if it hadn't been for the buzz of his gate alarm. I'd completely forgotten about the fire investigator's visit, so we had to scramble to make ourselves presentable. When Truman invited Dirk Bromley and one of his coworkers into the kitchen for coffee, I quietly asked if he wanted me to stay or leave.

For some reason this made him smile. "Stay, please."

I cleaned up the mess from earlier while he put on a fresh pot of coffee and got the two of them settled at the kitchen table.

Dirk gestured to the woman he'd brought with him. "Gail Brown is a member of my team. As you know, fire is a serious threat here in Colorado, so we do our best to understand the circumstances of every fire instance in order to better prevent them in the future."

"I appreciate it," Truman said. "I was shocked last night. I've never experienced any kind of house fire or fire at my business before."

Dirk nodded. "Well, I'm sorry to say, we did end up discovering signs of arson." I noticed he watched Truman's reaction to the news carefully.

Truman's face fell. "I was afraid of that."

Dirk glanced at me before looking back at Truman. "Do you have any idea who would want to set fire to your building, Mr. Sweet?"

Truman's hand reached for mine under the table, and I held it firmly. "Um. Well, it's kind of a long story, but..." He swallowed. "There is a man who's made threats to me before. His name is Patrick Stanner. He and his brother, Craig, have harassed me for a couple of years now. Most recently I was a witness to Patrick's deliberate destruction of property—Sam's motorcycle—and he threatened me against pressing charges."

I hadn't had time to tell Truman that I'd already told the investigator some of this, but Dirk handled it professionally. "Your friend Sam here said there was a note? Do you have that, and may I see it?"

Truman stood up and found the note. He put it on the table in front of Dirk, who gestured to his coworker to gather it into an evidence bag.

"Can you tell me other instances of this harassment?"

What happened over the next few minutes shocked me. Truman told Dirk about instances of physical intimidation around town, times when Craig and Patrick barred Truman from his own shop, the grocery store, and the diner. He explained about a time his tires were slashed, a night they barged into his shop and threw his inventory around, and a winter when they'd somehow had his road removed from the snowplow service route.

As he spoke, my heart started beating wildly like a caged, feral thing. I stood up to pace. I couldn't sit still and think about all the times this man was mistreated and left to fend for himself without any kind of support and no ability to rely on local law enforcement.

How the hell had he stayed?

Thankfully, Truman ignored my restless wander around the kitchen as he continued to tell them calmly about the time the brothers had cornered him behind his shop one night after closing.

He blinked over at me before continuing. "They, um, they told me their dad had been taken to the hospital for a heart attack and it was my fault because of the stress of everything from when he'd lost his job at the ski resort." He swallowed. "They punched me and stuff. This wasn't long before Mikey's, um..." He glanced up at the investigators before looking back at me. "Accident."

I could not bear this.

"They beat you up?" I asked, my voice almost breaking at the end. "Tru?" I returned to where he was sitting and squatted down in front of him. "They hurt you?"

I reached up to brush the tumble of curls back from his eyes so I could see them as he answered. He simply nodded. I wrapped my arms around his waist and pressed my face into his chest.

Fuck. Fuck, I was going to kill them.

This sweet man had taken this bullying long enough. And I wasn't going to let him have one more moment of pain at the hands of those abusers.

14

TRUMAN

I was embarrassed to admit all of this in front of Sam. The number of times I'd let the Stanner brothers take advantage of me was humiliating, but if I truly wanted them to pay for what they'd done to my shop, it was time to come clean. This investigator was from the state, not the county, so I had to assume he didn't have the bias local law enforcement had.

This was my chance.

"I went to the emergency room with bruised ribs, a sprained wrist, cuts and bruises on my face, and suspected head trauma. There should be records at the hospital. I know I had a CAT scan because I was relieved when it came out okay."

I gently nudged Sam back up into the chair next to mine. His display of emotion had taken me off guard, and I didn't have the mental energy to pick it apart right now.

I swallowed and continued. This was going to be the hardest part. It was something I'd never told anyone. Ever. "Like I said, they blame me for their father losing his job at the ski lifts. They thought my dad should have fought harder to keep the resort open, and they blamed me for the accident that had caused all the trouble in the first place." I glanced at Sam to gauge his reaction. "But it wasn't my fault."

Sam nodded, encouraging me to stop thinking a five-year-old was to blame for the accident. But that wasn't what I'd meant.

"The Stanner brothers were the ones who left the sled on the ski slope," I said.

I waited for the volcanic shift I'd always assumed would happen if I ever admitted the truth. It didn't come.

"It wasn't me. I was at home in bed," I added.

Sam took my hand in his. "I thought…"

"I know. They warned me if I told anyone the truth, their uncle would arrest me and put me in jail forever. I believed them. I didn't know better."

"How did they get your grandpa's sled?" Sam asked. Apparently he'd heard enough of the story from Tiller and Mikey to be confused by my admission.

"We'd been at school that day, and everyone was talking about the big snowstorm coming and how everyone was going to sled the next day on the big hill at Lewis Farm. I said I was going to ask my grandpa if I could finally try out his old sled which was this really cool metal sled with a steering wheel attached to control the runners. The Stanner brothers told me they wanted to test it out first, and then they threatened to beat me up if I didn't sneak it out of my house at midnight so they could try it out."

Sam's fingers rubbed across the top of my hands, gently encouraging me.

"So I did. And then… then I guess they left it on the slopes. I didn't know about the skier who'd run into it and gotten hurt. My dad came to me and asked why grandpa's sled was outside in the snow. I told him I'd taken it outside and left it by accident. I didn't want to admit to him that I'd let those boys bully me."

"But why didn't you come clean after you realized what had happened?" Sam asked.

"By then, Patrick and Craig had found me. They told me if I blamed it on them, they'd tell everyone my dad gave them the sled and he'd get fired and taken to jail. Then they told me I'd get taken to jail for lying. I know it sounds stupid now, but I was five. And their uncle was a cop. I was terrified."

Sam sighed. "I understand that. You must have been very scared. But what about later, once you were old enough to know better?"

I let out a humorless laugh. "I did. I told my parents after we moved to Durango. They didn't believe me. They thought now that I'd seen all the consequences of my actions that night, I was trying to pawn it off on those poor Stanner boys. And wasn't it bad enough their father lost his job? Then, when I moved back here, their uncle was the sheriff instead of a deputy. There was no way in heck he'd take my word over his nephews, and by then, who cared? No one would believe me after all this time, and the damage was already done."

It felt good to get it off my chest, but it also left me feeling exhausted and empty. Worse than when I'd woken up still half-drugged with artificial sleep. But I wasn't done yet.

"I'm tired of covering for them and being scared of them," I told the fire investigator. "I'm ready to fight."

He nodded. "Well, we will certainly follow up on this lead, but in the meantime, stay away from them. If that family had anything to do with the arson, it's going to be a big mess considering the connection to the county sheriff's office."

That was an understatement. But it was time for this all to be put to rest once and for all before someone got seriously hurt. I'd had the thought off and on all day that Chaya could have been inside doing inventory or Solo could have come by to use the shop's printer. Both of them worked part-time at the Honeyed Lemon and had keys to the shop. The idea they could have been caught inside when the fire started was enough to make me sick to my stomach.

"Let me know what other information you need from me," I told the investigators. "In the meantime, I'm going to hope this arson claim doesn't mean my insurance won't cover the damage."

Dirk leaned forward and met my eye again. "I need to ask where you were last night when the fire began."

Hadn't I already told them this? "I was home in bed asleep. Sam can tell you. He left after I was already asleep."

Dirk looked over at Sam. "What time did you last see Mr. Sweet here at the house?"

Sam's forehead crinkled in thought. "Maybe eleven thirty or twelve?"

The female investigator—I remembered her name was Gail—flipped back through her notes. "We believe the fire began a little after twelve which means he would have had time to leave here and get to the shop."

Sam's face turned stormy. "And what would his motivation be?"

Dirk tried to reassure us. "Property owners usually have several reasons to set their own property on fire, but insurance fraud is one of the most common. Regardless, it's standard procedure to investigate the owner, as I'm sure you can imagine. We need this information for our reports. It doesn't make you a suspect for us to ask these questions."

Gail turned to Sam with her pencil poised over her notebook. "And you? Where did you go when you left Mr. Sweet?"

"I drove back to Rockley Lodge where I'm staying with friends." He gave them the address of the property.

Gail continued. "So you had to drive through town? Did you notice anything at the shop?"

Sam shook his head. "No. I didn't even think to look. I was lost in thought. Sorry."

She made a hum of disapproval as if she didn't believe him or she found him irresponsible. For some reason it made me want to laugh, as if he should have been paying close attention to a particular storefront on a midnight drive through town.

"Is that all?" I asked.

"For now," Dirk said, standing up. "Hopefully you'll be around if we have more questions."

"Of course. I live here. Where would I go now that I have a laundry list of extra work that needs to be done?"

I stood up and led them to the front door before closing and locking it behind them and letting out a deep breath.

"Do you want me to get out of your hair?"

I turned around to see Sam standing in the kitchen doorway, leaning against the doorframe with his arms crossed in front of his chest.

"Not only no, but heck no," I said. "I was hoping we could get back in bed."

Sam's grin was slow and devastating. "I like the way you think, Mr. Sweet."

I let go of the rest of the residual stress from talking to the fire investigators and led the man to my bedroom. I had high hopes and big plans. There was going to be naked skin and questing tongues, hard dicks and happy trails. There was going to be a textbook full of new experiences for me in bed with the sexiest man I'd ever met.

Ten seconds after I slid between the cool sheets, I fell dead asleep.

I woke up sometime later to a large erection nudging my ass. Sam's mouth was trailing kisses along the back of my neck, and his hands had found their way under my shirt. One spread wide over my lower belly, and the other softly brushed one of my nipples.

I let out a long groan of approval without thinking, and it was answered by Sam's low chuckle.

His hands—and my body's response to his touch—made me feel powerful. Sexual. I pressed my hips back against his erection.

"You feel so fucking good," Sam murmured behind my ear.

"That's an accurate statement," I teased, noticing my voice was rough from sleep. "Can't remember the last time I felt this good."

He turned me onto my back and propped himself above me. "What can I do to make you feel even better?"

"Take off your clothes. Take off my clothes. Kiss me."

Within moments we were naked and rolling around the bed, kissing like the end of the world was coming. Sam's hands were everywhere—grabbing my ass, brushing my hair out of the way, gripping my chin to kiss me deeper. I humped against him desperately, too far gone to even feel self-conscious about it.

I wanted him. And feeling the evidence of his own desire made me dizzy with excitement. I'd never felt this way before. It was energizing and empowering, about as far away from scary and intimidating as one could get. I'd never in a million years expected I'd feel comfortable in bed with someone like Sam Rigby. His serious, stoic face and his wide, muscular shoulders were a combination that usually rang warning bells.

But not this time.

This time I wanted more. So much more.

I wrapped my legs around his hips and arched up into him. I wanted to come, and I wanted to bring him with me.

"You have lube, baby?" he murmured against my mouth.

My stomach jittered with nerves. "Mmhm. In here." I gestured to the drawer next to the bed, forgetting that the drawer with the lube also had a zillion toys in it. A wide swath of afternoon sunlight lit the side table up like a beacon.

As soon as Sam opened the drawer, I gasped and lurched for it to try and hide what was inside. Sam's arms came around me to keep me from dive-bombing the bedside table.

"Easy, easy. What's... oh. *Ohhh*. What have we here?" Sam's voice held amusement, and it was enough for me to drop my head and squeeze my eyes closed in embarrassment.

"Can we just... pretend you didn't see that?"

He tightened his arms around me while he moved to get a better look. "Not in a million years, Truman. This is so very interesting."

I turned to hide my face in his chest. "Not interesting. Embarrassing."

Sam's hands rubbed up and down my back. "Are you kidding? Feel how hard I am right now. The thought of you using any one of these toys makes me so horny I can barely see straight. What's your favorite one?"

I thought of the drawer full of dildos and plugs. Did I tell him what he wanted to hear or what was actually my favorite? Truth won out. I pointed to a slim black plug.

"I like to wear it out sometimes."

He reached for it and studied it. "Wear it out?"

"I mean... like in public. Not for very long, just... long enough for me to feel..."

"Naughty. Like you have a secret," Sam added.

I nodded. "Everyone thinks I'm a kid, that I'm this pure innocent baby. I, uh..." This part was embarrassing, but for some reason I wanted to tell him. "I liked to wear it when I was out with Barney because he would look at me like I was his angel, like he'd have to teach me what sex was and be patient while I learned about sexual pleasure."

Sam's grin was devilish. "And you were really sitting there getting hard every time this bad boy rocked against your special spot. Then you'd come home and shove one of these monsters in your—"

I clamped a hand over his mouth and felt my face heat. "Stop," I said with a nervous laugh. "Don't make it sound like I was getting off to the thought of Barney."

"If you were already experienced with all of this, why not have sex with him? Or... or did you?"

"No. I didn't. I've, um, never had anal sex before." *Or a blow job*, I wanted to add. *Until you.* "But there was something about him that made me nervous when things between us got physical. He would..." I tried to think of how to put my feelings into words.

"Pressure you?" Sam suggested softly.

"Not really. Not too bad. It was more like... when we kissed and things began to go further. His hands would wander, and he'd start talking to me about what I needed to do to please him, how to touch him the way he wanted and how to treat him the way that brought him the most pleasure. It was all about him, almost like he was training me for a future of service to him. It made me very uncomfortable. I think it's his age, maybe? An old-fashioned thing?"

Sam's eyes narrowed. "Or an egotistical jackass thing," he muttered.

"Don't get me wrong. I loved being the center of his attention. He was very affectionate and attentive. He made me feel cared for and looked after."

"Which is something you needed. Something you deserve."

I shrugged. "It was something I craved, anyway."

"Talking about your ex while I'm holding a butt plug isn't the way I envisioned spending the afternoon," Sam said, breaking the tension and making me laugh.

I leaned in to kiss him through my smile. He tossed the plug back in the drawer and flipped me onto my back in bed. We made out in a fun kind of sensual grappling. It was almost like the horny daydreams I'd had in high school when I watched a wrestling match.

Things didn't go further than kisses and possessive hands, and when he finally found the lube in my drawer, he used it to slick us up and stroke us both at the same time. I watched and felt the slide of our erections against each other in his large grip, and it was enough to send me over the cliff in moments. When I saw his release land on my body and mix with mine, it sent another shudder through me.

After a long, lazy recovery followed by a quick shower, we went outside to work on some of the remaining planting I wanted to get done. Sam commented on how beautiful it was in Colorado in general and how gorgeous the farm was specifically. I could tell he enjoyed the physical work, and having someone to share it with was like something out of a dream for me.

I watched the sun stream over his dirty-blond hair and the muscles move along his wide shoulders and back. Periodically, I caught myself drooling over him like I was watching my very own porn video. I secretly wondered how much I could make by capturing his sexy, shirtless body in blue jeans simply tilling soil and hauling debris.

"Why are you laughing?" he asked on his way back from the compost pile.

"If I had a video camera right now, I could start my own farmer porn channel."

Sam's face broke into a wide grin. "I'm wearing too many clothes for that."

I shrugged and batted my eyes innocently. "I could probably fix that for you."

He laughed, bright and clear. The sound filled the space around us and made me feel light as air.

"You're killing me," he said before stalking over and pulling me in for a kiss, garbling any sense I had left in my brain and taking away my ability to care about it one way or the other.

Eventually, we came up for air and finished the work. We met Mikey and Tiller for dinner at a pizza place in town, and I was surprised by how normal it felt to be with him as if we were on a real double date. As if a man like Sam Rigby would want to date a man like me.

Mikey and Tiller were engaging and fun as usual, and we ended up running into Winter and Gentry, who joined us at our table. The six of us ate pizza, drank wine, and shared easy company for several hours. It was such an incredibly normal night, like something out of a movie or television show, I wanted to cry with gratitude.

Finally, *finally*, I had the beginnings of a group of friends. I'd already been included in several of their get-togethers before, but this was different. Maybe it had been the outpouring of support after the fire, or maybe it was knowing that we had a shared enemy in the pension fund scheme, but I finally felt like I was part of something.

During the evening, Sam periodically glanced over or squeezed my hand to make sure I was doing okay, but he never told me I needed to leave to get some sleep or cautioned me against having too much wine. He simply sat beside me and enjoyed our time together as equals. When I was finally ready to go, I turned to him with as much courage as I could muster and asked, "Will you please come home and spend the night with me?"

The look in his eyes was liquid fire, and it burned me all the way through.

"Wild horses couldn't keep me away," he said, leaning close and brushing a kiss along the edge of my ear. His murmured words slid into my ears, too soft to be heard by anyone else. "It's taken every ounce of my patience not to throw you over my shoulder and steal you away to someplace private. You're the sexiest man in this room, and I want to strip you down and make sure you know it."

I let out a nervous laugh. "Oh-ho. Oh. Ho. Yes, well. It's past time for us to go. Goodbye," I said, standing up and addressing the group. I accidentally knocked the table with my hip and almost spilled several full water glasses.

Sam bit his lip and looked at me with a smirk. "Maybe we should pay first, real quick."

Heat rushed to my face as I sat back down. "Tiller Raine makes over twenty million dollars per season with the Houston Riggers," I blurted. "That means while we were sitting here listening to his delightful story about the difference between wing nuts and washers in regards to IKEA furniture—of which, by the way, he probably has none—he earned four thousand dollars. Pretty sure he can cover us for the pizza and wine tonight."

My eyes widened as my own rude words hit my ears. What had I just said?

Mikey's eyes widened, and he let out a laugh. "Get it, girl! I was wrong. The man knows football after all."

Tiller nodded and winked at me. "I got you, cutie. Be safe."

Gentry leaned forward with a grin. "And if he can't, I will."

"I'm sorry," I muttered, sitting back down. "That was rude. Of course I don't expect you to pay for our dinner. And I appreciate your extensive knowledge of Swedish engineering. Although... IKEA prefers to use barrel nuts if you want to know the truth. In fact—" I stopped myself before holding up the pointer finger of pontification. "Never mind."

Sam stood and thanked everyone for a lovely evening before picking me up and tossing me over his shoulder. We left to the hoots and hollers of a table full of kind-hearted men who would have covered the cost of a pizza for any friend in need.

And I was in need.

Despite my big plans for a long night of delicious mutual

orgasms, I barely got my pants down before Sam and I were humping each other to completion against the side of the car in my driveway. The cool night air chilled my hot skin, and the sound of Sam's heated groans made me dizzy.

His murmured "Come for me, sweetheart" almost drove me to my knees, but before I could even think about taking our interlude a step further, I was crying out and coming into his hand while clutching his shoulders and trying not to tip over.

Sam's words were like fire licking blazing stripes across my skin. "Fuck, fuck that was hot. Christ." Then Sam was grunting his own release, and I stared down at our bare dicks sliding against each other sloppily in his big hand. I gave another shudder of relief and wondered again why this incredible specimen of a man would want to do this with me.

Maybe he was desperate.

I laughed at the ridiculous thought, and then I just kept laughing.

"Not the reaction I was expecting," Sam said, yanking off his shirt to use as a rag. "But I could listen to you laugh all day for any reason."

I sighed with contentment. "Just happy, that's all."

Sam grinned wide. "Then so am I."

We went inside and slept curled around each other. It was beginning to feel delightfully familiar, and I vowed not to second-guess how long it was going to last.

I would simply enjoy it regardless.

I awoke the next morning to a handsy octopus determined to make me feel even more amazing than ever before. He kissed and sucked every square inch of my body before making me come like a bottle rocket.

Before I'd even fully regained my breath, Sam turned to me and raised an eyebrow. "Have you ever been on a motorcycle?"

I pictured the way he'd looked the day he'd ridden into town. Leather jacket and dark helmet, the rumble of the bike's engine getting louder on its approach, giving me hope that someone might witness Patrick Stanner's harassment.

It had been like a scene out of a movie.

"No. I would probably crash it the minute I thought about climbing on the thing," I admitted with a soft laugh. "But I liked watching you ride one."

Sam leaned in and kissed my jaw. "Hop up. I'm going to take you for a ride."

I watched his pale ass as he climbed out of my bed.

"Isn't that what we just did?" I teased before following him. Apparently Sam Rigby knew how to distract me from the fact my life was in shambles.

Because I found I didn't care nearly as much as I should have.

15

SAM

I drove us to Rockley Lodge in Truman's Subaru since I'd left the rental bike at Tiller and Mikey's place. Truman chatted nervously the whole way there, even after I'd reached for his hand and held it firmly. Finally, I looked over and said, "Baby, if you don't want to ride on the bike, that's totally fine with me."

His eyes widened behind his glasses. He was fucking adorable. "I can want to ride and also be nervous as heck about it."

"Point taken."

He looked ahead at the impressive exterior of Tiller and Mikey's lodge. "I've always loved this place. But you know what I love better? Mikey's peanut butter cookies. Do you think he's made any recently?"

If he hadn't, I'd bribe him into making some while we were on our ride. If that would make Truman happy, I'd do whatever it took to make it happen.

And that was a scary-ass thought. I was falling for this sweet man when the last thing I needed in my life was another person to care about and another reason to consider uprooting my life in Texas and moving miles and miles away from home.

"We can ask him," I said, trying to put those thoughts out of my mind. I didn't need to make any long-term decisions right now. Right now was simply about getting the bike and enjoying a morning ride in the mountains with a beautiful man.

But our plans were foiled as soon as we got inside.

Tiller gestured us into the kitchen with a sense of urgency. When we walked in, I saw Mikey on the phone. As soon as I saw his face, I knew something awful had happened.

He waved me closer. "Sophie, he just walked in. Hang on."

Mikey covered the microphone. "It's your mom. She's been in an accident."

My stomach dropped, and I grabbed the phone. Guilt flooded my gut since I'd put Mom and Sophie's numbers on mute in my phone earlier. They'd obviously needed me, and I hadn't been reachable. Instead, I'd been selfishly indulging in Truman's body.

"What happened?" I asked when I got the phone to my ear.

Sophie was crying. "She's alive. But she's real hurt. I need you. Kira's still in lockup, and I'm all alone here. I don't want to call Ethan because things aren't all that great with us right now, and I just... can you please come home?"

She sounded so scared, so unsure of herself. It reminded me of all the times she'd asked me to hold her when our dad was in one of his rages.

"Was it an auto accident? What kind of injuries does she have?"

"I don't even know yet. All they'll tell me is she's in surgery. If... if it's bad news, I don't think I can handle this by myself."

I closed my eyes and took a breath. The familiar warmth of Truman's body pressed against my back, and I saw his hands on the front of my shirt, holding on to me. I covered one of his hands with mine. "I'll be there as soon as I can. Call me as soon as you know something."

"Your phone wasn't picking up," she said, the accusation bitter in her voice.

"It will now, unless it's turned off on the plane."

"Okay. But... hurry, Sam. We need you."

I ended the call and pulled out my own phone to make sure I'd hear it when she called again. Sure enough, there were several missed calls.

"I have to go," I told Tiller and Mikey before turning to Truman. "I'm sorry."

He looked up at me, suddenly a little hesitant the way he was when I'd first met him. "Do you want... I mean... what can I do to help?"

"Just look out for yourself, okay? Ask Tiller and Mikey for help if you need it."

Truman looked suddenly annoyed. "I'm talking about you. You shouldn't have to go down there to deal with a family emergency by yourself."

I saw Mikey press his hand to his chest out of the corner of my eye. He was such a fucking romantic.

"I'll be fine," I said.

"I'll go," Mikey said. "I agree with Truman. You shouldn't be alone."

I nodded at him and turned to pack my things, trying hard not to feel swamped with guilt over not being there for my family. Whether I liked it or not, I was the steady one, the strong one, the one they all relied on to carry us through hard times.

And I wasn't there.

Truman followed me back to the bedroom. An awkward silence fell between us until he finally broke it.

"Are you coming back?" Then he quickly added, "Never mind. I'm sorry for that. You shouldn't have to even spare a thought for—"

I grabbed him and kissed him hard on the mouth, trying my best to punish those lips for ever uttering a single word that implied I wouldn't rush back here to him as soon as I was able. Because there was one thing I was quickly figuring out.

Despite not being relationship material, I was having surprisingly strong feelings about attempting a relationship with this particular man.

How was it possible I could go from knowing with complete clarity I didn't want or need a man in my life that way to obsessing over this near stranger? I'd never ached for comfort and companionship the way I ached for more time with Truman Sweet. The timing was awful. The last thing I needed right now was another person to care about, and the last thing he needed was someone else acting like they had a say in his life.

I stepped back from the kiss and bit back the words that were threatening to spill out of my mouth.

Truman's hands clutched my shirt in fistfuls of fabric that caught some of my chest hair in his grip with a sharp sting. I didn't care. I wanted to feel the pain along with the pleasure, to imprint every sensory detail of his touch onto my brain to carry with me back to Texas.

I could no longer hold back what I wanted to say.

"Be strong," I said, meeting his eyes. "Be fierce. Don't let anyone fuck with you, okay? If you don't feel safe at the farm, you come here and stay with Tiller."

Truman's eyes were huge behind his glasses. "You think I'm not safe?"

I cupped his face in my hands. "I don't know what the hell is going on, but I do know that someone deliberately burned down the shop and someone left you that threatening note. So you might want to either sleep with a baseball bat under your pillow or consider staying somewhere else."

I was trying so hard not to boss him around. He needed to follow his own gut, but fuck if it wasn't hard to keep from insisting.

"Maybe I could stay with Chaya," he said.

I nodded. "Perfect. She's scary as shit."

That surprised a laugh out of him, but he didn't disagree. I kissed him again. "And call me or text me to tell me how it's going. You won't be interrupting me. You'll be putting my mind at ease."

His face softened into a shy smile. "You too?"

I nodded. "Promise." And then kissed him again until Mikey called out for me to get a move on.

Before boarding the plane in Denver, I tried calling Sophie, but there was no answer. Mikey did his best to distract me, but my mind went to horrible places, imagining the worst.

When we finally landed in Houston, I realized I didn't even know what hospital to go to. I tried Sophie's phone again, and this time she picked up.

"What hospital?"

"What?"

"Soph, I'm here. What hospital do I need to come to?" There was a beat of silence, and my stomach dropped. "Sophie, is she okay? Is she...?"

"Come to the house."

No. No, no, no. "Is she gone?" I couldn't ask it without my voice breaking. Mikey reached for my hand and held it so tightly it cut off all circulation.

"No! No, she's not. She's fine. Come to the house."

I dropped the phone into my lap and felt my head spin with gratitude. Mikey must have heard enough of my sister's words to give the driver my mom's address. When we pulled up to the small house on Reinhardt Street my family had lived in as long as I could remember, I felt a bitter kind of nostalgia. Despite being the site of my father's brutality, it had been our home. Buying that little house was the one good thing my father did. I'd paid off the mortgage a little over a year ago, and knowing the only expenses my mom had on it now were taxes and utilities was a giant relief.

"Do you want me to go?" Mikey asked. I knew he didn't really mean it, but he was trying to give me options.

"Get your ass inside."

He grinned and hopped out of the car after throwing the driver a smiley thanks. We gathered our bags and made our way to the front porch. I knocked before opening the door and stepping inside. I stopped so abruptly, Mikey ran into the back of me and practically bounced off.

There sat my mom and both sisters, wearing pajamas and lounging on the sofa with a table full of sodas and snacks.

"Mom?"

I heard Mikey utter a curse word under his breath. As much as my fists wanted to clench, I forced myself not to jump to conclusions.

"What's going on?"

Mom jumped up and came over to hug me. "Oh, thank goodness you're here. I feel like you've been gone for ages."

"I've been gone less than a week," I said into her hair. It smelled clean. The coconut scent of her Suave shampoo was familiar, and it was hard not to sink into the same familiar role of dutiful son when I was surrounded by all the cues that put me right back in that mental place. "What's going on? I thought you were in the hospital? In surgery?"

She pulled away and headed back to her spot on the sofa, waving a hand over her shoulder. "No, that was just a little white lie to get you home. But now that you're here, you can help us come up with a plan. Kira has found—"

I didn't let her continue. "Wait, *what*? You weren't in an accident?" I stared at Sophie. "You... you lied and told me she was seriously hurt and in surgery, and she was really just... you..." I couldn't even get more words out. The truth of the situation was horrifying.

Mikey shifted behind me, reminding me he was there. He knew the humiliating truth of the lengths my family would go to in order to manipulate me. Our fucked-up parental relationships had been one of the things the two of us had in common. It had been one of the things that had helped us bond so early on. If things were shitty at home, at least we had each other. And it had been a godsend.

Still was.

My face flooded with heat. "Holy shit."

Mom held up her hand as if that would stop me from jumping to all the right conclusions. "Now see here, just wait a minute. We have some ideas. Kira found out about a lawyer who will only charge six thousand to—"

"No. No! I can't believe you lied to me to get me here so... what? So you could get me to pay for this lawyer? After I said I was done getting Kira out of her messes?"

"That's not fair," Kira said with a pout.

And that's when I completely lost my temper.

"Not fair? Not fair? You mean like having my sister show up high as a fucking kite in front of my crew and my client? Like having to leave in the middle of a job to save my other sister from getting her ass beat by her own fucking boyfriend? Like having to cover my mother's bills when she can't get her ass out of bed to make it to work on time?" I took a breath. "Like having to leave someone I care about while he's going through some major shit just because my selfish fucking family can't solve a single goddamned problem without my help?"

I felt Mikey's comforting touch as he ran his hand over my back. It was enough to keep me from completely losing control, but it was a near thing.

My heart was breaking, suddenly and without warning. Here were three women who'd never been the least bit maternal toward me. They didn't remember my birthday or ask me over for dinner. They didn't tease me about when I was going to get married or ask to meet my special someone. In all these years of being "the man of the house," I'd never once felt like I could ask them for *their* help. And I'd thought I hadn't even needed it or wanted it. What utter bullshit.

Of course I'd needed love and support. We all did.

I'd spent so long pushing down my desire for support, for an empathetic ear, for someone to drop everything and run to me when I needed it, and I'd forgotten that I'd actually had it.

I turned to Mikey and grabbed him up in a tight hug. "Thank you for loving me," I croaked into the side of his neck. "I don't think I ever told you how much I needed you. And you were always there for me."

"I love you," he replied calmly and softly. "Always."

I took a deep breath and squeezed my best friend one last time before letting him go. "Arrange for a car to pick us up, please."

He was rock steady. "Where are we going?" he asked, even though he already knew the answer.

"Home," I said firmly. "To Aster Valley."

As he pulled out his phone to arrange for the car, I pulled mine out to arrange for one last bank transfer. After a few clicks, it was done.

I looked back up at my family. "I've transferred two thousand dollars into each of your accounts. Spend it however you want. Mom, Sophie, pool it together for the lawyer, or use it to help your own damned selves. I don't care. I'm done."

The noise the three of them made as I turned to leave the house was deafening. They followed us outside and made a scene.

Mom tried to guilt me. "Samson Aaron Rigby, get back in here and stop being so selfish!"

Sophia cried. "I'm sorry for lying, but we need your help!"

And Kira taunted me. "Oh, it's like that, huh? You have so much fucking money you can throw it at us and bolt? Must be nice. Meanwhile, you've always treated this piece of shit better than us. Mikey and his rich family. You always wanted to be one of Coach Vining's sons instead of Mama and Daddy's boy! So go! Go be someone else's brother!"

As if I'd ever want Mikey's asshole of a father. I ignored them and reached for Mikey's hand, relieved when I found it dry and steady. Unfortunately, he was used to my family's theatrics. After we became friends, he'd offered for me to sneak into his family's finished basement to sleep on the sofa if I ever needed it.

I'd only ever taken him up on it once, and my mother's sudden crocodile tears reminded me of that night.

"This is all your father's fault. I never should have given you a Biblical name. So much for 'god-given strength.' I should have known. Sin leads to consequences. Samson was too strong, too violent. Just like your father. He betrayed God, and then look what happened."

The night my father had been arrested, my mother had spouted her convenient Bible bullshit. She hadn't darkened the door of a single house of God in all the years of my memory, but she was the first to spout about the good book when she didn't get her way. I remembered her accusing him of defiling their marriage bed, and then she'd turned the blame on me for not honoring my parents.

Thankfully, the car came quickly, and we got inside. We were halfway back to the airport before I realized Mikey was crying.

"Jesus, what's wrong?" I blurted. Here I'd been trying to keep from losing my composure, and Mikey was the one to lose it.

"It's so unfair. You had a shit family. You deserved better."

I laughed at that and leaned over to kiss his forehead. He was so damned sensitive. I loved that about him. "You had a shit family, too. Many people do."

He sniffled. "Still not fair."

I put my arm around him and squeezed, sending up a silent prayer of thanks for Tiller Raine giving Mikey a new home, a better family. "But now you have a good one. The family we're making on our own. By choice."

He glanced up at me with wet, spiky eyelashes and a devilish smirk. "You think we can add Truman to our family?"

I shoved him away from me with a laugh. "Now you're fishing. Don't bat those eyelashes at me and try to get me to declare my undying love to someone I've known for all of five minutes."

We rode in silence for a few more minutes before he said, "He's good for you. But more than that, I love how you are with him."

"How do you mean?"

"I remember you dating Will a few years ago. You were protective of him, too, but in a different way. You wanted to carry his burdens, and man did he want you to as well. He used to preen whenever you got all controlling and possessive."

I thought back to the guy I'd dated for a few months one summer. He'd been harassed by an ex, and it had taken me a long time to discover he'd actually loved every minute of it.

"He had problems," I muttered.

"That's an understatement. But you tried solving his problems for him, and that's not really how you are with Truman. It's nice."

I didn't really follow what he was saying. Of course I wanted to solve Truman's problems. I'd do anything to solve his problems.

"He's a grown man," I said. "Will was twenty. There's a big difference."

Mikey nodded and grinned. "Four whole years. I don't think Truman's used to being seen as an adult. And I can tell it's hard for you not to take over and bulldoze him over this Stanner brothers' threat."

"I want to beat those fuckers into the ground," I grumbled.

My phone pinged with a million texts and calls from my mom and sisters, but I put all of them on ignore. That left a few messages from Truman.

Truman: *I know it's late there, but I wanted to tell you I ended up staying at Tiller's. He opened a bottle of wine and asked me if I wanted to hear stories about you. Needless to say, I kept asking for more wine and stories until I was too drunk to drive home. Wish you were hair.*

Truman: *OMG. No. I wish you were here. Not hair.*

Truman: *But I also really like your hair.*

Truman: *It's very blond.*

Truman: *And thick and stuff.*

Truman: **tries to stop talking about hair*

Truman: *I've never dated a blond man.*

Truman: *OMG not that we're dating ha. HA!*

Oh my god. He was so fucking cute. I turned the phone so Mikey could see the text. When he was done reading, he showed me his.

Tiller: *Truman is adorable and we need to keep him.*

Mikey: *I believe I said that the minute I first saw him.*

Tiller: *I got him wine drunk and told him about the time Sam threw up when your appendix almost burst.*

Tiller: *Then I told him about the time Sam saved those kids from drowning.*

Mikey: *??? What kids?*

Tiller: *So I made some shit up. Sue me. Truman wasn't the only one drinking the wine.*

Tiller: *Now he's in Sam's room singing Beauty School Dropout.*

My heart filled with joy, and I let out a breath of relief. Knowing he was safely tucked into my room at Rockley Lodge with a giant, hard-bodied NFL player watching over him gave me peace of mind I didn't know I needed.

"God," I groaned. "Thank him for me. Jesus, that makes me feel a thousand times better."

Mikey tapped at his phone for the rest of the drive as I began to realize just how late it was. "Not sure there are any flights this late to Denver," I finally said out loud.

"No worries. Tiller hooked us up. He's just drunk enough to get bossy and throw his money around. We're flying on a charter."

Sure enough, we flew in a sleek private jet direct from Houston to the Yampa Valley Regional Airport where a driver was waiting to take us to Rockley Lodge. I'd dozed most of the flight home between bouts of waking up enough to stress over the confrontation I'd had with my family.

I had so many mixed feelings. Guilt, confusion, anger, frustration, betrayal, sadness. But I didn't have a single moment of regret. I knew I'd done what I needed to do to protect myself, even though it hadn't been easy. And I knew that more than anything else, I wanted to be in Aster Valley right now with my friends and with Truman.

When the driver pulled up in front of Rockley Lodge, Mikey was dead on his feet. I helped him into the house and nudged him toward his bedroom before heading to mine.

Truman was sprawled out like a half-naked starfish on top of the covers. The light from the hallway was enough to reveal he was wearing my oversized T-shirt that was rucked up under his arms and a tiny pair of royal blue briefs I wanted to stick my face in.

God, he was beautiful. His face without his glasses looked young and vulnerable, but his body was as hot as a thirst trap picture on social media.

I kept my eyes on him as I began removing my own clothes, but after realizing I smelled like an airplane, I headed into the bathroom to take a quick shower.

When I finally got back to the bedroom and pulled on a fresh pair of boxer briefs, I moved him under the covers and slid into the bed beside him, pulling him into my arms and inhaling his cherry smell that was only partly edged with the scent of alcohol.

I moved my hand under the T-shirt to rest it on his chest, and I fell asleep to the steady thunk of his heartbeat against my fingertips.

It seemed like no time had passed at all before I awoke to the hot, wet suction of a mouth on my dick.

16

TRUMAN

Waking up to Sam's arms around me was a shock. The best kind of shock. I didn't care how it had happened, only that he was there and already almost naked.

I started by sneaking just a few glances at him while he slept. Then a few caresses of his warm skin. After that, my lips wanted a quick taste of his mouth, his shoulder, his chest. I nudged his underwear down just a tiny bit to see the blond curls hidden there.

Before I knew it, I was giving him a blow job like some kind of porn star.

Well, like some kind of amateur porn star who didn't really know what he was doing. But Sam's dick was hard after all of my touching and kissing, and I wanted to see what it would be like to kiss it, too.

He groaned in a deep, sleepy voice and stretched his muscular legs. Sam's hand landed in my hair and yanked gently on the curls. "Fuck that's a nice way to wake up."

His voice was so sexy, it was enough to make me even more desperate. "This okay?" I asked quickly, to be sure.

The only answer was his rumble of laughter.

I grinned and licked his shaft again, watching how it jumped when I tweaked a certain spot by the tip. Sam's hand tightened in my hair.

"You're killing me. Feels so fucking good."

I continued experimenting, licking and sucking, teasing his balls, until he leaned up and grabbed my hips, twisting my body around until I felt his own hot mouth on me.

Sixty-nine.

If I'd had a wish list of sexual firsts, Sam would be checking things off like a madman.

It was impossible to keep paying attention to his erection while he was pleasuring mine. I became a whimpering blob of goo, so much so that Sam ended up laughing. The vibration of his laughter against my body made me feel even better, and I suddenly arched up, pushing myself deeper into his throat without warning and coming on a hair trigger.

"*Aghh!*"

Sam laughed and sputtered, trying to stay ahead of my release, but it was no use. When I glanced back down at him, there was cum dripping from his beard and coating his lips.

I let out another cry as my body convulsed again. How in the world was I allowed to be with this man sexually? There should have been a threshold one needed to pass, and I assuredly would never, ever have passed it.

I reapplied myself to my own task and sucked him down as quickly as I could, bobbing up again when I gagged. If I couldn't give him talent, I could at least offer as much enthusiasm as possible.

It worked. But as soon as he started coming, I quickly pulled off out of fear of being drowned. I didn't exactly want my inexperience to lead to sudden death right in front of him.

I heaved in a much-needed breath and smiled at my success.

"You're so beautiful," he said, sobering up. "I could watch you come all day every day."

I stared at him like he'd lost his mind. "Um, okay. I'm cool with that."

He laughed again, and it was a joy to see. Until I remembered where he was supposed to be.

I scrambled around and reached for my discarded shirt before using it to wipe his mouth off. "What happened with your mom? Why are you here? What happened?"

I'd wanted so badly to offer to go with him yesterday, to ease his pain or somehow attempt to comfort him while dealing with his family emergency. But it hadn't been my place. I barely knew him, so I'd forced myself to bite back the ridiculous offer before it could have escaped my lips.

He took the shirt from me and dropped it over the edge of the bed before taking me into his arms. His face was suddenly stormy. "It was all a lie to get me to come home."

My heart sank. "You're kidding?"

Sam shook his head. "Wish I was. I'm so angry. And hurt. I watched Mikey go through his own family shit last year, and I remember feeling sorry for him. But I guess I just didn't want to see how bad it was with my own family. It's probably why he and I developed such a close relationship. We both needed someone."

I was envious of their relationship. I'd never had a friend like that. I had Chaya now, but it wasn't quite the same. She was an extrovert, friends with everyone. Or maybe I was the reason we weren't as close as we could be. Often, I stopped myself from sharing things out of fear I'd sound like a whiny baby. I'd spent years being told to stop feeling sorry for myself and keep my complaints quiet. My mom was even known to throw out a "You think you have it bad? Imagine that poor skier who lost his chance at an Olympic gold medal" from time to time.

I quickly learned to keep my feelings to myself.

But here I was feeling grateful Sam was sharing his feelings with me. It made me second-guess my habit of keeping my own feelings locked inside.

"I'm glad you have such a good friend," I said lamely. "But... I still can't believe your family did that to you. I thought..."

My head spun with so many thoughts. The confusion must have shown on my face.

Sam brushed my hair back and met my eyes. "You thought what, sweetheart?"

"Are all families like this?" The emotion of the question and simultaneous realization hit me suddenly, causing my voice to crack. "I thought... I thought families were supposed to love you. I thought..."

Woah. My eyes flooded. It was too much. The conversation was supposed to be about him. About his family troubles, not mine. I lurched off the bed and hurried to the bathroom to try and get control of myself.

I should have known Sam would be right behind me.

"Hey, hey," he said softly, grabbing me from behind and pulling me against his front. He wrapped his arms around me and bent his head down to brush a kiss against my ear. "What just happened in there?"

I shook my head and tried to get out of his hold, but he didn't let me.

"Take a breath," he murmured. "Take a breath, but please don't ask me to let you go."

Instead of trying to pull away again, I turned in his hold and laid my cheek against the soft hair on his chest. "I think families suck," I said angrily. "So badly. It's so freaking unfair your family did that to you. I thought families were supposed to love you, to think of your needs above theirs, to be there for you and build you up." As my rant increased, so did the roughness in my voice. "And it's all lies. Families are awful. They're horrible. Why don't people call them out for what they are? It's so unfair. Look at Mikey. His dad tried to keep him from being with the love of his life, and he doesn't even care that his son doesn't want to talk to him anymore. He doesn't even care!"

I barely noticed Sam's attempts to shush me because I was on a roll.

"And after everything you've done to help your mom and your

sisters, they reward you with lies. To lie about being hurt? And it wasn't true? That's horrible. So awful." I shuddered. "And Sheriff Stanner sits back and lets Patrick and Craig commit actual crimes instead of trying to teach them to be better people, to find more productive ways to spend their time. No one helped Gene find another job after the resort closed. They've had years to help him get back on his feet, and yet they're so hell-bent on revenge... And then what about me?"

At this point the crying was too much for me to keep talking. I clung onto Sam with everything I had, fully realizing this breakdown would most likely be the end of whatever it was we might have been starting between the two of us.

"What about me?" I repeated over and over into his chest as he held me tight and tried to soothe my broken heart.

I didn't even notice when he carried me back to bed and laid me down. I didn't notice when he found a soft hand towel and tried to dry my tears.

But I did notice I'd taken his moment of heartbreak and turned it into my own.

"I'm so sorry," I said, changing my mantra on a dime. "I'm so sorry. It's not about me. I'm so sorry."

I felt like the lowest scum. How could I have been so selfish? I pulled the towel out of his hands and used it to finish sopping up the mess on my face before getting up the nerve to look at him. I expected an expression of forced patience on his face or maybe even pity.

But that's not at all what I saw.

"I think you're incredible," he said. The expression on his face was part tender adoration and part... pride? "And it's about time you realized you were dealt a super-shitty hand."

"We weren't talking about me. And I made this all about me. I'm the worst."

Sam smiled, changing his face from his signature intense gaze to a soft and tender affection. "You're the best."

"I'm sorry," I said again.

"Truman, you've been pushing down this pain for so long. You've spent years trying not to make waves, trying not to expect much of anyone. It's about time you realized you deserve better. You deserve better now, and you for damned sure deserved better then."

"But what about you?" I said with a final sniffle.

Sam ran his hands into my hair again. "I deserved better then, too. And I deserve better now. That's why I came back to Aster Valley. And now I think we need to shower off these tears and go face the day. I'm bound and determined to put my family out of my mind today as we tackle your to-do list."

I thought of everything I needed to do today and groaned. "I don't even know where to start."

Sam met my eyes and held my face in his hands. His smile made me feel like I could conquer the world. "You start with your family." My stomach dropped until he continued speaking. "Me, Tiller, Mikey, Chaya, and the rest of the Aster Valley crew who were here yesterday. Didn't they offer to help?"

I thought back to Pim's strong hug and Bill's quiet reassurance. Solo's offer to help with cleanup and Mia and Mindy's suggestion they could make some phone calls when their shop was slow in the afternoons. Nina even offered for me to use one of her ranch pickup trucks to haul supplies.

Maybe Sam was onto something.

Family.

Was it possible? Had I finally created a community for myself I could count on? Just thinking about my Aster Valley friends made me realize Sam was right. I had people who cared about me, people who'd proven they were there for me when the chips were down. People who ran to check on me even before I knew I needed them.

It was an amazing feeling.

"But first," Sam said, hopping out of bed and yanking me with him. "We scrub your naked body very carefully. Can't exactly face the day without making sure every single part of you is… spit shined."

I snorted at his waggling eyebrows and followed him into the bathroom. While we waited for the water to heat up, I thought about how much my life had changed in the span of less than a week.

A week ago, I was imagining losing my virginity in a quiet missionary encounter with Barney Balderson. I was trying my best to stay invisible and off the Stanners' radar. My biggest goal was to plant some wildflower seeds on the side of the highway without getting into trouble with the county council.

I wondered what the county council would think when they realized meek little Truman Sweet had finally managed to pin something on their precious Stanner family. Patrick and Craig would go to jail for arson, and Sheriff Stanner would no longer be able to protect them from the law.

If only the world worked like that.

After we showered and made our way back to the kitchen where Mikey and Tiller were fixing breakfast, I received a call from Dirk Bromley.

"I just wanted to let you know the Stanner brothers have an alibi for the night of the fire," he began. I opened my mouth to tell him they had to be lying when he continued. "The entire Stanner clan was at the hospital for the birth of Michelle Stanner's baby. I understand she's Craig's wife. The baby was born a little after eleven, and one of the nurses on the maternity ward can place the sheriff, Barb, Gene, Kimber, Patrick, and Craig Stanner all there in the waiting room or the patient's room until after one in the morning."

"Oh," I said stupidly. My high deflated into the lowest of lows.

"We will be investigating every lead, Mr. Sweet. I just wanted to update you to put your mind at ease that this family didn't perpetrate a crime against you."

As if that put my mind at ease. Better the devil you knew than the one you didn't. Besides, it didn't make any sense. The Stanners had been gunning for me for years now. There was no way it wasn't them. If they had an alibi, it only meant they'd found someone else to start the fire.

"Let me know what else you find," I said.

"Will do. I need to follow up with Mr. Rigby again today to ask him a few questions that have come up. I'll be in touch."

He hung up before I could ask him what he meant. I glanced over at Sam, who raised an eyebrow at me.

"Was that the investigator?"

"He wants to ask you more questions."

Sam looked at the phone and back up at me. "Right now? Is he still on the phone?"

"What? Oh. No. Sorry. He mentioned wanting to ask you more questions based on something that's come up. He's going to call you, I guess. But why would he want to ask you questions?"

Sam and Tiller exchanged a look that didn't make any sense to me.

"What?" I asked.

"He probably questioned the Stanners and got pointed in my direction. If they want to claim they didn't do it, who better to pin the crime on than a stranger passing through town?"

Tiller added, "Someone who knows construction, no less."

Mikey sighed from where he was working in the kitchen. "Assholes," he muttered.

"The Stanners didn't do it," I said. "That's why he was calling. They were all at the hospital for the birth of Craig's baby."

The three of them stared at me. I shrugged and felt like crying again. "If they didn't do it, that means someone else hates me enough to burn down my shop."

Sam pulled me over onto his lap. "No. It might mean it was a random act of vandalism. Or maybe it wasn't really arson."

"What if the investigator thinks you did it?" I asked.

"I don't have any motive for that kind of crime. They'd have a hard time pinning it on me with no evidence."

My phone rang again. This time it was Barney.

"There you are. I've been buzzing at your gate with no response."

"I'm not at home," I said, moving back over to my seat and taking a quick sip of coffee. The wine hangover wasn't too bad, but I was still looking forward to drenching it in whatever the heck Mikey was making that smelled so good.

"Where are you? I found something important at the shop."

"You went to my shop?"

Tiller and Sam exchanged another look. That was beginning to annoy me.

"Where are you?" Barney asked again.

"Rockley Lodge. I spent the night at Tiller and Mikey's."

Barney sighed. "I wish you'd called me. I would have come to stay with you. I told you that."

I was tired of telling him no over and over again, so I didn't. "Feel free to leave what you found. I'll be home later."

"No need. I'll run it up to you at the lodge."

I stared at my phone. "Why do people keep hanging up on me before I can respond?" I muttered.

Mikey slid a plate full of a steaming serving of egg casserole in front of me. Tiller vibrated with happiness. "Egg surprise! Truman, you need to stay over more often."

If they fed me like this, maybe I'd consider it. I dug into the food without waiting.

Sure enough, right as we finished up breakfast and I'd convinced Tiller to let me do the dishes, there was a knock on the door. Mikey brought Barney back to the kitchen. He was carrying a large paper grocery bag that he set down carefully on the island.

"Oh sweet pea," he said, bustling over to kiss me on the cheek. My hands were dripping wet with soapy dishwater, so I simply stood there and accepted it. Out of the corner of my eye, I noticed Sam watching every move.

Not going to lie, I kind of liked the scowl on his face.

"How are you bearing up?" Barney asked, cooing over me and murmuring that I looked just awful. "You must not be sleeping. I knew this would happen."

Mikey offered him a cup of coffee, then asked, "What's in the bag? Did you bring us some cookies? I happen to know Truman has a soft spot for peanut butter cookies."

Barney's face wrinkled in confusion. "Truman only eats organic plant-based foods."

I wanted to laugh. "No, I don't."

Sam couldn't resist. "Pretty sure peanut butter is plant-based anyway."

"Be that as it may," Barney continued, "I brought something super special for you from the shop. When I remembered how dear it was to you, I couldn't resist going over there to look for it."

I dried my hands off and opened the paper bag, pulling out a familiar, albeit soot-dusted, spiral notebook. "Oh my gosh! It's Aunt Berry's recipes." I glanced over at Barney in surprise. "How in the world did you find this?"

"And how did it survive?" Tiller asked, stepping closer to take a look.

It was a good question. The spiral was definitely covered in ash and soot, but otherwise, it didn't look like it had been harmed at all. I searched my memory to figure out where I might have left it the last time I'd used it.

"I could have sworn I had it here at the house from when I made the last batch of thyroid drops for Dee Lorens," I murmured, brushing off the dust into the kitchen sink. "No, wait. I took it to the shop to grab the ingredients for the eczema cream. That's right. I guess I must have left it there."

Mikey dampened a paper towel and brought it over to help clean off the soot.

I glanced back over to Barney. "Thank you so much for thinking of this. I can't believe I almost lost it. I have the recipes backed up on my computer now, but having them in her own handwriting means so much to me. I really appreciate it."

Barney relaxed and smiled under my expression of gratitude. "I'm so glad. I hated the thought of you losing something so special. I know you don't have much to remember her by. It would have been a shame to lose this in that horrible fire."

"Was there anything else?" I asked. "Berry's mala beads?"

Barney opened his mouth to say something, but then his eyes flicked to Sam for a beat and then back to me. "I'm afraid not."

Mikey frowned. "Were those the colorful beads that hung behind the register counter?"

I nodded. "It kind of looks like a rosary, but the beads are all different kinds of stones. Some were rare and precious gemstones. The mala is used in meditation."

Barney shook his head, more sure this time. "It definitely wasn't there. Most everything is ash or broken glass, I'm afraid. And it stinks to high heaven."

Sam nodded from where he stood a few feet away. I'd begun to notice when Barney was around, Sam seemed to keep his distance. I wondered why. Was he afraid of interfering in some perceived relationship of mine?

Sam cleared his throat. "I didn't see anything like that when I was there either, but then again, the investigator didn't let me very far into the building because it was considered a crime scene."

"You went to the shop, too?" I asked him.

Sam's eyebrows furrowed. "I boarded it up. Remember?"

"Of course. I'm sorry. I'm just turned around... When you were there, did you see anything else worth saving?"

Sam glanced at Barney, then back at me. He spoke carefully. "Truman, there wasn't even a single square-inch of wood from an interior wall or piece of furniture that wasn't burned. Nothing survived that fire in one piece."

I met his eyes and saw the truth in them.

This notebook hadn't been in the fire.

17

SAM

I wasn't sure what the older man was playing at, but I didn't like it. Barney had obviously lifted the notebook from Truman's house while he was creeping on the guy the other day. It was clear Truman had understood what I was saying about the notebook not being in the fire, but he did a good job changing the subject before Barney caught on.

"Do you think the insurance company will send out an adjuster?" Truman asked Barney. It was the perfect distraction. Barney puffed up and began giving Truman advice on how to handle the insurance adjuster. Meanwhile, Tiller raised an eyebrow at me and nodded his head toward the back door.

"Will you come check out a rotten board I found? I wanted you to tell me if I should replace it."

I nodded and found my boots next to where I'd tossed my saddlebags in the corner of the kitchen by the back door. I shoved my feet into them before following Tiller outside.

"That guy is a meddling prick," I muttered once we reached the privacy of the backyard.

"No kidding. Also a pompous windbag, which is an expression I've always wanted an excuse to use."

I took in a deep breath of cool, clean mountain air. This really was a beautiful place. The ski mountain sat right behind their house, and the trees were beginning to bud. "You don't really have a rotten board, do you?" I asked.

Tiller shrugged. "Probably. This place is huge. I'm sure something's rotten somewhere."

"That notebook wasn't in the fire," I said.

"No. It wasn't. Seems to me the guy swiped it from the farm and is using it to try and be a hero. What an idiot. Not sure I could have stayed in there without laughing in his face."

He was right. It was embarrassing. Barney was so intent on winning Truman over, he was willing to use the fire as a way of appearing the savior. If he wasn't such a plodding Goody Two-shoes, I might have suspected him of actual arson. Instead, I mostly suspected him of being pathetic.

I was grateful there were plenty of other people in town Truman could rely on besides Barney Balderson. It was a good community, and this visit had confirmed it for me. Tiller and Mikey had moved from Houston into a much better social situation.

I envied them their future here and wondered if now was a good time to ask Tiller how serious he'd been about an opportunity for me here.

"When you decided to move to Aster Valley, did you... how did you make such a big decision that quickly?"

Tiller thought about it for a little while as we walked down into the yard and across the grass toward the tree line. "I didn't decide to move to Aster Valley," he said with a soft smile. "I decided to do whatever it took to make Michael Vining happy. And Mikey was going to move here with or without me. So I bought this place to make him happy. And I moved to Aster Valley because that's where my Mikey was."

"You make it sound so easy."

"Because it was. I would give up my NFL contract for him, Sam. And you know it."

I did. Tiller would do anything for Mikey, but the feeling went both ways. Which was why they were able to have both Mikey's future resort in Aster Valley and Tiller's current NFL career in Houston.

I thought about my life back in Houston, my family, my company. None of it meant very much if Mikey and Tiller were here.

And if Truman was here.

"I never saw myself settling down with someone," I admitted. "I thought I was shit at relationships."

Tiller glanced over at me. "You were shit at relationships," he said with a smirk. "Because you always put your family first."

"I thought that's what I was supposed to do," I said, throwing my hands up. "I was told my whole life that family came first, blood was thicker than water. I was the man of the house after my father was sent up, and it was my responsibility to be there for them."

Tiller nodded in understanding. "But relationships can't be one-sided."

"I know that now. I would never choose my family over Truman. He deserves better than that."

He reached out and put a hand on my shoulder, turning me to face him. "I mean *family* relationships can't be one-sided."

That distinction stopped me in my tracks. "Family relationships can't be one-sided," I repeated under my breath, testing the words as they sank in.

Tiller started walking toward the woods again. "You know better than anyone how much effort Mikey put into trying to please his parents. But they always treated him like the runt of their litter. How long should he have kept trying to please them, Sam?"

I thought of Mikey's asshole of a father. The fact he remained Tiller's coach and boss couldn't have been easy on Tiller.

"Any amount of time is too long," I grunted. "Should have left that bastard years ago."

Tiller shook his head. "Don't say that—then I wouldn't have met Mikey. But I'm sure glad he's left him now. It's better for him to take himself out of that disappointment loop, don't you think?"

"Of course it is." Why was he stating the obvious?

Tiller turned to me again with another annoying smirk. "Haven't you been in a disappointment loop of your own?"

God, he was right. I tried so hard to rescue my family time and time again just to find myself right back in a mess one of them had made. Now that Sophie had finally found Ethan, maybe I could stop worrying about her so much. And since I'd decided to cut Kira off, as hard as it was to do, that left my mom.

The queen of the disappointment loop.

I loved her. There was no doubt about it. She'd had a shitty time of it with my father. But it had been years now, and it was time for her to stop treating me like his stand-in.

I noticed Tiller watching me as I made the connections between Mikey's family's manipulations and my own.

I thought about punching the cocky footballer in his smug face. "Shut up," I muttered instead. "You made your point. But it's not that easy."

His smile dropped. "No. Certainly not. Mikey spent two hours crying on my shoulder last week because his mother had called to tell him she'd heard an exciting rumor he was writing a cookbook. Never mind the fact he's told her about the book many times in the past five months. Unless he completely cuts his parents out of his life, he'll have to deal with her obliviousness and his callousness."

I sighed and leaned over to pick up a fallen twig to fling it into the woods. "Enough about my family. What do you think about the business owners going after the sheriff over this pension fund? Are we leading these guys into more trouble?"

"No. I pulled Pim and Bill aside and made sure they know I'll cover Julian's attorney fees. It's in our best interest to get this shit sorted out before we even think about opening the resort. We can't ask new vendors to come into Aster Valley as long as this extortion scheme is in the works."

"Good point. At least everyone seems to appreciate you and Mikey being here. I know Mikey was afraid of what the people of Aster Valley would think when they found out you wanted to reopen the ski resort."

"Most everyone is thrilled, actually. They recognize how much new business it will bring to town, and the locals who've been around long enough to remember how things were have assured the others that it's a good thing. For the most part we're actually being urged to speed up our original plan."

Tiller turned to me again, and I could tell what the look on his face meant.

"And speeding it up means needing a right-hand man," I suggested.

"No. It means needing someone to take complete charge of it. I don't need an assistant. I need a partner."

"You have Mikey."

"Of course. But he wants to focus on the lodge. I'd really like you to come on board as a stakeholder and the chief operations officer for the ski resort." I opened my mouth to tell him I didn't know what the fuck that was, but he stalled me by raising a hand up. "Before you argue, just hear me out. Phase one is getting the pieces and parts in place. Julian is coming on board to handle the legal and financial side. Contracts, investors, real estate holdings, working capital, and a bunch of other shit I don't know beans about. His dad runs a mining company, and he raised his kids to take it over one day. Julian hates mining, but his sister's a crack shot at it. So he's got the business know-how and the money side, right? He's got the fancy education. Meanwhile, the retired skier I told you about, Rory Pearson, will help us with that side of it."

"Shit, Tiller. Sounds like you've already pulled together some great guys. You've been hard at work since the Super Bowl."

Tiller nodded. "Mikey and I have been working our asses off. Ever since we met Rory, we realized what a big opportunity we had to launch this with his help. But we need someone to handle the construction and repair to get this place up and running sooner than we'd planned. You've been hiring specialty laborers for years. You know how to find the right person for these jobs. We need lift maintenance and repair, land clearing and grooming, and who the hell knows what else. You also know how to get the right permits and zoning shit handled. I need someone I trust to manage this part of it. And you can hire all the help you need, but the man at the top of operations needs to be someone we trust. That's you."

It was a big job, but god, it was exciting to consider. "I don't have capital to invest. I mean, once I sell my place in Houston, I'll have a little something, but…"

"No," Tiller shook his head firmly. "Hear me out. I wanted to talk to you without Mikey because he gets emotional, and this is about business."

I nodded in agreement.

"Right now this mountain investment has cost me peanuts. I'm not joking. They were desperate to off-load it because the family is old money, and they were horrified at what the scandal did to their reputation after the resort was sued out of business. They weren't here full-time anyway. It was owned by a larger investment holding out of Chicago. Truman's dad managed the resort itself, and another man operated the ski side of the business. I paid as much for this entire mountain as Peevy paid for his house in Boca. I want to put a hefty chunk into fixing it up and doing this right. But if I do that, someone needs to make sure it's running to plan. I can't do that while I'm still focused on the game."

He was right. As the league's highest-paid receiver, even after his injury last season, he needed to stay in top shape and focus on winning. At least for a few more seasons.

Tiller continued. "If you'll be the man on the ground here year-round, we'll offer you an equity share of the business as an incentive. It's not special favors. It's standard business practice. Julian's already written up an official offer for you and made it all legal. We're serious about this, Sam. But we don't want you making this decision out of friendship debt. Make it because it's going to be fun as shit and lucrative as hell. Do it if it makes sense for you logically. And that's why Mikey's not out here right now," he finished with a wink.

And he was right. Mikey would have begged me and used our friendship to pressure me to say yes. But it didn't matter.

I was going to say yes anyway.

I reached out my hand to shake. "I'll have to close things out back in Houston."

Tiller's face split into a wide grin, and he yanked the handshake into a pounding hug. "Fuck yeah. Thank god."

I felt the relief in his body and realized just how much he'd meant his words about wanting someone he could trust and trusting me. It made me feel appreciated and capable, like the hard work I'd done all these years was finally paying off with the respect of someone I cared about.

I cleared my throat. "I'm going to tell Mikey I said no, though."

Tiller laughed. "Why would you put me through that?"

As we walked back toward the house, Tiller reminded me I could make one of the chalets my own. "Or you're welcome to stay with us at the lodge. I just figured you might want more privacy."

I wondered if there would ever come a time when I could make a home with Truman at the farm or if he even wanted a relationship long-term like that. We'd only known each other a handful of days, so it was ridiculous to even think that far ahead.

But I couldn't help myself.

I felt lighter as we returned to the lodge. The future was exciting and challenging. For the first time in my life, I thought about what it would be like to live in a small town where I recognized people on the street and had a community to call my own.

Mikey shushed us when we entered the kitchen. Barney and Truman were at the kitchen table with a legal pad full of notes as Barney spoke authoritatively to the insurance adjuster on speakerphone. That was an important task ticked off the list. Maybe I needed to give Barney more credit despite his being a controlling asshole and blatant liar.

It was time to get to work to put the Honeyed Lemon back to rights. That meant finding out when the fire investigators would give us access to the shop again to begin clearing debris. Since I'd expected a call from them anyway, I checked my phone. Sure enough, there was a voicemail from Gail Brown requesting a time to interview me about the case.

I stepped back outside and called her back. After the requisite pleasantries, she got right down to business. "Dirk had a few questions for you and wanted to know if you could meet us sometime today to go over them."

"Anytime is fine with me. Truman also wanted me to ask when the building safety inspection will clear him to start work on the property."

I heard her rustling some papers around before getting back on the line. "We have a tentative date for the inspection on Friday, but until the investigation is complete, I can't confirm—"

I stopped listening as I caught sight through the window of Barney leaning over to kiss Truman. My heart sped up as I reached for the kitchen door, but then I saw Truman put his hand on Barney's chest to push him off.

I exhaled and turned around to catch my breath to keep from storming in there and making a scene. My heart was in my throat, and the strength of my reaction grabbed me by the balls.

My reaction hadn't been protective concern for Truman as the recipient of an unwanted advance. It had been complete and utter jealousy along with a healthy dose of possessive rage, something a caveman would feel if he found another asshole stealing his fresh kill. I'd never felt that way about another man before, and I'd scoffed at people who did. To me, jealousy had always been an indicator of mistrust. There was no need to feel jealousy when you trusted someone not to stray.

I let out a desperate laugh. How was it possible to feel jealousy when I didn't even have an official relationship with Truman from which he *could* stray?

It was entirely his prerogative to kiss anyone he wanted to. We weren't dating. We weren't in a relationship. I'd known him for only a matter of *days*. What the hell was wrong with me?

I rubbed my face with a hand and realized someone was talking to me. My phone. Gail.

"I'm sorry," I muttered. "Dropped my phone. So sorry. Can you repeat that?"

"We'll be in touch with Mr. Sweet about the inspection. Meanwhile, Mr. Bromley and I will meet you at the crime scene this afternoon. See you there."

I nodded stupidly and ended the call before taking another breath. *Slow down.* I didn't need a new job, new hometown, and new relationship all at once. One thing at a time.

I turned around and entered the kitchen, trying my hardest to remind myself that Truman could handle one measly little town librarian.

But then I saw Barney's hand pressed intimately against Truman's lower back as he led him out of the kitchen toward the front door of the lodge.

And everything I'd promised myself about staying calm and allowing Truman to fight his own battles went completely out the window.

"Are you leaving?" I asked, trying to keep a steady voice, if not a casual one.

Truman turned to me with a smile. "Barney wanted to look at your motorcycle. I told him it was a rental, but he said he still wanted to see it. Maybe you can show it to us since neither of us knows beans about motorcycles."

It was an odd request, but I followed them out front and showed them the Versys, explaining the basics for about half a minute before Barney interrupted with an excuse for needing to leave.

"I'll swing by and check on you later, Truman," he said before shuffling over to his car and driving away.

"That was weird," I said.

"Really weird. He hates motorcycles. Thinks they're death traps."

I glanced at him to see if he was pulling my leg. "Then why in the world did he... He was trying to get you alone outside."

Truman blushed and shrugged. The pink in his cheeks was enough to make me salivate. "Maybe."

"Then I'm glad I interrupted," I said without hesitation. "I'd rather be the one to get you alone outside."

Truman was silent for a moment, and he looked flustered like maybe I'd put him on the spot. Maybe I'd been too forward in my attempt to interrupt them.

Things between us were awkwardly silent for a few minutes until we both spoke at once. I said, "I'm sorry," at the exact same time he said, "I want to have sex with you."

"I'm sorry, what?" I asked, pretty sure I'd heard wrong.

"I want to start by giving you a blow job," he said hesitantly. "But no sixty-nining me this time."

The request surprised me. "Did you not like—"

"No! Oh gosh no. That's not it at all. *Like*? Of course I liked it. But I couldn't do my thing while you were doing your thing, and I'd really like to do…"

I lifted an eyebrow while he decided whether or not to finish the joke.

"*Your* thing," he said with pink cheeks and a grin.

Hot damn. The man was flipping adorable and all mine for the next few hours.

"But what about what I did back there with Barney? I was rude," I argued.

Truman shrugged. "He was the one who was rude. And he wasn't listening. He asked if he could take me home, and I said no several times. I told him I had orders to fill and some other work to get done, and I wasn't feeling up to entertaining. Since talking clearly wasn't working, a different approach was warranted."

"The interrupting jealous caveman approach," I suggested.

"Is that what you call it?" His grin was contagious. "Me like."

"So I shouldn't offer to take you home?"

"You should, actually. And you can use my car, too."

We were in his Subaru within minutes. I had to ball my fist to keep from fondling him with my free hand as I drove us across the valley to his farm, but when we got inside his bedroom, all bets were off.

"Get your ass on that bed," I growled, ripping my pants open and stripping off my shirt.

As he climbed onto the bed, he grumbled something about

thinking he was supposed to be the one giving the orders. I watched his slim body move across the rumpled sheets and imagined the day when I could grab his cheeks and eat his ass.

That would be an incredible day.

"Your, um... p-penis got excited just then," he said. "Are you having thoughts?"

"Lots of thoughts, Tru. Lots and lots of thoughts." I climbed onto the bed and began kissing his body wherever I could. He made sighing sounds of pleasure until his memory caught up with him, and he scrambled to shove me onto my back.

"Hey, this is supposed to be my show. You stay still. I'm in charge."

I settled onto my back and crossed my hands behind my head. "At your service, Mr. Sweet."

Truman rubbed his hands together and straddled me before examining my chest as if unsure where he wanted to begin. It didn't take him long. He put his mouth on one of my nipples and licked. I squeezed my eyes closed with a groan.

"I want you to fuck me, too," he said as he moved down my body. He kept his eyes on mine as his mouth wandered across my skin. His hair was an absolute curly nest after going to sleep with it wet last night, and seeing him without his glasses on always made him look even younger than he was. "If you want," he added a little cheekily.

"You ready for that?"

He got to my happy trail and ran his nose down it, closing his eyes and almost talking to himself when he answered. "Beyond ready. Long past ready. But only with you."

His words made me even harder, and I groaned and arched my cock up into his chest. "Don't say shit like that."

Truman laughed softly before finally putting his wet mouth on my dick. Maybe I should have waited until we'd had a chance to talk about things. Maybe I should have given him more time. But the minute his tongue stroked hesitantly down my shaft, I knew I would find a way to get inside him before I came.

"Oh fuck, baby, Jesus. That feels... *oh god*." I couldn't think straight. His mouth was wet and warm on my dick, and his own erection brushed against my leg as he shifted around.

I threaded my fingers into his hair and held him gently as he licked and sucked and made humming noises. It didn't take much for him to get me right to the edge. I gently tugged at his hair, and he lifted his head. His lips were dark pink and covered in saliva. There were tears in his eyes from the couple of times he'd gagged trying to take me deeper.

My head swam with desire, hot and pulsing from my chest down into my balls. I wanted to pound into him, shove him into the bed, and slake every filthy fantasy with his body. But part of me also wanted to treat him like the spun glass he hated being compared to. I didn't want to treat him like a fragile flower as much as like a beloved treasure.

"Stop," I said gruffly, leaning up to kiss his mouth hard. "Let me get the lube and... do you have condoms?"

He blinked at me in a daze. "Condoms... I've never, um..."

I reached for his chin and held his face until he looked me in the eye. "Tru. I'm on PrEP, and I haven't slept with anyone in months. Are you comfortable with me going bare? If not, we'll wait, and that's okay. Completely okay."

He nodded. "Considering you were trying to protect me from harm the moment I met you, it's hard to believe you'd ever put me in jeopardy."

And he was right. I would never, ever cause him pain if I could avoid it.

I retrieved the lube from his toy drawer and turned the tables on him, licking, sucking, and kissing all over his sweet body until he was begging me to do *something*.

"Like that, baby?" I murmured against an inner thigh.

"I..."

I slid my tongue behind his balls. "Like that?"

"Muhhh..."

I chuckled and moved my tongue up the crease of his leg before lubing up my fingers and reaching for his hole. "Relax, baby," I said softly as I continued to kiss him everywhere. "Just let me feel you."

His hole was tight and warm against my fingertips, and I had to lecture myself to go slow with every move I made to soften and stretch him. The sounds he made drove me crazy, and it was nearly impossible to keep from crying out my need to be inside him, to make him feel good. Hell, to make *me* feel good.

But I was terrified of hurting him and giving him an experience he wouldn't want to repeat.

So I fingered him to the edge and back, over and over again until he was thrashing his head back and forth and precum made a steady slick trail down the head of his pink dick onto his stomach.

"Sam," he breathed. "Sam, please."

I moved up to kiss him on the mouth, taking his lips a little too hard with mine. But he gave me the same fierce kiss, nearly gnashing our teeth together in the hard press of his mouth against mine. His hands clenched my face as he was afraid I was going to suddenly leave if he didn't keep holding on tightly.

He was passionate and fearless, open and free with his body in a way that surprised me considering how poorly he'd been treated by most of the people in his life.

His virginity was a gift, and I wanted to be worthy of it even if that sounded corny as hell to my own ears. If it was important to him, it was important to me, and if there was one thing I knew for sure it was that Truman Sweet deserved respect. He deserved to feel important.

Because he was.

"I want to be inside you," I mumbled against his mouth. "But if you—"

He reached down and grabbed my cock, pulling it toward him while his whole body curved up to meet it. I quickly grabbed some pillows to shove under his hips and tried to make him as comfortable as I could.

When I finally began pushing into him, I watched Truman's eyes like a hawk for any signs of discomfort. His eyes were wide and his cheeks were pink, but he didn't look to be in any pain. I remembered all of the toys in the drawer and realized he would be familiar with the stretch and burn even if he'd never done it with another man before.

His unruly curls surrounded his head like an adorable halo. I imagined fucking him from behind and holding all of those curls clenched tightly in a fist.

I groaned as the image melded together with the tight, hot squeeze of his body. "Ah, fuck." I swallowed. "You okay?"

He nodded and bit that poor abused bottom lip, which nearly caused me to lose it and shove the rest of the way in without stopping. By the time I finished taking my time with it, sweat had broken out on my back, and my breathing came short and shallow. I wasn't going to last long.

"Sam." Truman's voice sounded choked and desperate. "Sam, right there. Right there. Harder. *Please.*"

I reached for his dick and shuttled my fist over it while thrusting into him harder and faster. I had to trust he knew his body well enough to ask for what he needed, and from his reaction, he definitely did.

He was fucking gorgeous like this. Skin flushed and neck tendons prominent as he struggled for his release. His eyes were screwed shut, and the edges of his hair were damp with sweat. Truman's lips were cherry red from my kisses and his own nervous bites. His fingernails dug into the skin of my chest as I railed him into the bed.

It was the hottest sex of my life.

I spit into my hand and returned it to his dick, trying to push him over the edge so I could finally let go. He let out a cry and threw his head back, pulling his knees back in the process, which allowed me to push even deeper into his body. I choked out my own release as his body squeezed impossibly around me.

How could I ever walk away from a man who made me feel like this? From a man I wanted to pleasure this way over and over and over again? The look on his face, the body language of complete and utter abandon... he was the sexiest man I'd ever been with, and watching this shy man ask for what he wanted had nearly made me swallow my tongue with need.

I was lost to him, this kind and quirky human with the big eyes and crazy hair. He could crook his little finger, and I would come running. Anytime, anywhere.

Was it really possible to fall for someone this quickly? To catch an accidental glimpse into someone's heart and suddenly recognize it as the home you didn't know you were searching for?

It seemed impossible.

It took me a while to stop shuddering, but I made sure not to squash Truman under my dead weight. I lay to the side of him on the bed and noticed his fingers drawing lazy shapes on my arm.

His voice was soft but steady. "That made me feel powerful."

I turned to meet his eyes. He looked sated and happy. Calm. Confident. "You are powerful. You had me completely... you *have* me completely at your mercy. Don't you know that?"

We watched each other for a moment before he moved his hand up to cup my cheek. "But do I *have* you?"

He bit his lip again, radiating insecurity.

If only he knew.

18

TRUMAN

I didn't stop at that. "Does this mean something to you the way it does to me? Does it... *can* it mean we're together?"

It was one of the bravest things I'd ever done, asking Sam to define our relationship.

Sam's intense gaze, which was often intimidating, was as affectionate and loving as I've ever seen it. Granted, I hadn't known him for very long, but I could tell he cared about me.

And I was having more feelings than I could ever admit, no matter how brave I felt. Sam was the first person who made me feel like... me. He made me feel like I was exactly who I was meant to be and that maybe that person was amazing.

I'd spent plenty of time having sex with myself. In fact, I loved the freedom to express myself sexually when I knew there was no one around to judge me. In a way, my solo sex life was like my little secret. I could be as experimental or edgy as I wanted without having to worry about what anyone else thought.

I'd never expected to be able to share it with anyone. It was another reason I'd resisted getting physical with Barney.

But Sam didn't make me feel dirty or strange for wanting sex the way I wanted it. And I knew without even asking that he would be up for whatever experimenting I wanted to do with him in the future.

If there was a future. I was terrified of his answer.

"I would love it to mean we're together, Truman," Sam said softly. "I want to tell everyone in town that Truman Sweet is my boyfriend." He rolled toward me and lay on his side, reaching out and brushing the curls out of my face. "I've been trying to find the right time to tell you I'm moving here, to Aster Valley, but I..."

As his voice trailed off, my stomach began to knot. Did that mean he'd ultimately decided not to? "But you?"

"But I didn't want to pressure you. We've known each other a hot second. I don't ever want you to feel obligated or pushed. I want whatever you're willing to give. Nothing more."

My heart almost shoved its way out of my chest to dance happily on the bed between us and then smack kisses all over Sam's body.

"I'm willing to give you head," I said with a straight face, trying so hard not to throw myself bodily at his person and beg for him to glue me there like some kind of strange appendage.

It took him a minute to get that I was joking, and then his reaction was hysterical.

"Did you... did you just make a sex joke?" Sam's voice almost reached a Trumanesque squeaking pitch.

"Did you just hit puberty?" I teased.

"Oh my god," he said with a laugh, rolling over to squash me after all. "I can't believe who's suddenly mister jokester."

I was so happy, I felt almost manic.

"Now that I know the key to making Sam Rigby beg, I feel like the king of the world," I admitted with a smirk.

He reached around to pinch my ass. "Insubordinate punk. I didn't beg."

I laughed. "Are you kidding? You had a constant stream of chatter going under your breath. Things about how my body felt, how you were going to have to build a sex dungeon and name it after me, and how you would beg me to get back inside of my body if you had to."

Sam stared at me in disbelief, but his cheeks turned pink. Clearly part of him believed the truth I spoke. His words had empowered me. They'd made me feel high and free.

It was amazing what having sex with a man who respected and appreciated me felt like. I was full of mixed emotions. Gratitude for Sam's patient, steadfast regard. Resentment at all the years I'd thought I hadn't deserved someone like him. Joy at finally learning how it felt to have a man inside me, thrusting into me and shifting around until my body sang in just the right way.

And hope. If Sam Rigby was moving to Aster Valley, my life had the potential to crack wide open like a spring rain cloud succumbing to a burst of summer sun.

"Okay, it's true," Sam finally admitted. "All of those things are true. Except the chalet I'm going to move into at the lodge doesn't have room for a dungeon. So I'll have to make do with sex handcuffs."

I nodded agreeably. "You may use mine."

His eyes bugged out again. This was getting fun.

"I'm joking. I only have solo toys," I admitted. "But you're kind of fun to tease. And I'm clearly the much better liar between the two of us."

"Little Truman Sweet. You have anal sex one time and suddenly you're a tiger." Sam looked at me like inspecting a new species. "The Truman Tiger."

"Rawr," I deadpanned. "Now hush and let me pretend like I don't have things dripping from... places."

He laughed loud and deep before pressing another kiss to my lips and hauling himself up to get a cloth from the bathroom. I let myself lie there and bask in the role of pampered one even though it darned near killed me. When he returned from the bathroom, he reached out to wipe me down, murmuring something about being surprised I hadn't followed him to the bathroom and insisted on cleaning my own self thank you very much.

"I'm trying to keep you guessing," I said as my face ignited with embarrassment. I'd never had another man wipe me down before, and when the cloth got close to my private parts, I snatched it out of his grip and took over. Apparently, my ability to withstand pampering had hard limits.

Once we were both cleaned up, Sam spooned me under the covers again. "You feeling okay from the sex?" he asked after a few minutes of snuggling.

"I'm feeling boneless and giddy after the sex," I admitted. "And relaxed enough to doze off."

"Mm. I thought we came back here because you needed to work. Orders to fill and whatnot? It turns out... you just wanted to seduce me."

Sam's voice was deep and languid, the perfect backdrop to the floaty way I was feeling. "You found me out."

We drifted for a little while, fingertips brushing softly against each other's skin until my body began to react more strongly and I wanted him again.

I let out a little whimper of need without realizing it.

"You're killing me," Sam murmured against my ear. "Please let me have you again. Are you sore? It's okay. I can do other things." He proceeded to do lots of other things while my brain scrambled to put thoughts into words.

"Have me again," I managed. "Please."

This time it started off slow and breathtakingly sweet. No frantic rush of desperation like before. He treated me like I was the most valuable treasure on earth, and I wallowed in it. No one had ever made me feel so beautiful and sensual. He ran his hands over my body like he wanted to learn every inch. His mouth sipped at my skin like he was thirsting for it, and his murmured endearments sent the drunken hummingbirds flapping wildly around my stomach.

As soon as he pressed inside again, this time from behind, I could tell he was holding way back. He was afraid of hurting me.

"Move," I said. "More."

"S'okay. Good like this."

But I wanted it harder, and somehow I found the guts to tell him so. "Harder. Faster. Fuck me."

My words made him groan, and his body responded immediately.

The slap of his hips against my ass was so hot, it made me even harder. Listening to his grunts and feeling his hard body tense and flex behind me made me feel hot and sexy, powerful and masculine. Desired. Appreciated.

I felt like I was flying.

Sam's hand came down and wrapped around me, stroking in time with his thrusts until I was crying out my release.

Was this really my life?

I collapsed face-first into the mattress and grinned like a loon.

"Get up, lazyass," Sam murmured as he kissed me awake. "If you're not going to pack orders, then we're going for a ride on the motorcycle."

He was so excited about it, I agreed happily and washed up before getting dressed in clean clothes.

Sam drove us back over to Rockley Lodge and ran inside to grab the extra helmet he had.

When it was finally time to climb onto the bike, I was having second thoughts.

"Maybe it makes more sense for me to—" I began, but Sam cut me off by lifting me up and plonking me on the back of the seat and slipping his leather jacket over my shoulders. I nodded. "Okay. We're doing this. It's happening. Yes. I am riding a motorcycle."

Sam grinned as he leaned in to kiss me on the lips. His movements slowed as his mouth met mine, and he kissed me as if we had all the time in the world and he wanted to savor the very taste of me.

He finally rested his forehead against mine. "I have to tell you I'm having some feelings."

My heart jumped around like a puppy catching sight of his leash. "What, um, what kind of feelings?"

His normally stoic face turned soft, but his mossy-green eyes were just as intense as they always were when they met mine. "Positive feelings. About you. Possessive feelings." His hand moved from my cheek to my hair as he brushed my messy mop out of the way and slid the helmet on my head. "I don't want to rush things, Truman. But I really like you, and I hope you'll give me a chance to spend more time getting to know you. I'm really happy you asked if we could define what this is between us. I like that. You and me."

I nodded, noticing my head felt heavier with the helmet on it. "Me too," I said with as much courage as I could rustle up. "I'm having feelings, too. Strong feelings."

Sam's grin was as bright as the midday sun, and it gave me permission to trust his words. He really meant it.

Sam Rigby was having feelings for me. Truman Sweet. The guy who was nothing very special and about as sexy as a toilet brush. What in the world had I done to attract him?

When Sam threw his leg over the bike and knocked back the kickstand, the bike tilted precariously to one side. I yelped and wrapped my arms around him as tightly as I dared. The low rumble of his chuckle vibrated against my chest, and I decided I might be okay with risking my life if it meant spending a few minutes plastered to this big warm body.

When he started the engine, it added a completely new rumble, and we set off down the driveway. I closed my eyes as tightly as I could and focused on breathing. This was obviously not his usual bike, but he rode it like it was. His body was loose and easy as he leaned into the turns. Mine, on the other hand, was a tight ball of strained elastic band on the verge of snapping.

The cold mountain air was mostly buffeted by Sam's much larger body, and I eventually noticed the warmth of the sun on my back through the thick jacket. We rode away from the town and up into the mountains, slowly rounding the curves and catching glimpses of the valley far below until finally stopping at an overlook. Sam parked the bike and helped me off.

"This is gorgeous," I said, referring to the view of Aster Valley below. I could barely make out the meadow behind my property across the valley. It was a tiny bare patch among the trees. I recognized the small white farmhouse and tidy grids of my farm plots.

I squatted down to investigate a patch of small pinky-purple blooms. The air was crisp and clean, and there was a special kind of hush around us, only interrupted by the gentle mountain breeze and faint trickle of snowmelt somewhere.

"*Phlox subulata*," I murmured. "Did you know the roots of this plant were used to make an eyewash in early native tribes? The Cheyenne also used it to treat body numbness. Like a kind of stimulant. They'd make it into a bodywash. I actually use *Phlox* in my eczema mixture. There's an edible version of *Phlox*, but it's not this. This is the wild creeping *Phlox subulata*. Definitely not edible."

I stood back up and glanced over at Sam, wondering if my sudden burst of plant knowledge had turned him off. He stood right next to me, pointing his phone at the small flowers and taking a picture. Then he pointed it at me and took another one.

I blinked in surprise, moving a hand up to uncrush my overgrown hair. "I must look awful. Helmet hair and whatnot."

Sam's fingers took over and brushed through my curls. "Love your hair. And you never look awful."

"You're one to talk," I muttered, trying not to preen under his attention.

"I don't think I've ever actually taken a selfie, but can we take a picture together? Maybe commemorate our first ride together?"

Sam looked adorably unsure of himself, a state he was probably completely unfamiliar with.

"Only if you can make my hair look decent," I said, knowing it was impossible.

He got a devious look on his face. "What if I can make it so you don't care what your hair looks like?"

Within seconds, he was kissing me with full tongue and sneaky hands. Somehow he had octopus hands because he managed to get his phone out at the same time and snap a picture the minute he stopped kissing me. I sputtered and flapped my hands, demanding to see the photo so I could delete it into oblivion.

But it was amazing. One of those magical shots no one could ever capture on purpose.

My eyes were closed as if I was savoring the moment, and Sam's gaze was riveted on me with a combination of affection and self-conscious awareness. As if he cared about whether or not I was okay with what he'd done.

The entire valley was laid out behind us in a swath of golden sun.

I clutched his phone to my chest and looked at him. "Cripes," I breathed.

"Is it good? Let me see."

First, I texted it to myself in case I accidentally deleted it somehow. *The day Sam Rigby changed my life.* Then I showed it to him and watched the smile take over his face. "I've never seen myself look that way before," Sam said.

"Like what?" Did I even want to know?

"Like I had everything I've ever wanted right in front of me."

I sucked in a breath and met his eyes again.

And that's when I heard the squealing of tires as a familiar vehicle came barreling toward us.

19

SAM

I was in the middle of a magical moment when Truman's face suddenly paled and his eyes widened. "*Run!*"

Instead of doing what he'd said, I stared at him a beat too long. The beat-up pickup dropped a tire off the edge of the road which seemed to set everything else into motion. Suddenly, the car swung around until it was coming straight for us.

Truman yanked my arm, and I lurched after him, racing out of the way of the vehicle as it connected with the motorcycle and sent it crashing into the guardrail. It tipped over the rail and hung precariously with one wheel over and one still on the roadside while the driver of the truck threw the car into reverse and sped backward.

Within seconds, the driver was aiming the giant grill right at us again. I shoved Truman ahead of me as we aimed for a stand of trees up ahead. Just as we reached the safety of the first tree trunk, I hit a thick root with my boot and lurched forward until I'd tumbled poor Truman face-first into the forest floor and landed on top of him.

It took us a minute to untangle ourselves. I flipped Truman onto his back and brushed dusty dry leaves off his face and out of his hair. He was covered in smudges of dirt and bits of debris, but he was safe.

"Thank god," I said, yanking him into my arms and holding him tight. "Fuck. Fuck."

His entire body trembled in my hold. "It was Gene," he finally said between chattering teeth. "He did it again."

I sat on the ground and held him half on my lap. I was surprised he'd recognized the driver considering the sun had reflected blindingly off the windshield, but it was a distinctive truck. I thought I remembered seeing it at the Chop Shop the first day I came to town. "Gene Stanner?"

Truman nodded once in confirmation. "Craig and Patrick's dad. The sheriff's brother. That was his truck. He's the one who..." He clamped his mouth closed, but I shook my head.

"No, Tru. No more keeping this to yourself. Tell me."

"He's the one who hit Mikey and Pim last December." Truman's eyes filled with tears. "And I didn't tell anyone."

He looked so small and vulnerable. His glasses were bent, and his hair went every which way. Smudges from the dirty ground marred his cheeks and chin. I wanted to bundle him up and secret him away somewhere, but I knew that wasn't possible.

It was time for him to stand up. And I was going to make sure he knew this time there was an entire army of people who had his back.

"I'm a horrible person," he whispered, almost to himself.

"You're a scared person," I corrected, brushing some of the dirt off his cheek with my thumb. "And you're allowed to make mistakes. Tell me what happened."

The pickup was long gone by now, and we were alone on the roadside again. I wondered how the hell the man had found us or if somehow it had simply been a lucky opportunity that had fallen in his lap while he was out for a joy ride.

"I was closing up the shop when Mikey, Pim, and Bill showed up. Suddenly, they were shoving me out of the way. I looked to see what was happening and saw Gene's truck peeling off down the road. I didn't know what had happened until I heard Pim groaning and they were both on the ground."

His tears had overflowed and run a clean streak through the dirt on his face. I held him closer and tried comforting him as best I could, but I could feel the tension as his body continued to shake with adrenaline and fear. "Why didn't you tell anyone what you saw?"

I already knew the answer, but I wanted to be sure I understood his fear.

"It all happened so fast. What if I was wrong? What if the sheriff didn't believe me? What if he did believe me and he didn't do anything about it? What if he didn't hold his brother accountable and Pim and Bill and Mikey hated me for it?"

Truman swallowed around his tears. "It's just another example of how I've failed everyone. Part of me wants to leave, Sam. And make a fresh start somewhere else."

I stayed quiet so he could, hopefully, get to the next stage of processing this. He finally sighed. "But then how would I feel about myself? It's already been so freaking long of feeling like the world's biggest fool. And I can't... I can't keep all of this inside anymore. It's killing me." Truman let out a humorless laugh. "Heck, it's literally killing me. First the hit-and-run in December, then the attempted beating the day I met you, then the fire at the shop, and now—"

"He could have killed us. Especially if he was drunk. And if he's driving drunk, he could kill anyone."

Truman sighed and met my eyes. "We need to call the state police."

I nodded. "Or maybe the state bureau of investigation like Mindy suggested about the pension fund. But after what just happened, we can't afford to wait."

Truman stood up and brushed himself off before noticing what had happened to the bike. Suddenly, he started laughing, and he laughed so hard he nearly fell down again.

"I hope you had insurance," he said through his laughter. "Two bikes in one week, Sam. I don't know..."

I pulled out my phone to call Mikey for a ride. I couldn't help but smile as I watched Truman laugh through his tears. He was going to be okay.

I'd make sure of it.

I left Truman at Rockley Lodge with Mikey and Tiller. Their friend Gentry and his uncle Doran were expected to stop by for a visit to help Truman get in touch with someone in state law enforcement. Since Doran supposedly managed Gentry's music career, I figured he probably had friends in high places and could help Truman find the right person to talk to.

I knew that Truman wasn't ready to tell Mikey and Tiller about their hit-and-run in December until after he'd spoken to the state police, but we'd told them about what had happened to us on the mountainside with the rental bike and that Truman had recognized Gene's truck.

As I left, Mikey was fussing over Truman's dusty clothes and insisting on changing him into some comfortable clothes from Mikey's own stash. I fully expected to return to a Truman decked out in navy-and-orange Rigger gear.

Before heading to the Honeyed Lemon to meet the fire investigators, I stopped at the Chop Shop to check on my own bike and inform them about their rental. Jim Browning was behind the counter, squinting at an old calculator covered in years of shop grime. As soon as the bell over the door chimed, he looked up.

"Well, if it isn't our new troublemaker," he said with a friendly grin. "You're good for business."

I let out an unexpected laugh. "Sorry about that. How did you hear about it so fast?"

"Newt Coney came by to pick up some parts and told me he saw the Versys hung up on a guardrail halfway up the mountain. You didn't seem like a green rider when I first saw you, but looks can be deceiving, I guess." He winked at me to let me know he was only kidding. "But I'm glad you're here. Got your bike ready."

I was shocked at the news. "You... sure?" I couldn't believe how fast he'd been able to fit me in. My mechanic in Houston was booked out for weeks at a time.

"Sure as can be. Come take a look." He led me to the first bay where my bike stood as good as new. I stepped closer to look at the fork. "Brand-new. I had to go into Denver for a family thing, and I picked up the part while I was there. I know you were in a hurry this time, but if you decide to get fancy one day, I'd love a chance to upgrade her suspension."

He looked at my bike with hearts in his eyes, and I knew I'd be in good hands once I moved here. I reached out a hand to shake. "Thanks, Jim. I really appreciate it."

We went over some insurance claim information on the rental, and I settled up with him for my own repairs so he wouldn't have to wait on payments from both insurance companies. Then I rolled the bike out to the parking lot and left it for pickup later, pocketing my keys since I wasn't quite "Aster Valley" enough to trust leaving my keys with the bike in the middle of town.

I pulled out of the Chop Shop and turned toward the center of town, driving only a couple of blocks until I got to the burnt-out shell that had once held Truman's shop and his aunt's before that. One of the sheets of plywood over the front door had spray paint on it that read, "We luv U Mr. Sweet!" I took a picture of it with my phone and texted it to him. Leave it to a town like Aster Valley to have teen vandals who used love instead of slurs. Hopefully, that would remind Truman that not everyone in town had it out for him.

I parked Tiller and Mikey's SUV around back and found Dirk and Gail sitting in their state vehicle finishing a takeout lunch. Mikey had shoved a sandwich in my hand before I'd left, but I selfishly hoped he had a big dinner planned so I could gorge myself on some of my old favorites when I got back to Rockley Lodge. And if I was really fortunate, I could convince Truman to stay overnight with me there again.

But the look on Dirk Bromley's face when he noticed me made me wonder if I was possibly spending the night somewhere else tonight. Somewhere like a jail cell. I hopped out of the SUV and kept my movements easy and obvious.

The two fire inspectors eased out of the vehicle without taking their eyes off me. I had a sudden desire to turn and flee at top speed, but I forced myself to remember I hadn't actually committed a crime.

"There's a cafe just down the street if you'd like to grab a cup of coffee," I suggested.

They agreed to walk back down to the coffee shop with me and even greeted the woman behind the counter with familiarity. I blinked when I recognized Truman's friend Chaya.

"I didn't realize you worked here," I said.

She grinned. "I didn't either, until about ten hours ago. Yasmin needed some help because of a family emergency, and since I usually pick up part-time hours with Truman, I'm free at the moment. What can I get you?"

The three of us ordered and took a seat at a small table off to the side of the pickup counter. Gail pulled out a notebook, while Dirk craned his neck to get another look at Chaya. She was tall and beautiful with a mane of dark, curly hair. The woman would attract attention even without saying a word, but she had such an effervescent personality, her personal greetings and periodic laughter lit up the room around her.

Someone had a crush.

"What can I help you with?" I asked to get this conversation going. I didn't want to spend more time in town than I needed to. There was too much work to be done helping Truman organize the cleanup, not to mention the work at the lodge I'd specifically come to town to do for Tiller and Mikey.

Dirk hopped up to grab our drinks when Chaya set them on the counter and returned to our table after she left him to greet the next customer.

I took a sip and almost groaned in pleasure. God, I'd needed that. It had already been a hell of a day.

"Where were you at midnight the night of the fire?"

It took concentration to stay relaxed, but I did my best. "I believe I've already told you this. I returned from Truman's farm to Rockley Lodge where I'm staying with friends."

Gail nodded and scribbled in her notebook.

Dirk tried asking it a different way. "Describe the route you took from one place to the other."

I described the simple drive from Truman's down through town and up the other side of the valley to the lodge.

"So you drove past the Honeyed Lemon," Dirk suggested.

I nodded. "As I have previously mentioned, yes."

"And why were you seen in front of the Honeyed Lemon that night?"

"Didn't I just answer that?" I asked, unsure of what he was asking. "I was on my way back to the lodge."

Dirk clarified the question. "On foot. Why were you on foot at the shop?"

He asked it so casually, I almost second-guessed myself. "I... wasn't? After I got the call from Truman about the fire, I couldn't get within a block of the place. I pulled to the side of the road in front of the newspaper office, I think."

Gail didn't raise her eyes from her notes. "He means before the fire."

I knew what they were asking, but I still gave it serious thought in order to be precise. "I didn't go anywhere near the Honeyed Lemon on foot that day," I said carefully. "In fact, the only time I've ever even entered the premises at all was when I first met you after the fire."

Dirk's eyes widened in surprise. "You expect me to believe that you've never been to your boyfriend's own place of business?"

I let out a soft chuckle. "While I appreciate being thought of as Truman's boyfriend, we actually only met a few days ago. I came into town to help my friends with some construction work and came across Truman in the process. We hit it off quickly, but I assure you, I haven't been around long enough to have any kind of motivation to burn down his place of business."

Dirk sat back and crossed his arms in front of his chest. "You have an assault record in Texas."

My stomach dropped. "I do."

"So far, you're the only person associated with this arson who has a criminal record," he added.

I chose not to respond since he hadn't asked a question. Suddenly,

I wondered whether I should even continue this conversation without an attorney present.

Gail read from her notes. "There is also a report of you holding Mr. Sweet against his will earlier this week. A scene in town in which the local sheriff's office responded."

That was just plain ridiculous. "There were no charges filed, and you're welcome to ask Mr. Sweet whether I was, in fact, holding him against his will." I took a breath and decided to extend a small amount of trust to the investigators. "Listen, the assault charge was several years ago. My little sister was underage and drunk at a fraternity party. Her best friend called me to come get her. When I arrived, I found my sister being taken by a group of men into a back room. A fight ensued. That has absolutely nothing to do with arson or any other kind of willful property destruction. You're wasting time if you're looking at me for this."

Dirk sighed. "I understand your frustration here, but it's our job to question everyone."

"Did you question the Stanners? Ask if maybe any of their associates got a little too close to the Honeyed Lemon that night with a blowtorch?"

My patience was nearing its end.

Gail said primly, "We're not at liberty to share information gathered in the course of our investigation."

But Dirk leaned forward and spoke calmly. "We are interviewing everyone remotely concerned with this case. I assure you we're doing everything we can to find the person or people responsible, and we will not jump to conclusions because of your record."

I appreciated his ability to remain professional, but that was about it. I didn't feel confident in their ability to find a ghost, and if the Stanners weren't responsible, then it would be practically impossible to discover who was. Unless… were there other Aster Vallians upset enough by the closing of the ski resort to harass Truman this many years later?

If so, what would have changed to make them suddenly want revenge after all this time?

After a few more questions, in which I emphasized they were more than welcome to corroborate my whereabouts and character with Michael Vining and Tiller Raine, they thanked me for meeting them.

I stood and thought of one more thing. "Was there really no video from a nearby business? I've heard several Aster Valley business owners complain about vandalism. I would have thought some of them might have put up simple surveillance cameras afterward."

Gail surprised me by answering with specifics. "The janitorial company across the alley in the back of the shop has video from that night. There is no sign of anyone entering the shop through the back door."

That information stopped me in my tracks. "The arsonist entered through the front door? In full view of Main Street?"

Dirk and Gail both nodded. Gail continued. "But it's a very small town without much nightlife."

"Still," I thought out loud. "It was a Saturday night. Midnight isn't that late on a Saturday night in spring. Sunset is later, and the weather isn't as cold. Surely, someone saw something."

"Well," Dirk said with a nod. "One would think. We're working with local law enforcement to canvass the locals. It takes time. Meanwhile, we need to be patient."

I waved and called out a goodbye to Chaya, inviting her to come up to Rockley Lodge for breakfast in the morning if she was free. Mikey had planned another gathering of the Aster Valley business owners whether or not there was new information to share since there was now a plan in place to talk to a state law enforcement entity.

Chaya grinned wide and said she'd be there with bells on.

As frustrating as it was not to know who set the fire, there was nothing I could do to create information where none existed. But the conversation about surveillance video reminded me I'd wanted to put in some simple video cameras by Truman's gate and front door at the farm.

I stopped by the big home store on the edge of town and picked up a surveillance camera kit I'd used on a jobsite several times before. It was easy to install, affordable, and practically indestructible. Instead of heading to the farm, I headed back to the lodge to pick up Truman.

I called to let him know I was on the way.

"Hey," he answered breathlessly. "How'd it go?"

"Fine. They said whoever set the fire didn't enter through the back of the shop. The business behind yours has cameras. That was the only thing I was able to learn. How'd it go with finding someone at the state level to get help with the hit-and-run?"

His voice lowered until it was a soft whisper. "I didn't tell Mikey and Tiller yet about what happened back in December."

My heart nearly broke hearing the nerves in his voice because I knew he was terrified Mikey and Tiller were going to be upset with him. He didn't know them well enough to realize they'd understand.

"It's okay. You'll tell them when you're ready."

"But Doran is putting out a call to a contact he has with state law enforcement from when he had a security issue at one of Gent's concerts."

"Good. Listen, I'm almost to the lodge, and I wondered if you wanted to go over to the farm. You can take some time to think about how you want to approach it, and I can work on a few repairs I wanted to tinker with."

Truman let out a breath. "Yeah. That sounds good. See you soon."

When I got to the lodge, I noticed several cars out front. I loved knowing Mikey and Tiller already had a community here despite living in Aster Valley such a short time.

I walked into the kitchen and spotted Truman immediately through the window. He was standing outside on the deck close to a sexy-as-fuck blond man, and they were both belly-laughing about something. As soon as I saw Tiller and Mikey's friend Gentry gazing at the blond man like he was the second coming of Christ, I realized he was most likely Gentry's husband, Winter.

Sitting next to Gentry at the kitchen island was an older man with thick white hair.

Gentry spoke up. "I don't think you've met my uncle Doran yet."

After greeting the man with a handshake and a few pleasantries, I asked where our hosts were.

"Uncle Doran decided to share a particularly racy porn clip on his phone, and suddenly the two of them claimed they needed to fix some kind of gate," Gentry said. "I think that's some kind of weird Texan euphemism."

Doran muttered, "I offered to help hold someone's pole, but they didn't seem to want a third in their gate efforts. Shame."

I barked out a laugh and felt my face heat. Gentry shushed his uncle through his own laughter.

The two of them were sitting at the island in front of a laptop while an abandoned cutting board sat with a half-cut pile of onions on it. Nearly one whole countertop was covered with mismatched vases of wildflowers, tins of fudge, and several kinds of homemade baked goods that Mikey said Mia, Bill, and even Barney had apparently brought by that morning.

Music played softly from the speakers around the big TV in the kitchen's comfortable sitting area, and through the giant picture window past the kitchen table, I could see the burgeoning yellow green of the aspen trees blooming between the wide expanse of the lodge's backyard and what would soon become a ski slope again.

This town—this property—was poised on the edge of something exciting and new. I kept trying to remind myself that I actually had a life and a home back in Houston, a business that needed to be moved which would require any number of time-consuming steps and critical conversations with loyal clients, crews, and vendors I'd used over the years.

I didn't even want to leave Aster Valley long enough to do any of that. This place, this very kitchen, was so welcoming, so comforting and exciting all at once, that I wanted to settle in and make a little part of it my very own.

Truman and Winter came back inside at the same time Mikey and Tiller returned. Mikey called out my name and asked if he was going to have to come bail me out of "fire jail" later or if it would be traffic jail instead. Everyone glanced over at me, and Truman nearly knocked Gentry's husband over as he raced over to say hello.

Halfway across the kitchen, he remembered himself because he came skidding to a stop in his socks about three feet away from me.

"Oh, hi," he said awkwardly as if I were delivering a package he'd forgotten he'd ordered.

I smiled at him. "Hi."

A tiny tremor shook its way through his body, but he tried ignoring it. "So, you're... not arrested? I mean... no... fire jail for you or anything? That's good, because jail in general is a very unhealthy place to spend time. Unfortunately, people in jail experience more disease. For instance, incidence of sexually transmitted diseases is significantly higher among..." His eyes widened, and he cut himself off with a choking sound. "Of course, I didn't mean to imply that you..." He stopped and swallowed, his face becoming a little blotchy. "Help," he squeaked.

I stepped closer and grabbed his face, leaning down to kiss the man silly. Truman's hands grabbed at my shirt and fisted the cotton so I wouldn't pull away.

God, I loved kissing him. I could have seriously stood there all afternoon exploring his mouth at my leisure. But we were in a room full of people, and I'd embarrassed him enough as it was.

I pulled away and met his eyes. "No fire jail crabs for me, sweetheart. I'm all clear."

He closed his eyes and groaned, moving even closer to me and hiding against my chest. "I'm not fit for polite society," he muttered against my shirt.

"Then maybe I'll have to keep you tied up in my dungeon lair," I said softly into his ear.

"You already told me the chalet doesn't have room for a dungeon," he reminded me, looking up with a smirk.

"It doesn't now," I agreed with a wink, "but I'm a builder."

Truman pulled me over to introduce me to Winter and catch me up on the insurance help Doran had given him while I was gone. Gentry had described Doran as an expert in all things contractual, and he'd been correct. Doran had discovered the part of the policy that definitively showed the shop would be covered despite the arson finding. That was enough of a relief to explain why Truman had been so happy when I'd walked in, but then he also told me a funny story about Gentry being mistaken on an airplane once for a popular televangelist. Truman could hardly hold his giggles as he retold it.

As the group socialized around us, I realized that this was way more beneficial to Truman's well-being at the moment than surveillance cameras or even tending his farm would be. So I sat down next to him at the kitchen table and listened.

There were times he became self-conscious and stammering, but for the most part, he seemed to shine under the affectionate attention of the other men in the room. Somehow he'd recognized everyone here as a friend, and it allowed him to come out of his shell more than I expected.

It wasn't until someone mentioned the "motorcycle accident" that I saw Truman's mask slip.

Mikey's eyebrows furrowed. "I can't believe Gene Stanner is allowed to drive without a license and there's no one around to stop him. People could be killed. What if he'd hit one of you?"

Truman's breathing had shallowed, and he looked like he was about to faint.

"Hey," I said. "Why don't we head back to the farm for a bit? You still have those orders that need to go out."

I didn't care about his orders, but I wanted to get the cameras installed before making a call back to Houston to touch base with the Harding brothers about moving my business to Colorado. I knew they'd take good care of my clients in my absence, but I needed to notify them and get the ball rolling.

"Oh, uh, yeah. That's... a good idea."

"I picked up some security cameras I wanted to install at your place if that's okay with you. They're really easy to use, and you can even check them from your phone."

He looked at me in surprise from where he sat next to me at the kitchen table, shredding a paper napkin with nervous fingers. A half-empty baggie of peanut butter cookies sat in front of Truman at the heavy wooden table, and Doran's collection of wine bottles he was emptying "for an art project" took up most of the rest of the tabletop space.

"You didn't need to do that," he said.

"I know. But I'd like to. Do you want to come with me and get those orders done?"

He nodded. "Yeah. And maybe lie down. I'm feeling drained all of a sudden."

We stood up and said our goodbyes. Thankfully, Truman's Subaru was out front, so we were able to leave Tiller and Mikey's SUV at the lodge. We drove toward the farm in what I originally thought was companionable silence, but I quickly discovered was not.

"I lied to everyone," he said, shoving the words out like he'd spent several minutes trying to get them to leave of their own free will first. "I think I'm going to be sick."

20

TRUMAN

After Gentry had brought up the motorcycle hit-and-run, which of course everyone simply thought was a case of regular drunk driving, I'd been swamped with guilt. I'd asked Sam not to mention that we thought it had been deliberate until I was ready to talk to them about what happened in December, too.

But the guilt was eating at me. How could I be in Mikey's kitchen acting like one of his good friends after I'd kept the identity of his hit-and-run driver a secret all this time?

Because of me, Mikey and Pim had never gotten justice.

The guilt was a poisonous ball in my gut that was never going to go away. Not only had I kept the secret, but I'd also allowed myself to get closer to Mikey as a friend during this time. How could I have done something so horrific?

I was a terrible person, just like everyone had tried to tell me for years.

I pulled the car over to the side of the road and jumped out, barely making it into the trees before I began throwing up. At first, I assumed it was the guilt that had upset me to the point of nausea, but then the vomiting didn't stop.

Sam had rushed over to help, which basically consisted of gently rubbing my back until I squawked about wet wipes in the glove compartment.

He brought the wipes and a bottle of water which helped me scrape together a tiny speck of dignity again.

Eventually, I was too weak to keep leaning over, so I moved to a cleaner spot and sat down in a heap. Sam looked horrified, but I quickly realized he was scared for me.

"Let me call an ambulance," he said.

I shook my head weakly. "No. I'm fine."

That bold-faced lie was almost enough to surprise a laugh out of me. Instead, I closed my eyes and groaned as another wave of nausea rushed over me in a cold, clammy sweat.

"What have you eaten?" he asked.

I thought back to the tuna sandwich I'd had for lunch which was a graphic enough memory to bring up another harsh attempt at emptying my stomach.

"Oh, shit, baby," Sam said, realizing what he'd done. "I'm sorry. Horrible question, never mind."

After it was clear the bad stomach wasn't simply a delayed hangover, I admitted maybe I did need to go to the hospital. Sam found a couple of plastic shopping bags in the car from the stuff he'd purchased at the home store, and we made a makeshift vomit receptacle for me before getting back into the car.

At this point, the only thing still coming up was bile, but I was making such horrific noises, I wouldn't have been surprised if Sam had dropped me off at the ER and bolted back to Rockley Lodge.

Of course, he did the opposite. He carried me inside the hospital and demanded I be seen as soon as possible. Thankfully, the emergency room wasn't very crowded, and we were shown to an empty bed in one of the triage bays fairly quickly. Throughout the whole time, Sam kept a tight grip on my hand.

"Hi, my name is Summer Waites, and I'll be taking care of you this evening," a young nurse said. She had the same dirty-blonde hair as her brother. We'd met a couple of times, but I wasn't sure if she'd remember. "I hear you've been vomiting." She bustled around the bed to take my vitals.

"You're Winter's brother," I said.

She grinned, revealing a dimple. "Sister, but yeah."

I felt my face heat. "Sorry. Brain not working."

She reached for my hand and squeezed it as she took my temperature with the other. "That's okay, sweetie. We've met a few times. You own the spice shop and a particularly sweet bow tie collection, if I'm not mistaken."

At the reminder of the shop, I felt another lurch in my stomach. Things were not going my way.

Sam chuckled. "How come I haven't seen any of your bow ties yet?"

Summer told him he'd have to stick around long enough to see them, and then she turned to me. "Truman, did you take any medicines or strange substances today?" When I spent too long thinking about it, she turned to Sam. "Is he under the influence of any pharmaceuticals that you're aware of?"

Sam shook his head. "I don't think so. He prefers homeopathic remed... wait." He brushed my hair back from my face where it was damp from cold sweat. I felt like an ugly mess. "Have you taken any of your herbal supplements or teas today?"

I remembered telling Sam the other night about the various homeopathic teas I made. He'd asked a ton of questions and listened with active interest as I'd told him all about the ancient stories that went along with the healing properties of many of the botanical elements. "Nothing."

I really didn't want to be alone right now. I felt vulnerable and lost, wrong-footed and untethered. Everything that had seemed within my grasp only a couple of days before was suddenly nothing but a poisonous fog.

My friendship with Mikey and Tiller would end as soon as they discovered my culpability in the December hit-and-run. Same with the affectionate paternal relationship I'd always had with Pim and Bill. Obviously I couldn't rely on Barney anymore, and I even felt like

Chaya might feel differently about me when she found out about the secrets I'd been keeping.

Sam's face was tense with worry. "Anything else you ate that you can think of?"

He was so sweet. No one had treated me with such careful attention and concern before. Well... maybe Barney, but his attention had been suffocating. But why was Sam being so nice to me when I was a horrible person?

I burst into tears.

Summer acted like it wasn't happening. She kept chattering on happily, probably because she was used to patients losing their minds in the emergency room, and it was her job to stay as upbeat and calm as possible.

But Sam looked horrified.

"Tru? What... what's happening? Are you in pain?"

I nodded and immediately shook my head which only made his thick blond brows furrow deeper. He looked up at Summer. "How can we find out what's wrong with him? Is it food poisoning? We were at Mikey's house, and there was a ton of food there."

He'd whispered the word "food" so softly, I almost laughed through my tears.

"We're going to get an IV going to get some fluids started. Meanwhile, I'm going to need to ask you some questions when you're ready," she said to me. "No rush. Why don't you take a minute while I gather everything I need?"

As soon as she was out of our little curtained area, Sam stepped closer. "What can I do? I feel so helpless."

I reached for my phone with shaky hands and unlocked it before pulling up Chaya's contact info. "Text her and ask her to come sit with me so you can go back to the lodge."

"What? Why?" He took my phone and did as I asked.

I shook my head as more tears came out. "This is going to take a long time, and I don't want you to have to sit around here all night. I don't want you to miss dinner at the lodge and everything."

Sam's jaw dropped. "Are you kidding? I thought we already

defined things this morning, Truman." He almost sounded angry. "Do you even know how hard it is for me to hold back from telling you how much I—"

A familiar voice screeched through the curtain, "Tell me where he is right this minute!"

"Barney?" I asked, genuinely surprised to hear his voice in the emergency room.

He threw back the curtain and blew out a breath of relief when he spotted me. "Thank god. Oh, thank god. I was so worried."

He bustled over and put his hand on my forehead as if checking for a fever. I flinched away from his touch at the same time Sam jerked his hand into a fist and held it tightly to his thigh. He didn't move from his chair, though, and I was impressed with his display of self-control. I knew he hated the man.

"How did you know I was here?" I asked.

He reached for my face again to try wiping my tears away, but I held up my hand to block him. He sighed and reached for the box of tissues on a nearby shelf instead. I took a few tissues from the box to wipe my face.

"Mrs. Danielson called me the minute she saw you come in. She's here with Henry's angina. Are you okay? What happened?"

Before I could answer, a hospital administrator bustled in to take down all of my insurance information for their records. Barney took great pride in knowing the answer to almost every question, so I didn't have to exhaust myself answering the poor woman.

By the time she had everything she needed and Summer had finished inserting the IV, Barney had forgotten what we were talking about. He asked me about the insurance claim, the fire investigation, my plans for the shop, and a whole host of other topics I was way too tired to care about.

"I don't feel well," I said, finally reaching the end of my manners. "So I'm going to... stop talking now."

"What happened? What are you here for, sweet pea?"

"Just a touch of food poisoning. I'm sure it'll be fine," I said. "Go on home."

My attempt at a dismissal failed, but then again, he might not have heard it over the sound of Chaya forcing her way into the room.

"Holy fuck on a fiddle, what the hell happened?"

Her hair was wild, like a physical manifestation of her mood. It was a relief to have her here.

"Vomits," I said, unable to say more about it without feeling sick again.

Sam snuck his hand back in mine where it rested next to my leg on the bed. His skin was so warm and his grip gentle. If he'd done what I asked and left me there to go back to the lodge, I would have cried even more.

Barney tried to nudge Chaya out of the way so he could reach for the hand Summer had put the IV in. Thankfully, Chaya bodychecked him.

Barney mumbled about this being caused by stress. "I'm sure it's because of the fire. Those Stanners set that fire. I'm sure of it. And look at the stress it's causing you."

Chaya turned to him. "The Stanners have an alibi. They were here celebrating Craig and his wife having their new baby."

Barney's eyes widened in surprise. "That's impossible."

As Summer began collecting her supplies to leave the room, she stopped and crinkled her brow. "No, sir. All the Stanners were here the night of the fire. I remember my friend Diya complaining about how loud they were. The men had all been out drinking somewhere when they showed up around ten or eleven for the delivery. And I know they were here until at least one because the maternity ward night manager finally booted them out so the new moms on the floor could get some sleep. I remember because she said later, after they were gone, 'I don't care who the sheriff is, my patients need their rest.' And Diya specifically mentioned finding Gene's ball cap in the parking lot after her shift next to the pile of cigars they'd gone outside to smoke after the baby arrived."

Sam's hand brushed gently along my forehead, pushing my curls out of my face. "Is there anyone else in town that would have committed arson for them? Anyone else who feels that strongly about your supposed role in the resort closing?"

Barney answered before I could even think. "Impossible. It has to be them. Especially after the hit-and-runs."

I was inclined to agree with him since I'd seen Gene's truck both times. How could there possibly be yet another person who wanted to harm me like that. But... then again... what if I was wrong? What if it had been someone else driving Gene's truck? I hadn't actually seen the driver either time. Had I?

My head pounded, and my throat felt raw. Summer had given me a minty swab to help freshen my mouth, but it still felt like I'd vomited a million times.

"It's too late for me to think about any of this right now, okay? I just... I just want to sleep a little bit." I closed my eyes and took a mental assessment of my stomach. It felt empty almost to the point of hunger, but there was no way I was putting anything in it anytime soon.

I let myself doze off by focusing on the strong, warm grip of Sam's hand in mine. He'd been rock steady since I'd met him, and I wondered if he was possibly as wonderful as he seemed. At every turn when he could have decided I was too odd, too quirky, too meek, or too high-maintenance, he'd still stuck around.

"Too good," I whispered.

I let the sounds of the hospital melt together to form a general background buzz. I didn't really fall asleep because I perked up a little when Barney left and again when I noticed Sam talking to Chaya. I noticed the tender way in which he periodically ran his fingers through my hair and murmured reassurances to me. And I noticed more than anything the familiar lemony pine scent that clung to him despite everything he'd been through today.

My brain rifled idly through what ingredients I could use to recreate that scent and sell it in the shop. I'd make a killing.

After a while, he called to tell Mikey what was going on. I heard him say, "I'm worried about him. Maybe I should try and take him with me to Houston for a little while to get him out of danger."

Tired and weakened as I was, the reminder of Sam's life in Houston hit me hard. Sure, he'd said he wanted to be with me, that he was thinking of moving to Aster Valley, but that seemed easier said than done. And if Mikey was as horrified by my behavior as he was bound to be, would Sam regret that he and I had defined our relationship so quickly? If Mikey didn't want to be friends with me anymore after I confessed about the hit-and-run, then how could I expect to date his best friend?

At some point I must have actually fallen asleep because they had to wake me to talk to the doctor. He was an older man with an overgrown salt-and-pepper beard, a pale pink bald head, and kind brown eyes. "How are you feeling, Mr. Sweet?"

"Like I've been turned inside out," I croaked. "But I don't feel like I want to vomit anymore, thank goodness."

He smiled and asked to listen to my heart and lungs before crossing his arms and studying me. "You were definitely dehydrated, so I'd like you to stay long enough to finish this bag of fluids, but I think after that you can go home and rest there. As for what caused the vomiting, your friend mentioned others having the same kind of sandwich you did today which rules out food poisoning from your lunch. Breakfast would most likely be too far in the past for such an acute reaction, but I understand others had the same foods there, too. Is there anything at all you ingested that no one else did?"

I thought back to the day spent mostly at Tiller and Mikey's. "No. I was with friends all day. We ate the same things like Sam said."

"I've had a couple of cases in the past where—and it's usually a terrible prank—someone slips ipecac into someone's drink, but it's very difficult to sneak past a person because of its bitter taste. The most probable cause for your episode is a stomach virus, but I haven't seen anything causing quite as violent an episode and sudden onset the way your friend described. Which is what leads me to wonder if you could have possibly consumed an emetic without realizing it."

"*Myrica pensylvanica*," I muttered, trying to clear my head enough to think.

"He's a botanist," Sam added proudly. No one had ever described me that way. It was surprisingly sweet.

"Plant geek," Chaya coughed into her fist.

"The root bark is an herbal emetic," I continued. "But you have to take it in very large doses for that. I grow it to use in a throat gargle."

"Would it be possible for someone to slip the 'Merica Pennsylvania into something you consumed?" the doc asked. I didn't correct his pronunciation since I couldn't tell if he was trying to be funny or not.

I was too tired to think straight. "I can't imagine how, especially if no one else I was with today got sick."

The doctor nodded. "Then I'm going to go with a suspected stomach virus. But if you don't feel better in the next couple of days, follow up with your regular doctor to see if something else could be going on."

I nodded and glanced over at the IV bag hanging from a nearby pole. Almost empty, thank goodness.

The doctor left and sent Summer in to start the process of getting us out of there. "By the time we get the paperwork finished up, you should be good to go with the drip."

Sure enough, after saying good night to Chaya, who'd told me very sternly that we'd be having a talk about my life choices *very soon*, we were loading back up in my vehicle within thirty minutes and on our way to the farm. Sam must have known, without me needing to say anything, that I wanted to sleep in my own bed that night.

When we got to the house, I was relieved to see nothing amiss. Sam forced me to take a shower and brush my teeth before sliding into bed, but when I finally did, I groaned in relief.

"I'll be right next door in the guest room," he murmured, pulling the sheets up past my shoulders and reaching to turn off the lamp.

I didn't want him in the guest bed. I wanted him plastered to my body as tightly as humanly possible.

"Stay," I said in a rough voice that sounded way too desperate. "Please."

He didn't say a word. He simply stripped down to his underwear and slid in beside me. I shifted over and lay against the warm, solid length of him before finally exhaling and letting myself go.

Several hours later, I awoke from a tangle of twisted dreams. "Smoke!" I cried out, sitting up fast enough to make me almost tumble off the bed with dizziness.

21

SAM

At first, I assumed he'd been having a nightmare about the fire, but once I woke up enough to really listen to what Truman was saying, I realized that's not at all what he was talking about.

"They went outside to smoke! The baby was born after eleven, and the men went outside for cigars."

It took me a minute to wake up enough to process what he was implying.

Gene Stanner, or any of the Stanners, really, could have left from there, set the fire, and then come back in for the rest of the celebrations. The nurses who'd claimed to see them there wouldn't have necessarily kept track of *which* Stanners were there during which of those several hours.

"Jesus, babe," I said in a sleep-roughened voice. "You're right. But I'm not sure we can call the fire inspectors at..." I glanced at my phone. "Three in the morning."

"No, no, of course not. No. But, god. I was starting to think all kinds of things about who could have set the fire. I even thought after last night that maybe Barney had," he said with a soft laugh.

I had to admit to having had the same thoughts, although I wasn't sure what his motive would be exactly, and it was hard to think of the older man as a felon after a quiet life spent as the town's librarian. I had to admit that at least part of my bias against the man was caused by my possessiveness over Truman.

I lay back and rubbed my face. "Maybe he wanted to marry you for the insurance money," I teased. "Convince you to become a househusband and see to his every literary and sexual need."

Truman shuddered and snuggled close to me. "I can't imagine closing the shop. Besides, he's independently wealthy. His parents own some important company somewhere, and he grew up rich. So maybe he would want a househusband, but that's definitely not me."

I didn't particularly want to talk about Barney Balderson in the middle of the night while in bed with Truman, so I was about to change the subject. But his stomach rumbled loudly before I had a chance to say anything.

"You must be starving," I said instead. "How do you feel?"

He took a minute to think about it before nodding. "So much better, but yeah. I'm hungry."

We got up and made our way out to the kitchen to forage, pulling out eggs and bread for toast and pouring large glasses of ice water. I wanted to make sure Truman was staying hydrated, and I returned to his bedroom to retrieve a sweatshirt once I realized how chilly it was in the kitchen.

I urged him to sit down while I scrambled some eggs for us. "It makes sense it was Gene all along," I said. "You recognized his truck last year when Mikey and Pim were hit. You recognized it again this week with me on the mountain. And thanks to the nurse, we know his alibi wasn't as tight as it could have been the night of the fire. Now all we need to do is find someone willing to arrest him."

"Mikey's going to never want to speak to me again," Truman said miserably before laying his head down on the kitchen table. "I've ruined everything." He pulled his head up again and met my eye. "You're his best friend. Tell me how to make this right."

I knew he was referring to keeping the identity of the vehicle secret from Pim, Bill, and Mikey last December, and honestly, I wasn't sure how to counsel him on it.

"I think you need to sit down with Tiller and Mikey and tell them what you saw and explain why you didn't speak up. You need to describe the fear you felt and the years of harassment. It's probably not necessary to remind them that reporting the identity to the sheriff would have resulted in your witness statement being deliberately downplayed or ignored, and it certainly would have meant the sheriff finding a way to protect his own brother from legal trouble." I shrugged and stirred the eggs in the pan. "Mikey and Tiller really care about you, Truman. I think they'll understand even if they're disappointed."

"So you do think they'll be disappointed in me."

"I think they'll be disappointed you didn't feel you could trust them to help you fight the Stanners sooner. But it's understandable considering you didn't know them very well at the time. They also were simply tourists back then. They were going to be in and out of town whereas you're the one who had to live here under the Stanners' thumb."

Truman took a minute to think it through before nodding decisively. "I want to tell them. I want to go over in the morning and tell them before I chicken out."

"Good man," I said, turning the stove off and plating our meal. "Voilà. First breakfast is served. It's not nearly as good as second breakfast will be, but it'll at least get you started with something easy on your stomach."

As we ate, I decided to lighten the mood a little in an effort to distract him.

"Little-known fact about Samson Rigby," I said. "I was once a bartender at a place called Bum Shakers."

Truman's eyes widened, quickly followed by his lips. "No kidding?"

I shook my head. "A *dancing* bartender, actually. It's a huge club in Houston with scantily clad servers. It's actually called Rum Shakers, but no one calls it that. I wore cutoff jean shorts with enough holes in them to necessitate waxing. Never again, Truman Sweet. Never again will I have a perfectly friendly stranger rip the hair off my junk to make a quick buck."

He started giggling, and I wondered what I could possibly do to keep him that happy for the rest of his life. I felt my entire chest warm with satisfaction that I'd made him forget all about the fire, the hit-and-run, and everything else bad that had ever happened to him.

"Pretty sure Mikey has pictures," I added. "Every time the DJ played the sound of ice in a cocktail shaker, we had to stop what we were doing and perform a little dance number."

His laughter made his eyes water. "Do it for me. Please. I'll pay you whatever it takes. Shake your booty for me, Sam."

I shook my head and took a bite of eggs. "Hell no. I don't even remember how it goes."

Which was a lie, of course.

"Aw. Who knew such a stoic tough guy could be such a terrible liar? Hm. Weird."

I blinked at him and noticed the teasing glint in his eye. Game on.

"I once rode a bicycle all the way to Beaumont, Texas, just to have sex with a Dallas Cowboy cheerleader. I was once paid to paint a real-life vagina onto the wall of the ladies' room at an OBGYN office I was renovating. I have a severe allergy to marshmallows." I tilted my head at him and batted my eyelashes. "Which one of those was the lie?"

He pinned his lower lip with his top tooth which made my dick take notice. I shifted in my seat as he continued to study me.

"They all are."

I stared at him in disbelief.

"I told you you're a terrible liar," he said as he started giggling again.

"How the hell could you know that?"

He held up an index finger. "One. According to Mikey, you bought your first motorcycle when you were sixteen. It was a crappy five-hundred-dollar bike you bought used off one of his brothers, but it was still good enough to get you to Beaumont, Texas. Hence, no bicycle. Two. Doctors aren't stupid enough to hire a general contractor to do detailed labia work. Three—"

I snorted. "Truman Sweet just said 'detailed labia work.' The world is ending."

His face bloomed dark pink which only made him sexier.

"Three. People with marshmallow allergies are actually allergic to the gelatin which means you wouldn't have been able to scarf down the giant pack of gummy bears I found in your saddlebag."

"Gummy worms. If you're going to be such a smarty-pants, might as well go for accuracy."

"Is there a difference?"

Now it was my turn to tick off several points using my fingers. "One. Gummy worms have less surface area which means more gummy center and less weirdo exterior texture. Two. Gummy worms allow you to make things interesting with sexual innuendo as you eat them—"

"I think you mean awkward," Truman suggested.

"Three," I continued. "There's not quite as much murder guilt involved."

He looked at me blankly.

"The sanctity of worm life is arguably held in less regard than—"

Truman lurched forward and kissed me, throwing his arms around my neck and going all in. I felt like it had been ages since we'd kissed, even though it hadn't been. I was grateful he had the energy for it, but I was careful not to overdo it. When I finally pulled back, he was dazed and flushed.

"Can we go back to bed now?" he asked.

I shoved the last few bites of food into my mouth before grabbing his hand and pulling him after me toward the bedroom. When we got there, he surprised me by peeling off his sweatshirt and removing his underwear.

He was hard and beautiful and stunning, and my brain couldn't even work well enough to do more than grunt my frustration. "Baby," I managed to croak out.

"I want to make out." He looked at me with mischievous eyes. "Really badly."

"As do I. But if we do, I'm going to take it too far, and you are still recovering from your sickness."

Truman glared at me. "Don't treat me like a child, Sam."

I held up my hands and stepped closer. "I am not treating you like a child, and you know how I know? My dick is hard as fucking nails, and all I can think about is pounding your ass right now." My voice sounded rough to my ears, and my blood thundered down to my cock. "I don't get hard for children. I get hard for sexy, stubborn men who show me their hot dicks and tight bodies. And so help me god, I'm going to *mpfh*."

He jumped at me and kissed me, trying to climb my body the way he'd done before. I held on to his bare ass with my hands and reveled in the feel of him. Healthy, happy, horny. *Home*.

I kissed him for seconds or minutes or hours, until both of us were short of breath and my head began to spin. "Jesus, god. You're going to make me lose all sense of responsibility," I muttered, nudging him back down onto the bed and out of my hold. "Get in the bed."

"I want to see the dance first," he said with gleaming eyes.

"What dance?"

Truman mimed shaking a martini and made a piss-poor attempt at the sound of tinkling ice cubes. "Shake your bum for me, Samson."

Without giving myself enough time to chicken out, I went through the motions of the old routine, shaking my ass and twirling around before stomping three times and tipping my imaginary cowboy hat.

Truman giggled and shivered a little as he slid between the now cool sheets.

"You're freezing," I muttered, pulling up the extra blanket from the foot of the bed and laying it over him. I climbed in next to him and pulled him against me. "And what were you doing going through my saddlebags in the first place?"

"I was sneaking a bottle of the wild-harvested black cumin in there," he said sheepishly. "As a gift. Something to remember me by when you went back to Houston."

The gesture squeezed my heart. "Stop being endearing," I warned. "Because I find it incredibly sexy, and we're not doing that right now. Instead, I'm going to tell you more about my day job. Construction. It's going to bore you to tears, and you're going to get more sleep before it's time to go to the lodge for breakfast."

"I would never fall asleep listening to you talk about your life," Truman said hotly.

He was snoring within three minutes.

After waking up again and stopping by the Chop Shop to pick up my bike so I wouldn't be hassled anymore for using Mikey and Tiller's SUV, Truman and I made our way up to Rockley Lodge for Mikey's breakfast.

Mikey outdid himself and was clearly thrilled to be cooking for a crowd again. He'd invited the same group of business owners as before, even though Julian wasn't able to come to town to meet with everyone for a few more days. The kitchen was full of Aster Vallians all talking at once, regardless, and the topic of conversation moved from Truman's poor stomach to the evil hush money conspiracy in town.

At one point the doorbell rang, and Tiller came into the kitchen leading Deputy Stone into the mix. Everyone immediately shut up as if we'd been holding a secret meeting of felonious coconspirators. Someone's final snapped words of "the sheriff's corrupt pension scheme" echoed around the room as everyone's words ground to a halt.

"Morning, everyone," he said with a slight nod. "I don't mean to interrupt. I only stopped by to have a quick word with Mr. Sweet."

At the confirmation there was no general round-up of criminals imminent, the townies went back to their chatter while Truman stood and welcomed the deputy.

"We can sit in the sunroom. Is it okay if Sam comes with us?" he asked, gesturing to me. "He's my... boyfriend." As soon as the word was out of his mouth, he shot a nervous glance at me as if waiting for me to correct him in front of everyone. I noticed a little squeal of excitement coming from the general direction of where Mikey stood at the kitchen island.

"Sam Rigby, nice to meet you," I said instead, holding out a hand to shake.

Stone shook my hand. "Declan Stone. And that's fine."

Tiller handed the deputy a mug of coffee and thrust a plate of pastries at him as well. "No breakfast, no entry. Sorry, but those are Mikey's rules. Apparently."

The deputy's stern face finally softened into a smile. "I'm certainly not going to turn down something that smells this good. Thank you."

After we got settled in the sunroom around a wooden pedestal table most likely meant for card games or puzzles, the deputy explained the surprising reason for his visit.

"I got a message from the fire investigators first thing this morning and stopped by the hospital before the shift change to reinterview the witnesses."

I glanced at Mikey. I hadn't known he'd reached out to the fire investigator already about the cigar break. Could we trust a Rockley County deputy to run down the discrepancy?

"And you were right," Stone continued. "Most of the Stanner men took a long cigar break in the parking lot sometime between eleven and midnight. Any of them could have made it to your shop and back during that time. I'm sorry, Truman."

He seemed sincere. A crease of concern appeared between his brows as he took a moment to collect his thoughts. "Can you tell me more about what I heard back there in the kitchen? About a pension scheme?"

Truman glanced at me as if looking for a sign of whether or not he should trust the deputy. I wasn't sure one way or the other, but I did know that at some point, it would cease to matter. And it would be better to know which side of good and evil this deputy was on.

I nodded slightly, and Truman went on to explain to Deputy Stone what had been going on with the sheriff's department, vandalism, and the demand for contributions to this sketchy program.

As he spoke, Deputy Stone's professionally bland expression showed signs of cracking. I could tell he was both horrified and somewhat unsurprised. He finally leaned toward Truman with a heartfelt promise.

"I will get to the bottom of this. Regardless of whether or not there is such a fund and the collection of monies for it is legitimate, no resident should feel unsafe around their own local law enforcement professionals." He looked uncomfortable with the position we'd just put him in.

"Are you sure you're the right person to handle this?" I challenged.

He let out a combination of a laugh and sigh. "I don't have a choice. But considering I left my previous position after blowing the whistle on a bribery scheme involving some of our officers, it looks like I've found a new calling."

Truman seemed relieved by the news, but I was more concerned. "Will that hinder your credibility in this case?"

Deputy Stone shook his head. "Just the opposite. I made some good contacts at the FBI during the investigation, so I know exactly who to call. We'll get to the bottom of this as quickly as we can."

"There's more to this story," I added. "It goes back a long way with the Stanners and encompasses more than the fund."

With a shaky voice, Truman explained what had happened back in December, why he hadn't reported seeing Gene Stanner's truck, and some of the other things that had happened that the sheriff would have never pursued. Then he touched on the fire and finished up by telling him what had happened to us on the side of the mountain.

"And you're sure it was the same truck?" he asked, scribbling notes quickly in a little notepad.

Truman nodded. "Yes, sir. I didn't see the driver either time, but it was Gene Stanner's old truck. It has a red bumper sticker on the back with some kind of acronym on it and the outline of a ski lift."

He nodded and sighed. "Well, shit. I don't even know what to say to all that. I'm so sorry for all you've been through, and I assure you I'll pursue this as quickly as possible. Give me a little time to contact the right players before I get myself involved by questioning you any further. That could be seen as interference since I'm in the department. In the meantime, if you feel unsafe or have any need of my help, please don't hesitate to contact me." He gave Truman his card and shook both of our hands. I wasn't sure what his plan was, but it was clear he was in for a challenge. Being new in town and not knowing who to trust couldn't have been easy.

When we returned to the kitchen, Mikey took the opportunity to introduce the deputy to the various locals in the room. He'd always been social like that and wanted nothing more than for everyone to get along. Mikey was like a natural public relations firm for the future ski resort even if that wasn't his intention.

The deputy accepted another cup of coffee and took a seat at the kitchen table where several other people had gathered around platters of muffins and sausage rolls.

Since no party was complete without a grumpy librarian, Barney showed up and joined the fun. His face made no secret of his feelings about seeing Truman surrounded by so much activity this soon after his visit to the hospital.

"What in the world is going on here?" he asked, rushing over to Truman and putting his hand on Truman's forehead like a worried mom.

Truman's face crinkled in confusion. "What are you doing? I'm fine."

"You were just in the hospital! You need to be at home resting. Why are these people—"

Truman cut him off. "I said, I'm fine. And I needed to meet with Deputy Stone anyway. Come sit down and have a cup of coffee."

I expected Barney to decline or to try to get Truman out of there, but he surprised me by moving over to take a seat at the table near the deputy.

He introduced himself to the man and joined the conversation, politely asking Deputy Stone where he'd moved from and what he thought of the area so far.

As Truman fixed Barney a cup of coffee, Tiller leaned over to me and spoke in a low voice. "Is he simply going to be a necessary evil now?"

I shrugged. "Truman is desperate to stay friends with him, and I can't decide if it's because of his guilt at not dating the man or his big heart at wanting to include someone who clearly doesn't have many friends."

Mikey stepped in close to us to join the whispered gossip session. "At least he didn't try and yank him out of here like he did before."

When Truman walked the coffee cup over to Barney, Barney thrust his chair back suddenly so he could reach for it. Too late, I saw the chair legs tangle in my saddlebags and shove them right in the way of Truman's feet.

"Wait!" I cried, trying to warn him before he got hurt and hot coffee went everywhere.

But it was too late. Truman's foot hit the saddlebags, knocking them over. He lurched forward to try and grab the table with his free hand, and Barney was able to save the coffee mug from going flying.

Deputy Stone jumped up to get out of the way and almost slipped on something that had rolled out of my now open saddlebag.

"Aunt Berry's mala!" Truman cried, recognizing the colorful string of beads next to the deputy's foot. He crouched down and reached for them before realizing where they'd come from.

My saddlebags.

I stared at him as his gaze lifted to mine. The room suddenly went quiet.

"Sam?" Truman's voice was unsure. "Why... why were these in your saddlebags?"

Barney's face darkened. "I knew it. I knew he couldn't be trusted. Did you know he has a record? I wasn't going to say anything because I didn't want to upset you, but I heard it from Ellen Amana, who heard it from Jane Dempsey, whose husband works at the sheriff's office. That man is a criminal. And now this!"

Deputy Stone's eyes flicked between Truman and Barney and me. "Can someone please tell me what's going on here?" he asked carefully.

"I don't know how those got in there. I didn't take them," I said to Truman. "Someone must have put them in there."

Barney's eyes widened, and he spluttered. "Someone planted evidence right where the sheriff's deputy was sitting? That's quite a charge, sir."

I could see the confusion in Truman's eyes, and I didn't like it. He stepped closer to me with the beads still wrapped around his fingers. "Is it true? Do you have a record?" he asked softly.

This was one of my biggest fears. Finally finding someone I cared about and losing them because of my own damned stupidity.

"Yes."

Mikey stepped up next to me. "Tell him what for," Mikey said angrily to me before turning to Truman. "Ask him why."

"Does it matter?" I asked Truman instead.

His eyes filled with tears, but before he could say anything, Barney interrupted again. "Truman, you have known most of the people in this room for years. You've known this stranger for a matter of days. We all saw those beads come out of his bag with our own eyes. Do you really think someone came here to plant evidence on him? Who? The Stanners? Don't be ridiculous."

Chaya lifted her chin. "Maybe it was you, Barney. We never did hear where you were the night of the fire."

Finally, someone had said it.

Barney's face paled before turning florid with anger. He turned to her and barely kept his cool when he responded. "I'll have you know I was at a model train meeting until half past midnight. I was almost home when I saw the fire trucks outside of the shop, so I turned right around to pick you up at the farm."

I felt my shoulders drop in defeat. If the Stanners really had been the ones to set the fire, then who the hell had planted the beads in my bag?

The saddlebags had been in Mikey and Tiller's kitchen all week, and any number of people could have had access to it.

That meant there was someone here we couldn't trust.

I looked back at Deputy Stone, who'd been sitting right next to the bags. He could have planted them on behalf of an angry sheriff.

He narrowed his eyes at me as if trying to read my mind. Before either of us could say anything, Truman stepped forward and said, "No. It doesn't matter."

And then he stood up on his toes and wrapped his arms around my neck before kissing me full on the lips. It took me a minute to remember what the question had been.

No, it doesn't matter you have a record.

I exhaled into the kiss and held on tight. No matter what happened after that, I would be okay. All I needed was to know Truman Sweet didn't think the worst of me.

I could handle the rest, whatever that ended up being.

22

TRUMAN

I knew I was taking a risk. My brain agreed with Barney. Why in the world would I trust someone I'd barely known a handful of days? I had a history of being proven time and time again that people weren't trustworthy.

But I refused to give up trusting people. And I refused to tell my heart—the heart that had never gotten what it wanted, what it *deserved*—that it had been wrong about Sam.

Besides, why in the world would he have burned down my spice shop? He had no motive, and his best friend was one of my best customers.

I pulled back from the kiss but stayed close enough to enjoy the feel of Sam's arms wrapped around me. "I know you didn't burn down my shop. Besides, I went into your saddlebags for the gummy bears the other day, remember? And the beads definitely weren't in there then."

Sam's eyes closed in relief for a moment, but when they opened again, he looked warily at Deputy Stone as if waiting for the metal slap of cuffs against his wrists.

I belatedly realized Barney had made a choking, gurgling sound, so my eyes flashed to him in time to see his apoplectic response to my kissing Sam.

"You've lost your mind," he sputtered. "This man has brainwashed you. How could you... how...?" He suddenly sat down hard in his chair and dropped his face in his hands. He looked like he was going to pass out. I felt a little sorry for him.

Deputy Stone looked around at the group gathered in the lodge's kitchen. "Would someone care to explain the significance of the beads?"

Thankfully, Chaya jumped in to explain while I gently extracted myself from Sam's embrace and went over to Barney. "Let me walk you out."

He looked up at me with an expression I'd never seen on him before. Defeat.

"Yes. Fine."

I felt Sam's eyes on me as I led Barney through the kitchen and outside. He didn't follow me which was a testament to his self-control. I knew he wanted nothing more than to boot Barney off the lodge property, but he respected me enough to let me handle it myself.

When we got to Barney's car, he turned and grasped my upper arms. "I just want what's best for you."

I shrugged out of his grip. "I know."

"You shouldn't have to carry these burdens alone. You deserve someone to take care of you, to treat you like the precious man you are."

I offered him a small smile. "Thank you. I agree."

"I don't understand how..." He sighed and dropped his shoulders. "It no longer matters. Clearly you have chosen your preferred course. I can only caution you to be careful."

I nodded. "I will."

His hands shook as he lifted one to run it over his hair. A few thin wisps caught in the breeze and blew the wrong way, making him look older and more vulnerable somehow.

"I'm sorry," I added softly. "I never meant to hurt you."

Barney stared at me for a moment as if trying to memorize my features. It wasn't like we were never going to see each other again. We lived in the same small town, and I even hoped to be able to volunteer at the library again someday.

"Nor I, you," he said gently. His eyes softened. "I only wanted to keep you from harm."

"I know. And I'm grateful for everything you've done to care for me."

Because I was. He'd been there for me many times when others hadn't. Now that it was pretty clear the Stanners were probably responsible for the fire, and we knew they were the ones who'd done both hit-and-runs, I realized Barney was the one who'd tried to protect me from them the most. Even though I didn't agree with his heavy-handed methods, I was grateful for his attempts.

"Alright," Barney said, taking a deep breath. "I'll leave you and your... friends alone. But please promise you'll call if you change your mind and need anything at all."

"Of course I will. Thank you."

There was a pause, and then Barney said, "I think... I think I'm going to take some time off. Head to a cabin and catch up on some reading." He moved toward the kitchen door. "So if you can't get a hold of me, I'm probably out of range. But you have Chaya, and you have... other friends, so..."

"I'll be fine, Barney," I urged. "Enjoy your time away."

He looked at me again for a moment before leaning in to kiss my cheek. And if he pressed his face against mine for a few beats too long, it was easily excused as the final gesture of a chapter that was long overdue for an ending.

I turned back to the lodge and walked eagerly toward the new chapter.

The one that opened with my need to pin the Stanner family to the wall for everything they'd ever done to me.

23

SAM

While Truman was sending Barney off, Chaya was calming Deputy Stone down. Not that the man needed calming. He took everything in with the same cool detachment he'd had before. Once the significance of the beads was explained, he promised to update the fire investigators and let them determine whether beads that clearly hadn't even been in the fire were evidence in an arson investigation.

Even though it was clear Barney hadn't had time to plant the beads in the few moments he'd been sitting at the table, I still wondered if he'd done it. The bead situation seemed awfully similar to the miraculous discovery of Aunt Berry's notebook. But then why not just offer them to Truman the same way he'd done with the notebook?

And when the evidence was so clearly indicative of the Stanners' involvement in the arson, why would Barney attempt to frame me for it? It didn't make any sense which was the only reason I didn't think he was a reasonable suspect for planting the mala in my bag.

So then, who else would have done it?

I looked around the room at so many familiar faces. Pim and Bill from the diner, who'd been nothing but kind and generous with Mikey and Tiller since they'd arrived in town. Their son, Solo, who was scrolling through his phone like a typical teenager. Mia and Mindy, who seemed to dote on Truman like a pair of big sisters. Nina from the ranch, Gentry, Winter, and Doran, who had absolutely no motive whatsoever considering Gent's music career had made him millions. Winter still happily worked as an OT at the hospital clinic, and Doran continued to manage Gent's career the way he'd done for years. That left Deputy Stone, who was definitely hard to read.

I noticed him paying close attention to the discussion Pim and Tiller were having about opening the ski resort.

Pim's eyebrow lifted at Tiller. "Mikey said you guys were thinking about getting it up and running sooner than you planned," he said, pouring another cup of coffee.

Truman walked back into the kitchen and snuck under my arm to wrap his hands around my waist. I dropped a kiss on top of his head. "Okay?"

"Yeah. It's over." He sounded relieved which was enough for me to say a silent prayer. Hopefully he was right.

Tiller nodded at Pim and explained about having some investment interest that had sped up his timeline. He didn't share the name of the well-known skier yet, but he gave everyone as much detail as possible about what the plan was. "And Sam has agreed to come on board to manage operations, which we're thrilled about," he said with a grin in my direction. Everyone cheered and congratulated me, but I only had eyes for Truman's reaction.

Even though I'd told him already, it still obviously made a difference to him to hear it confirmed. His cheeks flushed pink, and his mouth curved up in a smile. I couldn't help but pull him more tightly against my side and lean down for a kiss, which of course made for more cheering and excitement.

"Also," Tiller continued, "my agent has hooked us up with some high-end PR agency to ensure that any media coverage about Aster Valley and the Rockley Ski Resort will be positive and focused on the future as much as possible. To that end, they're in contract negotiations on our behalf right now with a film producer who wants to shoot most of his movie on the mountain later this summer."

I could tell this was news to Mikey. His face lit up with excitement, and he began asking a million questions. Tiller shrugged. "I don't know much yet since the agency is in charge of all that. I just figured it would start giving the mountain some good news coverage well before the resort opens back up. That way when we launch the resort and open the mountain for skiing, there will be more for the media to cover than just the accident and subsequent shutdown."

It was a good plan, something I never would have thought about in a million years. "That means we need to get those chalets ready," I said. "Offer them as rentals for the cast and crew."

Tiller laughed and pointed a finger at me. "Earning your keep already. I like the way you think."

Deputy Stone cleared his throat. "If you wouldn't mind keeping us updated so we can help with crowd management and whatnot, that would be much appreciated. Meanwhile, I'm going to head out. Thank you for your hospitality this morning."

The deputy's departure broke up the party with most everyone else admitting they needed to get back to work. Mikey cheerfully showed everyone out while Tiller asked if we could talk about some business logistics for transitioning into my new role.

It was an exciting way to spend the rest of the morning, and I enjoyed sneaking glances at Truman from time to time. He was happily helping Mikey clean up from breakfast by washing dishes and putting leftovers away.

I fell into a kind of daydream haze of imagining plenty more days and nights like this, hanging out with friends and enjoying watching Truman thrive among people who loved him.

"And then we can craft tiny space rockets and send messages to the aliens on faraway planets," Tiller said.

I blinked at him, trying to figure out what in the hell I'd missed. Was he suggesting a themed restaurant on the mountain? "What the fuck are you talking about?"

"You're in lurve," he said in a singsong whisper. "With a capital *L*."

I waved a hand of dismissal. "I'm just tired. Tell me what you think about renting out the lodge to the movie folks."

"I'm not sure whether it's a good idea. It's our home, you know?"

I nodded. "But you'll be in Houston for preseason, and you could always offer it at an obscenely high rate. I'll bet they'd be willing to pay for the convenience of walking to the set. Besides, by that time I should have a work crew, and we can always move your personal belongings into one of the storage rooms in the basement and lock it up."

"I'll see what Mikey says. I don't particularly care, but I know he feels strongly about his kitchen."

He was right. But the money from the rental could pay for a kitchen renovation a million times over, especially if one's best friend was a general contractor.

"Think about it. It's a good idea to establish Rockley Lodge as the place to stay if your plan is to open it as a bed-and-breakfast when the slopes open."

We talked about it a little more before Tiller and Mikey disappeared back to their bedroom, leaving me blessedly alone with Truman. I nudged him out the back door and across the yard to where Tiller had installed a giant hammock between two trees at the edge of the woods.

It was a glorious spring day with bright, clear sun sparking off the new green growth in the grass and nearby aspen trees.

Once we were settled together on the hammock, I asked him how it had gone with Barney.

"He said he'd only ever wanted what was best for me but that he'd leave us alone. It was kind of sad."

I agreed. But it was also a relief to hear the older man had finally quit the field.

"He's coming to terms with the reality of my feelings," Truman continued. "I guess. And I really wanted to find a way to stay friends with him. It was sweet of him to make me those peanut butter cookies yesterday, even if he *did* have to make a point of gloating about how all the ingredients were organic and plant-based. It was a shame you weren't there to see him brag when he dropped them off, as if he's the only one who can make a decent peanut butter cookie."

Listening to the lengths the man had gone to in order to impress Truman almost made me pity him.

Almost.

"I'm ready to tell Mikey and Pim about the hit-and-run," Truman said, changing the subject. "It's going to come out anyway once the Stanners have to answer to state law enforcement, and I don't want them to hear about it from anyone else. They're going to meet me for breakfast tomorrow at the diner."

I ran my hand up and down his back while he changed the subject back to the mala beads.

"Who could have put them in there?"

"Anyone, really," I admitted. "Tiller and Mikey have had tons of people over, and before that, the bags were still on my bike at the Chop Shop."

"Ugh, you're right. You haven't searched through them since then? You didn't look inside them after you retrieved them from the shop?"

I shook my head. "I thought the only things in there were a few snacks and an extra jacket. I took my backpack out when we walked into town that first day. Remember?"

Truman sighed. "Yeah."

Before we could talk it through, Tiller poked his head out the back door.

"You, me, 5:00 a.m. tomorrow. Road trip. Be ready," he shouted across the yard with all the cocksure attitude of a pro baller.

"Like hell," I hollered back. I had plans to be naked in bed with Truman Sweet at five tomorrow morning. Besides, if he was going to finally tell Mikey and Pim about the hit-and-run, I wanted to be there for support.

"First job of the COO. We got a lead on a snow gun."

My brain couldn't follow his words or logic. "A... snow gun?" I murmured.

Truman laughed and shrugged. "Don't ask me. I'm a plant man."

Tiller kept shouting rather than step his precious bare feet off the deck. "It's the thing resorts use to make snow. They're not cheap, and there are a couple used ones for sale in Breckenridge. The movie people want us to be able to make snow for the film, and I'd prefer not having to pay full price for them before we know what the hell we're doing."

I hesitated, trying to figure out how to turn down his first request of me in my new role. Truman grabbed my cheek with one hand and angled my face to meet his eyes. "It's fine," he said with a smile. "I can handle the breakfast on my own."

"I know you can. Doesn't mean you should have to," I said softly.

"But I want to. And I want you to start your job here so you'll be locked into staying here in Aster Valley," he teased. "Besides, now that Deputy Stone has all the information about the Stanners and the fire investigators know they don't have an alibi, maybe we can forget about all of this stressful stuff for the rest of the day."

"Mm-hm." I leaned down and kissed him softly, taking my sweet time tasting his mouth.

"Dude!" Tiller called from the deck. "For real?"

"You're one to talk, asshole," I called, running fingers through Truman's curly hair where his head rested on my chest. "Fine. But those things probably not small enough to fit in the SUV either. We're going to need a trailer."

His voice sounded as excited as a little kid on Christmas. "New snow machines and a big-ass new trailer? Don't mind if I do."

I laughed when I should have said no to the whole damned thing. But I didn't.

And it turned out to be a dangerous mistake.

24

TRUMAN

That night back at my place, I decided to attempt to tick off several more items from my sexual wish list.

After running the sprinklers and letting Sam do whatever it was he was doing with the new surveillance system, I made my way inside and tried to come up with a plan. I'd meant what I'd said about wanting to put all of the stressful events of the day and week out of my mind, at least for the night. Trying to determine how the Stanners had planted that mala in Sam's saddlebags was driving me crazy, and second-guessing my friends was awful. And then of course my brain couldn't help but continue to remind me that if I was going to second-guess my friends, I needed to second-guess Sam, too.

Which was ridiculous. And allowing my mind to spin around in those circles was also exhausting. Instead of worrying, I wanted to do something that would take my mind off everything.

I wanted to have lots and lots of sex with Sam Rigby.

After going into the bathroom and prepping myself, I showered and dressed in a crisp white button-down shirt, a yellow bow tie with tiny blue dots, and absolutely nothing else.

Then I texted Sam a selfie of me in my favorite Truman costume.

Five seconds later, I heard hard boots land on the wooden boards of the porch before the front door slammed open and Sam's voice boomed out. "Where are you?"

The flushed and frantic look on his face when he slid into the bedroom on his socks made me laugh. "In here?"

As soon as he saw me, his eyes went dark, and his entire face looked predator-like. "Mine," he said in a low voice.

I bit my lip and nodded.

He stalked closer. "What've you been doing in here, sweetheart?"

I took a step back toward the bed. "Cleaning."

His forehead crinkled. "Cleaning what?"

"Myself."

If it was possible, his eyes became even more intense. The mossy-green color deepened until the green was dark enough to muddle together with his wide pupils.

"Is that right?"

"Mm." I turned over and leaned over the bed as if to straighten the covers. The slight draft from the room swirled under the hem of my shirt as it rode up the back of my thighs and over my ass. I heard Sam's low growl as he moved closer.

"You're feeling spicy today," he murmured as his warm hands landed on my hips and moved up under my shirt to my sides.

Goose bumps prickled along my skin.

"Very spicy," I admitted, sucking in a breath as I felt his body lean over mine. "I've been having some thoughts."

"Mm, I like thoughts." He nibbled the edge of my ear and pressed the bulge of his jeans against my bare butt. The denim was rough on my smooth skin. Sam's hands moved around my front and reached down to stroke my dick and fondle my balls.

"I want," I said in a shaky voice. "I want you..." It was hard to concentrate when his big hands were on me like that. "I want you to do it to me like this. Bending over. From behind."

The deep groan he made rumbled against my back. I squeezed my eyes closed and inhaled the sunshine and lemon pine scent surrounding me. "Please," I added in a whisper.

Sam's hands were large and rough. They ran all over my body as he grumbled words into my ear.

"S'fuckin' sexy. Want you. Gonna fuck this sweet ass. Bend over for me, sweetheart, just like that… that's it. Let me see…"

His words made me harder, and my breath came in eager pants. I bit my tongue against the desire to keep begging him, and I squeezed my eyes closed to try and keep from coming just from listening to his voice and feeling his hot strong body all around mine.

He shoved my shirt up under my arms and knelt down behind me.

"Oh," I breathed. "Oh, please. Yes."

I'd fantasized about someone doing this, putting his lips between my cheeks and swiping his tongue over my hole. It had always seemed forbidden to me, but incredibly hot. Every scene I'd ever seen with rimming had made it seem so freaking good.

And it was.

"Oh!" I cried. "Sam!" His thick hot tongue pressed against the tender skin behind my balls and swiped up over my hole.

I almost swallowed my tongue. My hands fisted the bedclothes to keep me from sliding to the floor, but Sam's hands held my ass cheeks in a firm grip.

"God, this ass," he said with a groan. "Want to eat it, bite it, fuck it. Could stay here all night like this."

His tongue teased me, bringing noises out of my throat I'd never made before. By the time he moved up to trail kisses along my spine, I was a whimpering puddle of desperation on the bed.

Sam finally found the lube and moved from using his tongue to his fingers. I could have come ten times over just from that, but I wanted more. I wanted the feel of his strong body thrusting into me from behind. I wanted to have to brace myself to keep from being slammed into the bed. And I wanted to hear his grunts as he used my body for his pleasure.

Sam teased me with his dick until finally pushing it in. I cried out in relief and reached back to grab his hip and pull him closer.

"Sam," I said, not really knowing what I wanted to say. *More, harder, please, god.*

"Y'okay?"

I loved how his Texas drawl showed up only when he was drunk with need.

"Fuck me."

He leaned his hot, damp chest over my bare skin where my shirt was most likely ruined already with sweaty creases. I didn't care. Not one bit.

The crisp brush of his chest hair against my back and the scent of his sun-warmed skin excited me. I moved my hand from his hip to his head and grabbed a handful of his thick blond hair before turning my face to brush a kiss against his mouth.

"Want you. Don't be careful."

"I'll always be careful with you."

His words sucked the breath from my lungs. I murmured his name again and again like a plea.

Maybe he was careful in his own way, or maybe all he'd meant was making sure I was okay while he did it, but Sam cranked up the intensity exactly how I'd asked. He slung his hips against my ass hard and fast until the slapping sound of hot, damp skin filled the room and brought me closer to orgasm.

But it was when he pulled out and leaned back in with his mouth, sliding his finger inside me and working my hole with his tongue, that I finally lost it.

My brain blinked off as every muscle seemed to contract in my body at once. I cried out Sam's name and scrambled to reach for him with one of my hands. He grabbed it and held it tight as my release rocked through me.

When I started to breathe easier, I felt the warm splat of Sam's cum on my back and heard the low, sustained grunt of his own orgasm.

As soon as his orgasm finished, he gently moved me onto the bed fully and lay beside me, brushing my hair back and pressing soft kisses on my cheeks, lips, and eyelids.

"You're so beautiful," he whispered. "So sexy. I'm so lucky to be here with you like this. When you... when you trusted me, even after Barney told you I had a record... no one has ever had blind faith in me like that before."

His vulnerability was a gift, and I was grateful to see it. It was easy to think he was the one bringing everything to the table in our relationship, so hearing I was able to touch him in that way was special.

Sam drew a finger down the side of my face. "It was an assault charge. My sister was—"

I cut him off with a hard kiss. "It's okay. I want to know the story if you want to tell me, but later. Okay? Right now I just want you to hold me like this and maybe tell me again how beautiful I am," I teased.

This was all too good to be true, but I decided to relish it while I had it. But the longer we locked eyes on each other, the more I thought maybe it wasn't too good to be true. Maybe it was exactly right.

And maybe it was time I learned to accept that just maybe, I deserved to have someone as kind and loving as Sam Rigby all to myself.

∼

I offered to drive Sam to Rockley Lodge early in the morning so I wouldn't chicken out before my breakfast confession to Mikey and Pim. I was, indeed, a little too nervous to go it alone, so I also begged Chaya to join us there.

After kissing a sleepy Sam goodbye and sending him off with Tiller to get the snow guns two hours away, I gestured for Mikey to hop in the Subaru with me so we could catch Pim before the breakfast rush.

As soon as we entered the cozy diner, I asked Pim if he could join us long enough for a cup of coffee. Since Solo was working this morning, he happily agreed and got us all settled with coffee in a back booth.

"Um..." I began.

Chaya squeezed my leg. "Spit it out, babe. Mama's got a day off and cowboys to ride."

Mikey chuckled, and Pim made an encouraging remark. I finally found my tongue. "I know who hit you with the truck," I blurted. "Back in December."

Thankfully, no one else was within hearing distance. I continued talking too fast for anyone to interrupt. "The hit-and-run was meant for me. And it was Gene. Gene Stanner. After you pushed me down, I turned to look and recognized his pickup. Then... then he tried it again on the mountain. It wasn't an accident. It had to be deliberate. Sam and I were on a motorcycle, and he ran the truck right at us. I realized I can't... I can't keep this to myself anymore because what if someone else got hurt like you two were hurt? I couldn't live with myself. Knowing all this time I kept it to myself and didn't tell a *soul*."

I forced myself to keep facing Mikey and Pim. "I'm so sorry. I can't even begin to apologize for not giving you the information you deserved to bring your assailant to justice. There are explanations for why I withheld the information, but they're not excuses. There's no excuse for what I did."

Pim's face was soft and paternal. He reached out a hand to hold one of mine. "You were scared, honey. Everyone here understands how awful that family has been to you. Of course we understand. But I appreciate you telling us now. I'd like to see him go to jail, if not for my own injury, then for all the pain he's caused you over the years."

It was too kind. His words brought tears to my eyes, and I willed them back inside. I wasn't used to a kind and understanding paternal figure.

Chaya wasn't as touched. She muttered into her mug. "You mean you didn't tell a soul except your new boyfriend. And your pal Barney."

I turned to her in confusion. "I never told Barney."

She nodded and swallowed a sip of coffee. "You must've, because he mentioned it at the hospital. Said 'It has to be them. Especially after the hit-and-runs.' Runs, plural. Believe me, I noticed, and I was not pleased that you shared with *him* and not *me*."

"But..." I thought back to when I would have told Barney about recognizing the truck at the hit-and-run. "No. No way. I did not tell him. Ever since that moment, I swore to myself I would take the secret to my grave. And I kept that promise until I told Sam yesterday afternoon."

"Then how'd he know?"

I opened my mouth to explain but then closed it again. How *did* he know?

"Maybe you misheard him?" I asked.

She shook her head. "I know I didn't because he muttered something under his breath about whether it was 'hits-and-run' like 'attorneys-at-law' or 'hit-and-runs' like 'glad hands' which I don't understand at all."

"It's a model trains thing," I muttered. "But..."

"Wait," Mikey said. "Model trains. Wasn't he at the model trains meet-up until after the fire was started? Wasn't that his alibi?"

I nodded. "Well, that's what he said. But in all the time I've known him, I've never known a model trains meeting to go past nine forty-five."

Pim leaned closer. "What was his reaction after the December incident? Was he upset? Guilty? Worried?"

"Definitely worried and stressed, but I assumed he was worried for me because I was so upset about it myself. I remember telling him how scared I'd been," I began. "When you guys pushed me and I heard the honking and squealing of tires... I was really shaken up afterward. He was supersweet. He made sure I wasn't alone. He slept over in my guest room for several nights and made me breakfast. Then he'd stop by the shop every day just to say hi. We ended up spending so much time together, we were kind of dating, even though I kept telling him I didn't want to be in a relationship."

Mikey clasped his coffee mug between two hands. "But when I was first here in December, someone told us you two were dating, and that was before the hit-and-run."

Pim nodded. "Probably me. We all thought you two were dating."

"No," Mikey said. "I think it was Winter. When he and Gentry came over for dinner."

"Why? We were just friends before that. I volunteered as a reader at the library," I explained.

Pim thought back before answering. "He told Lew Bristol, who told Bill at cards one night. It was Black Friday because Bill was bragging about the deal he'd gotten on an immersion blender that morning."

Chaya cut in. "And I remember Mindy mentioning it around then, too. Remember, I asked you about it?"

I'd just assumed it was one of those funny, small-town rumors. But I never would have guessed it had come straight from the source. The lying source.

"But, why?" I asked, feeling like a fool.

Pim shrugged. "Tale as old as time, isn't it? Lonely older man and a young, respectful cutie with good manners and a tight little bod."

Bill cleared his throat loudly from behind him before setting a platter of muffins down and pinching Pim's side. "Watch it, old man."

Pim grinned at his husband. "I was watching it. I believe that's what got me into trouble."

Bill leaned down and kissed Pim gently on the lips while smoothing down an errant strand of hair. "You okay?" he murmured softly.

Pim nodded. They shared a beat of eye contact before Bill returned to the kitchen. Pim watched him walk away before turning back to the table and fanning his face. "Lordy, that man."

Chaya was pissed. "Barney would have wanted to push Truman into needing him. Make him scared and lonely. Make him need an older man to look out for him. That asshole. I knew he wanted you barefoot and pregnant like a good little wifey."

I ignored her even though she was kind of right. He'd made plenty of statements implying I'd be better off at home, without my shop.

Mikey met my eyes. "Did you see Gene Stanner behind the wheel either time?"

I closed my eyes and shook my head. "No. At the shop, I only saw the tail of the truck as it raced off. But I recognized the beige-and-orange truck and the red bumper sticker. And then yesterday, I recognized the truck and bumper sticker again, but the sun was glaring off the windshield."

"So it might not have been Gene," Chaya added. "Which gels with what Kimber said at the drunken girls' night. That Gene hasn't gotten behind the wheel since losing his license. Wait. Hasn't that truck been sitting over at the Chop Shop? Beige with an orange stripe down the side? Not a very common combo."

Pim lowered his voice. "Supposedly Gene wrecked it and got a DUI at the same time. Jim fixed it up, but Gene probably can't pick it up from the shop without a license, and Kimber doesn't want it sitting in the driveway anyway. So there it sits with no one driving it."

Except I remembered Sam joking about Aster Valley being a small enough town to leave the keys in the car at the auto shop.

"You mean where *anyone* can drive it," I corrected with a groan. "Jim Browning leaves all the keys in the trucks once the service has been paid for. That means it could have been anyone. We're back to square one."

"No," Chaya insisted. "Barney knew it was Gene's truck, and he knows you're scared of Gene for good reason. Let's talk this through as if it's Barney. He takes the truck, tries to scare you in December. Accidentally hits Pim and Mikey which does its job of scaring you anyway. You cling on to him—*ouch!*"

I pulled my hand back from poking her. "I did not cling."

"You agree to let him coddle you," she semi-corrected. "And he gets the dating scenario he'd already begun to tell people about. All goes fine for him until Sam arrives. Patrick does his usual shitty harassment on the highway. Sam enters the picture. Barney recognizes him as a threat and decides to scare you back into his own arms again."

Pim tapped his chin and continued the narrative. "Barney starts the fire. He probably didn't mean for it to burn the whole building down. Maybe it was meant to be small, but you probably had plenty of flammable items in there."

I cut in, nodding. "Essential oils, garlic, cinnamon. Heck, even orange peel has limonene which is a known…" I drifted off when I caught myself digressing. "Anyway, yes. It could have easily gotten out of hand."

Chaya jumped back in. "He was careful to save Aunt Berry's notebook before setting the place on fire."

Mikey sighed. "And brought it to you like a damned hero."

I thought through more of the week's events. "The fire was started by someone who went in through the front door of the shop. Barney had a key."

Mikey was getting angry. "And then he had the gall to take Gene's truck again and run you two off the mountain road? Is he a monster?"

I nodded slowly, putting the pieces together. "Yes. I think he is."

"Damn. Now I really wish I'd brought this up at the hospital," Chaya said worriedly. "I just thought it was bad best-friend behavior to yell at you when you were busy tossing your cookies."

Tossing my… oh god!

I looked over at Mikey. "He poisoned the peanut butter cookies."

Chaya asked what I meant, so I explained. "Barney brought me some organic, plant-based peanut butter cookies yesterday to prove there was such a thing. I ate several and then vomited."

Mikey frowned. "But I had one, and Tiller had one, too."

I shook my head. "I had like four or five, since he kept talking about how much trouble he'd gone to and wondering if I'd *really* liked them. But if he used the compound I'm thinking of—"

"The America Pennsylvania one!" Chaya said excitedly.

"*Myrica pensylvanica*," I corrected, "which he could easily have taken from my shop. It only works to induce vomiting if you take a higher amount of it. That would explain why you could have one or two and not get sick."

Chaya was pissed. "And that's when he planted the beads in the saddlebags. I'm going to kill the little toad."

Mikey nodded enthusiastically, but Pim shook his head. "Children, children. This doesn't call for some kind of slapdash payback attempt. This calls for a magnificent, well-planned, and expertly executed vengeance extravaganza."

We all stared at the older man in awe before nodding our allegiance to the master.

Of course, I was the one a little less sure of everything. "But what if he didn't actually do it?"

Chaya snorted. "Oh, he did it."

Pim took my words into careful consideration. "We're going to lay a trap, Mr. Sweet. And only the guilty party will feel the cold metal bite of its teeth when it snaps closed."

If I'd felt like a player in an overly dramatic production of a stage mystery then, it was nothing compared to how I felt after we'd concocted our actual plan and Chaya had suggested using costumes, "In order to get the full effect."

I really loved costumes, but now definitely wasn't the time for them.

The one saving grace was everyone's agreement to wait for Tiller and Sam to return from Breckenridge so we'd have some big muscle on our side in case things went wrong somehow. Like... if the Stanner brothers had conspired with Barney and were waiting in the wings to beat me up as soon as I'd gotten a confession out of Barney.

But then the plan went completely out the window when Solo casually mentioned boxing up a to-go order for Mr. Balderson, who was picking it up on his way out of town.

The four of us scrambled like idiotic coconspirators. Mikey called Tiller in a frantic rush as Pim wondered aloud whether or not to slip a sleeping pill into the man's breakfast order. Chaya pointed out that might put other drivers in jeopardy when the man got on the interstate, and I simply sat there thinking a silent version of "Ack! Ack!" until I actually saw him come into the diner.

And then everything became crystal clear. I knew exactly what to do.

"Excuse me," I said calmly to my lovably nutty friends before sliding out of the booth and making my way over to Barney. "Um, hi."

He glanced at me and then back to the bag of food Solo had placed in front of him. "Hello, Truman. How are you feeling today?"

"Actually, not great. I mean... physically I'm fine, but..." I bit my lip and looked at him. "I was wondering if you might come up to the farm and talk to me for a few minutes before heading out of town. I'm confused about something, and I would like someone to help me sort through it. Would you mind?"

His eyes widened in surprise. "Of course not, sweet pea. My car's right out front. Why don't you let me take you home?"

I shook my head, trying not to get nervous. This next part was important if my plan was going to work. "No, I need to stop and get some gas on the way home. But I'll meet you there in a little while? That okay?"

He studied me for a minute before smiling. "Tell you what. Why don't you let me fill up the Subaru, and you can take my car. You shouldn't have to get your hands dirty for something like that."

"I couldn't ask you to do that," I said with what I hoped was a shy grin. "Besides, I wanted to pick out a candy bar, and if you go instead, I won't have an excuse."

Barney winked at me and nodded. "Sure enough. See you soon."

I started to turn away, but then turned back and brushed his arm. "Barney? Would you...? No, sorry. Never mind."

"What is it, Truman?"

I sighed. "Would you mind running by the shop and seeing if there are any updates on the investigation? I want to know what they know, and no one will talk to me. Maybe they'll talk to you."

Barney nodded in understanding. "Of course."

I had no idea if Dirk or Gail were at the shop today, but it didn't matter. I only needed a little head start.

I waved goodbye to my friends, who all scrambled to follow me outside without looking like that's what they were doing. Pim went out the back door, Mikey followed me, calling out about grabbing his jacket out of my car, and Chaya just threw up her hands and enigmatically called out, "Costumes, goddammit!"

"Go away," I hissed. "I got this if you clowns don't tip the man off."

Mikey's eyes widened before his face split in a grin, and I had to pause for a second to wonder who the heck I was in that moment. Meek, unassuming Truman Sweet would never talk to his friends that way before going off to confront his arsonist, attempted murderer, former almost-boyfriend.

But then again, that old Truman would never have considered these folks his friends, let alone confronted anyone.

I liked the new Truman way better.

Chaya narrowed her eyes at me. "I will be hiding in your goat shed. Bark twice if you need me."

"Whatever," I muttered, reaching for my door handle.

Mikey grabbed my elbow. "Wait for Tiller and Sam. They can help."

"You know I can't wait that long. He's leaving town. It's now or never, Mikey." I gently pulled my elbow out of his grip. "I've got this. Trust me."

And I did. I knew I would give it my best shot, and no matter what happened, I'd be proud of myself for trying.

"I know you do," Mikey said softly. "And I love the hell out of you, so don't get hurt." Then he pulled me into a quick hug before practically shoving me in my vehicle. I wasn't stupid. I knew Mikey was way too nosy to stay away. I could only hope he didn't park his SUV where…

By the time I remembered I'd driven him to breakfast, he was already lying on the floor of my Subaru under a jacket that barely even covered his ass. "You won't even notice I'm here," he said in a stage whisper.

I sighed and slammed the door. "Don't quit your day job," I muttered, but secretly I was feeling all warm and fuzzy inside from his claim of loving me. I finally had a true family, like Sam had said. And it felt incredible.

As I drove toward the farm, I picked up my phone and made a call to Deputy Stone. I wasn't stupid enough to try and confront someone without backup, and Deputy Stone was the only person I even remotely trusted within a close enough distance to get there in time. I got his voicemail and explained everything as quickly as I could, hoping like heck I could trust him.

I was relieved when my phone stayed silent after that. If there weren't messages and frantic attempts to contact me coming from Sam, perhaps Mikey hadn't tattled on me after all.

Or maybe Sam's simply driving back here too fast and recklessly to waste time on messaging.

I ignored all thoughts about Sam and focused on what I was going to say. When I parked in front of the farmhouse, I hissed at Mikey to get his ass in the house and stay out of sight. "Try the guest room. And lock the door!"

I made sure the surveillance video cameras were online and working and then sent off the login information to Deputy Stone before slipping my phone back into my pocket. Hopefully, Barney wouldn't turn violent, but after everything I now suspected of him... it was hard to know for sure.

When his car finally bumped up to the gate, I took a deep breath and marveled at my steady nerves. Even though this wasn't the Stanner family I'd always imagined an eventual showdown with, I still felt that this conversation had been a long time coming. No matter what happened, it would be a relief to finally get some of these things out in the open.

Barney leaned out of his window. "Can you open the gate for me?"

After he parked and got out of his car, I gestured for him to follow me to the rocking chairs on the front porch.

"Thank you for coming," I began, clutching my knees nervously. "I didn't know who else to talk to about this."

"You were right to come to me. Anytime," he assured me.

I groaned and closed my eyes, resting my head back on the rocker. "I feel like such an idiot. I think..." I opened my eyes and looked at him before glancing down at my lap. "No, I *know* I was wrong to trust Sam."

I held up a hand. "Wait. Before you say anything, please don't be disappointed in me for trusting him in the first place. I feel like a fool..."

Barney sighed and reached over to place his hand over mine. I tried not to cringe. "We all make mistakes. But... what happened to change your mind?"

"I should have seen it. And you tried to warn me. He's just so crass. And he pressured me to ride on his motorcycle. I was terrified, but I didn't know how to say no, and we almost died! And then he told me that he thought I should take the insurance money from the fire and use it for something decadent, like an expensive motorcycle. Can you imagine? When I asked about what I would do with the building, he said I could probably make money by tearing it down and making a parking lot there instead since the town is going to boom after the ski resort opens."

Barney's eyes widened comically. He was a sucker for historical buildings. Or so he'd said. "A *parking lot*?"

"Right? It seemed kind of... disrespectful. Of my aunt Berry if not of me directly. That's when I realized you would have never suggested such a thing to me."

"Certainly not!"

"And it made me question some other things he's said, too. Like I think he's thinking of skimming money off the ski resort somehow. I didn't really understand what he was saying—you know how business stuff just goes over my head—but it sounded illegal."

"I told you there was something off about him, didn't I?" Barney squeezed my hand tighter and shook his head, clucking over me like a mother hen. "From the very first day. I warned you to stay away from him, and now you see the proof yourself."

I nodded and tried to come up with a tear or two. "You did. And I didn't listen. And now I feel so stupid. You've always been there for me. Through everything. When the Stanner brothers beat me up behind the shop that time, you were the one who brought me flowers and my favorite salad from Bolo's Market. You looked out for me and helped guide me on how to stay out of trouble. I just feel like... I feel like..." I sniffed and looked away.

Barney's hand came down on my shoulder and squeezed as if trying to reassure me. It took all of my self-control not to shudder under his touch. No wonder my gut was always trying to warn me away from hooking up with him. He was an awful human being. My body had known it, even if my brain hadn't.

I glanced at him quickly and then darted my eyes away. "I feel ashamed of how stupid I've been," I whispered, and it was the first true thing I'd said since he'd arrived.

"Sweet pea. We all make mistakes. Of course I understand. You're young. You're easily led astray."

I forced myself to smile wanly. "I just hate that I made you have to go so far out of your way to guide me back to the right path. You tried so hard to get me to realize how good you were for me, and I didn't listen. I abused your trust in me."

"Sometimes love means doing the hard thing, Truman. And I love you enough to do the hard things."

"I can see that now. I see how much you love me." I looked at him and tried to appear lovestruck. "You loved me enough to come up with an amazing plan. And I messed it up. I messed it all up."

"What do you mean?"

"When you tried to set a little fire to get my attention, I'd failed to ship out a big delivery of essential oils that day. If I'd just done my job instead of being lazy, the fire would have never gotten out of hand. Oh, how you must have been so upset! I feel terrible." I let my true feelings of regret and anger bring real tears to my eyes. "It could have been contained if not for my stupid, stupid procrastination. It's all my fault. All you wanted to do was..." I faked a big gulping sob, and Barney stared at me for a few beats.

I assumed he was trying to determine whether or not to continue trying to pin the arson on Sam or accept my understanding and let it be.

This was the moment of truth.

Barney finally pulled me in for a hug.

"Shhh, shhh. It's okay. There, now. It's all over. It is what it is. Although that certainly does explain why it got out of hand."

That wasn't enough. It wasn't an actual confession. I needed more.

"But then the motorcycle crash in the mountains. I feel like I misunderstood what I was supposed to do. Run? Should I have stayed there and made sure he was standing by the bike? I felt so stupid, Barney. I didn't know what you wanted me to do. Tell me what I should have done." I cried on his shoulder.

"Of course you should have run, sweet pea. I didn't want to hurt anyone. I simply wanted to scare him away from here and remind you how unsafe and unreliable a man like him is. You did the right thing. Of course you did. There, now. Stop the waterworks. It's alright now."

"After the time in front of the shop, I wasn't sure. But I should have known you didn't want to hurt anyone. I knew it had to be a mistake."

"I wasn't expecting those other two to interfere," he said peevishly. "And I certainly wasn't expecting some imbecile driver behind me to honk and scare me to death."

"I'm relieved to know that," I said softly. "Because when I think about how close I came to being in the shop the night of the fire..." I shivered.

"I would have never set that fire if you'd been there. Surely you know that. I'm not stupid, Truman, and that is hardly the first fire I've set."

Suddenly, I remembered the timing of Patrick Stanner's shed burning to the ground. It had happened a week after the Stanner brothers had beat me up behind my shop.

I pulled out of Barney's arms and stared at him. "You burned down Patrick Stanner's shed."

The glint in his eyes was a combination of pride and pure malice. "He hurt my sweet pea."

"Did you... did you really do all of these things... for me?" I couldn't believe it. How was it possible I'd caused all of these horrible events in Aster Valley after already being the town pariah from years ago?

His eyes bore into me. "I did. Don't you know I would do anything for you, Truman?"

"Even the cookies?"

"Well, you forced my hand."

"And is that when you snuck the mala into the saddlebags?"

He looked put out. "You needed to understand why he wasn't right for you. He's a criminal, Truman."

Suddenly, instead of feeling angry and vengeful or even horrified and betrayed, I felt... tired. Tired of one more person in my life thinking they knew better than I did about what I needed in my life. One more person thinking they could control me by lying to me or for me or simply not listening to me when I tried standing up for myself.

"But why didn't you listen to me when I told you I just wanted to be friends?" I asked in a soft voice. "Why didn't you trust that I knew what was best for me?"

His eyes narrowed the tiniest bit. "Because you don't. You have a long history of making the wrong decisions."

Okay, now I was angry. "How can you say that? What decisions have I made that were wrong?"

He stood and began pacing. "Oh, I don't know. Let's start with loaning the sled to the stupidest boys in town. Then lying about it. Then moving back here like nothing had happened and expecting people like the Stanners to just let it go. Why couldn't you have just been quiet about it instead of putting yourself out there in front of the whole town all the time?"

I flapped my arms out to the side in disbelief. "Putting myself out there? I spent the first couple of years here too scared to speak! I went to work, kept to myself, and went home to the farm. The only thing I did was work and volunteer at the library with kids. How can you imply I was somehow attracting attention or causing anyone problems?"

And why was I arguing with a madman? Did it matter? I was trying to use logic with someone who had literally poisoned me.

Barney must have seen the fear on my face as soon as I remembered how high the stakes were.

"You must think I'm stupid, Truman," he said calmly, stepping closer. "I'm not. I'm actually quite smart. I know more than you think, including how to read about emetic compounds from your aunt's notebook. Including how to place the same accelerant I used at your shop in the middle of a shed full of silly costumes and take care of them once and for all."

I opened my mouth to scream a warning to Chaya, but Barney cut me off.

"And including cutting the wires to your security cameras before this little meeting of ours in case you tried to get me to confess any of these things on camera."

My stomach dropped.

He knew.

I scrambled out of the rocker and bolted for the goat shed.

25

SAM

I was going to kill Truman for doing this when I was so far away from home.

Why in the world had he decided to confront a dangerous asshole when Tiller and I were halfway down the road toward Breckenridge?

I crept up the edge of the meadow toward the back of the house as quickly as I could. I'd never seen Tiller drive so fast or been so grateful for his spending an obscene amount of money on an SUV with a giant engine.

I'd never make fun of him for it again.

Why Truman would choose to confront a crazy man without backup was beyond me, but it had been his call, and he'd obviously made it.

I had to trust that he knew what he was doing. But that didn't mean I had to sit idly by while he did it.

My plan was to listen and wait to see if he needed me. And at first, it had seemed like he didn't. But then I heard him shout.

I scrambled forward to the corner of the house and peeked around. Truman was hauling ass toward his costume shed on the far side of one of his garden plots when Barney grabbed the back of his shirt. Man, that old man could move.

Part of me... okay, *most* of me expected Truman to go down in a heap of shy, trembling plant geek. But my man surprised me. He swung around with the fire of heated vengeance in his eyes and roared as loud as his little lungs could possibly manage.

And he punched that fucker square on the nose.

I wasn't sure who was more surprised: me, Barney, Truman, or the weirdo in the goat costume stepping out of the toolshed.

"Punch him again!" the goat cried in Chaya's familiar voice.

"Chaya! Leave the shed, leave the shed!" Truman cried. "He's going to torch it!"

"It's fine! Beat the shit out of him," she replied.

"Don't beat the shit out of him," someone else warned from behind me. I didn't stop moving long enough to say anything, I simply reached my arms around Truman's body as soon as he followed up the jab with a right hook. I pulled him back away from the older man and held tight as he scrambled to get out of my arms and pummel the librarian to death.

"No," I said calmly.

"He did it!" Truman cried. "He did all of it! He did it!"

His shouts turned into sobs until his body collapsed in my hold. I let his weight take us to the ground and held him as Deputy Stone appeared from behind me and secured Barney. He spoke into his radio before reading Barney his rights.

Meanwhile, I turned Truman in my arms so I could check out his poor knuckles. The goat came skidding over to us, falling on her knees and shoving her giant furry snout into my face as she attempted to hug Truman.

"That one looks good on you," Truman said through sniffles. "Especially since you're not burned up in a f-fire."

Chaya pulled off the headpiece and grinned wide. "I know, right? I think we should plan a skit party or a costume charades night. You've got the best shit in there. And I didn't see any sign of fire stuff."

Mikey came racing across the lawn only to be obstructed by a waiting Tiller. Tiller grabbed him up and kissed him, looking him over for injuries before learning that Mikey's role had been more "consultative" than "participatory."

"Thank fuck," Tiller muttered.

When the sirens and lights finally came streaming through the gate, I was surprised to see they weren't the familiar Rockley County Sheriff's vehicles. Instead, they were state police. I glanced over at Stone.

"You can trust them. They're good officers, and they know everything. Sheriff Stanner has been put on paid leave while the investigation takes place. There will be a formal announcement later this morning. I can't say much more than that right now, but you have my word everything you told me is in the right hands. And Truman gave me the app and login to the cameras before Balderson arrived. I have it all recorded on video."

Barney spluttered. "What video—there's no video! I cut the feed."

I looked over at him and smiled wide. "There are no wires to cut on a wireless system. You cut the feed on the backup set."

Truman snugged even closer against me, holding on to me as tightly as he could. He was trembling, but he'd stopped crying after Chaya's masterfully ridiculous costume comments, and he was watching everything with an intense focus.

"He told me I needed someone to protect me," Truman said, watching Stone take Barney away. Then he looked back at me. "But I don't."

I nodded. "You certainly proved you're more than capable of protecting yourself," I said in agreement. "You used your brain, your circle of friends, your technology, and your community resources. Not to mention your physical strength and agility. I'd say you proved yourself, babe. Not that you needed to. Not to me. Ever."

He went quiet for another few moments as law enforcement moved around us.

"But what if I *want* someone to protect me?" he asked in a low voice.

I let out a breath of relief and kissed his hair. He smelled like sun-ripened cherries, and I would never get enough of it as long as I lived.

"Then I would say I know someone who's looking for the job. Permanently."

Truman sniffed and met my eyes. His lashes were spiky with tears, but his face was clear and his jaw was set. He looked determined, although I wasn't sure about what.

I reached out and cupped his cheeks. "I love you, Truman Sweet."

His face dropped into shock. "You do?"

I grinned at him. "I'm so damned proud of you. You're brave and happy and kind. You give everyone the benefit of the doubt, and you take on the world's burdens to keep others from feeling pain. You're smart and hardworking. You're adorably quirky and fun. And talented. And so damned sexy. I... I'm head over heels in love with you." He still seemed shocked. "If that's okay? I know it's fast. Really fast."

Truman's jaw snapped shut. "Not too fast. Not too fast at all."

I leaned in and kissed a tender spot behind his ear that made him hum. "Good. Because I get the feeling you have a few more things on your bedroom wish list I might be able to help you with..."

His eyes widened comically. "How did you know about my bedroom wish list?"

I blinked at him with as much innocence as I could muster. "Well, I know you wanted beadboard in the kitchen, and I'm pretty sure you want a new picture window in the bedroom. Maybe some paint. Maybe some..."

Truman bit his lip to keep from grinning at me. "Maybe some...?"

"Spice?"

He flushed deep pink. "I'd like that. And Sam?"

"Yeah?"

"I love you, too." He spoke the words with confidence, as if he knew how much they'd mean to me.

I wasn't prepared for how they made me feel. They flooded my heart with a heady combination of love, peace, excitement, and relief.

"Even if I can't even keep a fake plant alive?" I admitted.

Truman lifted an eyebrow at me. "I called your drill a hammer."

I leaned in and kissed him softly before speaking against his cheek. "I don't care if you ever learn a thing about construction as long as you continue to bloom and grow."

Chaya's goat mask shoved its way between us and knocked Truman's glasses askew. "Sorry to break up the kissfest, but Deputy Stone has been trying to get your attention."

I looked over to see the stoic deputy looking a little bit uncomfortable. "Sorry to interrupt," he said, "but I thought you'd like to know I pulled that video you asked me about."

Truman's brows furrowed since the deputy was talking to me instead of him. "From my surveillance system?"

Deputy Stone shook his head. "No. Sam asked me to take a look back through the surveillance video from the business located behind your shop. They gave me access to everything they had, and sure enough, I found the night of your assault. Craig and Patrick Stanner are clearly identifiable on the video and have been taken into custody as a result."

Truman's jaw dropped. "You're kidding?"

The deputy looked upset. "I can't even begin to tell you how sorry I am that you had to go this long without justice for what you went through." His eyes flicked to me and back to Truman. "I saw the assault, and it was awful. I'm grateful you're with us today, and I hope you know that I will continue to monitor the case as it makes its way through the system."

Truman looked up at me. "It's... it's over. They're in jail."

Deputy Stone nodded. "And the state police are unraveling the pension scheme. We should have an update on that in the next couple of weeks for you. In the meantime, you know where to find me. There will be plenty of changes in the department, obviously, but you can rest assured, I'll be here as long as I'm needed."

A nearby deputy snorted. "Gonna be longer than you think, Stone. You're the only one they'll even think of appointing in the sheriff's place before they can elect a new one."

I could have sworn Deputy Stone rolled his eyes and muttered, "Lord help us all," before glancing down at his watch. "It's not even ten in the morning yet and it feels like midnight."

Pim came bustling over and grabbed Truman out of my arms to squeeze him in a big bear hug. "Christ, I thought they'd never let me over here to check on you. How are you? Okay? Did that good-for-nothing lay a hand on you?"

Bill caught up to his husband and put a hand on his shoulder. "He's in good hands, hon."

They tittered around him, making sure he was truly unharmed.

I watched as our friends gathered together in a giant group hug. A sassy-mouthed chef, a laid-back footballer, an overgrown goat with wild-ass hair, a jolly diner-owner slash coconspirator, a pair of lesbian knitters who looked more like sisters, a famous musician, his beautiful husband, and their oddball uncle, a stern-faced deputy whose watch face surprisingly had a tiny rainbow flag on it, and a beloved spice merchant with bruised knuckles.

And me. The man who'd finally found his heart and his true family in a small town in the Rocky Mountains of Colorado.

EPILOGUE – SHERIFF STONE, TWO MONTHS LATER

I shouldn't even be here.

I glanced around at the party in full swing behind Rockley Lodge. Mikey had arranged a giant marquee tent that was strung with fairy lights and housed a scattering of round tables with votive candles and wildflowers in fat glass jars even. A wooden dance floor had been erected under one half of the tent, and a DJ was setting up on the small stage behind it.

Everyone had come to celebrate the successful release of Mikey's cookbook, and they'd invited Aster Valley's "new sheriff" to join in the festivities. I thought it was more likely they wanted Aster Valley's *gay* sheriff there since the party seemed to be overrun by the town's rainbow contingent. And, honestly, it made me feel welcome for the first time since moving here half a year ago.

I was certainly not in the market for a boyfriend, but I appreciated feeling welcome among such an interesting and caring group of men regardless. If there was one thing I definitely could use after my recent trouble back in California, it was a group of friends I could trust.

Tiller held up a champagne glass and wrapped his arm around Mikey's shoulder. He and many of his guests were already happily tipsy, which made me grateful for the lodge's many bedrooms and the hosts' invitation for anyone and everyone to stay the night rather than getting back on the mountain roads in the dark.

"To my favorite chef in the whole wide world," Tiller called out across the cluster of friends and family. He'd pulled Mikey up to the front edge of the stage to get everyone's attention. "And New York Post bestselling author!"

"Times," Mikey said under a cough. He knew Tiller was teasing him, and I was fairly sure this would earn Tiller a few well-placed comments about his football "field match" or his impressive "tackle free throw percentage." The two of them had invited me over for dinner one night a few weeks ago, and I'd laughed so hard I'd almost pissed myself listening to their sports banter.

But now I was back to feeling like an outsider. It wasn't easy balancing being the new sheriff with making friends, especially when I had to work so hard to maintain the highest professional standards after the last idiot who'd held the position.

"That's my son," an older man said to me from where he stood next to me at the small bar stand.

I knew Mikey and his father didn't get along, but I'd heard great things about Tiller's family. I assumed this was his father, who'd come in from Denver for the party. I smiled. "Does he get his football talent from you?"

The man barked out a laugh loud enough to draw attention from a few people around us. "Mikey? Play football? I wish. He would have been an incredible kicker if only he'd let me convince him to train for it. He was a star on the soccer field until he gave it up in middle school."

He gazed wistfully at the men on the stage as I mentally scrambled to adjust my thinking. This was Mikey's father. The football coach.

"You must be Coach Vining, then," I said, holding out my hand. "Declan Stone. Nice to meet you."

He nodded and shook my hand. "Likewise. He doesn't know we're here yet. Tiller invited us." He spoke gruffly, turning back to look at the men as Tiller continued to wax romantic about Mikey on stage. "Damned proud of him, though. He's, ah... always been a good cook."

A woman stepped up and reached for one of the two drinks in the coach's hands. "Did we miss the proposal?"

Mikey's dad shook his head. "Don't think so. He's working up to it. The man is cool as a cucumber in triple coverage against the meanest safety in the league, but seems to be sweating buckets up there trying to get up his nerve to pop a single question to my baby boy."

The woman, who I assumed was Mikey's mom, smacked him gently on the arm. "That means he cares more about your baby boy than he does about football. Isn't that sweet?"

"Mpfh." The man grunted into his drink, but I could see he hadn't taken his eyes off what was happening on the stage.

I introduced myself to Mikey's mother and turned back to the stage in time to tune into the good part.

"Michael Vining, will you cover my home base and swing at all my pitches? Will you be the hooker in my scrum and ace all my wild serves? Will you promise to tackle every... *ooof*."

"What the hell is he talking about?" Coach Vining grumbled.

Mikey elbowed Tiller. "Skip to the good part."

Tiller's eyes sparkled as he pulled a ring box from his pocket. "Will you make me the happiest man on earth and agree to marry me?"

Mikey's tears caught the light, but even I could see from this distance that they were happy tears. His mom sniffled next to me, and I turned around to seek out a few paper napkins from the bartender before handing them to her.

"Thank you, dear. They're just so perfect together. Aren't they, honey?"

Mikey's dad's voice was rough when he answered. "Tiller Raine is a good man. And so is Mikey."

It seemed like those were words he wasn't used to saying out loud. I leaned over to advise him in a low voice even though it was truly none of my business. "You should go tell them that, sir. Congratulations."

He nodded awkwardly and led his wife away to approach the happy couple.

Mikey's eyes widened in surprise when he saw them. After a few more awkward moments of his dad's attempts to congratulate them, Mikey threw himself at his dad and hugged him tightly. After a brief pause, Coach Vining hugged him back just as tightly.

I let out a breath and turned around, just to catch sight of Truman Sweet sobbing behind a giant potted plant.

"Shit," I muttered, reaching for more napkins. I hurried over to him and offered him the stack. "You okay?"

He looked up at me from under his mop of curly hair. His eyes were wide behind his dark-framed glasses. "Ignore me. I'm a sucker for a grand gesture."

I looked around to see if I could find Sam, but he was over by the newly engaged pair. The tall blond man stood silently by Mikey and watched Mikey's parents like a hawk.

"Do you want me to get Sam for you?" I asked.

Truman sniffed and gave me a watery smile. "No, that's okay. I don't want him to worry. They're happy tears, but he will still cluck around me like a mother hen."

I scrambled for a safe topic of conversation to help get us past this odd encounter. "How are things going with the rebuild? I drove by and saw the new windows are in. What a difference it makes."

His smile widened. "It's amazing. I think Sam's crew is scared to disappoint him, so they're working extra hard to impress him since they know his personal connection to the project."

That was an understatement. Sam Rigby had taken every chance he had to make it clear to the people of Aster Valley that Truman Sweet was not to be messed with. He'd also encouraged Craig and Patrick Stanner to set the record straight about what had happened years ago with Truman's grandpa's sled.

According to Tiller and Mikey, the result was... anticlimactic. Apparently, way fewer people in town cared or even remembered why the resort closed. And since it was reopening soon, the excitement for the new celebrity ownership eclipsed any of the negative feelings remaining from the past.

"Well, good luck with it, and let me know if you need help at any point. I'm sure Sam has it well under control."

Truman sighed. "He's working too hard. That movie crew is scheduled to arrive next week, so he also has crews working at the chalets and over on the mountain where the old slope-side restaurant is. I guess the movie people paid extra to have that building up and running with working bathrooms and everything so the crew and craft services people would have a place to be. I don't understand why they couldn't just bring in trailers. Don't actors usually have trailers on a movie set?"

I couldn't hold back a laugh. "The set isn't usually halfway up a ski mountain. It was probably cheaper for them to pay for updates to the building, but I think Tiller negotiated to share the expense since he's going to reopen the restaurant anyway."

I'd spent way too much time this week in political discussions between the newly installed head of the county council and the production assistant from the movie crew to want to discuss that damned movie tonight. I'd left Los Angeles for a reason, and it was to get away from the bullshit surrounding celebrities and their overblown sense of entitlement.

So far, I'd discovered Tiller Raine and Gentry Waites were two exceptions to the rule, but in general, I found celebrities—actors especially—to be toxic and spoiled. And discovering how easy it had been for them to bribe their way out of any and all legal trouble back in LA, I'd been doubly glad to leave there.

But now here I was having to deal with Hollywood nonsense again anyway. In tiny Aster Valley, Colorado.

I couldn't wait until this film shoot was done and the cast and crew fucked back off to California so the rest of us could go back to normal. Between the extra work of dealing with the upcoming production security needs and the locals losing their shit over some hotshot actor coming into town, I was seriously reconsidering accepting the promotion to temporary sheriff. But it was only for two years, and then the position would be up for re-election.

I could do anything for two years, and it would give me a chance to meet plenty of the locals and settle in. After that... well, I could simply take it one day at a time.

Sam leaned over to say something to the DJ before heading over to find Truman. He reached out a hand to shake and clapped me on the shoulder. "Glad you could make it. I'm surprised Mikey didn't try to introduce you to every single gay man here already."

I let out a laugh and shook my head. "Not Mikey. Pim. I think he tried auctioning me off to the highest bidder. Even offered all-you-can-eat pancake specials at the diner for anyone willing to show me a good time tonight."

Truman giggled and tucked his head against Sam's shoulder to try and hide his laughter. Sam wrapped his arm around Truman's shoulders and pressed a kiss into his curls.

"Go on and laugh," I told him. "I explained my idea of a hot date tonight was reading the new M.P. Blackfoot mystery out on the new sectional sofa I got for my screened-in porch. Heaven."

Truman's eyes lit up. "I'll have to look and see if they have it at the library. I'm volunteering on Tuesday, so I can check then."

"I heard they may have found a new permanent librarian," I said, remembering the county council meeting where it was discussed for an abnormally long time. "She comes from over in Salt Lake, I think."

Truman nodded. "She's awesome. I met her when she toured the library. She has tons of ideas for getting more kids into the library, but I can see you don't want to hear about that right now."

My eyes had picked out the sound of tires squealing and gravel spraying from around the other side of the house. I held up a finger. "Excuse me for a moment. Sorry to cut you off."

I jogged around to the front of the house and stopped in my tracks. There, in the middle of the tidy row of local vehicles, was a Paris Blue McLaren 720S Spider with electronic dance music blaring from its speakers and a man in mirrored sunglasses and a backward ball cap sitting in the driver's seat nodding his head to the beat. In the passenger seat sat a fashionably petite yet scowling man with bleach-blond hair partly covered by a silk scarf.

"Is this it?" the passenger asked with a sniff. "Where's the vodka, darling? This looks more like a beer-on-tap place, if you catch my meaning."

Good god, the movie people were early.

As soon as he saw me, the driver lifted his head and snapped his fingers. "Hey, you. You there. Can you park this for me? I'm late, and I kind of need you to help me out here. I'll look out for you, man, even if you're not the valet. Feel me?"

He flashed me a million-dollar smile and waited for me to jump to do his bidding.

I stood up taller and crossed my arms in front of my chest, wishing like hell I were in uniform.

"Sorry, no. I don't *feel you*." Although, I had to admit, now that I saw the driver a little more clearly, I wouldn't mind feeling him, as long as I could do it with my hands on his bare skin. He was on the smaller side but fit as fuck. His eyes were wide-set and flashed with an energy I could barely remember from when I was his age at least fifteen years ago, if not twenty. The kind of energy that would fare quite well in bed. Or out of it if he was the adventurous type.

And if I wasn't the sheriff of a small town where everyone was all up in everyone else's business.

"You'll have to park on the street," I suggested, lifting an eyebrow.

His mouth opened just a little. I tried not to notice how lush his lips were. I'd put big money on this being the actor everyone had been losing their minds over. In fact, he looked vaguely familiar, but I wasn't a movie buff, so I wasn't surprised I didn't recognize him right off. The other man was a groupie if ever I'd seen one.

And I'd seen plenty.

"You want me to park a half-million-dollar *McLaren*. On the street."

I shrugged. "Or you could park it at your hotel in town. And walk back."

He turned off the engine with the car right there in the middle of the driveway, where it was blocking absolutely every single car already parked in front of the lodge, including mine, and got out. The man was wearing clothes that probably cost the better part of my annual salary, but he was completely barefoot.

"Safety regulations suggest driving barefoot is ill-advised," I said, cursing myself before the ridiculous warning had finished erupting from my stupid mouth.

The corner of his lip curled up. "Is that right? Who are you, the safety patrol?"

"You could say that." Why did I sound like such a prick?

He pulled off his mirrored lenses, revealing light blue-green eyes ringed by another line of dark blue. Freckles covered the bridge of his nose which might have explained why he looked so young to me.

The sun still hadn't set despite the late hour, but it was low and rosy warm, and the long evening beams landed on the man like God himself knew this kid was all that.

Jesus fucking Christ, I was hard for this asshole punk.

"I'm the sheriff," I finished in a gruff voice before pointing to my SUV which was emblazoned with all of the golden decals explaining who I was in addition to multiple light bars, bull bars, and spotlights, not to mention the laptop mounted on the dash. The SUV that was now blocked by his expensive-ass car and his little piece of man candy. "Now get your fucking car out of the way so I can leave."

The man sauntered around the car and right up to me with the same annoying smirk on his face. He pulled off the ball cap before running his fingers through longish hair and resetting the cap on the right way around.

It said *Hot as Heller*.

And that's when I recognized the little fucker.

Finn Heller. Child star from the long-running family rom-com series, *Cast in Clover*, and the very definition of an entitled actor.

He opened his mouth to say the words, and I winced before they even hit my ears. But when they came, they came from his groupie instead of himself.

"Do you even know who this is?"

I looked between the two of them before settling on Finn. "I sure do. He's my next guest at county lockup if he doesn't move his car out of my damned way."

Up next: Will Sheriff Stone keep his cool now that flashy entitled Finn Heller is in town? Pre-order *Hot as Heller* to find out. *Hot as Heller* goes live June 1, 2021!

LETTER FROM LUCY

Dear Reader,

   Thank you for reading *Sweet as Honey*.

   In the next book, newly-appointed Sheriff Stone is looking forward to the slow, easy pace of Aster Valley. Grateful to have escaped Los Angeles and the society of spoiled Hollywood celebrities, he's content to fill his days responding to petty vandalism and small-town hijinks. But then former-child-actor Finn Heller roars into town with his expensive sports car and entitled attitude. This was not at all what Declan Stone had in mind when he left LA far behind him.

   Hot as Heller comes out June 1, 2021, and you can pre-order it now for the earliest delivery.

   All Lucy Lennox novels can be read on their own so find a story that appeals to you and dive right in!

   Please take a moment to write a review of this book on Amazon and Goodreads. Reviews can make all of the difference in helping a book show up in book searches.

   Feel free to stop by www.LucyLennox.com and drop me a line or visit me on social media. To see inspiration photographs for all of my novels, visit my Pinterest boards.

Finally, I have a fantastic reader group on Facebook. Come join us for exclusive content, early cover reveals, hot pics, and a whole lotta fun. Lucy's Lair can be found here.

Happy reading!

Lucy

ABOUT THE AUTHOR

Lucy Lennox is a mother of three sarcastic kids. Born and raised in the southeast, she now resides outside of Atlanta finally putting good use to that English Lit degree.

Lucy enjoys naps, pizza, and procrastinating. She is married to someone who is better at math than romance but who makes her laugh every single day and is the best dancer in the history of ever.

She stays up way too late each night reading gay romance because it's simply the best thing ever.

For more information and to stay updated about future releases, please sign up for Lucy's author newsletter here.

Connect with Lucy on social media:
www.LucyLennox.com
Lucy@LucyLennox.com

WANT MORE?

Join Lucy's Lair

Get Lucy's New Release Alerts

Like Lucy on Facebook

Follow Lucy on BookBub

Follow Lucy on Amazon

Follow Lucy on Instagram

Follow Lucy on Pinterest

Other books by Lucy:

Made Marian Series

Forever Wilde Series

Aster Valley Series

Twist of Fate Series with Sloane Kennedy

After Oscar Series with Molly Maddox

Licking Thicket Series with May Archer

Virgin Flyer

Say You'll Be Nine

Visit Lucy's website at www.LucyLennox.com for a comprehensive list of titles, audio samples, freebies, suggested reading order, and more!

Made in the USA
Monee, IL
16 April 2021